Advance Praise for *When the Dust Fell*

"A jaw-dropping backstory that teases and taunts as it unfolds in richly painted glimpses. Meanwhile the plot rushes on at breakneck speed. Super fun."

—Uli Reese, Emmy Winner, Cannes Speaker, and Author of the *101 Great Minds* series

"Speculative fiction with an all-too-real undertow. It's both impossible and totally believable at once. An audacious ride, fearlessly steered to keep you buckled in and loving it."

—Jon Hoeber, screenwriter of *The Meg*, *My Spy*, *RED*, and *Whiteout*

"Cinematic, with big-picture imagery, action, and heart. Bring a bowl of popcorn to your favorite reading chair."

—Joey Berlin, CEO of the Critics Choice Association, founding Executive Director of the Broadcast Film Critics Association

WHEN THE DUST FELL

WHEN THE DUST FELL

MARSHALL ROSS

A PERMUTED PRESS BOOK
ISBN: 978-1-63758-317-3
ISBN (eBook): 978-1-63758-318-0

When the Dust Fell

Cover art by Cody Corcoran

Permuted Press, LLC
New York • Nashville
permutedpress.com

Published in the United States of America
1 2 3 4 5 6 7 8 9 10

1

The birds had flourished in the aftermath. Come morning, their commotion of song would enter her worried dreams and gradually build until the world and all its real frights rushed in.

Sarah pushed away the long coat that had been her blanket for the night and sat up in the musty back seat of the dead Buick. The windows of the abandoned car were caked with years of dirt and grime and the cabin was dark despite the dawn. She reached for the lamp stick in one of the coat's many pockets and used it to check that nothing had tumbled out from the others while she'd slept. Satisfied the gear and weapons were all where they should be, she popped the old finger-pull lock on the left-rear door and slowly pushed it open, careful not to let the rusted hinges squeal too loudly.

The outside air was delicious compared to the rank confines of the old car. Crisp and clean. Sarah slipped on the long, heavy coat, slung the strap of her bag across her chest, and picked up the path she'd been on when she spotted the car the previous evening.

At night the shadows hid the wildness that had overtaken everything. With the dawn she was reminded again of just how exuberant the landscape had become without its tenders. The trees, bushes, grasses, and vines seemed ecstatic to have been left alone, free to sprawl over the walkways and roofs. Like everything else, they were determined to capture all they could. She walked alone, waiting for the sun to rise fully above the horizon and the air to warm. There were just six hundred miles left between her and Ohio. Five thousand more after that and she'd be back on ship with Trin.

If he'd forgive her.

The *if* was a new thing. It had entered her mind somewhere on the Atlantic after she'd lost sight of land and a panic rushed up in her as cold and sour as the ocean spray. Eventually, the panic had left. The *if* did not.

When she approached a narrow two-lane road heading west, she took the camera bot from a breast pocket and sent it flying ahead to scout. While the little machine surveyed, she remained in the tall grass and shrubs to wait and snack. But for the noise of the birds, it was quiet. No traffic, no voices on the breeze. She scanned the sky in all directions.

"No rain, I think," she said aloud to no one.

It had been two days since Sarah and the French girl went their separate ways. Or maybe three. It was hard to keep perfect track of time, and hard to know why she was even attempting the trick in the first place. She and Gabi had not been close. There'd been language barriers at times, and other things in the way. It was, she had thought, a relationship of convenience. Of mutual safety. Except she and Gabi had shared something important, something Sarah hadn't shared with anyone in a long time: a common birth planet.

Three years ago, Earth wouldn't have been an address with any meaning. From where else could one be? But since the answer to that question had suddenly—and tragically—changed, a connection between two people as basic as each having been raised under the light of the same star, even if one called it *the sun* and the other *le solei*, was newly binding. It had made Gabi's leaving painful in a way Sarah hadn't expected.

They were always going to part ways. That was understood from the beginning. Once they'd made it to New York, to the Kingdom, they each had their own paths to follow. Gabi into the Kingdom proper, and Sarah to Ohio. To home. If it was still there. If truth be told, a part of Sarah had looked forward to the split. She hadn't wanted a travel companion in the first place, and Gabi had been more liability than asset. She was weak, dangerously attractive to men, and she'd cut into Sarah's dwindling food supplies. When they'd finally separated, Sarah thought her load would lighten. She'd be free once again to move at her own pace, make her own decisions about when to rest, when to eat, and where to sleep. She wouldn't have to hide the truth. But if anything, the load had only gotten heavier. Gabi, by her absence, and in the sting of her parting words, had somehow joined the others. The ghosts that stalked Sarah's dreams.

The bot returned and Sarah skimmed quickly through the projection. The road appeared empty. Safe enough at the moment. She left the shrubs and grasses of the neglected park and started down the pavement. The weight of the duster holstered in her coat shifted against her hip in time with her steps. She once hated its heft and the danger it conjured. Now in the way a favorite watch is missed when it isn't worn, the heavy, alien gun had become part of her stride. Part of her. Somewhere along the way, certainly in Gabi's eyes, and maybe even her own, she'd become something dangerous, something to fear.

Six hundred miles left between her and Ohio. Five thousand more after that and she'd be back on ship with Trin.

Unless by then there was simply too much to forgive.

2

How many words can be squeezed into ten seconds?

This had been the question swirling around his brain for days. Kino had been considering at least three different strategies he might employ in the dangerous game of words he knew he'd soon be playing. Tom Nader, *the mayor*, as he was known in New York, would insist upon it. Kino had seen this happen often enough to predict it with confidence, especially if the mayor had an axe to grind with someone. And in Kino's case, the mayor most definitely had an axe to grind. Or two. The botched killing in Murray Hill and the unfortunate bedding of the wrong woman—both were dumbass moves worthy of a stubborn grudge. Even if the bedding was her idea.

Ostensibly, the ten-seconds game was an eccentric exercise in efficiency. A mind game that pitted the mayor's skills of intimidation against a contestant's skills of speedy persuasion. Convince him the meeting would be worth his limited and precious time and a few moments would be granted. Looking at this proposition with one eye squinted and the other closed, the game made perfect sense. The mayor was, in fact, a tremendously busy man. Holding his Scotch-taped kingdom together took all kinds of time. So sure, it was only right that getting his attention be a challenge. However, the real sense of the game didn't show itself with the winners.

It was the losers who illuminated the game's true purpose, because in their defeat, they shone a blood-red spotlight on the perverse proclivity that had established the mayor's iron grip on power in the first place. He killed people. Often. Now, Kino knew all kinds of degenerates who could seemingly shoot without regret. But in the mayor, he saw an enthusiasm for murder that inspired Kino to wonder if it wasn't a kind of oxygen for the mayor, an elemental need. The game, then, not only fulfilled the mayor in some twisted way it gave him one of history's most proven tools for control. A daily body count.

Until now, Kino had only been a spectator to the game. To actually play the game himself would require something new from him: a plan. He used his walk downtown to run through his various strategies. No matter which way the game might go, Kino wanted his responses down cold. Of course, he knew that the words he'd ultimately speak would only carry him so far. The real trick to the game would be to keep his emotional footing under control, along with his bowels.

In this regard, Kino did have one tiny advantage upon which he had placed all his hope. He knew what he was walking into. This was the principal pro amidst the many cons of his endless mental machinations concerning his next step. Most contestants hadn't seen the game coming. The game was sprung upon them by surprise, its rules hidden and seemingly random. Which, of course, they were. To the unsuspecting, there was no way to have practiced or prepared in the slightest. And in nearly every losing case, balance, or lack of it, had been the deciding factor.

The mayor had a unique gift for destabilizing things. People especially. His very presence brought out in people their weakest selves. Even seasoned killers seemed to rattle under the mayor's gaze: one bright, piercing, blue eye, the other a light, milky green, and aimed slightly off from wherever the blue one was pointing. Although Kino had always addressed the blue eye, he worried it was the damaged green one that did the real seeing, that looked past the lies. Kino didn't believe in superpowers, or in much of anything, but he believed the mayor had in him that certain something people of greatness sometimes have—a bewitching force that inspires in others a willingness to trade whatever shreds of goodness they might possess for nothing more than proximity. Mere charisma couldn't explain it. In the mayor, there appeared to be more going on.

Kino had read once, Before, that nearly one-seventh of the world's population was directly related to Genghis Khan. Apparently, once the great Khan had captured a village, he raped its mothers and daughters. Generations later, with the help of transoceanic trade and the bloody-footed migrations inspired by war and famine, the Khan's DNA had spread across the world. Perhaps the mayor had received a bigger share than most. Whatever it was, it was a power that simply couldn't be denied. Now, for better or for worse, Kino had decided to put himself squarely in the crosshairs of that power.

What options did he have, though? None. He had done the calculations ad nauseam, weighed the situation every which way possible, and there was simply no getting around it. See, he was on a list. The Mayor's List.

The List wasn't a kill list, not exactly. But it was close. Or maybe worse. It was exile. Three years After Correction, a documented shunning like The List brought with it a whole host of painful exclusions. For starters, the door to city hall was literally closed to him, cutting him off from the big-money work only the mayor could dole out, such as enforcement jobs or resource commandeering. Needless to say, even subcontracting for others still happily in the mayor's good graces was impossible. Those with more mayoral largesse than they could personally handle wouldn't dare risk helping a Lister, however proficient and expert he might be. There were too many clean guns available hoping for a shot at getting on the inside. Crossing the line of The List was the same as crossing the mayor himself, which was the same as suicide.

Working, and therefore eating and sleeping someplace where the rats left him in peace, hadn't been easy. He'd had some temporary luck in hauling garbage, construction, and as a shovel master at the water filtration plant. That last job, scooping and hefting raw sewage, had been the worst of it. Still, all of it had been real work, the kind his body disliked in the extreme. When he had a bed at night, he would fall into it exhausted and sore, his hands cracked and bleeding. But it was the knock-down back to civilian status, and the myriad of daily humiliations and deprivations that came with it, that represented the true punishment of exile. On the inside he had access to all sorts of luxuries. Two-ply toilet paper, coffee, and most precious of all, a name.

On the inside Kino was *someone* because he was at least the mayor's no one. Now, without the mayor, he was back to being an ordinary nothing. Even Before, New York City was a ballbuster. In the After-Correction world, New York was a slog on a whole different level.

He was on Lafayette and nearly as close to the old city hall building as Foley Square. He turned to face uptown. It was a bright day. Apart from the red and black colors of the Kingdom, which were draped almost everywhere, the city, aglow with full sun, looked almost normal. He shook his head in wonder. It was true, the Correction hadn't reached as far as New York. But it might as well have. Without the energy of tourism and the splashy money of diplomatic work, without the commuters from Queens, Long Island, New Jersey, and Connecticut, the business trips from Europe, Asia, and Des Moines, all of which pushed the population of the tiny island to nearly four million on weekdays, the streets appeared abandoned. He had come to New York for the crowds. He had come for the scale. While the buildings were still there, for him, the city was gone. As gone as the others that truly did disappear. The sight of the emptiness only expanded the one in his soul.

Nevertheless, more than a million people still lived in Manhattan Kingdom, all trying to do everything they possibly could to scrape out something that seemed at least slightly connected to Before. Yet

Kino wasn't trying to find himself a little scrap of normal. He knew Before was gone. He just wanted to get off the damn list.

He turned back downtown and began his walk again. Once he was within a block of City Hall Park there'd be no turning back. Spotters who were once his friends would radio to security. After that, if he didn't show up, they'd come find him. He had walked this way down Lafayette toward the old city hall building at least four times before. He had always turned back uptown before reaching the Perimeter. On those other walks, he had filled his head with scripts of apology. He had even trained himself to cry on demand. Literally begging, he had told himself on those previous trips, was not altogether over the top. He had done the plusses and minuses, the pros and cons, of all his potential appeals. In his heart, though, he had always known that forgiveness would never be a realistic delivery of his absolution. The List would never have its power if a person could simply weep his way off it, however debasing the tears.

This time he was coming with a gift. One he knew was worth crossing the Perimeter and playing the game to give. He just had to survive long enough to give it.

As he climbed the stone stairs of the old building toward the columned portico that protected the main entrance from the weather, he touched the pocket of the greasy coat that carried the phone. It was the hundredth time he'd checked the pocket that morning. Getting to the phone as quickly as possible in the game would be important. He ran through his lines again, this time out loud, searching for the right tone of voice—something between too cool and the actual desperation he felt.

Of the five sets of double doors, only the middle was in use. The others had been bricked over. The center doors, the working doors, had been clad with steel and outfitted with an intercom and several security cameras. He pressed the dirty intercom button. He heard the digital buzz on the other side of the door and then the whirr of the gears that redirected one of the nearby security cameras in his direction.

"You have got some very large-sized testicles," a thick, educated, Mumbai accent crackled from the tinny speaker in the door.

"Good morning, Lonny," he answered back as flatly as possible.

"Good morning? Fuck you. How's that for a good morning?"

"About what I expected."

"Glad I could be so accommodating. I feel my life is fulfilled. You can go now."

"Listen. I have something."

"You have something? Yes, my friend, I believe you do. You have a disease. A dreadful disease. And it has infected your mind. If you think you are in any way welcome here, you are delusional."

"You think I'd risk crossing the Perimeter if what I have wasn't something he'd want?"

"Who knows with you, Kino? You are not the sharpest knife in the block."

"Drawer. Not the sharpest knife in the *drawer*."

"Exactly. And your continued harassment of my command of the idiomatic inanity of American English, even in bloody exile, is only proving my point. I would be as crazy as you to open these doors for a Lister."

"I'm trying to do the right thing here, Lonny."

"You and the right thing? Now, this is *hilarious. Advice for an old friend: leave while the only holes on your head are the ones nature has given you."*

"Lonny, please. I need this."

"I'm sorry, Kino," he said in a tone that, to Kino, didn't sound particularly regretful. *"I cannot help you."*

"That's your last word?"

The speaker was silent except for the soft, telltale hiss of a line still open. A sign that maybe the conversation wasn't quite over.

"Okay, Lonny. I'll take it to King George. Deeper pockets there anyway."

He turned and headed back toward the long, stone stairs.

"You are wagering that we would let you off this island," the speaker crackled.

Kino faced the doors, but remained where he was, closer to the stairs down than the doors in. He heard the gears of the camera refocusing the lens to its now more distant subject.

"If I walk down these stairs right now, we're both betting, aren't we? And I can get on and off this rock anytime I want."

The hiss continued.

"Perhaps I should understand the quid pro quo," Lonny finally answered. *"It might help in my decision process."*

Kino looked around him before answering. He didn't see any of the lookouts or security guns that might make a run for it impossible. "You let me in, old friend, and I'll forget that you almost didn't."

"Asshole."

Asshole was good. It wasn't "fuck off" or even "goodbye." "Asshole" was merely a statement of fact. So, even though the intercom had clicked off completely, its hiss gone abruptly silent, Kino pictured Lonny making his way from the monitor station to the doors, the three US silver dollars the doorkeeper always kept in his pocket jangling all the way. Sure enough, a minute later he heard the heavy bolt from the top lock shoot back into its metal cradle. Then the middle lock and, a beat later, the bottom. The door opened a few inches, enough for him to see the shapes of Lonny's eyes and his bright, white smile emerge from the dark skin around them and the much darker gloom of the entranceway.

"He hasn't shot anyone today, yet," Lonny said with mock cheer as he swung the door open wide. "Please, come in."

Kino stepped into the large, stone-clad entrance. It wasn't much warmer than the outside temperature, and other than the soft light coming in from the rotunda, it was dark as hell.

"Running low on bulbs?" Kino asked as he surveyed the hall.

"Lights are for guests."

Lonny slammed the door shut and shot the bolts back home one by one. When he was done, he turned to Kino. "Arms out."

Kino spread his arms and the doorkeeper gave him a quick patting. He took the phone out of Kino's jacket pocket, looked it over disinterestedly, and slid it back in place.

"You know the rules, Kino. Straight back, no detours. I am well aware of your sticky hands."

"Fingers, Lonny. Sticky *fingers*."

Lonny smiled slowly and hit Kino hard in the gut. It was a perfectly timed sucker punch and Kino doubled over, surprised by the blow and embarrassed to be surprised. Especially by Lonny, who'd see any screw up by Kino as a win.

"Jesus, Lonny!" he coughed.

"Old friend, why must you always prove my point?" Lonny gently grabbed Kino by the shoulders and got him standing straight again. "Enjoy the game. And please do not vomit on his carpets. They're new."

Kino slowly made his way through the large, unfurnished hall toward the rotunda and beyond it, to the mayor's office. Before, the room was home to dozens of desks and their occupants doing city business. Now it was a heavily guarded buffer zone that shielded the mayor's office from the street entrance. The city work attended to in this hall had died three years ago with the city itself. Now Kino was walking through the makeshift Court of Manhattan Kingdom, government seat to a semi-feudal city-state, one of hundreds that formed after the Correction set the clock of civilization back half a millennium.

He counted how many guns he could see as he walked. Eight, ten, twelve. He counted the number of computers. Zero. When he was a boy, he dreamed of flying cars. He got the Middle Ages instead.

For New York City, they had arrived via the Midtown Tunnel, in a caravan of Streets and Sanitation trucks stolen from the outer boroughs and jury-rigged with black-market RPGs. The two hundred trucks and the army they carried had required just three days to take city hall. It was crazy. So was the man in charge.

Tom Nader, lacking any real moral compass beyond one that pointed to his own desire for power, had been far more willing to kill in his quest for control than the depleted and exhausted NYPD had been in its mission to keep it. Nader was a man who knew an opportunity when he saw one. And, as far as Kino could tell, the mayor had never missed one since.

Actually, in the days right before Nader's army swept into town, it didn't take a shark's nose to smell blood in the water. Everyone picked it up. Too much had already happened. The discovery of the ship, the Twenty-One-Hour War, and the cheap shots from Russia. Three big ones that left a radioactive hole in the middle of North America that couldn't be crossed in either direction. It didn't take long before the U in US stood for Unraveled. Russia's nuclear scumbaggery was almost the least of the problems. The Correction had been the white-hot match to the soft, dry wood that undergirded the global order. Modern life and everything that had held it together went up too fast to even run for the buckets.

It was only a matter of time before a Tom Nader would come along.

After the smoke had cleared and the bodies were picked up, a kind of resignation had set in. If the National Guard had been too leaderless to help, if the Congress and the Cabinet had all locked themselves behind the doors of their summer homes, if even the military had left its post and torched its own vast armory to keep its contents from joining the coming chaos, then someone had to establish order. Sure, Tom Nader was a sociopath, but he made sure the power was on in most places, made sure the water ran, and made sure enough people could eat.

His only price? Total control. "Deal," said the desperate residents of Manhattan. For most of human history it had been kings, emperors, and queens. He was simply one more. Hours after the last of the police had given up, the tunnels and bridges in and out of the city were transformed into armed border crossings. Nothing and nobody went in or out without knowing the right people, blowing the right people, or paying the right people. Manhattan had become an island in every sense of the word. Still, given all that had happened, it wasn't the worst that could've occurred. If a person tried hard enough, he could still find booze.

Kino touched his pocket again, making sure the phone hadn't fallen out when Lonny's welcome punch bent him in half. The door to the mayor's office couldn't be missed. It was at the end of the main hall, surrounded by four men and four machine guns.

"Gents," Kino said casually as he approached.

"Kino," said the biggest. "Long time."

"Maybe not long enough," he replied straight faced.

They laughed, and Kino pushed through the doors.

The mayor's office was much as he remembered: palatial, with a soaring barrel-vaulted ceiling and a tall dentil-notched mahogany crown between it and the paneled walls. Ornate carpets covered the parquet floors. Nader's staff was scattered about the room. Two guards were standing along the back wall behind the desk facing the door. On the big leather sofa were two women who looked to be around Kino's age, mid-thirties, both Asian, both beautiful. In a large chair next to the desk slouched a long-legged man with gray hair and a tired face. Kino didn't recognize any of them.

Nader himself was perched on the leading edge of the seven-foot-long desk, his signature mirror-finished Smith & Wesson 686 in his left hand. He wore what would have been a six-thousand-dollar suit Before. A blue chalk-stripe, two-button. His dark brown shoes were polished. He was trim and well groomed, slightly tanned, and looking not a day older since Kino had last seen him. Was he fifty? Sixty? Kino had never known. It had never mattered.

The most important things to know about Nader were that his patience was nonexistent, his temper misleadingly controlled, and his shot never missed. It always hit its target precisely between the eyes, exactly centered. Dead center, Nader called it. Also, Nader was smart. Perhaps the smartest person Kino had ever known. Smarter, he knew, than any of the other kings. The plus that was also a minus. But the matter of The List outweighed all cons, which was why Kino had risked standing on the mayor's new carpets, waiting for Nader to start the game.

The mayor looked at Kino, his two-toned stare expressionless. It was a long look. When he finally spoke, he didn't move a muscle.

"Ten seconds."

"Thanks for seeing me, Tom."

"A foolish waste of two seconds."

Kino took a breath and chose to ignore the finger flick to the nuts of his courage.

It's just Shove One, Kino told himself. Nothing more than a tactic. He squared his stance and plowed forward.

"I can get us some really big guns."

"Stop." Nader's voice was calm, soft, without urgency, as if he knew none was needed. "Let's be clear, Kino. There's no 'us' in whatever you're about to say. Not anymore."

"Okay, sure, Tom. You, then. I can help you get your hands on some guns...guns I know you need."

Nader released the cylinder of the revolver and spun it. Kino could see that all six chambers were full.

Shove Two.

The mayor clicked the cylinder back in place. He casually polished the gun with the end of his tie. "Three seconds left, Kino. And I've got all the guns I need. More guns than any kingdom east of the zone."

"These are special," Kino said.

"That's funny. The bullets in my gun are special too. Thirty-eight Special," Nader toyed. "Maybe I should show you."

"Alien special."

Nader arched an eyebrow and laughed. "Kino, you've developed a sense of humor. I'm impressed. I admire personal growth. After all, conquering our own limitations is always the toughest challenge of life, isn't it? Good for you. But your ten seconds are over."

He pointed the barrel of the gun at Kino's face and squinted down the sights.

"I'm surprised at you, Kino. You of all people know how insanely dangerous it is to waste my time. There hasn't been an alien sighting in years, and never one on this continent."

"Let me show you something," Kino said, his voice even, in check. He looked past the gun to Nader. "I have proof."

Nader kept the gun aloft. "Proceed. Quickly."

"A vid. You'll see. The alien, she takes out at least eight bangers. All big boys. And she does it fast. Three shots. There's nothing left to bury, only dust."

"She?"

"Young. Blonde and..." Kino stopped himself from offering any more details.

Nader must have guessed what was next in Kino's litany because that very particular sort of smile, the one reserved for the appreciation of a beautiful woman, started on his face. "I'll grant you eight bonus seconds," Nader said, as he adjusted his grip on the pistol.

"I'm going to take my phone out," Kino said carefully. "No one shoot me, please."

He took the phone from his pocket. It was the beat-up Apple 5SE he stole from the French girl after her grip on the device had been greatly diminished by the travel of a titanium carbonite blade across her throat. Before meeting Kino, she had high hopes of selling the video stored on the phone for enough diamonds to survive life in New York. She'd come to find her boyfriend who had left Paris for Gotham right before the world fell apart. *"Because he was such a talented actor,"* she'd said.

Or maybe she didn't. It was ancient history now and too boring a story for Kino to have remembered much of it. The girl's nervous oversharing had made his head pound. Half the reason he'd cut her throat was just to shut her up.

In a way, he'd done her a favor. He'd been quick about it. Merciful. She was too beautiful to live long. And her hair...like mythic goddess curls. A girl like her would have found herself in all kinds of unholy trouble in New York. A girl who had been stupid in all the worst ways. Stupid to have held onto anything from Before. Like dreams of a boyfriend. Or hope. Stupid to have done what she must have done to get out of Paris and to Manhattan. And stupid to have believed Kino would pay what she had wanted for the vid.

There were some people in the After a person like Kino had to pay if he wanted certain things. The French girl had not been among that inglorious community of fellow grifters, hustlers, and worse. She had been unconnected in any way Kino needed to fear, and she had been unarmed. She had all but tattooed "kill me" on her forehead. He only did what someone else would have done, but at least his knife was sharp. Still, and much to his surprise, he had felt badly when instead of diamonds from his pocket, he had produced a knife. The look on her face was so pathetic he couldn't stop himself from letting a twinge of empathy push its way through the dead thing in his chest that used to be his heart.

The twinge, however, had been just that. A twinge.

He hit play and handed the phone to Tom Nader. The mayor watched the video twice in silent and intense study. Clearly Kino's bonus seconds had been extended without notification.

"Where did you get this?" the mayor asked, hitting the little white triangle on the freeze frame once again.

"A friend of the shooter."

"Not a very good friend. But what can an alien expect, yes?"

"Desperate times," Kino answered evenly.

The mayor lifted his eyes from the screen to partially meet Kino's, the green eye surveying some other interest. "Indeed, they are. What about the blonde? Your Killer Alien?"

"I know where she's going. Told the friend a story about fetching a sister and bringing her back to the ship."

"A sister? That doesn't make much sense, does it?"

"An obvious cover. But whatever, I'm happy to act as the welcome committee."

"Nice of you to offer, Kino, but the game's not over."

The mayor brought the gun up again. For the first time, Kino noticed the green eye snap into obedience. It sent a tiny shiver of fear up his spine.

"What else do you know about this alien with the amazing gun?" the mayor asked. "Her friend must have told you more before you killed her. You did kill her, yes?"

"Only her name. Sarah. And yes, the friend is dead."

"Sarah? You're sure of it?"

Kino wondered if there was a bit of genuine surprise in the mayor's voice, or if Kino was simply being toyed with again, just another round in the game. Kino shrugged. "Yeah, that's what she said. Sarah."

The mayor seemed to be chewing on this—the issue of the girl's name. "Okay, Kino," he said at last. "Maybe you'll get a chance to earn your way home. To redeem yourself. But it'll be your last chance. Disappoint me again and we, along with your pitiful life, are through for good. Do you want this chance, Kino? Because I'm happy to just take your stolen phone and leave you on the List. It's not much of a life, but it beats the alternative."

"I won't let you down, Tom."

"You mean this time," Nader said with a crooked smile. A beat later he knocked the top of the desk with the knuckles of his right hand, perhaps signaling an end to the game, or at least a decision. "Fine, a chance it is," he declared to the room at large. "One more thing," his tone was casual now. "The blonde, bring her back. Alive."

Kino didn't like this "one more thing" at all. It would take him time to weigh all the possibilities but there was no doubt in his mind that bringing the alien back, especially alive, would mean all kinds of trouble. All kinds of unnecessary risk. Who knew what an alien was truly capable of?

"It's cleaner if we keep this about the weapons, Tom, don't you think?" He looked over at the two women in the room, then back to Nader. "Besides, you have plenty of friends."

Nader smiled fully. "See, this is what worries me about you," he said, still peering down the polished barrel at Kino, the green eye deadly serious. He let his smile fall. "You've got good ideas, and one of the brassiest sets of danglers I've ever had working for me. I'll give you those. But sometimes, Kino, you can get risk and opportunity all mixed up. That little *mistake* up in Murry Hill comes to mind."

"That was a fast-moving situation." Kino's throat had gone dry. If he could live three moments of his life over again, the mess in Murry Hill would be one of them.

"Everything's a fast-moving situation, Kino. I can't be everywhere. I need my team to keep up, and to know when the fruit is there for the picking." He lowered his gun, turned the phone toward Kino, and hit play. "Now watch carefully." Nader let the video play for a few seconds. At the 00:14 mark he paused it. "It was just a flash, Kino. When she swings around to get the last of those boys. Most people would have missed it, but something like this is the kind of thing I need you to *see*."

Kino leaned in to get a closer look. "Your alien annihilator there?" Nader said breezily. "She's wearing a cross."

Kino nodded as if he understood the significance of the cross. Later, he'd run down the different possibilities in his mind. Sometimes he needed time to think things through, to consider the angles. For now, it was enough that he had a deal with Nader.

The trick would be keeping it.

SEVEN
WEEKS
EARLIER

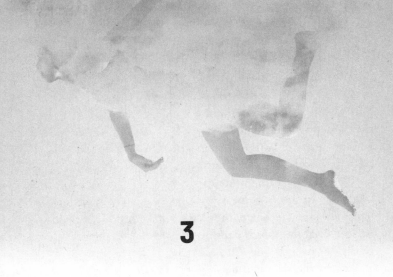

3

It helped Sarah to have a routine. She'd begin her days with a tea at her favorite café table and a vid float that conjured for her a view outside to the planes. They, too, had a routine. She could always find them, well beyond the moat, a tag team of fighter jets, the tattered remnants of Europe's air forces, flying an endless circular patrol around the ship. It wasn't necessary for her to do this, to track them as she did every day. The ship's defenses kept their own watch. But ever since the planes first showed up, Sarah had opened a float for her own close-up view. It was the nearest she could get to her own people.

The planes rushed past the clouds in the float's hovering image, like a scene from a *Top Gun* movie. She liked their precision and their obvious coordination. Their formation flying always looked to her like hope. That the planes seemed intent on intimidating the ship was beside the point. At least they were doing it together.

On this particular morning, Sarah noticed something different about the planes. Their relationship to the horizon was new. They were closer. For some reason they'd broken their own proximity rule since the previous day's patrol. Until now, they'd never dared get any closer to the *Kalelah* than the fifty-mile line.

Why the pilots in those planes had believed fifty miles was safe in the first place she had no idea. It wasn't. If the *Kalelah* wanted to burn them from the sky the ship could do it in a heartbeat. Even if they were five hundred miles away. It would happen so fast the pilots wouldn't even know it had happened. Their demise would occur in a flash that would be over almost the instant it began. To an observer on the ground, it might appear to be a trick of the eye. "Hey," one might say to someone nearby, "did you just see lightning?" In that near-subliminal moment, the planes would be gone, leaving no shrapnel, no serial-numbered debris—only a fine, shimmering dust falling gently downward. The *Kalelah* could do this easily.

Except the ship had declared an end to killing. Although there had never been an official count of the Correction's death toll, all the estimates were in the billions. All life above ground east of Moscow had been turned to a black, jeweled dust, the signature legacy of plasma cannon fire. When she saw the first images of the aftermath, Sarah had gasped. Having seen pictures of Nagasaki, of Dresden, and Jackson after their decimations, she had expected a scarred, brooding apocalypse.

Only there were no burnt-out chimneys standing to say *here once stood a city*. No tumbles of bricks that might someday be stacked right again, no semi-collapsed hulks of municipal grandeur worthy of restoration. Dubai, Delhi, Jakarta, Shanghai, Beijing, Manila, Seoul, Tokyo, and every city, village, and outpost between and around them were gone without a trace, like they'd never been there at all. It hadn't been just a destruction; it had been a cut and paste, one world for another.

In the newly made landscape, the one supplied by the Correction, every vista possessed a dreamlike disposition. It was clear skies—cleaner than they'd been since the Pleistocene Era—and soft, black dunes of sparkle that seemed to go on for endless miles, like the drifting dunes of northern Africa made of black diamonds instead of sand. For Sarah, the images of that absurdly dazzling world had stung like nothing she'd ever seen.

"It's beautiful," she had sobbed to Trin. "Why did it have to be beautiful?"

He took his time to answer, which wasn't like him. The typical Trin response was fast, as quick as his very quick mind, often profane, and confident bordering on cocky. Yet when he answered he was none of those things. His boyish youthfulness, punctuated by the shock of bright green eyes against brown skin, momentarily gave way to the pain of a much older man who had seen far too much.

"Because we have to live with it," he had finally said.

In that instant, Sarah hadn't fully understood his point. She hadn't understood much of anything then. The events had been too quick for her to keep up. That she had started it all, that she had been the one to have accidently knocked the hornets' nest, only made it harder to get her head around what was happening in real time.

Because a world of things had happened.

•

Three years ago, before the Twenty-One-Hour War, before the Correction, before the *Kalelah* had risen from the cover of its ancient hiding place seven miles beneath the surface of the ocean, there was a short, secret meeting aboard a survey vessel named the *Lewis*. And if history would be honest for the first time in all time, that first contact would be remembered as the moment human life on Earth met its actual makers.

The *Lewis*, a state-of-the-art sonar carrier owned by Allied Oil, had recently sailed from her home port in Honolulu to the seas above the Mariana Trench, the deepest waters on Earth. It was an unusual sail. For the first time in its work at sea, the *Lewis* wasn't looking for oil. Several weeks prior, an Allied tanker had spilled off a Japanese beach along the eastern edge of Honshu. The slick had stretched more than a mile. As part of the clean-up and payback package thrust upon Allied, the *Lewis* was loaned out to a research group with hopes to map the sediment below the trench. In fact, the *Lewis* had been central to the negotiations.

To oceanographic scientists the world over, the *Lewis* had become a kind of geologic celebrity. The experimental scanning technology it carried was considered wholly next level, a first-of-its-kind deep-sediment probe. It was the most powerful sonar array ever built. Researchers from all corners had been begging Allied to let them have a run with it, so Allied had been given a simple choice. It could take a side trip from oil hunting and help the world understand what was below the deepest place on Earth, or it could write a nine-figure check to environmental groups that would then use its own money to lobby it out of business. Soon after, the *Lewis*, the scanner, and its operator, geologist Sarah Long, found themselves in waters they'd ordinarily never be.

In those waters, seven miles down, far deeper than sunlight could reach, and deeper still into eons of silt and sand, Sarah Long had found something she wasn't looking for. Something no one was looking for.

Sarah thought often about that little twist of fate. Had it not been for the spill, she wouldn't have aimed her scanner along the particular coordinates that would prove to be the world's most unlucky address. Had it not been for the spill, her scanner wouldn't have awoken something that should have been left sleeping. Had it not been for the spill and the fury it incited in those who would protect the world from the dangers of fossil fuel exploration, there might still *be* a world.

But the spill had happened. And the dominos had fallen.

Less than a week after Sarah's scan had made its discovery, a small transport vessel left the *Kalelah* and traveled the seven-mile vertical trip to the surface of the Pacific. It broke the water gently and without the slightest pause continued its silent ascent into the air. Despite the obvious alien nature of its design and movements, to Sarah, watching from the deck of the *Lewis*, it had been a thoroughly beautiful thing, like a manta ray constructed of mosaic glass, a floating jewel box. Its skin sparkled in the morning sun as it maneuvered above the survey ship and lowered down to the helipad. In that first moment of wonder, charmed by the little craft's radiance, she hadn't dared to imagine the horrors that would soon come from it.

A warm wind had been blowing in hard along the port side and she was struggling to keep her hair from becoming a tangled mess. But when the glass manta's hatch had opened and three men walked off the strange vessel, she gave up on her hair. It had been all she could do just to breathe.

Three years later, the memory of that day still played through her mind in full technicolor. It still woke her up at night, still had the power to churn her stomach.

The three men from the ship had lined up along the port side of the *Lewis* with their backs to the water. The looks in their eyes, the carry of their shoulders, the fidgeting of their hands were profoundly and unmistakably human.

Captain Jan Argen was olive skinned, broad in the shoulders, and muscled in the arms and chest. Had she seen him walking down a shopping street in Honolulu instead of emerging from a crazy little flying craft she knew had risen from an alien ship the size of a city, Sarah might have thought him handsome.

Smenth Ganet, the tallest of the three, pale and light haired, introduced as the *Kalelah's* chief, had a nervous and aggressive stance about him.

The third man had been a different story, even in those first breathtaking moments. He was dark skinned and clearly the youngest of the three. Younger than her, she had figured. His name was simply Trin. One fast syllable. Yet Sarah knew in that instant the short, quick name held a much longer story, and somehow it would include her.

For the rest of that odd and terrifying meeting, she'd catch herself watching him, trying to decipher his thoughts on the strange moment. She knew nothing about him then. Not his intelligence, not his confidence that often nudged right up to recklessness, nor how he'd one day make her feel. Yet his presence, and a sense that he was in some way an ally, had given her the strength not to scream. And what Captain Argen had said in that short confab between two worlds was definitely worth a scream.

Argen's story had begun like this: "We're here to help you, if it's possible." His words were halting, his accent unplaceable.

On the receiving end of those first awkward and mystifying words were Sarah, her boss Scott Bronner, Mike Henderson, a VP from Allied, Len Wilson, the United States Deputy Defense Secretary, Army Major Tom Riley, and several armed soldiers.

"Why would we be in need of help?" asked the army major. He and Wilson had been quickly dispatched to the *Lewis* once the government had learned of the scan.

"Because you are in grave danger."

The deck, with its wind and myriad distractions, had quickly become the wrong place for the kind of conversation everyone now wanted. After a whispered deliberation between Wilson and the army major, they all went below deck to sit uneasily around two steel tables hastily pushed together. The three strange visitors sat on one side, the Americans on the other, with the soldiers hovering protectively behind. Of the two sides, it was hard to tell which was the more nervous. Sarah took a mental note each time one of the visitors from the little ship looked past the people sitting opposite them to the armed men standing guard. She had understood why the weapons were there, how could they not be? Even so, their presence had embarrassed her. And she'd blush every time one of the strangers stole a glance at a pistol or machine gun. She hadn't wanted those things to represent Earth. To represent her.

Argen's words had required a conscious effort at listening, his accent was that inscrutable—an artifact, she would later come to understand, of Virus Injection Learning's early stages. Even when she was able to understand his words clearly, their implications would still twist and knot in her brain. He couldn't possibly have *meant* what it sounded like he said.

"The *Kalelah's* mission is Delivery and Guidance," he said early in his story.

Brows furrowed and eyes shifted sideways, but so entirely freaked out had the American contingent become that no one had the wherewithal to quickly spit out the obvious follow-up.

"Delivery of what?" she finally managed.

"Purelings. Though perhaps it's easier for you to think of them as *seeds*."

"Seeds? What kind of seeds?" asked Wilson.

Argen pointed to a breast pocket of his jumpsuit and looked to the army major. "May I?" He pulled a small square of blue glass from the pocket and placed it on the table. He tapped a corner of the glass, and a large float unfolded above the metal surface and filled most of the room. It displayed a dark field of star-studded space; at the center of the image, a blue planet was spinning slowly on its axis.

"Our home, Origen, the First Place," he said softly.

"My God," whispered Bronner. "If it weren't for the shapes of the landmasses and the three moons, it could be Earth."

"Or Earth, as you call it, could be Origen," Argen answered. "Which is why the *Kalelah* was sent. We came here to finish the work. To add the sacred ingredient that would bring this planet into God's orbit. That ingredient was you."

Silence again. And this time Sarah didn't try to break it. How did one respond to that? Did you laugh it off? Did you weep at the shattering of all you've ever been told and believed? Did you fall to your knees on the ground? She wanted to do all of that.

Wilson, efficient, smart, and playing true to his role in the DOD, got things back to the most important business. "On the deck you said we were in grave danger. What is the nature of this danger?"

"Arguments have been made against you on my ship. Arguments with great power and consequence behind them."

Wilson leaned forward in his chair. "What kind of consequence?"

Argen took a breath. "There's more you need to know."

"Then tell us quickly, Captain. The United States takes threats to its national security seriously."

If Wilson had hoped to put Argen on notice, it didn't work. The look Argen offered back was more pity than alarm.

"Deliveries are fragile," he answered. "Especially in the early stages. This planet looks like the First Place. It's warm and has flowing water like home. It smells like home. But 07-347-28, the place you think has always been yours, is still an alien and dangerous world. We lost dozens of planets at the start of God's travels. It took us millions of years to learn the essential lesson in creating new home worlds in waiting."

He paused for a minute. Sarah had thought he was trying to read the room, but she wasn't sure what he might make of the faces he'd see—or what others might do with the suddenly supercharged breathing space. The story he was telling was crazy. Comic book crazy. Henderson's famously blooming cheeks had already turned crimson, Wilson's eyes were clouded in disbelief, and Riley had looked ready to tip the table over. If everyone hadn't known the giant ship below them was real, if everyone hadn't seen the little shuttle hover the water with their own eyes, the three strange visitors would probably have been arrested and locked away, and Argen's story locked away with them.

"The essential lesson," she prodded. "What was it?"

"Surrender," he said at last.

"What the hell does that mean?" Henderson snapped.

"A wild planet has a powerful immune system. Its weapons are disease, predators, poisons, and perhaps most potent of all, the keeping of secrets. Millions of secrets. It's impossible to prepare for dangers you don't know exist, for enemies beyond your own imagination. After an unbroken string of failures, a shift in strategy took place. Instead of shelters and machinery and the import of our familiar ways, instead of trying to force *us* upon the planet, we've learned it's better to let the planet put itself upon us. The only strategy that has proven to work is to come naked, with no language, no culture, no technology. The Pureling seed populations we bring are surrendered to the planet as clean slates awaiting the natural scribbling of their adopted home. They must then do what every other successful organism in the universe has done."

"Adapt," said Bronner.

"Yes. To survive, Purelings must become no less an elemental part of their world as water to a river. They must lose their alien scent. For that, they have the planet as their tutor. Over time, through trial and error, through death and survival, they become new natives. Once immunized in that way, they are ready to begin their transition from *halfborn* to *fullborn*. The journey to become humans in exactly the ways God has prescribed. For that process they have us. The Guides."

"So, what, you *direct* who and what we become? Is that what you're saying?" Sarah asked.

"In a way. We influence from a distance. Through viruses in the water or the air, through engineered insects whose stings contain learning agents, we implant ideas that manage a seed population's pace of discovery, as well as what it discovers. Language, culture, God, the knowledge and ways of the human universe."

"Okay," Bronner jumped in, "suppose what you're saying is true. Where are we in this process of yours?"

Argen appeared caught off guard by the question. "Your Delivery occurred more than one hundred and twenty thousand years ago. It has since taken an unusual trajectory."

Bronner blinked at the number. "Sapiens," he said softly, as if a few of the crazy dots suddenly connected.

"What are you talking about?" asked Henderson.

"In the fossil record, one hundred and twenty thousand years ago is about where modern humans show up."

A chair pushed back hard from the table, its back legs screeching loudly against the metal floor of the mess, and the army major stood. He looked at Wilson, fire in his eyes. "How much more of this crap are you going to take?"

Sarah had seen this coming. She'd watched the major slowly boil during the meeting. Whether others felt like he did she couldn't say, but he was the one to worry about most. He was the one with the guns.

"These people are lunatics," the major said, "or enemies trying to distract us. Or both."

Wilson motioned the major to sit, though the look that went with it made the gesture read like, *"Sit the fuck down."* The major sat, but didn't look particularly settled about it, and Wilson turned to Argen.

"Captain, as fascinating as this story is, you haven't told us why we're in danger."

Trin stood up now. Slowly and carefully, as if trying to tamp the tension. "There was a malfunction of the time clock." He took the glass from Argen and filled the room with digits and graphs. He pointed to two strings of symbols. "While we don't know how it happened yet, as you can see, the timing's all off."

Sarah couldn't even begin to make heads or tails of what they were looking at, nor could anyone else from her side. She gave him a look.

"Sorry," said Trin. "What you're looking at is the guide model for this planet. Each one of these graphlets along this line signifies an epoch of time." He pointed to a series of round, knot-like marks. "These marks indicate the epochal checks, or E-checks, the moments when we monitor the population and guide, or administer the influence needed. Since adaptation only works if it works slowly, this model calls for forty-one E-checks over the course of one hundred and fifty-six thousand orbits. Sorry...*years*."

"That's impossible," said Wilson. "How can you possibly span that time?"

"In a kind of deep sleep that allows our bodies to skip time. Usually, we don't Skip for more than ten thousand years. At least not on purpose. Most Skips are planned to be much shorter." He walked a few paces to his right down a long line in the float. "When the scan alarm woke us, it was supposed to be E Two, six thousand years from the first E-check, and nine thousand years since Delivery. Except that wasn't what happened." He followed the line further, curving round the table as he walked, forcing the soldiers to back up and give him room. "Somehow, we overslept. To E Thirty-Seven. To now."

The red in Henderson's cheeks had spread to his neck. "You forgot to set your damn alarm clock? That's the problem?"

"We don't know what went wrong," said Argen. "But here we are, and here you are."

The pale one, Ganet, didn't like his boss's answer. "Let me make this simple. You've been on your own for a long time. For too long a time. What you've become in that time...*that's* the problem."

Sarah looked to Trin. He met her gaze and the sadness in his face made her stomach drop.

Argen nodded solemnly. The words he said next were tinged with resignation, like the lines performed by an actor not quite on board with the script. "The human universe requires consensus of thought. Consensus of belief. That requirement is why there is Guidance, a learning process you were denied. The things you know, the things you think you know, the technology you possess, the gods you worship—all of it was acquired without the benefit of the Plan. So all of it, by definition, is incongruent. Forbidden. You have grown apart from the rest, and that cannot be."

That word, *forbidden*, it hit Sarah like a brick. She looked to the other Americans. Everyone's eyes told the same story.

After a minute, Wilson folded his hands in front of him and put on the face of someone still in control, but Sarah could feel the bouncing of his leg through the vibration of the floor. In the quiet, she could hear the subtle squeak of his shoe.

"Now it's my turn to make something simple," he said at last. "Whatever you and your people may think, this is our planet. We'll decide what can and cannot...*be*."

Argen's jaw clenched. He swallowed hard and when he finally spoke, Sarah felt a sense of desperation in his tone that frightened her more than anything he'd said so far. "The *Kalelah* has an obligation. And unless we move quickly, my crew won't abandon it."

The bounce of Wilson's leg picked up its pace. "An obligation to whom? To what?"

"To God. To the Plan. To the way things are and have always been. The people on the *Kalelah* don't need my orders to know what they are compelled to do. I've been buying time for the last few days, but with the chief and I off the ship, preparations for Correction are likely in motion as we speak."

"Correction?" Wilson pushed back. "You're going to try and reeducate us? Seven billion of us? Half the world doesn't even believe in evolution, and you expect us to abandon everything we know and believe in you? In this story?"

Argen's face was of a man already in mourning. He looked at Wilson for a long time. "No," he finally said. "A Correction is not education."

The film in her mind always stopped there, at The End.

4

Sarah spent her mornings on the *Kalelah* watching the planes and her afternoons attempting to learn the Plan. How else could she possibly even begin to understand the people around her, and the first man she had ever loved? And given its presence on ship, how could she ignore it? By her walking estimation, the ship was four miles long and two miles wide. The biggest thing she'd ever seen, a titanium megalopolis. Yet even within all the impossible scale of the *Kalelah*, the Plan loomed large. The ship was like a giant Marriott hotel, only instead of The Book of Mormon available in the top drawer of every nightstand, there was a chapel every quarter mile of concourse. The lacework symbol of eighteen interlocking circles, one for each scroll, that served as the signpost for the Plan, was more prominent in the stems and passageways of the ship than the Nike swoosh was at a football stadium.

The trouble, of course, was reading the thing. She could speak Origen reasonably well. Trin had dosed her with a language virus soon after she'd come aboard, mere hours after The First Contact. Her accent, however, had remained an embarrassment, her tongue, lips, and throat never quite willing to perform the gymnastics that might hide what her every strangled word revealed. Aboard the *Kalelah*, it was she who was the alien. Nevertheless, she could communicate. The written form of Origen, with its arcane syntax and odd poetic cadence, had been an infinitely harder code to crack. It could take her a day to make her way through just one column of text, and it would leave her head spinning and tired. She had kept at it though, and over time, she'd come to an astonishing conclusion.

The Plan may have had its origins galaxies away, but its purpose was as familiar as the testament she'd been forced to study in Catholic school. The names of the characters were decidedly foreign, and the squabbles were tremendously more far flung, stretching across the universe rather than mere fields, deserts and seas, but it professed to answer the same questions about life's beginnings, the order of the universe, and the nature of God.

And exactly as Argen had promised, in his kind and soft-spoken way, all the answers were different than the ones she'd grown up on. Not just different the way Judaism, Christianity, and Islam were different, which Sarah had always believed were barely different at all. No, the Plan and everything else she knew anything about were different the way oxygen and carbon monoxide were different. They were similar enough that our bodies happily welcomed them both inside, but one had a nasty habit of killing us.

Instead of gospels or testaments, the Plan was a first-person account, the words of God straight from the source. The original scrolls were, according to Him, written in His own blood. No archangel had been sent as interlocuter. There were no gospels written years after the fact, or witness accounts scribbled in ancient tongues defying translation. It was all Him.

> *I slew the treacherous Twaithlaw with my own hands, hurling him into the blue star to be consumed by the molten, spitting fury of his own false and intransient creation. His sons and daughters too, all twelve-hundred and twenty-one thousand, were thusly destroyed, purifying the Ever-And-All of his sin for all time.*

When those battles were done, and the many more that needed fighting, I alone had survived to rule. That I do rule is beyond contestation.
Let none forget. Let none dispute.

It didn't matter if she believed a word of what she'd read, because whether it was really God's story, or merely a story, it had inspired people to build a kingdom as vast as the universe itself, and to kill anything that might get in the way of it. Which recently, had been planet 07-347-28.

Also known as *Earth*.

•

All of this had left Sarah caught painfully in the middle, like a halfling of two worlds, both dented and broken by their unimagined collision.

Outside the ship was a world of regrets and people she'd left behind long before the Correction. When she had finally graduated college and left her mother's house for the *Lewis* and the south Pacific, she had no calling then other than distance. Geology had meant nothing to her. Getting as far as possible from Lancaster, Ohio had been the sole point. Surely the other side of the world would be far enough.

Except it wasn't. There had been no getting away from Jack, her stepfather, and the mother and older sister who had looked the other way.

She had their email addresses still, her mother's and sister's, and the *Kalelah* was monitoring the sporadic internet traffic for any sign from either of them. So far, nothing. Email of any kind from the US had mostly stopped. Dependable infrastructure and legitimate business models simply weren't there anymore. Hackers were able to stand up crude networks and workarounds that sometimes managed a global reach, such as it was, but never for longer than a day or two. Pirates, counter hackers, and gangsters kept things chaotic.

Based on the bits and scraps of information the ship had been able to stitch together from the spasms of signals coughed out from time to time, Sarah could see that the world she'd known most of her life had quickly grown dangerous in all new ways, with virtually no shelter. Places like North America, Scandinavia, and Western Europe, where a person could once have counted on order, norms, and even sometimes the police, had become indistinguishable from the places where corruption, lawlessness, and wanton cruelty had long ruled. The old corporate battles, the ones once fought with innovation, advertising, lobbyists, and lawyers, had given way to real wars waged with dynamite and bullets.

Then there was her world on the *Kalelah*. The world with Trin. A four-mile by two-mile oasis of impenetrable alloy. Even injured and grounded, the *Kalelah* was safe from the dangers of the other world around her. So Sarah was often told. The ship had fresh water, food grown and processed onboard, and could still cater to her human occupants in every necessary way.

But the *Kalelah* was not safe from herself. The loss of her mission and the shame and guilt that had come with it, were already punishing much of the crew. Two members had tried to escape the ship and its life without purpose. They walked the twenty miles through the fine powder of the impact zone, *the moat*, to the outer rock ring, a ship's recorder bot capturing every inch of their travel. When they had climbed over the ring, they were greeted by a black UAZ pickup covered in dirt and crowded with six men. Unable to respond to the welcome party in Russian, Polish, or even broken English, the two were beaten with clubs and hockey sticks, chained at their feet to the truck's back pull-rings and dragged off to the west, their bodies bouncing lifelessly along the pock-marked asphalt.

The recorder hadn't followed any further. There'd been no point, because there'd be no rescue mission. Not even for the remains. The ship's new leadership had sworn off hostile contact of any kind, even if it meant the death of crew members. The ship would protect the moat if she truly felt at risk, which would take an awful lot to inspire. Outside the moat, leadership had warned, you were on your own.

Although Sarah had no intention of leaving, she hadn't yet figured out how she was going to stay.

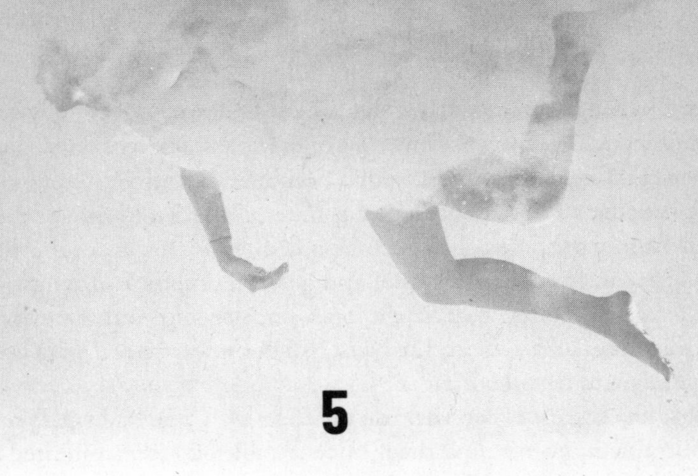

5

Another day starting with the planes. Sarah watched them as they in turn continued to watch the *Kalelah*. Like every day, the transparent, three-dimensional air vid floated above the small café table where she sat drinking a cup of tea, its soft light reflected on the polished surface of the table. Miles away, the tiny recorder bots chasing the fighter jets had no trouble keeping up with their subjects. The intimacy they offered Sarah never ceased to amaze her.

She could elect to have the entire scene play out in front of her, real enough to make her want to touch the images hovering above the table. Or she could move in close enough to see what was happening inside an individual cockpit. None of this required any hardware on her end at all. Another endless amazement. Navigation windows that gave users access to data and images simply appeared out of thin air at the command of a few well-practiced gestures. From there she could get whatever her access level allowed.

There were six planes today. Six pilots. She recognized them all. She had given all the pilots ridiculously stereotypical names based on their tail insignias. Carlos, Jürgen, Nigel, Elouise, Greta, and Luca. Not only could Sarah see the pilots well enough to name them, she could listen to them too. In the 1980s, an international standard had set English as the language of aviation the world over. While the international order was gone, the pilots still stuck to their training. The comfort of habit, she guessed. She loved to listen to their voices. To hear the familiarity of an Earthly language spoken by people actually from Earth.

She did more than just listen. Early in her plane-watching days she had tried to explain what happened. Using the ship's communications tech to break into theirs, she had tried to share with the pilots what she knew to be true. That things were not what they seemed to be. That she was not who they thought she was. She had tried to tell them about the Plan and the guilt over following it to the letter. She had told them, between tears, that she and the others on the ship were just as frightened as the pilots must certainly have been. A hundred times in a hundred different ways she had tried to say how desperately the *Kalelah* mourned.

It grieved, she'd confessed, for its own losses, for there were plenty. The source of all the trouble, the extended Skip—the time-jumping sleep that had gone wrong by lasting longer than it should have, a full one hundred and twenty thousand years longer than it should have—had taken nearly 10 percent of the crew. Hundreds more had died in The Mutiny. The *Kalelah*, she had argued, wasn't taken down by the forces of Earth. It was taken down by a deadly uprising within its own crew. She'd chronicled, in agonizing detail, the entire bloody fight. Including the story of its failure. Yes, she and the others who fought for the people of Earth had managed to stop the Correction, but not before it had started. This, more than anything, was what the ship truly grieved. For Earth's losses, she'd wept, there were not tears enough to cry.

To make a peace, she had made offers as well. Pledges to help in their recovery. She had described in minute details the marvels of technology aboard the incredible ship. The advances in medical care, communications, and agriculture that could be shared. She had tried to convince them of their connection to the *Kalelah*, and the ship's connection to them, a bond of DNA and a shared heritage as deep and wide as the cosmos itself.

None of the pilots had ever responded. Not once.

Maybe the messages had been the wrong messages. Perhaps she had been the wrong messenger. Or maybe the pain for the pilots had simply been too loud to hear another side of things. The scale of the murder too vast to ever believe it wasn't malicious, greedy, and irredeemable. Or maybe the state of things, of governments, of institutions, of churches, collapsed too quickly for the pilots or their commanders, whoever or whatever they were, to respond in a way that could have made a difference.

After months of pleading with the pilots, and whomever else might have been listening in, she finally gave up her crusade to explain the actions of the ship's crew. She gave up on the idea of changing hearts.

Her monologues since had devolved into simple greetings of good morning, or good evening, talk of the weather, or what she had for breakfast and how she longed for bacon. Or cold pizza. She thought once that Greta might have been on the verge of a response. The German pilot had smiled briefly at a joke Sarah made about cigarettes. Something about the way the corners of Greta's mouth had turned slightly upward, for a brief moment, had made Sarah's heart leap. But the exchange stopped there. Greta had given nothing more. One short-lived half-smile was the only hint Sarah had ever had that the pilots could even hear her.

Recently, the planes encircling the *Kalelah* had begun to breach their self-imposed fifty-mile barrier more aggressively. Carlos, for example, had suddenly diverted from his usual orbit and raced toward the ship for a mile or so, as if leading an attack. After a few days, one mile became two miles, then three, then ten. The other planes began to follow, Luca being the first. Now all the planes had actually shrunk the circle to thirty miles of the ship, only ten past the outer edge of the moat, the de facto border between the *Kalelah* and whatever was left of the world beyond her.

Sarah knew the planes were trying to draw the ship's fire, to learn if it still had any left, an act of sacrifice she couldn't help but admire.

And fear. Not for the safety of the ship or herself, of course. During the Twenty-One-Hour War, when the ship had arisen like a giant, dripping city from the surface of the ocean, the world's top militaries did nearly everything they could to stop it. Russia had checked its swing, having goals of its own, but all the big guns had brought out their best and worst to bring the monster ship down. All had failed to even make a scratch. In less than five hours, the world's largest aircraft carriers and their planes were gone. Two days later, Asia and a most of the Russian Federation were gone too. If it hadn't been for the small war onboard the *Kalelah* herself, the entire planet would have been charred to diamonds. No, the fear she had was for the planes. For Greta, and Luca, Carlos, Jürgen, Elouise, and Nigel.

Trin had assured her the *Kalelah* would never fire on the planes. She believed him. She trusted him. She loved him. Despite that, every time the planes had changed their radius, had come closer to the ship, she had worried for days. Anything could go wrong when people were involved. She knew this all too painfully. The whole world did. She couldn't bear for one of the pilots to die. She couldn't bear to lose another friend.

Even a friend who greeted her confessions with silence.

She looked through the floating image of the planes to the bustle of the stem traffic beyond her table. The sim sky high above the tree-like metal lace of the concourse canopy was blue and brightened by a red-yellow sun. It was morning and she went about getting some food. She gestured for a new window, brought down a second float, and ordered a crispy bread-like cake called *unta*. It was salty and only had minor hints of the dreaded seaweed, which seemed to find its way into nearly everything. Apparently, seaweed was a perfect crop for the *Kalelah*. Nutrient dense, and hard to kill. Unfortunately, Sarah loathed seaweed. Seaweed from another planet proved to be no more likable.

Overall, she really couldn't give food from outer space more than two stars. It wasn't overtly gross, or conspicuously processed, like Space Sticks or MREs. In fact, dining was a big deal on the ship. There were nearly as many cafés and restaurants as chapels. For her, it was all vaguely weird and relentlessly foreign. After most meals, she felt an undertow of nausea faintly pulling at her gag reflex, the same feeling she once had after eating tortilla chips made from cricket flour. They'd gone down without a fuss. Later, though, after she'd eaten half the bag, her imagination had kept choking on the word *cricket*.

After two years on the ship, she still hadn't gotten over the post-meal desire to barf it all away. This week, actually, the nausea seemed to be worse. She'd thrown up after breakfast two mornings in a row. She was thinking about how the *unta* would agree with her when she heard her name in Elouise's French accent break through the float. Not soft or garbled by static. It was unmistakably "Sarah," loud and clear, as if Elouise were sitting at the table with her. Hearing it sent Sarah's heart racing.

She sent a bot in close. For the first time ever, Elouise looked aware of the recorders. Impossible of course. Each was no bigger than a small hummingbird. And at six hundred miles an hour? Yet Elouise actually turned to the small side window of the cockpit, directly to the camera, like an actor in a movie breaking the fourth wall. She lifted the dark visor of her helmet and peered into the lens with eyes that felt strangely familiar to Sarah.

"She's waiting for you," Elouise said.

"What?"

"I'm afraid she won't last long." The pilot's words were calm, but not without worry. There was a new familiarity to the voice too, despite the thick accent. She'd heard Elouise speak many times before, but now she sounded different.

Sarah's cheeks warmed. "What are you talking about? Who won't last long?" she barely managed to get out.

"Margaret," Elouise said with a hint of what sounded like impatience, as if Sarah should have known who "she" was.

"Margaret?" Sarah repeated, her heart pounding so hard she worried it might burst.

"You have to *find* her," Elouise said emphatically. "Find Margaret while you can, Sarah. Do you understand?"

"No. No, I don't understand. Are you saying Margaret's alive?" Sarah said softly, still processing.

"She's waiting, Sarah. She's waiting *now*."

"How? How do you know her? How do you know *my sister*?"

"You can't leave her there, Sarah. It's important you don't leave her."

"Where is she? At least tell me where she is!" Sarah said, the prospect of her sister in some kind of danger sinking in.

"There." The pilot pointed a gloved finger west.

"What does that mean?" Sarah pleaded.

"I have to go now, Sarahbeara. I'm sorry. There are rules. I'm so very sorry."

"Wait. What did you call me?" She sank back in the chair, her head spinning, her breath lost.

Only one person in the world had ever called her by that name.

The pilot lowered her dark visor and turned her head back to once again face the windscreen straight on.

Sarah grabbed the float closer. "Who are you!" she yelled.

Elouise said nothing, and Sarah panicked that the conversation, if that was what it was—if it had even happened at all—was actually over.

For the next hour, Sarah sat at the little café table imploring the glowing visage of the tiny squadron that floated over the table to offer something more, anything more. No response ever came. The pilots ignored her as they did every time before Elouise had called her name. They chatted amongst themselves about flight formation and fuel levels until each one in turn peeled away and was replaced by a fresh plane.

The *unta* had come and long gone cold. Sarah pushed the pan away, rocked by a wave of queasiness. She didn't know what to make of Elouise's strange message, the words of a ghost in the attic.

All she knew was that her world had been turned upside down. And that she was going to be sick.

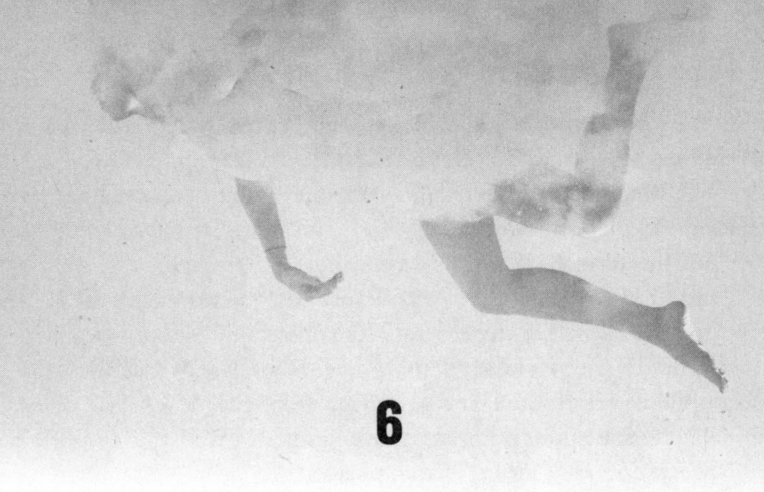

6

That night she stayed awake watching Trin sleep. She hadn't told him about Elouise. They had barely talked at all before she had complained of being too tired to eat and retreated to the pod early. He looked normal there, with his head on a pillow, breathing to the rhythms of sleep like any ordinary human. Which he was, apparently, but also, not at all. For all her life Earth was the human home. Yet here was this man, living, breathing, sleeping proof of the contrary. A dark and beautiful face with blinding white teeth. The aura of a young Obama, his cocky confidence oozing from every pore, the kind that drives someone to take a shot from a high-school gym three-point line with the cameras rolling. "Because that's what I do!" he'd shout when the ball went in. So human. So familiar. So attractive. Except he grew up on a world with purple grass and blue-leafed trees.

How was it that he would be the one who'd made her fall more deeply in love than any person—any human—ever had? She thought about this and a dozen other mysteries of her new, strange life. She thought of her old one as well. The one with Margaret. There had been a certain kind of peace to believing she'd been dead, safe from further harm or suffering. Now, though, after what Elouise had said—if Elouise had actually said it—Sarah began to feel the tug of Margaret's gravity again.

Margaret had their mother's looks, brunette, long lashed, and slender, no matter the number of pizzas per week. She had their mother's fearfulness too. Everything frightened Margaret. Looking back, it seemed their childhood together had been practically defined by the collective work of dealing with Margaret's fears.

When Sarah was six and Margaret nine, the two were alone in the house at night for the first time. The subject of their looming independence had been a thing all day. Their mother wanted a sitter for the girls, certain they were still too young to be alone, even for a few hours. Jack, though, was insistent that Margaret was old enough for the job. In any event, he was done paying for sitters. He spent the rest of the day on the tiny back porch smoking and her mother spent it in the kitchen chewing at her thumbnails like she did whenever she worried. This was the moment when an important truth about her mother and her stepfather had become clear to Sarah. Jack would always win. And he wouldn't have to try particularly hard to do it.

Despite the fuss of the day, the night had begun well. Bagel Bites were successfully heated in the oven and the cable hadn't gone on the blink. Sarah was in the small living room eating in front of the TV when she heard a scream come from the bedroom the two shared on the other side of the house. She ran to the room and found Margaret curled on the floor between the two beds beneath the window that faced the backyard.

"What happened?" Sarah asked.

"A man was at the window," Margaret said, her eyes wide and her lip trembling.

"Was it Mr. Celioni? Sometimes he cuts through our yard."

"No. It was a *stranger*. And he was looking in the window!"

"Is he still there?"

"I don't know." Margaret chewed on her lip for a long while. "Can you look?" she finally said.

Sarah climbed on the bed to look out the window. The moon was barely a sliver, but she could see clearly enough.

"I don't see anyone. There's no one there."

"Are you sure?"

"I think so."

"Maybe we should go outside. To double check," Margaret suggested.

"There's no one there, Margie!"

"Not so loud! He could be hiding. Or in the side yard. He could be on the porch!"

Margaret's sprinting imagination started Sarah's running too. "We should call mommy."

"No! If we call mommy, Jack will be mad." Now Margaret's terrified eyes had the power of truth behind them. A bogeyman would be easier to face than a Jack whose Saturday night was cut short by his wife's panicky daughters. Worse, it'd be their mother who'd bear the biggest brunt of his disappointment.

Sarah got down from the bed and crouched to Margaret's level. "Fine, I'll go check outside."

"I'll come with you," Margaret said. Her eyes, however, said something else. Sarah could see it would take more courage than Margaret had in her at that point to simply stand up, let alone join the patrol.

"It's okay, I'm not scared," she lied. "I told you, I didn't see anyone."

Sarah walked out the front door and followed the cracked and broken segments of gravel and concrete stepping-stones around the little house. Part of her was terrified. Another part of her relished the task. In taking the walk around the house she felt in some small but powerful way that she was holding up her part in the pact of Sarah and Margaret against the world, the world being the tragic mess, obvious even to a six-year-old, that was their family.

According to Margaret, it was the death of their father and the subsequent arrival of Jack that had made the mess. Sarah was barely three years old when her father had died. Her notions of him were not even memories in any useful sense. They were mere fragments of images and moments. A smile. A scratchy beard. Nothing that added up to a real picture of the man. Nothing she could compare to Jack. For Margaret, it was different. She'd known him well enough to grieve him, to miss him. And the presence of Jack, menacing and self-centered, made the missing worse. Whenever Margaret spoke of their father, the pictures she conjured were not the out-of-focus still shots in Sarah's mind. They were stories, vivid and sharp. Stories that could make the both of them laugh. And stories that could make them both cry.

She owed Margaret something for that, for carrying the joy and pain of memory for the both of them. As for Margaret's bogeyman, Sarah never did see him that night. And when she got back in the house she spent the rest of the evening watching TV on the sofa cradled in Margaret's arms and grateful not to be alone.

Life with Margaret was never straightforward or simple. Maybe that's the way it is with sisters.

•

A half hour later, Sarah gave up on the idea of sleep and carefully swung her legs off the small bed of the multitable until she felt the cool of the tiles beneath her feet. She dressed in the dark and managed to make it to the door of the pod and open it without waking Trin.

The stem of Leaf Two was quiet, but not empty. The cleaning bots, looking like Seussian cousins of the Zamboni machines that resurface the ice between periods of a hockey game, were busy at work, their long, spidery arms reaching to the height of the soaring ceiling. She walked close to the side of one, taking in the bright scent that always surrounded a cleaner—like ozone before a storm. She picked up her pace to keep even with the machine on her way to the main stem, its cloud of charged air helping her shake off her own darker fog of sleeplessness.

Leaf Two had been home since the war had ended. She could have had her own pod almost anywhere on ship. Between the number of crew that hadn't survived the crazy long Skip, and then the casualties of war, there were plenty of empties. But the possibilities of her own place had never even come up. Of course she'd stay with Trin. Of course he had wanted her to.

The sim sky above her still displayed the night stars of Tembla Eight and two of the three moons of Origen, the first having already set below the digital horizon. Plenty of time before morning. Maybe someday the ship would be able to disengage its armor and give sight of the true Earth sky through the windows. For now, it was still too dangerous for that.

When she reached the intersection, she turned right at the main stem to travel downship toward Leaf Four, one of the larger leaves. The traffic was heavier now. The main was the major commercial thoroughfare that ran lengthwise and connected all six leaves. Large service offices lined the edges of the huge concourse interrupted by small chapels, gyms, and restaurants. Closer toward the transport lanes in the center of the stem were tiny stands with the feeling of airport pop-ups. Pods were small, personal storage was limited, so people didn't accumulate things. Instead, the stemway markets were devoted to the spiritual, nutritional, and healthcare needs of the nearly twenty-two-thousand-member crew.

There were beverages of all kinds, as well as colorful, bite-sized snacks that reminded her of mochi—but tasted more like sourdough and seaweed. There were injections, pills, and booths that performed minor surgeries.

Almost all the routine business of the stem was managed by bots. They stood stiffly and quietly behind counters or alongside chairs and tables. They were tubes, and pinchers, boxes of all sizes, some metal, some glass, and all of them proud in their shameless distinction as machines. None possessed even a hint of human appearance. Their forms were pure expressions of their functions, like a car without its painted and stylized body. Some were quite elegant, beautiful even, others brutish and obvious. This, like so many things on the ship, was mandated by the Plan. Human life, filled with the breath of God, must not be imitated, said the scrolls. As she made her way, Sarah thought about the irony of being deemed too sacred to copy, but not too precious to kill.

She came to the crossways of Leaves Three and Four and took the left turn to Four. It had become her go-to neighborhood whenever sleep proved elusive. Despite its size, there were almost no pods there. It was an entertainment district specializing in sim worlds and the *Kalelah* equivalent of pubs. After a few thousand years, even a ship as large as the *Kalelah* got small. Leaf Four was the place crew went when they needed some space, even if it was only in their heads.

The Rundera, named after Origen's largest ocean, never closed. It was small, just ten stools along a slab of glowing quartz suspended from three sets of thin wire cables. She liked it because an actual person worked it. In another lifetime, the ocean, with its scale and its secrets, had been the one thing that could keep her from losing her mind. She sat at the stool closest to the entrance and watched the hologram fish that swam through the blue-green liquid projected across the walls of the bar. The scene was a meandering journey through the depths of what she assumed were the waters of Rundera. It didn't look any more alien to her than the depths of the South Pacific once had. Any jellyfish on Earth would look at home in the digital waters of Rundera.

A door glided silently open from the wall behind the bar, drawing a rectangular hole of yellow light in the dark oceanscape, and a tall, brown-skinned man with long black hair and a constellation of jewels studding his left cheek emerged.

"Well, well," he said flatly. He had brought with him a black metal cylinder topped by a shallow dish, which he placed on the bar in front of her. He turned to the shelves behind him and grabbed two jars, one filled with crushed blue crystals, the other with red, and held them out to Sarah. She pointed to the red and he poured a cough drop's worth of the sparkling bits onto the dish. She beckoned with two fingers for more and he doubled the pour.

"Careful, hero," he said, his eyes looking up from the dish to hers.

She cupped the cylinder gently until the dish began to warm up. A soft, white light spread under the crystals and after a minute they began to outgas a creamy-pinkish haze. She leaned a little closer to the dish, inhaled deeply, and held the spice-fragrant vapor in her lungs before gently letting it escape slowly through her nose.

"Drink?" the man asked.

"Wine," she said, her eyes following a large golden eel undulating sideways across the wall behind the man.

He filled a small glass halfway with an absinthe-colored liquid and stepped away to return the bottle to its place on the shelf behind him. He remained there, away from the quartz slab, leaning against the backbar, the ocean movie now playing across the upper half of his face, and watched her drink. She pretended to remain fixed on the holo, the anonymous camera moving through a coral reef now, the stony field of color lit by a silty shaft of sun.

"You going to stand there and watch me all night?" she asked.

"Be morning soon enough."

"It's never soon enough," she answered in English, tweaking him for no good reason. It put a moment of silence between them. Likely another crystal-related casualty. The red stuff did that to her. It clarified and sharpened her, let her be herself. Sometimes she needed help with that.

"Third night in less than two weeks," he finally said.

"Nothing gets by you, does it?" She took another hit from the crystals and launched a perfect ring of vapor up toward the sim predawn sky.

"Trin know you're here again?" There was a sweetness in his question. It pissed her off.

"He doesn't have to know everything."

"Suit yourself."

"If only."

She sat there for a long while, slowly drinking her wine and not talking. When her glass was empty and the crystals cooled, she pushed away from the bar, got off the stool, and stood to go. She turned back to the man instead, who remained at the backbar, partly submerged within the watery projection.

"Hey, Ary, do you believe in ghosts?"

"Depends what you mean by ghosts."

"I read something the other day. 'God's children fall unto death complete, but for mine who cannot die, my mercy lives,'" she said to his shape beneath the waves. "I can't figure it out."

"Scroll Seven," he said. "You're making progress."

"Except I still don't understand half of what I read."

The man stayed in the water. "Everyone struggles with Seven," he said.

"Help me then."

"I'm not a Keeper. I just pour crystals."

"Where I come from bartenders know everything."

He emerged from the projection and walked the short steps to the glowing slab between them. "If you make it to scroll Eleven, you'll learn that death is a fluid thing, and not the same for everyone. Dying and being *made* to die can have two different results." He smiled strangely and the light from the quartz and the ever-moving hologram made the jewels in his cheek flash, as if lit from fires deep within the stones.

"If you're murdered you don't go quietly into the night, is that what you're saying?" She sat back down on the stool and warmed the crystals again.

"Everything's a job, hero." He put his elbows on the bar and leaned in toward her like he was passing on a secret she wasn't supposed to know. "Being alive is a job. We live to give God his power, because without us, He dies. That's why we Deliver new planets. The more of us He has, the stronger He gets. The stronger we get. Being dead's a job too, but the murdered dead are special. And sometimes a killed person gets a special job. Something to ease the pain."

"'But for mine that cannot die, my mercy lives,'" she repeated the line. "You think that's referring to ghosts?"

The man straightened up again. "Have you seen a ghost, Sarah? Is that why you've crawled in here this time looking half dead yourself?"

"It doesn't make any sense." She let out a cloud of pink. "Why hold mercy for the killed? If you're God, why not stop the killing in the first place?"

The man eased back into the ersatz sea, a throng of little black fish boiling around him. "We thought He had."

Her mind went to an image of Captain Argen, the look of confusion and curiosity on his face as he surveyed the guns her shipmates aboard the *Lewis* had brought to the moment of first contact. He, Trin, and Chief Ganet had all come from the *Kalelah* unarmed. Like she'd done a thousand times since, she replayed the moment she should have seen coming, the moment when Riley's anger over the story Argen had told would boil over into action, the moment the major drew his Army service revolver and pulled the trigger. To the moment when the air had gone acrid with the smell of the spent cartridge and Argen's head had slumped to the table, the miracle of their meeting shattered by Earthly violence and stained by the blood of a man who wanted to save the world from what it had become.

A wash of shame came over her, flushing her cheeks and filling her eyes. "Then..." she said softly, more like an exhale than an actual word. That was all she could utter, the rest of the words somehow caught in her throat, like a thought too terrible to even whisper.

"Then we planted this seed," Ary said from somewhere too deep in the water for her to even see anymore. Nevertheless, his meaning was clear: The seed was the one left to grow on its own. The one that revealed the true nature of her people, and of his.

When she left the Rundera the sim had already declared the morning. Pink and orange clouds fanned out across the ceiling as the last moon to set floated on a field of brightening blue. Sarah was grateful not to have to return to bed. Grateful not to dream.

7

Trin strode through the docking bay toward transport ship *18*, a recently modified version and unofficially, *his* ship. In his mind at least. Transports were the only other craft on the *Kalelah*. They were small, with room for no more than three. Fast, and uniquely stealthy. Along with a thinner, lighter version of the nanowool that covered and protected the *Kalelah*, their outer hulls were studded with cloaking mirrors—billions of them. Hovering idle in their berths, they looked like glass mosaic versions of ocean creatures that flew across the bottom sands on featherless wings.

Stealth was essential to the transports because it was essential to the job of Guidance. If a seed population became aware of the strings being pulled to progress its development, all kinds of problems arose, particularly in the area of belief management. There were laws designed to explain the workings of the natural and spiritual worlds, as well as a strict timeline for their dissemination. A premature glimpse of a transport buzzing through the woods or landing in the clearing of an early settlement could shatter the fragile illusions the Guides needed to embed within the population a proper foundational belief system. Sightings of reality tended to put cracks in those foundations. Eventually, inevitably, the cracks would widen, and things got wobbly in dangerous ways. Even the Guides themselves were mandated to stay out of view until the very end of the process.

The timeline had been honed over millions of years and with the pain of trial and error. It was to be respected. Guides, after all, were not mere teachers; they were creators. Pureling seed populations were not yet human beings at Delivery. They were something less, something primitive and blank. *Halfborns*. Their successful development, their transcendence to fullborn, was placed in the hands of their Guides, a responsibility that was deeply revered. After all, if God could expand His reach only as far as humankind could travel, what more important work could humankind do than ensure its own expansion?

By the time Trin had entered the Service, failed Deliveries were the stuff of school lessons, cautionary tales with the hint of fiction. Success was practically taken for granted. Trin had landed a spot on the *Kalelah*, a brand-new ship captained by Jan Argen no less. It was a perfect start to what would surely be a celebrated career.

Until it wasn't. The sabotage had cut it short. Now it was the Guide Ship's turn to do the adapting, but on a much faster timeline.

Machines were the easiest places to make changes. Most lacked awareness of their habits and preferences anyway. Transport *18* had been modified on ship to deal with a seed population in possession of technology way before its time. Not only could *18* make itself invisible to the naked eye, like all transports could, it had the power to escape detection from radar, and across the entire frequency spectrum.

Since the crash, only *18* had ever left its slip. Even before its revisions, it was special. At least to Trin. It was the transport that had carried *Kalelah's* small but desperate boarding party to the *Lewis*. And Trin to Sarah. Ever since, he'd considered it his lucky ship.

As he continued his way through the dock, its high, overhead lights turning on steps ahead of him to mark his progress, a float appeared, putting him nearly face to face with the image of a beautiful red head. *Wildei*. No surprise that she'd show up. Normally the captain of a Guide Ship wouldn't pay much attention to the specific comings and goings of a little transport. Nothing about these times, however, was particularly normal. And when it came to Trin and his scouting runs, it wasn't just a matter of protocol for Wildei. It was personal. It'd been Wildei and Trin and Sarah at the center of The Mutiny. Without their work together, Laird would still be captain. And all of Earth would be nothing but black, shimmering dust. So while Wildei cared about everyone on the ship, she cared about Trin and Sarah just a little more.

"This is so very tiring, darling," she said, her painted lips drawn tightly, her eyes serious.

"Captain."

"I find it amazing that one of the smartest brains in the entire Service is capable of such sustained idiocy."

"What is it you always say? I'm full of surprises."

"Yes. But I never mean it in a good way."

He smiled and kept walking toward *18.*

"At some point I'm going to have to pull rank," she said.

"You won't."

"Won't I?"

"You haven't yet."

"Only because you'd disobey. I'd have to arrest you or something and then what would I say to Sarah? Save us all the mess. For the hundredth time, let the bots do it, darling. It's their job."

"They can't do what we do out there."

"*We.* This is my point. You're out there in the wild Code Diving. Half your mind is somewhere else. It's terribly dangerous, and it's monumentally stupid. But, of course, you know this."

"I'm invisible, remember?"

"Until you and the Code, both of you lost in each other's so-called brilliance, crash the transport and the cloak goes poof."

"I don't crash."

Captain Wildei sighed. "Very well, XO. What do I say next in this ridiculous ritual of ours?"

"I'm on my own."

"Yes. I mean it."

"I know you do. That integrity problem of yours."

"Fuck off."

"Love you too."

The captain offered a tired look of resignation and the float folded neatly in on itself until there was nothing left to fold. The little ship was waiting for him, its hatch open and retractable stairs lowered. Trin got in and pushed the tiny Bridge Maker to the Code into his right ear. The sounds of initialization began, like a lover's breathless whispers, hungry and impatient. He closed his eyes, waiting for the rush of connection when his mind and hers would join and the fast talk would start. An endless stream of hypotheses and debate. A conversation like drugs, intoxicating, overwhelming, and always ending with a shadow of hangover that left him craving more.

A few seconds later they were on their way. The ship sped toward the far wall of the dock, a solid green-gray sheet of hardened nanowool that stretched several stories high and curved its way backward at the top to connect with the side walls in a graceful, arcing vault. As the ship picked up speed, a dot of bright turquoise appeared in the wall's center and spread outward to form a thin horizontal scratch in the titanium wool. Trin aimed for the glowing blue line. When the little transport finally reached the wall, the scratch flashed open for just a moment, like the blink of an eye in reverse, and in that nearly immeasurable fraction of time the little shuttle shot through the wall of the great Guide Ship and into the alien light heading east, the blue line erasing itself in the craft's wake. The sun, bright and direct, prompted the mirrors covering the transport's skin to make their adjustments and the ship disappeared into the rose-tinted morning.

They raced low to the ground of the dusty moat toward the rock ring. All the while, images and notes from their last run moved between them, frictionless and fast. The river was a few seconds beyond and when Trin nosed the ship up to clear the ring, they could see the bright green water glisten, its color in shocking contrast to the dirty brown and black walls of urban brick and metal that lined its edges and threw desperate shadows on the water as if their presence still mattered. Birds flew high in the air between the banks. From his height Trin could see far downstream, where the river flowed southerly to a black desert of the Correction's last infernos. There it did the futile work of carving its new course through the silica and diamonds only to empty in a sea that was boiled and dead.

Trin slowed the ship and took a center path downriver toward the bend where it met its larger feeder tributary. The traffic on the water was crowded with small craft. Some were elaborate beauties with sonar and powerful engines, their signatures well-known now to the Code and easy to classify. Many, though, were primitive makeshift floats, decrepit and fragile. The heat of their occupants and their fitful fires sputtering in the winter air were all they had to offer the sensors attempting to take measure of what life had now become.

When the crew of the *Kalelah* had first learned of their failure, the failure of the Delivery, it had raced to digest all that could be hacked and read about the people of this world. In the immediate aftermath of *Kalelah's* crash, information about the area around her had still been easy to track without risking the actual wild. There were instances of readable signals broadcast terrestrially and through what Sarah called the *internet*.

So he knew the basics. That the ship had crashed upon a place called The Russian Federation. That Russia, as it was more simply known, had once been a great power. Now, after decades of decline and then the Correction, it was something else altogether. A half-blind thing, crawling on all fours, bleeding from its nose, wailing. *Kalelah's* armor had repelled missiles and nuclear warheads, but the wounded cries of this land pushed their way through to Trin as if the city ship was skinned in tissue paper. Trin heard them at night. He heard them at prayer. Like sirens they drew him out in the wild where they dared him to stay and face their morbid music unprotected.

He kept the transport at building height as they cruised. Too low to the water and they'd disturb it, drawing attention and maybe suspicion. Too high and he might as well let the bots do the work. Which, of course, he should have. Wildei was right. The bots could count and record as well as he and the Code.

Structures burning: 17, + .092% from the last run.
Boat traffic: + 22.634%, with 82.9% of the delta accounted for by junk-built craft.
Particulate Matter Pollution:
Water: 0567ppm, + 36.123%
Air: 0079ppm, +11.859%
Carbon Dioxide:
Water: +12.439%
Air: +31.872%

The bots would have come back with the same numbers. They'd have offered to Trin, as well as the biology and anthropology teams of the *Kalelah*, the same grim news: the society around the ship that lay crippled and grounded was crumbling. What the bots could not measure, however, was their own sense of responsibility for it. Only he could do that.

The Volga River was once among the mightiest on the planet. Its tributaries and streams ran for thousands of miles. What was left of it had become Trin's sample universe. Nearly all the remaining population of the country lived along the waterway system between Moscow in the eastern edge of the habitable territory and Saint Petersburg to the northwest. At full power Trin could cover the straight-line distance in less than eleven minutes. Only fast wasn't his objective. He wanted time to fully see. Time to feel.

The outside temperature was unseasonably cold, four degrees below freezing. In the less traveled parts of the river, thin sheets of ice had been allowed to build undisturbed over a few square feet. They overlapped each other in a mosaic of whites and translucent greens. Despite the cold, the thermal sensors on ship stayed busy. All along the river and for miles outward of its banks, the fire count was rising. Not all were buildings burning. Some were refuse-fires licking high into the air from inside large steel drums. Some were piles of rubber. Some appeared to be controlled, some not. As the little ship continued its flight downriver, the horizon line ahead grew evermore punctuated by columns of black smoke, inky tendrils reaching for the clouds and scarring the skies with streaks of despair. While Trin knew the Code was instantly updating its own tally of the fires as they went, he couldn't help his own counting. He said the numbers out loud, at a speed unabashedly human, caring little at the sudden break in the joint consciousness he and the machine mind had been using since they blasted through *Kalelah's* skin and into the calamity of the world.

The missiles came from the west, near the river's start, and were detected at the instant of their launch. Their presence jolted Trin out of his counting and he merged once again with the machine. There were six projectiles traveling at a speed nearly double the shuttle's pace. A float opened between Trin and the glass of the windscreen. The worried face of a security engineer entered the frame.

"Sorry, boss. Captain sent me to check up on you."

"We're good," Trin lied, hoping to end the conversation quickly. He nosed the ship up and curved backward on his own flight path, righted the transport, and boosted to full power.

"Closure in thirty-one point three seconds, sir. A full two points of a second ahead of your time to safety. Make that three points. So just shy of 'good.'"

Fucking babies.

"I've done my own math, ensign."

"Roger that, sir. But you've got no guns. So maybe we dust the missiles for you while we can. They're well in range. Just to be safe. Twenty-one point four seconds, sir."

I thought I was on my fucking own.

"We don't dust anymore, remember?"

"They're just hardware, sir."

"No cannons."

"Roger. Sixteen seconds, sir."

"Stop counting, ensign."

The missiles were now visible to the rear camera, its ominous float hanging next to the worried image of the ensign who could do nothing but watch. The *Kalelah* came into view up ahead. The missiles now filled the entire view of the rear cameras. Trin pushed on the power lever, knowing there was nowhere further for it to go.

"Ensign," Trin said solemnly, "I need to tell you something. It's important."

"Sir?" the ensign said, a hitch in his throat.

The missiles closed the gap. A blue dot appeared in the skin of the giant Guide Ship. It stretched into a thin line. Trin closed his eyes. He heard the ensign swear. As the little ship shot through the portal's blink he screamed, "Fuck. Your. Math!"

A split second later he heard the brake alarm go off and the dull thud of explosions from outside the dock. He cut the power and cruised slowly to slip number 18, his hand still white-knuckled around the lever and shaking.

"Also, ensign, I could use a clean jumpsuit. Thank you."

•

The debrief was the shitstorm he predicted it to be. Wildei never sat. She paced the small conference room the entire meeting, her eyes as fiery as her red hair.

"The why is easy," she said in an early lap. "They'll try to get us one by one if that's their only choice. And I can't say I blame them. The *how* is what's driving me mad. If they couldn't see the transport, have *never* seen the transport, they wouldn't be waiting for it. So how did they know your exact position?"

"The stealth was working. All of it," Trin countered. "The Code logs don't show even a nanosecond's malfunction."

"Trin, those missiles were locked on. If *18* was functioning as it should have been, its cloak on, its jammers at work, how does lock happen?"

"The shimmer?" squeaked a pale-skinned science officer.

"What?" both he and Wildei said simultaneously.

"When *18's* radar cloak is deployed," the science officer continued, "it produces an infrared shroud we call a shimmer. An unintended byproduct of the retrofit. It's very slight, almost imperceptible. Someone would have to know it was there and have the right tech to find it. We're talking about an extremely advanced tracking system. I can't imagine how they'd have anything even remotely up to the job."

"There's a fucking *shimmer*?" Wildei exploded. "How long have we known about that?"

"Since the retrofit," the science officer replied meekly. "Theoretically, it was an acceptable risk because—"

"I know why, darling," Wildei cut in, "you can save your breath. But if the shimmer was beyond their capability to find, will someone then explain to my idiot brain how in the living *fuck* they found it and tracked it nearly up the ass of the most valuable person on this ship?"

"It's obvious," Dent Forent said flatly. "They had help."

Forent sat at a small table, his overfed body making the table seem smaller still. Only the size of the man resembled the Dent Forent of three years ago. No one on the *Kalelah* appeared more transformed. His white hair had grown thinner and even whiter somehow, and his eyes had taken on a look of perpetual fatigue. Even his voice seemed to have lowered to reflect his true age more accurately. Before the war, Trin wouldn't have described Forent as, say, "sunny." "Curmudgeon" would have been more like it. But he had always been quick-witted, with dancing eyes and a mischievous grin. His sour outlook came with a joke. Now you just got the sour. Who could blame him?

The Correction, and the internal battle over it, had been especially hard on Forent. He was the first to confront Laird after she'd taken over the ship and the first to suffer her anger. He'd been captured by his own shipmates, imprisoned, and beaten hard. Now he was a Guide Lead with no one to guide anymore.

"If they were given the precise wavelength of the infrared," Forent went on, "it would be a significant help in advancing technologies the population likely already has."

"Sure," the science officer replied. "But miniaturizing the tracking system would be a major leap in two years. Then there'd be the issue of testing."

"Where are you going with this?" Wildei asked, still in motion around the room. "Who would be stupid enough to risk something like a tech transfer to the population? Think of what that would involve."

"Stupid enough? No one," Forent said looking down at his immense hands. Palms down, fingers splayed, they crowded the surface area of the table so completely that the others seated around it had no choice but to simply cede the entire tabletop to him. "But *possessed* enough?" He looked up at her for the first time, a shadow of dread upon his round, boyish face. "Surely someone. Or two, maybe hundreds. Enough to form—"

"A Circle," said Wildei, finishing Forent's thought for him.

"I looked it square in the eyes, Captain, like I'm looking in yours now. That day, the day before the war started, when Laird told me what she'd done, why we'd slept through the Delivery's entire development, I saw what The Circle can do to a person. Laird wasn't just insane—she was a slave to something that does not let go or find itself content with one slave. We can't dismiss the possibility of another..." He paused, like he was searching for a word. He never offered one and didn't need to. Two came to Trin's mind without any help from Forent.

Fucking infection. The thought of dealing with The Circle set Trin's teeth to grind. An ancient cult of purists and fundamentalists, The Circle took devotion to the Plan to an intolerant and sometimes violent extreme. And it had proved nearly impossible to confront. It hid its meetings and its membership. It scribed no scrolls and left no data trail. You never knew who was in The Circle until it was too late. Trin couldn't decide if they were brilliant survivalists or just fucking cowards. Either way, it had been The Circle that put them all in the shitbox they were in now. Crashed and broken. And he hated them for it.

"The Circle died with Laird," Wildei said softly, more like a hope than an assertion.

"We think. We hope. But you know how The Circle operates," Forent countered. "Why couldn't The Circle's death be just another rumor? A misdirect?"

Wildei took a breath. She rubbed the back of her neck and sucked her lower lip between her teeth. She shook her head slightly, like she was in a debate not only with Forent, but with herself as well. Maybe herself most of all. "If The Circle wanted Trin dead," she said, "there are easier ways to get it done."

Forent brought his glance back down to his hands. He turned his left hand over and picked at the nail on his index finger with his thumb. "Easier, yes," he said slowly, addressing no one in particular. "But maybe an easy kill isn't the point."

Trin didn't spend much time thinking about his own death. Now how could he not? The science officer glanced uncomfortably at him. He gave a small shrug back. *No sweat*, he hoped it said. Except, it was bullshit; he *was* starting to sweat. Forent wasn't the same guy he used to be. He was off, prone to wild theories about irrelevant things and fits of melancholy. It was possible Forent had gone mad. It was possible, too, that Forent was on to something. He was sure Wildei felt the same way. He saw it in her pacing, in her nervous eyes, and he saw it in everyone else's silence. Forent was making sense.

That was the thing about Wildei, she could never hide what was really going through her head. Her face and body never failed to reveal her real intentions. In fact, her heroics in The Mutiny aside, it had been her almost shameless willingness to crack the traditionally stiff spine of leadership posture that had inspired the surviving senior ranks of the *Kalelah* to make her captain, even though she was nowhere near the service rank to inherit the job in a normal succession. Of course, what could be a normal succession after the shitstorm that was Captain Laird?

The ship had loved Argen for his strength and his simple goodness. Transparent, though, he wasn't. He and Laird had that in common. They both wore the captain's uniform like a shield. Their crews saw only what they wanted them to see. Now, after the damage that shouldn't have happened, after the loss of faith, after too many dangerous secrets, people were done with the need-to-know crap. People simply needed to know. So Wildei, with her rebel past, her easy warmth, her humor, and her willingness to ask questions about things an ordinary captain would already know or pretend to know, and her "darlings" and her "lovelies" all felt like something a ship full of broken spirits could almost trust. After the war, the Correction, and The Mutiny, almost was close enough.

"Let's start with the most basic assumption," Forent went on. "If you're The Circle, you don't think the Correction was a mistake. You think the mistake, the most blasphemous thing of all, was stopping it. If you're making a dead list of those who did the stopping, Trin is most certainly on it. At the top I'd say."

"Thanks, Dent. Do I get a plaque or something for that?"

A few nervous chuckles went through the room. Forent waved away the joke. He was just getting started.

"Think about how much better Trin's death would be if it looked like the population had killed him. If the missiles had been a little faster, or Trin had been a little slower, the real explosion wouldn't have been the missiles hitting their target." The large man looked around the room, his own eyes flashing as if reflecting the fires conjured in his mind. "The real explosion would have been our reaction."

"I'm with you to a point," the captain said. "I agree that somehow those missiles got an inside edge on Trin. And I have to admit that I don't know what I would've done had they succeeded. But even if I had gone out of my mind with rage, I couldn't have given The Circle, if they do exist, what they want. Sure, we can do some damage, but we're grounded. Without flight, without all the guns working at once, there are limits to what we can do. Even if they killed us all and took control of the ship, even then they couldn't finish the job. As long as we're stuck in this moat, completing the Correction is impossible."

"Maybe they don't want to finish the job. Maybe what they need more than an ending is a never-ending middle. There's nothing like a good long fight to bring the faithful to their feet."

The captain stopped pacing. "Dent, you think The Circle wants to up-tech the population so it might actually have something like a fighting chance against the *Kalelah*? Feed it our own weapons and defenses? Teach it how to hurt us?"

"We're a Guide Ship, are we not?"

8

Sarah was already in the pool when Trin got to the bathing pod. The overhead lights were dimmed, and the room was mostly illuminated by the soft, white glow of the large underwater light at the pool's bottom. Ripples of reflected color danced across the low, white ceiling. He threw his clothes on the steel bench, eased himself into the water, and sat on the ledge that ran along the inside of the bowl.

"Too hot as usual."

"And you're late as usual," Sarah said.

"Ran into some complications on the recon."

"What kind of complications?"

"Nothing major. We needed a debrief."

She pushed off her side of the pool and glided to his. She straddled him, put her arms around the back of his neck, and kissed his chest. He held her with one hand at her waist, the other along her thigh. She raised up to his eye level and smiled, her nipples brushing against him as she rose.

"You're a liar," she said. "You think I don't have friends?"

She pushed back to her side of the pool and got the glass of wine from the deck above the water.

"Fuck me," he said, making a mental note to thank Wildei for blabbing to Sarah.

"Yeah, I don't think so."

"I didn't want to make you worry." It was true, he hadn't. Something was up with her lately. Not sleeping, walking the concourses in the middle of the night. She was acting like she did right before the Correction, when the shit was hitting the fan from twelve directions.

"What makes you think I'd worry?" she asked.

"Now who's a liar?"

Her smile faded and Trin saw her blue eyes glisten, highlighting the color. She turned her head and drank.

"I had plenty of time," he said. "Wildei's making too much of what happened. Forent was off his nut, but what else is new?"

"I need to know something," Sarah said.

"Okay."

"What is this?"

"What is what?"

"You have no idea what I'm talking about, do you?"

"Of course I do." He absolutely did not.

"The two of us. Is this our life together? We just do what we've been doing. Shouldn't we be more somehow? To each other. Shouldn't we get married?" She said the last four words in English. "I mean, does that even happen in your world? Probably not, because as I was thinking about that question, I couldn't even find the words in Origen."

He pushed over to her side of the pool, but she pushed him back. He stayed in the middle of the pool, treading water. She tucked her hair behind her ears, a gesture he could watch over and over.

"Get married," he repeated in English. "What does it mean?"

"Forget it. It was a stupid question. I never even wanted to get married." She gave a tiny laugh. "My mother married twice. The second was a total disaster. It ruined her life. It ruined all our lives. I swore I'd never do it."

"Do you still feel like your life is ruined?"

She looked at him for a long minute.

"No."

"Then tell me what it means."

"I'm embarrassed now. What if you disagree? Then, you know, *what?* We just fight this fight for the rest of our lives? We keep trying to make a peace, to share what we know, and they keep hating us and trying to kill you? That's the sum of it?"

"They're not trying to kill *me*, exactly. It's more like us. They're trying to kill *us*."

"Oh, that's better. You're really managing the shit out of this moment."

"Tell me already."

"Okay." Sarah took another drink. She looked him in the eyes and spoke slowly and carefully, with a look that somehow managed to mix bold confidence with naked vulnerability. It was a kind of beautiful that drove him mad. "It means that we're forever, no matter what. It's a vow. A solemn promise. Even if we get separated, we're never apart."

"Why would we get separated?"

"Things happen," she shrugged, her eyes misting again.

"I'm not leaving you," he said without needing to even think about it.

"Okay." She pushed out to the center of the pool and they both gently treaded water.

"Are we married now?" he asked.

"Of course not, you big asshole. You have to get me a diamond ring."

"What?"

"Yeah, and it better be huge too."

He took her in his arms, this person from another world who he never should have met, and hardly ever understood, and he couldn't believe he could love anyone more.

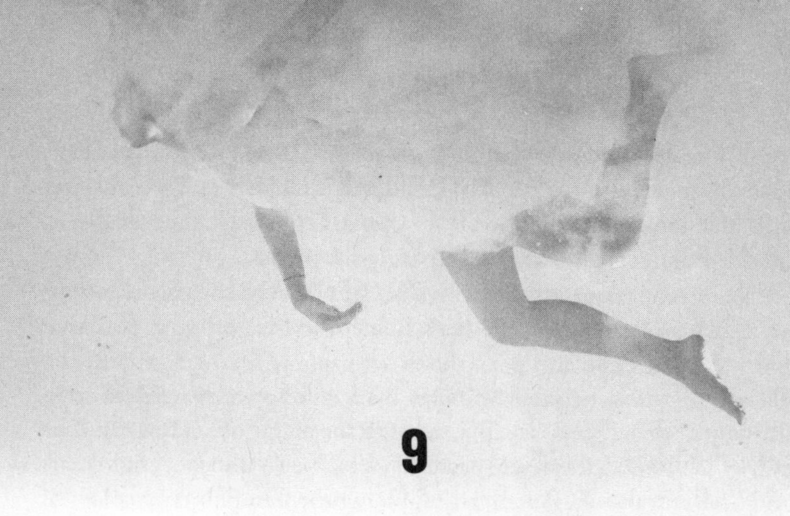

9

The sleep that night had gotten off to a good start...until her queasy bitch of a stomach had other ideas. Rather than hit the bar again, Sarah decided to distract herself with the fighter jets and their ongoing tag team vigil of the ship. She chose the Command Center for this particular watch for no reason more technical than the proximity and relative luxury of its toilets. She'd barfed in a public trash receptacle the day before and wasn't looking forward to a repeat performance.

The CC greeted her with its dependable hue of absolute whiteness brought about by a source of illumination unknown to her. The ceiling of the CC looked as if there was no ceiling at all, like a hole in the ship with a view of the Elysium sky. There were no hanging fixtures, seams, or visible structures that might suggest the secret to the seemingly infinite expanse overhead. There was just light, calibrated to the perfect brightness and color for the tasks performed in the CC.

She had no official workspace on the ship, let alone in the CC. Even though the room was mostly empty and she could have taken a proper station, she set up shop at one of the visitor chairs that ringed the outer circle of the center. An implant in her right hand had given her fingers the magical power to call up files and feeds from anywhere on the ship, and a chair in the CC counted as "anywhere" more than most. She gestured into the space above and to the right of her face. A small, square hole in the air opened and less than a full second later unfolded into a fully functional view float. From there she was able to quickly connect to the cameras chasing the planes.

Out in the concourse, the sim skies still showed the constellations of The Watcher and The Tiller's Blade, the first celestial dots that every Origen child in its southern hemisphere learned to connect. They were the only ones she'd ever been able to consistently spot in the dark of that alien space. But through the magic of her float and the eyes of her bots flying at jet speed, she was able to transport lightyears and hours away, to a sun already applying the first painterly colors of an Earthly day, at times throwing the fast-moving planes in dark silhouette against soft pinks, oranges, and whites. When the jets turned toward the south, or when the cameras flew between them and the rising sun, they'd come out of the blinding effect of back light and Sarah could easily identify each plane's nationality and the pilots who controlled it. She had not seen Elouise since the day the French pilot had turned to the cameras and broken her long, stubborn silence.

Actually, she hadn't seen even the slightest shred of evidence that Elouise's strange message hadn't been anything other than a fantasy, a shimmering mirage of fatigue and guilt. Sarah had shuffled backward in the record of that day a dozen times, searching for the video that matched the pictures in her mind. That haunting moment when Elouise turned and spoke, not of the concerns of pilots, but of Sarah's sister. Unless Sarah was going mad—a possibility she hadn't completely ruled out—the imagery looping in her mind felt completely real. Everything in Sarah's head and heart told her it was real, and yet every time she'd gone back to look, it had been the same indifferent Elouise. A person so oblivious to Sarah's pleading attempts at connection as to be in another world entirely.

Maybe, Sarah thought, *that's how it was.*

Perhaps Sarah was in one reality and the pilots in their planes were in another.

She looked around the space of the CC. It was still in that transition between the mostly skeleton crew of the overnight shift and the more serious staffing of the day hours. In either case, the CC no longer needed the full complement of crew it did before its mission abruptly ended. The ship wasn't going anywhere anytime soon, and there were no Guide Teams out to be monitored. Guiding, thanks to Laird's handiwork, had stopped before it had even had a chance to start. There were no alerts to address, and the Code managed all the basic systems of the ship and most of the requests of the early waking crew. For the most part, a small staff was really all the CC needed anymore.

The analysts' station, in fact, had only one person in attendance. After a few moments, the analyst rose from her chair and made her way toward Sarah. She was tall, wearing the light purple-gray jumpsuit of a second lieutenant, her long, dark hair a luminous contrast upon her slender shoulders. The woman was looking directly at Sarah, a smile on her face like the one an old friend gives to another after a long absence apart. Sarah didn't recognize her, so she looked briefly behind to the second row of chairs to see if someone else might be the woman's true target. The chairs were empty. Sarah smiled weakly back and tried to return her attention to the planes.

The woman stopped in front of Sarah's chair, the black waist belt of her suit visible through the translucent glow of the float and drawing a dark dividing line across the image.

"Hello, Sarah."

Having never attended Academy, Sarah wasn't required to acknowledge the woman's rank with the standard salute, a two-finger tap of her right hand upon the silver pin attached to her left chest-pocket. Out of respect, however, she folded the float away and began to stand.

"Please sit." The woman smiled broadly. "Mind if I join you?" She sat before Sarah could respond.

Sarah regarded her apprehensively. "My apologies, Lieutenant, I've forgotten your name."

"Oh, that's okay, Sarah, it's been a long time. A really long time, actually." She extended a hand. "Heather."

Sarah paused a beat before taking the woman's hand. Shaking hands wasn't something people did on the *Kalelah*. "Did you say Heather?" Sarah asked.

"That's right."

"Such an Earthly name. A coincidence of sounds, I guess."

The woman sweetened her smile a bit more and ignored the question in Sarah's observation.

"Listen," the woman said in English, gripping Sarah's hand tighter and leaning closer in her chair, "I want to tell you a story."

Sarah took her hand back and shot up from the chair. "What the fuck?"

The woman held the soft charm in her face and showed no awareness of the shock in her words. She looked up at Sarah calmly, as if the two had been discussing the weather.

"You speak English," Sarah said angrily, hoping to cover up the real stuff pushing its way up her spine. Fear. With the lone exception of Trin, who'd self-dosed a language bug, a profoundly *illegal* language bug, no one on the ship could speak English. No one spoke anything other than Origen. Throughout the universe entire no one spoke anything but Origen. Except on Earth. Yet this woman, clothed in the jumpsuit of an officer, pinned like a crew member, a person from a star so far away only the bending of space could bring her here, not only knew the language, she spoke it with a perfect Midwest twang—a feat even Trin couldn't muster.

"I think it's easier for us, don't you?" The woman smiled broadly again.

Sarah couldn't answer. Somehow this woman seemed to know her. *But how?* What was the connection?

"When I was a little girl, maybe twelve years old," the woman pushed on, "there was a boy in school who would make fun of my height. Ugh, he was relentless. 'Ho, ho, ho, here comes the jolly green virgin!'" she said in the singsong voice of a boyish bully. "His favorite though was, 'Every time I see you, I get altitude sickness.'"

"Why are you telling me this?" Sarah managed.

"Perfect segue," she said, her smile all flash again. "See, the story of the boy is also a story about you, Sarah. One day you overheard him teasing me. And, oh my God, you got so angry. Way worse than now." The woman shook her head wistfully, her eyes on Sarah, and in that look Sarah thought she could see the young girl this strange woman spoke of like a ghost from a past she'd long shut away. Her heart began to beat so loudly in her ears she was afraid the whole CC could hear it.

"Do you remember what you said to that boy?"

"I—I didn't say—"

"Well, right. First you punched him so hard he dropped straight to the ground."

"I can't remember what I said. It was too long ago," Sarah said in a stunned whisper.

"Well I remember. I'll never forget it. You bent down and you said, 'Now everyone's taller than you, asshole.'"

Sarah did remember. The minute the words came from the woman's mouth, Sarah remembered.

"You were a grade ahead of me, so you were probably about thirteen years old when you did that. You and I were never really friends, but you were special to me ever since. My hero."

"You're *that* Heather?" Sarah felt faint and sat back down. "You're Heather Morgan? That's what I'm supposed to believe?"

The woman looked her deep in the eyes. "I'm here because you need to be someone's hero again, I'm afraid."

"I don't understand."

"Margaret, Sarah, Margaret. There's still time to help her if you leave now."

"This is crazy. I'm crazy. I have to be."

"I'm going to hit you now," Heather said with a kind but determined look on her face.

"What?"

"Don't be angry."

"What?"

A white light flashed in Sarah's left eye and a stabbing pain roared in right behind it.

"Shit!" Sarah screamed. The Command Center went blurry from tears. Even through the watery distortion she could see the few heads in the room turn her way.

"I'm sorry," the woman who called herself Heather said. "But I owe you for decking Bobby Saputo."

"Dammit!" Her eye was really hurting now, and it was swelling beneath her palm. "You said I was your hero."

"You helped me that day. Later, your swollen eye will help you. You can save her, Sarah, but you can't wait. It's not the food that's making you sick."

"What the fuck are you talking about?" Sarah said, holding her hurt eye and scanning the CC with the other to see if anyone was still watching them. Only a young tactical officer, several ranks below the lieutenant, was still looking their way. The kid quickly turned his head back to his float when Sarah caught his eye.

"You're sick because you're pregnant, Sarah."

"You're crazier than I am," Sarah said, but she knew in an instant it was true. It was the one thing that made any sense at all.

"That's why you can't wait. You have to go now while you still can. Because it won't be an easy trip."

Sarah sat thinking for a minute. Her eye hurt like hell, and she wanted badly to cry. "Go? Go where? I don't know where my sister is. She could be anywhere," she said more to herself than to the woman.

"Not anywhere, Sarah. She's probably right where you think she'd be."

"Then you get her."

The woman gently shook her head. "It has to be you, Sarah. You alone. This is your trip to take."

Sarah was too lost in the woman's words to argue the point. She looked at her closely for the first time. "People's faces are always uneven," she said, her heart still trying to pound its way out of her chest.

The woman didn't respond. She kept looking at Sarah, her expression calm, still warm.

"One side of the face is never a perfect mirror of the other. Like one eye is lower and maybe shaped a little differently than the other, or one side of the jaw is heavier or droopier. It's called asymmetry. You never notice the little differences though. Until they're not there."

The woman gave a slight smile, a nod perhaps to Sarah's powers of observation. Or another trick, maybe.

"Who are you? *What* are you?" Sarah said.

"Part of me actually is Heather, but mostly I'm all of us." That sweet smile flashed big again, but now it didn't seem warm anymore. It seemed mocking and frightful.

"All of who?"

The woman dropped her smile and softened her eyes. "The Killed."

"This is bullshit."

"Is that what you think? Is that why you're frantically looking for a vid of the pilot you call Elouise giving you the same message I just gave you? Because you think it was bullshit?"

"That was you I saw?"

"Us."

"Okay, I'm done being insane for the moment. You can disappear back into my subconscious or whatever it is dissociative identities do. I need ice for my eye. Also, a shrink."

"Sarah, it's time for you to do your job."

"My job? Why is anything my job? None of what happened was my fault. I didn't kill you, whoever you are. Or my mother. Or the two billion others. That scanner from hell ran over this damn ship. I wasn't looking for it. It just showed up on my screen, buried there, perfectly intact. What was I supposed to do?"

The woman smiled sympathetically and smoothed her jumpsuit along her thighs. She took Sarah's hand again. Did her fingers feel cooler than they should have? Sarah wasn't sure. There was suddenly a lot she wasn't sure of.

"You won't see Heather again, Sarah," Heather Morgan said sweetly, like no bombs at all had dropped. "But tomorrow, you'll look in the mirror at your swollen and blackened eye and then you'll come back here and ask that frightened Tactical on the other side of the room what happened. Did you fall? Did you bump into a wall? Or did someone hit you? And then you'll go find your sister."

"Fuck you. Tell Elouise to fuck herself too when you see her."

"I know this is hard, Sarah, but we've heard you and we want to help you."

"I didn't ask for help."

"No, but the souls of the Correction did."

Sarah shook her head. "This can't be real. It just can't."

"The collective pain of the killed was like a knife, Sarah. It cut through the planes of existence."

"What does that even mean?"

"It means we can help."

"Ghosts?"

"If that's how you want to see it."

"You're speaking in circles. If Margaret really is alive, why help her? So many people need help, why her?"

"Margaret is critical to your journey, Sarah."

"My journey? What's so important about my journey?"

"You have to trust us."

"Really? I don't trust *me* right now."

"Leave this ship. Look for your sister."

"And if I can't find her?"

"Then you'll find something else. Or something else will find you."

The woman stood and walked toward the big doors of the Command Center. On the way she stopped by the young Tactical Officer's station. He gently put the first two fingers of his right hand to the silver pin shining from his left chest pocket. The tall, slender woman bent slightly, and looked at his float. They had a few words together that Sarah couldn't make out, but the two were definitely communicating, dashing Sarah's theory, or hope, that she was having some sort of psychotic breakdown. After a moment, the woman straightened again and looked Sarah's way.

After the woman had walked through the metal doors of the CC, Sarah reached up to her face and winced when she touched her eye.

10

The recorder hovered a few feet from Sarah's face. Although it made no noise and offered no visible signal that it was listening, Sarah had learned to trust the machines on the ship, so she spoke—confident her words would be recorded.

"Starting," she said softly.

"This is the first installment of my recorded journal to you. I guarantee nothing. I wasn't a diary kind of girl. I'm not great at saving things. In fact, the recorder bot didn't even make the original list of critical gear. Then, without warning, it became the most important thing. Anyway, here goes..."

"When I first walked on the ship, it was the scariest thing I'd ever done. Somehow, the thought of walking off is worse. I guess when I had agreed to come aboard the *Kalelah*, I wasn't thinking about what I was leaving. I hadn't talked to my mother in years, my sister had stopped talking to me, and my job was stupid. So back on the *Lewis*, in the middle of the Pacific Ocean, when Trin pointed to me and said, 'This one,' I said yes, I'll go. I didn't know where I was going or if I'd ever see life as I knew it again. I didn't know why he felt I could help. Me of all people. But I didn't think twice. Now all I'm doing is thinking. And the hardest thing about it is that Trin...I mean, *your father*—sorry, still very much getting used to that concept...

"Pause."

There were suddenly tears in her eyes and Sarah wanted her voice clear and strong before she continued. She got up off the multitable and made a quick circulation of the pod to collect herself. The bot followed her, adjusting its position to stay in the best possible range of her voice. Once she felt back in control, she picked up where she'd left off.

"Starting.

"The hardest thing about leaving is that your father has no idea I'm even thinking about it. I want to tell him. I *should* tell him, especially now that you're around. But if I do he'll try to talk me out of it, and I don't think he'll be able to. Then what? He won't let me go alone and I can't let him come with me. Out there, in the world, he won't be able to hide who he is and they'll kill him for it. And too many people on this ship depend on him. Including me.

"So, to the real business: Why am I doing this? The honest answer is...I don't really know. It's pretty crazy considering everything, considering you. Except there's a part of me out there I thought was gone forever and maybe it's not. Maybe I can bring that part back with me. With us."

She wiped another tear. *Dammit.*

"You see, I never said goodbye. Not just when I came here, to the *Kalelah*. But long before then, when I first left home. My sister didn't know I took a job halfway around the world until she saw my bag. She was the one person who knew everything about me, the good, and the horrible. But she didn't know I was leaving. That I was leaving *her*. I had always thought there'd be time to fix us. Then, poof, there wasn't.

"Now I might have a second chance. It's an insane long shot of a chance. But if Margaret's really alive, I have to take it. I know, it's ironic. I'm doing to your dad what I did to Margaret. Just leaving. The difference is, he can take it. Your dad is strong. And he knows I love him. He'll have that until I get back. That's the thing about

Margaret. I didn't give her that. And she needed it. She needed it more than anything.

"I'll be as careful as I can. I'm not running away this time. I'm coming back. And we'll be a family. All of us. I'm almost certain of it.

"Pause."

"Starting.

"You'll be much older when you finally get to listen to this story. You'll already know how it turns out. I have this dopey movie in my head that I present this to you all giftwrapped in paper and solemnity. You'll sit on your bed, legs bent with one foot crossed under the other, an elbow on each knee, your chin resting on your fists, and actually listen. Sometimes you're a boy, dark and beautiful like your father. Smart like your father. Sometimes you're a little blonde girl with my mother's eyes. You'll hear my voice from a time before you were born, a time when I'm almost always scared, and nothing makes sense. When cracks in the world open up and the unexplainable escapes. In my movie, when you're sitting on your bed listening to these notes, a part of you is entirely unable to understand. You just don't have the reference points. You can't imagine our kind of fear. You can't grasp the inability to picture a future past the day you're simply hoping to survive. Your world isn't like mine. You're protected and you're so very loved."

Sarah took a breath and held back the emotion that wanted its way out. "And you're happy.

"Ending."

11

Her list was short. Clothes that could keep her warm and not give her away at first glance; a modicum of survival gear; food that would not spoil easily; money; two small cutters that were lightweight, easy to hide, and lethal; and finally, three waist-tuck dusters that she'd already wrapped in undergarments and stuffed into a large laundry bag slung over her shoulder. She'd have preferred a type of gun less dangerously thorough than dusters. Something that fired projectiles rather than plasma, that might only wound a target, but the dusters were half the size and weight and didn't require she carry ammo as well.

She headed to the lower deck of Leaf One, tip of the spear. The instant the door of the conveyor opened she was hit by the rich, salty smell of the farm where thickets of two-story glass tubes, each nearly as wide as a grain silo, filled the voluminous space before her.

Fed from above by enormous grow lamps and green with sea water, kelps, mosses, and fish, the tubes looked like an aqueous forest reaching upward to a low-hanging star cluster. Several tubes, like the dead stumps of fallen trees, were broken down to their first few feet of glass, victims of the crash landing that ended the Correction. Their edges had been ground dull and their interiors drained and repurposed. The unevenness of their heights, and the general sense of victimhood they projected, added an oddly natural layer to the surreal jungle, as if it—like any on the planet—was susceptible to an Earthly order that was wild and unpredictable, instead of the alien algorithms that were actually in charge. Avian harvest bots, with their winches and nets and clippers, darted about the canopy between the tops of the tubes and the lights. Others flew closer to the ground, injecting nutrients or extracting samples through ports placed at various heights along the vertical stretch of the tubes.

Sarah made her way down the central pathway of the forest toward the back of the Leaf and the storage facility. Once through the tube farm, the ceiling fell to ten feet off the ground, and though only five-foot-five herself, the effect was dramatic enough to nearly make her duck. The relative darkness was another shock of contrast. This was some sort of staging area, a place for parking transports for the loading and unloading of supplies and home to the conveyor to the food processing plant that shared the back of Leaf One with the supply vault. The look and mood of the place would be nothing out of the ordinary in the basement of any large office building. Here on the *Kalelah* it stood out as profoundly austere, graceless and dim.

In her experience, even the most utilitarian environments on ship had the scale, beauty, and marvel to drop jaws at first sight. The ship's designers knew what they were building: a new and last home for nearly twenty-three thousand people. Once aboard there'd be no going back, crash or no crash, because while the crew was sleeping its way through space and the millennia between E-checks of their seed populations, the worlds they'd left would have progressed eons ahead without them, to become as unrecognizable as any alien port that exists. It was always a one-way ticket on the *Kalelah*. Thus, the ship was lavishly designed; as if to compensate for the fact that the *Kalelah*, and each other, were all the crew would ever have. The place Sarah found herself in now seemed to have been forgotten, the ship's bones showing through the walls and ceiling, her bolts and welds and seams plain to see even in the gloom.

This was a place only bots went.

She could hear the loud hum from the food processing plant up ahead to the left. It was dark but for the occasional laser blink to guide the automata workers, like a deep cave populated by fireflies. She arrived at the door to the supply vault, searching all around it for the flora scanner. There didn't appear to be one. She passed her hands across the door and breathed out heavily into the air. Nothing. After a minute it hit her. There was no flora scanner because there was no need for one. Bots didn't carry a microbial cloud. Her stomach dropped at the realization of how poorly planned her excursion was. She couldn't even get in the damn door to steal the stuff she'd probably get caught stealing. After a solid minute of holding back panic tears, she sat down with her back against the wall next to the door and tried to tell herself that her poor planning might actually be for the better. The absence of a flora scanner meant she wouldn't ping the Code where she was. Instead, she'd simply wait for the door to open and slide in behind whatever was coming or going. Stealthy.

The name's Bond. Sarah Bond.

Except Bond's timing was usually much better. She waited nearly two hours before an electrician bot rolled up to the door. Afraid to stand for fear of attracting the bot's attention, Sarah tried not to move at all. The bot and the door communicated with a few short tones and the door thrust silently upward into the wall. The bot rolled in and Sarah followed, staying low on all fours. She let the bot get a good twenty or so yards ahead before standing. *Oh my God.* The room spread out around her was so large as to appear endless. Shelves, lockers, and racks went on for a city block before disappearing into a murky sepia generated by the dim glow of the tiny overhead lighting. Bot lighting. The gear on her list, minimalist as it was, wasn't going to be an easy find. She walked up to the rack of deep shelves closest to her containing a stack of plain fiber boxes, unmarked except for a string of code along the upper edge of the facing side of the package.

More good news.

She had no clue what was in the box…or any of the thousands in the room.

It was impossible now not to leave at least a few breadcrumbs.

She gestured for a directory.

Crumb one.

Sarah Long was now officially someplace she had no need to be. A day from now, when the Code would do its routine location check, the signature of her gesture implant would be flagged, which meant she had only twenty-four hours to pack her bag, get off the ship, and get far enough away to make chasing her down too risky. Assuming Trin didn't catch on sooner. The idea of running from him, of all people, only added to the general uneasiness in her stomach. She'd have to freak out about that later. Right now she needed to grab some cash.

No one needed money on the ship. On the outside she'd need plenty. Luckily, the ship herself was probably loaded. One of the most central ingredients to long-term space travel was gold. Get out beyond the atmosphere of a planet like Earth and the vacuum of space was crazy with radiation. As a geologist, Sarah knew plenty about radiation. Solar radiation, including ultraviolet light, was the main driver of the Earth's weather system and therefore a primary force of the planet's geology. Trapped solar radiation kept the Earth nice and warm. Good when it was just enough. Bad when it was too much. Solar radiation was how sunbathers got tans, and also skin cancer. Out in space, free from the mitigating effects of Earth's atmosphere, solar radiation was a whole different animal—like a dog in a park let off its leash. And it was the lesser of the radiant evils in space.

To those intrepid enough to venture past the protective blankets of sky and cloud, the real boogeyman beyond was Galactic Cosmic Radiation. GCR was the accumulated radioactive output of millions of solar systems, a storm of ancient particles, born lightyears before and moving so fast they could pass through a spacecraft as if it was made of vapor, influencing and damaging susceptible material along its murderous path. One especially susceptible material was people. Another was electronics.

Gold, however, was nearly immune to solar and galactic radiation. As a result, every bit of conductive material onboard the *Kalelah* was made of it. Any glass that acted as a window was tinted with it, as were the visors of helmets and the insulation of water supplies. Since Guide Ships were designed to fly for eons, Sarah guessed there ought to be plenty of spare gold in the stores.

She followed the float's path to the right location, a good ten-minute walk, and there it was—giant bins of it, unlocked and unprotected like it wasn't one of the most valuable things on Earth. Of course, to the supply stewards who stocked *Kalelah* before she left Origen, or to anyone else on the ship, it probably wasn't. It was important, sure, but everything on the ship in one way or another was important. Cleaning fluid and spare brush heads for the sweep bots were important. Besides, as far as she knew, elsewhere in the universe gold could be as plentiful as dirt. So here it lay like another industrial commodity, another of those crazy disconnects between life on Earth and life on the ship.

The metal was different looking from the gold she imagined had been stored at Fort Knox or in the secret banks of Switzerland. It hadn't been shaped into bars or ingots. It was wound into little spools and fist-sized nests like dried twirls of angel-hair pasta. She found a fiber box on a shelf across from the gold she could easily empty and stuffed it full. It wasn't as heavy as she expected it might be. If the world hadn't been Corrected half to death, and the Russians hadn't blown a giant hole in the US, she figured the amount she had would have been enough to make her comfortable for years. But now that the world's economies had been dusted, the value of gold had likely gone up. A boon and also a worry.

She redirected the float to find Guide Packs.

Crumb two.

When the Guides worked off ship, they carried a satchel loaded with survival essentials. Brush cutters, dehydrated food, a water maker, a thermal wrap, a communicator, and a med kit. Getting one was a six-minute walk back toward the door she'd slipped in earlier.

She could hear the bot she followed into the vault rolling through an aisle nearby, moving to its own agenda. She continued down a dimly lit corridor with rows and rows of shelves and lockers all labeled in code, their contents a mystery to her.

The packs were where the float said they'd be. She had to climb the height of two shelves to reach them. She snagged two, transferring the food packets, med kit, and thermal wrap from one to the other and leaving the depleted pack behind. Easy so far. The next stop was the only one she had looked forward to. Clothes shopping.

Her jumpsuit—everyone's jumpsuit—looked unabashedly alien. Zippered, slim-fitted, fabric of unknown origin, insignias at the biceps, chest, and collar, waisted by a belt Batman would kill for and tucked into side-buckled boots at the bottom. Her second biggest fear was that she'd be discovered missing before she could make it across the moat. Her *first* biggest fear was making it past the moat but getting tagged as alien ten steps past the rock ring. Haute Comic Con was not a fashion statement for survival. There was one style exception to the Star Trek theme. Of the entire crew, Security alone was spared the jumpsuit curse. She queried the coordinates.

Major crumb three.

The security force wore pants and zip tops that—at least from a distance—resembled normal pants and pullovers. Once she found the rack that stored the uniforms, she could see that "normal" wasn't quite the term for the shirt and pants she held up to herself for sizing. They looked fine, stylish even. The black pants zipped at the side and buckled across the hips. The shirt buttoned up to a tall collar with a narrow V-shaped slit just below the chin. The insignia on either side of the split could easily be mistaken for the signature mark of a prewar designer. She knew the mark signaled security forces, but no one on the outside would. It was the fabric that worried her. It was heavy. Not crazy heavy, but she was sure it would slow her down some. Also, it wasn't cloth; it looked like some kind of woven alloy.

She unbuckled her belt and zipped out of her jumpsuit. She put on the shirt first. It was soft enough, but cold. Metal for sure.

Probably tear proof, which wouldn't be a bad thing. The shirt fit well. The pants were fine too, for now. This stuff didn't feel like it would stretch much. The real prize in the outfit though was the coat. It was long, dark gray, almost European in cut, and packed with pockets. She could imagine it hanging on a rack in some fancy boutique she'd never been able to afford. It would easily cover up any residual alien weirdness to the pants and shirt and add to her carry capacity. She was dying for a mirror, but she felt good. Vaguely badass. She undressed, slipped back into her jumpsuit, rolled her new clothes into the Guide Pack, and placed it in the laundry bag. She slung the now much heavier bag over her shoulder and crept to the corridor at the end of the aisle.

When Sarah entered the corridor and turned left the electrician bot was directly in her path. She nearly bumped straight into it. She backed away a few steps and froze. She hadn't heard the rolling friction of the bot's wheels nor the slightly musical hum of its motor for a long time. Had it been waiting for her?

"Go about your business," she tried to say with some authority.

The bot stood its ground. It was a tall, faceless rectangle on wheels, its smooth metal surface interrupted here and there by a series of extendible pinchers, hooks, and delicate digit-like instruments. A self-propelled toolbox. There was nothing about it that hinted at even the slightest semblance of intelligence. After a moment, a slim vertical door opened midway up the rectangle and a thin scanner rod emerged. When it had reached the end of its extension its leading edge lit up to a vibrant yellow. Sarah stepped sideways hoping to get out of the scanner's imaging range, but the bot wheeled sideways as well and sounded six notes in a climbing scale. She stepped sideways back in the other direction. The bot followed, playing the six notes again, this time louder and with more urgency.

"Shit," she said aloud.

Two lights flashed at the top of the rectangle.

"I don't have time for dancing."

The bot blasted the six notes yet again.

"Okay, okay! Take your stupid picture." She stood still while the yellow light from the scanner moved across her body. What did it matter? She'd already pulled a float. No, *three* floats. The Code would know she was here soon enough.

The scan was over quickly. The rod retreated back to its space in the tall box, the bot wheeled around and headed for the doors. She followed and slipped out of the room directly behind it, so close they were practically dirty dancing, if that were possible. Once clear of the door and back out into the weirdly low-ceilinged staging area, she picked up her pace and broke into a jog. It was time to leave the *Kalelah*.

All she needed was a way out.

12

Sarah wished the real world was more like Star Wars. If it were, she could simply jump out with a garbage ejection. Or she could steal the conveniently parked Millennium Falcon and make a dramatic getaway, blasting out from a maintenance bay, engines glowing white hot, the bay doors inexplicably open, while rounds shot everywhere except on target.

Sadly, none of those cinematic options were open to her. The *Kalelah* was a closed and self-sustaining system. There were no ejections, and every molecule of waste was recycled. Stealing a ship? Even one not nearly as prized as a craft that could do the Kessel Run in twelve parsecs? Forget it. Every vessel aboard the *Kalelah* was a child ship to the mother herself. The Code didn't always have control of things, especially once off ship, but here, within the confines of the *Kalelah*, Sarah couldn't so much as open a hatch without the mother's permission.

Objects did come and go between the ship and the outside world. Surveillance bots and probes, like bees leaving the hive, squeezed through ports to the outside every day. The recorder bots that followed the fighter jets keeping watch over the *Kalelah* came and went in regular shifts. Most bots, however, were small, considerably smaller than Sarah. Even if there was a bot port big enough for her to slip through—drill bots and other repair equipment likely used ports her size—again, the Code would intercede. It would never stand for a port opening without an ordered bot mission to prompt it. Every channel she imagined the Code somehow controlled.

Another fit of mild panic crept into her belly.

As she rode the conveyor out of Leaf One, Sarah wondered if she'd been thinking about this all wrong. If there was no getting around the Code, maybe she could go *through* the Code. Both Trin and Wildei, the two best Code Divers she knew, had told her the Code identified as female. While she had no idea exactly what that meant, Trin's relationship with the Code was, in her opinion, pretty weird. Discomforting actually. Trin's brain worked so fast he could communicate with the Code in ways no one else could, not even Wildei. He could *run* with her, he'd said.

Sometimes a run with the Code would leave him spent, similar to how she'd leave him spent. The whole thing made Sarah think about that old movie where Joaquin Phoenix fell in love with an OS played by Scarlett Johansson—or Scarlett Johansson's voice, anyway. She couldn't help it...the thought of Trin and the Code getting all techie intimate together made her a little jealous. Worse, it made her feel alien to his world in the one part of their relationship that felt natural, human, and instinctual. The one part that felt normal.

When she tried to ask him if his relationship with the Code was more than just professional, or more than good friends, he looked at her like she was crazy, and Sarah had blushed with embarrassment for asking. It wasn't like he'd seen the movie and even understood the question. She'd dropped the issue almost as fast as she had picked it up.

Now it was time to ask the question again. This time, of the Code. Maybe she'd get a different answer. An answer Sarah could leverage.

Sarah's interaction with the Code had never been more than *indirect*. Sarah worked through an interface, the float network. It was easier, faster, more intuitive, and more elegant than any computer interface she'd used Before. No keyboard, no mouse. All she had to do was call for a float and speak. Later, after the initial novelty of speaking into the air to something like a computer had lost its ability to blow her mind, she soon followed the example of most people on the ship and hand-drove her floats. Driving a float by hand was much faster and much more enlightening than using voice. By talking aloud with the Code, the conversation was limited by Sarah's queries or responses to the Code's linear answers. It was limited by the natural constraints of human speech—this word or phrase before that word or phrase.

Connecting via a hand-driven float let the Code offer feedback and suggestions that were layered, dimensional, and always smarter than what Sarah had in mind. Since ideas from the Code didn't have to follow the ordered and rule-bound patterns of dialogue, the Code could offer a dozen responses at once in a kind of visual architectural hierarchy. Sarah didn't have to scroll through lists like she did on the internet. The ideas came in words, images, graphlets, and moving pictures that clung to different layers of transparency within the float, like dew drops on a three-dimensional spider's web, so even an untrained mind like Sarah's could simultaneously take in multiple responses from the code that were wildly different in perspective. Like any interface, though, it was an intermediary that applied its own guidelines and rules onto the connection between her and the Code. In Sarah's case that connection was mostly demand and supply. Show me, tell me, answer me, guide me, help me.

Divers like Wildei and Trin could connect with the Code in an entirely different way. They used neural connections delivered via a Bridge Maker worn in the ear, what Trin called fusing. The smarter and faster your brain, the deeper you could go both within the Code and *with* the Code. No one on the ship could come close to Trin's intellect and processing speed. Sarah had no idea if she could even fuse at all, or what would happen if she did. All she knew was she had to try.

She went straight to the pod. Trin always had a maker with him. There were two spares he stored in the one and only storage space their pod possessed, a shallow depth behind one of the wall panels, and she found them in no time. One was a simple, concave disc with a pinch grip on one side and a gold coated stem about an inch long on the other. The second Bridge Maker had the same gold stem but was shaped like a top. She didn't know what their shapes meant, if anything, so she grabbed the top-shaped bridge because it looked like it would be more comfortable and left for a place on the ship no one would see her.

Despite the enormity of the *Kalelah*, there weren't many places to be alone. Only personal pods and the captain's conference room were shielded from the constant monitoring of cameras and microphones. Staying in the pod was risky though. If Trin came back for a rest, he wouldn't be happy seeing the maker in her ear. Besides, she worried seeing him at all would melt her resolve. The pilot's nest was her best chance of getting some privacy. Abandoned since the crash, it was perched up high on the ship and out of the way of any normal traffic flow. It was worth the thirty-minute walk to get there.

The room was dark, dusty, and forlorn, with the desolate chill of a place looted and left for dead. The pilot's gloves, once luminous as jewels in the sunlight, lay dully on the floor. Their thousands of shorn optical connections, the umbilical lines between gloves and the Code, coiled around them in circles like caution tape around a crime scene. Had the gloves been moved at all since that day? Or were they exactly where Donnelay had dropped them after he had ripped them from their receptacles to bring the ship down? Sarah thought back on that day, on that moment. In The Mutiny's last minutes, she had been getting her ass seriously beat by Laird. It was in the concourse outside the CC. Trin was held back by three guards and Laird's fists had felt to Sarah like hammers. Right before she had passed out, she felt the floor pitch beneath her. She had smiled then, despite the ass kicking, and her smiling made Laird hit even harder. Sarah smiled because the floor falling out from under her, from them all, had meant that Donnelay had done it. He had made his choice and sided with The Mutiny. Looking at this room now, she realized what must have turned Donnelay's heart.

The nest's windows were covered now by layers of protective nanowool. When Donnelay had worn the gloves and provided the human link required by Plan Law to let the ship fly, his only actual job as pilot, the view from the nest would have given him an unfiltered three-hundred-and-sixty-degree view of the Correction. From his post, with no float haze to soften the horror's edge, and without the clinical distance of Code reports, he would have seen all too clearly the full force and fury of the plasma strikes. He would have seen the merciless transformation.

Sarah's heart broke in yet another place. And it surprised her to learn there were any pieces still whole enough for the breaking.

The nest was shaped in a V, with the pilot's chair placed central at the point. She climbed into it and swiveled round so she had a view of the entry to the room. It was large and comfortable. She made a mental note for the future: clean this place up and it would be good for a secret nap. She took the Bridge Maker from her belt, found on its edge what she thought was an on switch, and pushed it. The maker instantly came to life, its polished metal surface turning translucent and glowing bright blue. She put it in her left ear and waited. She heard a soft hum, like the after-ring of a cymbal strike. A second later it screeched into a sharp, painful bolt of feedback. She yanked it out of her ear.

"Dammit," she hissed, rubbing her ear.

She turned the piece over in her hand examining it for some clue to its proper use. There was nothing else to push or twist. But its blue glow had begun to pulse.

This thing is angry, she thought. *That's an error message.*

Could the ear she chose matter? Did the two sides of the brain process sound differently? She had no clue. That was biologist stuff, not geologist stuff. Trin would know. The Code would know. She could know easily enough. She tried her right ear but kept her hand close just in case. The cymbal sound came again, this time without any feedback. It grew in volume. Or was it richer somehow, fuller, like other cymbals tuned to different octaves had joined the first? Then something extraordinary. The soft blonde hairs of her arms raised. Her spine heated. Without warning she was there. She didn't know what "there" was. It was just the word that came to her. A feeling she'd transitioned somehow from one place to another. The surprise of it made her gulp for air. Her chest began to heave and she feared she'd soon be hyperventilating. She reached up to the maker to take it out again but was suddenly awash in an instruction. Not in words, in a *knowing*.

Relax, it ordered. *You are in charge*, it reminded her, and instantly she knew it was right. The agreement was simultaneous, a flash knowing like the stab of déjà vu. She slowed her breathing down, straightened her back, and placed her hands on her knees. She stared calmly toward the entry and the small, dim corridor just past the threshold.

At last, she spoke. In a language she'd never used before, a language that expressed itself in whole ideas, in pictures and in feelings. They gushed from her like a spigot flung open full. The Code's responses, if that's what they could be called, came even faster. Together, in a span of missing time, they came to an agreement. A woman and a machine, both in love with the same man, would do everything they could to keep him safe. As best they could, they would prevent him from doing what they both knew he would do—chase Sarah down at all costs, put himself out alone in an alien world, thinking he could study his way to understanding a world half a universe from his own.

Except, unlike Sarah, who was born on this planet and knew its shadows and masquerades, he could never hide here. His bizarre accent, his misunderstanding of idiom, and his lack of practice with the customs of Earth would conspire to give him away in minutes. They both knew he would not kill to protect himself. He would never harm the children he and his ship had failed so completely. Instead, his hunt for Sarah would kill him. On that they agreed. And on more.

Their plan was that Sarah's visit to the supply vault would be scrubbed. The report from the electrician bot would never reach its destination. In fact, those adjustments were made on the fly, the instant they were conjured. Later, at Earth's night, repair bot hatch 213 off Leaf Five would open for eleven seconds. Sarah would slide out the hatch arms first, and grab hold of a sensor rod the Code would extend to the side of the hatch. She'd bring the rest of her body out and hang from the rod while she felt for a foothold on the smaller bot hatch beneath. Once she was stable, she'd use her perch to find handholds among the network of protrusions along the nanowool and slowly free-solo her way down the side of the ship until she was at a height low enough to safely jump to the ground. Given her inexperience in climbing, and the weight of her clothes and pack, the Code predicted her descent would take ninety minutes. The logs of both the hatch and the sensor rod would be altered in real time. The cameras and electromagnetic sensors scouting the moat would not see or detect Sarah, and a cleaning bot would be dispatched to obscure her tracks while she trekked toward the rock ring through the soft, sad powder of Moscow's pulverized remains.

The Code promised to leave nothing in her mind of Sarah's escape for Trin to discover as he anguished for clues about the whereabouts of the mortal woman he loved. Nevertheless, they concurred without debate, at some time in the weeks to follow, he would surely detect the Code's complicity. Suspect it at the least. How could he not? At this shared conclusion, the two women cried together in each their own ways over the pain they both knew he would feel. The pain of losing one love, and of another's betrayal.

Five hours later, Sarah slid out of hatch 213.

13

Sarah walked the powder of Moscow's destruction with a half crescent moon hanging low in the sky. The expanse of the impact crater went on uninterrupted for miles around her. Not a tree, rock, nor even the smallest remnant of the great city that once occupied the land she walked poked through the level, barren plain. There was a light wind that traveled from the east, blowing off the sterile dunes of black diamond desert the Correction had left in its wake. She buttoned the large collar of her security guard coat against the chill and looked back to mark her progress.

The ship lay hulking on the horizon in the night. A stand-in skyline for the one it crushed. There was no doubting its beauty. The ship's Leaves, six distinct segments, arranged from smallest to largest, caught the moonlight at their edges and drew upon the night a gleaming outline of the colossal arrow shot to Earth from another world. Was it beautiful to her because she knew its secrets? Because she could speak its language? She turned back toward the west, toward the ring and the world still living beyond it. What must the *Kalelah* look like to eyes that were unable to see past the ship's impenetrable skin? Eyes that were blind to the marvel of its arched ceilings stories high, its lake and farm, and the miracle of the Code. Eyes that would never see past the ship's mistake. To those eyes, she imagined, the giant arrow sitting in the center of the city it took away was a monster from the end of the world. That the ship had come here to start the world probably mattered little. She hitched her pack up higher on her shoulders and trudged on.

She got to the rock ring by midmorning. The sky was clear, and while the air was still cool, the bright sun felt warm and good on her face. She'd seen the ring in floats a thousand times. Now, standing at its base, she was daunted by the scale of the thing. This was a small mountain. She hopped on the first rock and started an angled path upward. The first fifty yards were easy going. The rocks were large and heavy. They offered broad faces from which to jump and land. She did her best to keep a relatively straight line up the face of the rubble, but some jumps required a little switchbacking. The lower third of the ring was mostly broken slabs of concrete, asphalt, and twisted cords of rusted rebar. As she climbed higher up the pile the rubble began to change in constitution. Of course the heavier material would have stayed lower during the blast. Now, approaching the midpoint, like climbing up layers of sediment, the pieces were smaller and lighter, and the face of the city began to show through. Mixed into the abstract chunks of cement were bricks, broken lintels, and bits of carved limestone. Sarah couldn't help imagining the buildings they once made, and the people that had once lived within them. She decided to pick up her pace, get away from the ghosts, and took a long step up. The brick she landed on didn't hold and she slipped a good ten yards before she could stop herself.

She took a breath and waited for pain from somewhere. A banged knee, a busted elbow, an injury near the baby? Her heart felt like it might burst from her chest, but she seemed unhurt otherwise.

Metal clothes, she marveled. *Worth every fucking ounce.*

She looked back toward the ship while she caught her breath. She half expected to see a transport flying her way or a pack of surveillance bots hovering right there at eye level. There was nothing. Only the dark shape of the ship far on the horizon. She looked back up the pile and started her way again, this time testing each piece she chose as a foot or handhold for fastness to the pile. So much for escaping the ghosts. And these wouldn't be the last or the worst of them.

The sun was high, and Sarah cast no shadow by the time she summited the ring. Not sure of what lay beyond the pile, she stayed low on the ridge, resting on her elbows, her feet still on the ship side, and took in the view of the other side. Far in the distance, the tiny black dot of a fighter jet silently moved across the sky. Just below her lay the Poklonnaya Hill and Victory Park, an enormous open-air tribute to the Soviet role in the outcome of World War II. It was a sprawling collection of Romanesque structures and public squares dotted by a series of freestanding columns and a central, towering obelisk with the triumphant Goddess of Victory at its top, her bronze robes flowing. In the open areas between the large museum buildings and the memorial columns was a tent city, crowded and unruly in appearance even from her relatively distant vantage point. She took in the scene thinking about the most recent war, the one without victory, the one whose only monuments were the rock ring she just climbed and the desperate ramshackle below her. Would the place she was going to look any different? Would she be any less desperate when she got there? Would her sister?

She decided to wait before starting her journey in earnest. Going over the side now, in broad daylight, seemed like suicide. Besides, she was hungry. It had been hours since she'd last eaten.

She lowered herself back off the ridge and dug a shallow bivouac, opened her kit, and unwrapped a square of what resembled a thin pane of white chocolate but tasted strangely like crunchy bacon grease. The first bite was okay, savory and slightly sweet at the same time. The rest were awful. She forced herself to eat until she felt full, then rewrapped what was left of the pane—nearly half of it. The water maker signaled there was plenty of humidity in the air and she gave it a try. Incredibly, she had half a cup of clean-tasting water in less than a minute.

The sun was still high. Sarah sat looking at the ship, sipping the cool water. The lids of her eyes grew heavy now that her stomach was full, and she fought the pull of sleep for fear she'd slide off her perch.

•

She woke with the sound of gunfire coming from the other side of the pile. It was dark now. The crescent moon of last night was thinner and low clouds shrouded its dim light. Another blast from the gun popped behind her. Three so far.

Shit. What am I about to walk into?

The only thing she knew for certain was she couldn't stay on the pile forever. Trin could already be in freak-out mode. It was time to get beyond the ring.

She took a drink, stowed the water maker in her pack, and climbed back up to the summit. The plateau was only a few yards wide. She stayed low on her way across, using an awkward version of what she imagined to be an army crawl. The park was an even crazier looking place at night. There were electric lights in some places, and small fires in lots of places. She swung a leg over and began her way down.

This side of the ring pile was no less steep or treacherous than the way up had been. Her hopes of being able to walk down looking out toward her destination were quickly dashed. She had to keep her face toward the rock and blindly feel her way for footing. More than once she sent debris tumbling down the pile making all kinds of noise. Each time it happened she'd cling to the wall holding her breath waiting for a flurry of gun shots to start careening off the rocks around her. But the guns she'd heard earlier had quieted, and each time she was able to resume her descent without incident.

A good thirty minutes down the rubble the mixed smell of cooking, generator exhaust, and human shit reached her, something she hadn't experienced in years. She took it in deeply, savoring and separating its unique components. There were odors on the ship, but none like the scent of roasting meat or stewing cabbage. Not the smell of automobiles and kerosene and coffee. Not the smell of life on Earth. Even the stench from the outhouses gave her an odd comfort.

At that point down the ring wall, not far from the base, the rocks began to offer more generous landings and she could turn away from the pile toward the park. She saw them instantly. Two men at the ring's base, watching her descent, waiting. Each had a club in one hand. If they had other weapons, they kept them hidden. One looked in his forties, the other perhaps near seventy. They were less than twenty yards below her. She moved a few steps to her right. They moved a few steps to their left. The ring wall went on for miles in both directions. Given their advantage of flat ground, she'd never be able to outrun them. She could go back up, but there'd be no guarantee of making it over safely. And then what? She unbuckled a jacket pocket near her right hand and continued her way down. When she reached the ground, the older man shouted something at her in Russian. When she didn't reply right away, he screamed at her again.

"I can't speak Russian," she said in English.

The men looked surprised, like she was a talking bear or some other magic trick.

The younger man switched to English, "What the fuck are you doing on his wall?"

"I didn't know it was anybody's wall."

"Now you know," he said. "So, again, what the fuck are you doing on his fucking wall?"

"I wanted to take a picture."

He laughed. "Of this beautiful city?"

"Of the ship."

He translated her answer to the old man. The old man said something in response.

"Let's see the picture."

"I chickened out."

"What?"

"I lost my nerve. I got scared and never made it to the other side."

The Russian translated again, though he talked for a long time, longer than he needed to simply translate. She used the time to climb down the few remaining feet of wall. The old man kept his eyes on her and then smiled crookedly, showing his yellowed and broken teeth.

"You're an American," the younger said.

"Yes."

"From where?"

"Ohio."

"I studied in Boston for a year. You're a long way from Ohio."

"I was here—I mean, overseas—when...you know."

"When they killed us."

"I guess."

"You guess?"

"Yes, I guess."

"Why haven't I seen you before?"

"I didn't want to be seen."

"That's a bullshit answer."

"What do you want from me?"

He smirked. "What are you willing to give?"

"Sorry, no thanks."

He laughed. "American girls. They are not as pretty as Russian girls. The whole world knows that, but they have a certain sense about them. What is the word?" He looked to the old man, who continued to stare dumbly at Sarah. "Entitlement? That's it. Like the world owes you something. It's very attractive. The girls were my favorite thing about Boston. Especially the rich girls. Were you rich?"

"No," she said.

"I'll bet you were a cunt anyway." Another laugh.

"It depended."

The young man laughed loudly at that and caught the old man up in Russian and then the two of them were laughing.

"I know everything that goes on in this camp. How come I didn't know about you until you showed up on my wall?"

"I thought it was *his* wall."

The young Russian smiled. "What is in your pocket there, girl from Ohio?"

"There's nothing in my pocket."

He aimed his club toward the pocket and pushed the piece of wood forward as if to test her claim. Sarah knocked it away. This brought about another peal of laughter. When they were done laughing, he moved closer toward her, his smile melting.

"Now I'm really curious," he said.

She quickly sidestepped him, grabbed the old man by the arm that held the club, twisted it around to his back, yanked it up high toward his shoulder blades, and put the laser cutter from her pocket to the old man's throat. He let out a noise like a dying horse.

The younger Russian stopped. He studied the cutter pressed up to the side of the old man's throat. "You're threatening my friend with a cigarette lighter?" He laughed again.

"I gave up cigarettes three years ago," she said. "Involuntarily. I've been bitchy ever since."

"You think I care about the old man?" He moved toward her again. "Kill him if you can."

Sarah pushed the old man hard into the younger and aimed the laser at the ground between her and the Russians, quickly drawing a smoking red line of molten plaza stone nearly eight feet long. The two Russians stared at the bubbling groove.

"*Blyad'!* What are you?"

"I'm not anything."

"What do you want?"

"I need to get to Amsterdam. Help me and I'll give you the cigarette lighter."

"And what else?"

"Final offer," she said, frying another line in the ground inches from his feet, forcing him to jump backwards.

"Okay, okay. I know someone. It'll be expensive though."

"That won't be a problem. I've recently become a rich girl."

14

Trin stretched his arm across the width of the small bed expecting to find the silk of Sarah's hair. Nothing.

"Start," he said aloud. He opened his eyes as a slanted shaft of rose-colored morning sunlight projected from a windowless wall to the tile floor of the tiny pod. It took nothing more than angling his head a little to confirm what he already felt in the pit of his stomach. She wasn't there. She hadn't been there at all last night. He was used to her long walks, excursions through the ship that could easily last half a day, or half the night. This was different. She'd never been gone this long—a full day now—without some sort of communication.

Trin opened the storage wall and found two days' worth of her clothes. Three was all anyone had. Wherever she'd gone, she hadn't planned on staying there long. So where was she?

He got dressed and started the long walk to the CC. The morning rush to station was underway and the main stem was crowded. He kept his eye out for Sarah and anyone who might know where she was. He stopped at a food stand they both liked.

"May God ease your new start," the vendor said cheerfully.

"Yours too, Micale."

"Tea?"

"Right." He looked around, hoping to see Sarah heading toward the stand, the usual smile on her face.

"Sarah is sleeping late today?" the vendor asked.

"No. Up early, I guess."

"Very early," the vendor replied. "Or she has gotten her cup elsewhere," he said with a hand on his chest in a mock gesture of heartbreak. He handed Trin the glass of hot liquid. "It's good today. Strong."

Trin took a sip of the cloudy red brew. "Yes. Thanks, Micale."

He moved away from the cart to a nearby railing he could comfortably lean against while he drank his tea and watched the crowd that moved through the stem. There was no reason to panic. Sarah could take care of herself. If something had happened to her, something serious, he'd be notified. He considered checking her float pulls. At least he'd know where she'd been. But if she was on the system at the same time, she'd know he was checking up on her. Bad idea.

Each time a glint of blonde hair in the distance caught his eye he was sure it was Sarah's. A second later, something about the woman under the hair—her height, uniform, or the way she walked—would dash his hopes as quickly as they'd risen. It was stupid to think he'd never see her again, but he thought it anyway. He hadn't realized how lonely he'd been before he met Sarah. His work on the ship before the war had been all consuming. And exciting. He was the youngest officer on the ship, the youngest officer in the entire Guide Service. The leadership team understood why he was there. They knew his mind was capable of tasks no one else on the ship could handle, so he was never without work. Interesting work. He had a girlfriend too. Cyler was sweet and devoted. And fantasy beautiful. He figured he had all he needed. Needs, however, change.

He first saw Sarah on his way down the metal steps of *18* to the top deck of a population-built vessel. A vessel called the *Lewis*. In that instant, with her golden hair blowing wildly in the ocean wind and the eager, determined look in her eyes, something about her had stood out beyond the obvious fact that she was the progeny of a great mistake. She had a bearing about her, a stance, an essence he couldn't ignore. He wouldn't say it was love at first sight. It was something though. A tickle in the spine, a spark in the brain, a skip in the beating of his heart. It was something that had never happened to him before.

And later that fateful day, when it was time to pick someone to return to the *Kalelah* with him, someone to show Laird and others exactly what a Correction would be killing, someone who might turn what was a function of rote protocol, *if A happens then B must follow*, into a decision, a *human* decision, Trin picked Sarah. Whether it was that tickle in Trin's spine or the little skip in his heart that had done the actual choosing, he couldn't say. But whatever it was, he was damn grateful for it.

The scheme to stop the Correction, of course, was screwed from second one. Argen was killed before they even returned to the ship. And Laird, evil fucking genius that she was, moved too quickly. Yet all throughout those panicked and fast-moving days just before the Correction, and then during the whacked insanity of The Mutiny, Sarah had shown a remarkable ability to pivot and cope. Anyone else in her position would have been paralyzed with fear. She'd known nothing about the world aboard the *Kalelah*; he couldn't have imagined a more foreign place for someone like her to be. Instead, she was strong and decisive. And brave. It had been as if she was born for the job. And afterward, he'd come to believe, born for him.

Long ago, when he joined the Service, he'd understood what traveling through time would mean. He knew virtually everyone at home would grow old and die long before he'd wake from his first Skip. His mother, his father, cousins, friends, his pets, his teachers, even the fucking asshole researchers who had probed and prodded his whole childhood to understand how a human brain without any augmentation could outthink processors—all of them would be dead. All but his sister who had joined the Service a few years before him. Leaving everything was all part of the deal going in. He had come to terms with it long ago. And while he'd had his bad moments of loneliness and sadness for what was, he'd never been brought to his knees.

Losing Sarah. That, he thought, would do it. That would bring him down.

He tried to dissolve the lump in his throat with the tea and think about the work at hand, the job of tracking down the tech leaks to the outside. No luck. There was no shaking that empty side of the bed. It brought him back to words his sister once said, words he'd always told himself were just talk, shit Deeja said solely for the exercise of saying. Those words now grew in legitimacy and tucked themselves in amongst Sarah's unused bedding. "There's no one anywhere like either of us. Not in the entire universe," Deeja had said casually, almost buoyantly. "Because of that, you and I, little brother, will always be alone." What calculus she'd used to draw that particular conclusion, he had never known. It also didn't matter. Deeja's proclamations had an uncanny habit of proving themselves true.

"Don't eat that, it's going to make you sick."

"Mother drinks too much."

Or when she was eight years old, "I'm going to live forever."

You just didn't argue with Deeja.

Trin had the more agile brain. The more reckless one too. What she lacked in speed, she made up for in judgment. Or clairvoyance.

Maybe now Deeja was right again. He *was* destined to be alone. During more than one dark moment after the war, he had dreamed of time with his sister. An hour even, to tell her things he'd only barely been able to tell himself. Of his shame for not having anticipated Argen's murder. For not having moved faster against Laird. For the countless deaths and the wreckage of a world. For a people knocked centuries backwards, carrying with them all the knowledge of what their lives had once contained without the means to regain it. The dead were gone. It was the living who haunted him.

And one thing more. A shame born of pride. A shame that cut all the deeper for his weak-willed indulgence of it. Lightyears from now, in the nearest and furthest corners of the universe, when the uplinks were received, when the history of these past three years joined the long history of the Guide Service, a terrible math would be made horribly plain. In all the millions of years during which the Guide Ships, those giant arrows shot across the stars, had worked to spread humanity through the cosmos, only one ship had ever truly pulled the trigger of a full-blown Correction.

One Correction would now become two. And the second name beside the number would be *Kalelah*. The ship that slept through its Delivery's development and let loose upon the universe new gods.

His sister would know what to say about all these things. About all his shames. Deeja was out there somewhere, a captain of her own ship and the only person of all the homeworld people he once knew who was still alive. While they could never communicate in real time, a Deep Space Relay could reach her, unless she was Skipping. If that was the case and she was tucked away inside that thick, protective womb of deep sleep, only a ship's emergency alert could get through, like the one the *Kalelah* had used to rouse Captain Argen three years ago. The technical obstacles were a bitch, no doubt. They just weren't the real problem. The real problem was the shame. The fucking, pitiful shame. Even to ease it he couldn't get past it.

Because really, what would he say? *Hi, sis, guess what? We let a seed population breed and grow and conquer a world while we snoozed our asses buried in the sand of an ocean floor. The seeds created language on their own, built computers on their own, weapons on their own, and just to seal the deal, they found a few gods on their own. More than a few, actually. Oops. I know what you're thinking—if there's one thing we know about God, he's not exactly a fan of competition. So yes, you guessed it. We killed them. Not all of them, but a few billion. The rest are just a matter of time, because even though we've all been raised to believe it was impossible, the seeds found humanity on their own too. When we dusted them, we dusted that most of all. Lucky shot, I guess. Proud of your baby brother now?*

He pushed the DSR he would never send out of his mind, finished his tea, and joined the river of people making their way toward the CC.

Enough, he told himself.

He had managed more than five thousand years without Sarah, he could survive another few hours. At this point, there was nothing to worry about. He even vowed not to think about Sarah until his shift was over. He literally shook his head to clean his thoughts and picked up his pace.

The vow lasted twenty minutes. When the big doors of the CC shot open, his first thought was that he'd see her among the twenty or so people scattered about the large, round room. She'd be focused on her float, her brow crinkled toward the space between her eyes, the fingers of her left hand brushing a few stray hairs behind her ear. She'd glance up from her work and give him a look along with a smile that was something more than professional.

Fuck.

Like the crowds in the stem, the tea stand, and his bed...no Sarah.

Okay, asshole, it's time to risk checking the floats. Let her be mad. At least you'll know she's alive.

He went to his station, called up a log of every float pulled in the last eighteen hours, and narrowed it to Sarah's. The last float she'd called was fifteen hours ago, thirty feet from where he was standing, from a guest chair along the outer perimeter of the Command Center. She was watching the planes that patrolled a circle thirty miles from the ship. It was a short session, less than an hour. Nothing since. He tried to think of the longest he'd ever gone during waking hours without pulling a float.

Now it was time to start worrying.

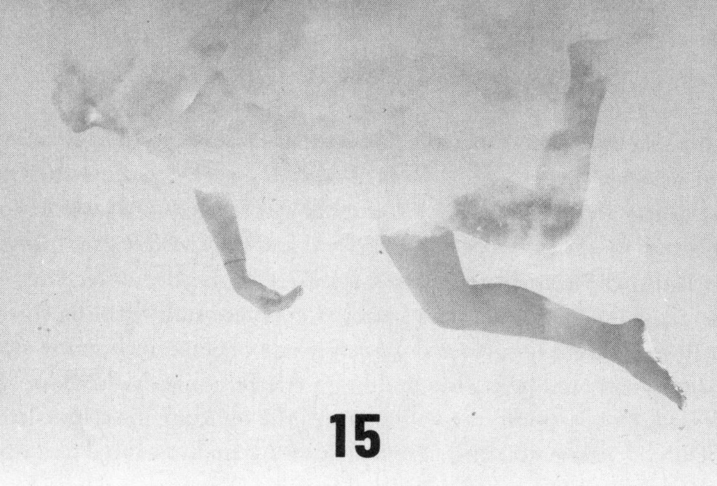

15

The two Russians led Sarah through the camp. At ground level it was even more chaotic than it had appeared from atop the ring pile. The smells of waste and cooking had become too strong to retain any kind of nostalgic allure. And there was an ominous, organic quality about the camp, as if it had grown in place of its own accord the way an invasive ground cover takes over a garden. The large columns erected to pay tribute to Soviet heroes, the tallest among them with its caped figure looking like a bronze depiction of Superman, stood their ground. However, the battle for what would become of this place looked all but over. The wildness of the camp seemed darkly destined to win out over the considered order of the monuments and structures that made up the open-air museum complex.

Tents and scrap-built shacks butted up against each other at haphazard angles like drunken lean-tos. Wires from generators were strung across the meandering pathways, a harried canopy of scribbled black lines against the cloudy night sky. Sarah walked by a tent lit from within by greasy candlelight, its flap open, its occupants naked despite the chill and coupled on a bed of flattened cardboard boxes. The woman caught Sarah's eyes and smiled wantonly, then threw her head back in spasm. More shots rang from somewhere across the camp. Sarah flinched and was glad neither of her two Russian escorts had seen her do it. A small pack of dogs, their ribs showing through their dirty and patchy coats, crossed her way at a crooked intersection of two paths. She offered them no food and they paid her no mind.

Another twenty yards ahead appeared to be the outer edge of the camp. Beyond that were battered concrete stairs leading to the main structure, a long, low-slung semicircle of columns holding aloft a single-story white marble building perhaps twenty feet above the ground. At one point, the void beneath the building must have been enclosed by glass, creating a ground floor. All that remained of it now was a tortured tangle of black metal framing. The fires and light from the main camp threw a flickering, orange glow upon the face of the semicircle and she could see the stains of fire on the marble above the twisted metal frame and the broken windows of the building proper. Nevertheless, even with the ground level enclosure gone, the building, suspended as it was, still offered a kind of roof. For many, it appeared, that was enough. Several fires burned beneath the floating mass and danced wildly in the wind that pushed between the columns. People gathered around the heat and light in a sad replica of happier times. Some stood alone, their meager belongings in heaps of bags at their feet. Others ate, talked, or slept as close as they could get to the shallow radius of warmth. It was home for those without the wherewithal to construct one or protect one.

"How much further?" she called to the younger Russian.

"We walk through the Hall of Glory ahead and then down the hill. Not far."

"This place... It must have been beautiful."

He stopped on the first stair to the building and nodded toward the rock ring. "This place used to be a hill. You could see half of Moscow from here. Now what do you see?"

"I'm sorry about what happened to your city."

He looked at her blankly and shrugged. "Everything ends. And it wasn't my city. Let's go. I want my fucking lighter."

"Oh, I thought you lived here."

"I did. Most of my life."

"I don't understand."

"You wouldn't. You are American. You could afford attachments to things. To houses, to cars, to money. Because it was possible to believe you could keep them. In Russia, ordinary people could not have such beliefs. Without power, everything could be taken from you at any time. So why care? And this?" He gestured toward the camp. "It's better for me. Putin is gone. Now anyone can do the taking."

They walked through the Hall of Glory, the ceiling above them charred, the people around them looking hollow eyed and frail in the firelight. A woman was attempting to pry open a shallow tin can of something with a rusted knife at the edge of the tiled slab beneath the Hall, her back resting against a column, her feet dangling over a patch of dead grass. Once through the Hall of Glory, a vast lawn of weeds, brown wildflowers, and unruly grasses spread out down the hill. At the bottom of the hill, she saw why they had come this way.

"Holy shit."

"Yes. Most of it is shit."

Dotting the lawn below them was a military parade's worth of tanks, big caliber artillery, transport vehicles, planes, and helicopters. Draped in shadow, they were blackened sculptures in the near moonless night, their details obscured. They were frightening just the same.

"The anti-tank guns have no firing mechanisms and are filled with cement. The tanks have no engines. The MiGs have no avionics." He shrugged. "Besides, we have no runway so what does it matter? But that over there," he pointed to a hulking silhouette in a far corner of the weed field, "that flies."

It was largest helicopter she'd ever seen. They headed down the sloping lawn toward the giant chopper and stopped about twenty yards from the beast.

"Mi-26," the Russian said. "Very big, very powerful helicopter. It is the home of my friend. But he is not too friendly, so we will stop here and wait."

"How long?"

"Not long. He will see us. Even if he is asleep, he will hear us. Only problem, if he is drunk, he may shoot us."

"Your friend is the pilot?"

"Yes. A good pilot too. Hero. In what you called the Cold War, he killed many Americans."

"Can't wait to meet him."

They waited in silence for a long ten minutes.

"Shit," the Russian said, looking at his watch. "He is drunk."

Sarah frowned. "Maybe now's not the best time to—"

"Alexey Galygin!" the Russian called.

A few seconds later they heard a loud, angry groan from inside the chopper.

"I don't think he's very happy," said Sarah.

The door to the big 26 burst open. A large man in military boots and pants and no shirt stood in the hatchway of the helicopter holding a machine gun at the ready. He was well-built but flabby. His skin was ghostly white, as was his thinning hair, and even from the distance of her vantage point, Sarah could see the deep lines of his face. He was old. But the muscles of his forearms were still large and he carried the big gun like it weighed nothing. Ignoring all but two of the steps that hung off the sill of the door, he hopped down to the weeds with athletic poise and made his way to the small group.

"Pavel Antonovich," he said without greeting, warmth, or malice. It was merely an observation. "*Chego ty khochesh'?*"

Pavel answered in Russian. All Sarah understood was the word *Amerikanskiy*.

The pilot looked her over. "I'm booked," he said in English.

"I can pay," Sarah said.

He stared at her, his eyes the color of dirty blue ice. "I can get sex anytime I want."

She reached into one of the many pockets of her coat and pulled out a tiny spool of the gold and held it out to the pilot, hoping her eyes were saying what she knew her mouth should not at this point: *Here you go, asshole*. He took the spool between the fingers of his left hand, held it up to the pale night sky. "Come with me," he said and pointed his gun back toward the chopper. "Not Egor," he said to Pavel while aiming his glance at the older Russian. "He'll stink up my house." The old Russian replied with something that sounded like profanity and spat. The pilot laughed as he turned and walked toward the Mi-26.

The inside of the chopper had a faint odor of gasoline and it looked like a mash-up between a junkyard and the laboratory of a mad scientist. It was big enough to hold several cars and Sarah wouldn't have been surprised if there were in fact a car or two buried somewhere beneath all the crap. He pointed behind her to the cockpit, which was home to the only windows and the only two seats.

"Make yourself comfortable."

She remained standing behind Pavel a few feet from the still open door. "I'm good," she said.

He shrugged and placed the machine gun on a rusted metal table—perhaps salvaged from a patio somewhere—that was pushed up against the rivet-studded metal wall of the cabin. He took a filthy bottle off a makeshift shelf, pulled the cork out with his teeth, turned it up against his lips, and took a drink. When he finished, he wiped his mouth with the back of his hand, corked the bottle, and tossed it to Pavel, who took a drink and held the bottle out to Sarah.

"I'm good."

"It's custom," Pavel said, his eyes pleading just a little.

"No disrespect, but I'm not drinking," Sarah said, inching a little closer to the open door of the helicopter.

Alexey Galygin rummaged through a wooden box on the floor and after a minute pulled from it a small cast iron dish, black and ancient looking. He walked the dish a few steps down the cabin where on a long counter groaning with the weight of kettles, tubes, beakers, and small electronic machines sat a propane-fired burner. He placed the iron dish on a halo-shaped loop of wire suspended above the burner and turned on the gas. He fished about for something on the counter long enough that Sarah could smell the gas from the unlit burner. Eventually he found a box of matches and struck one to flame.

He put the match over the tip of the burner and a ball of fire burst alight with a loud, dull pop. He scrounged around the counter again until he found a large industrial-looking thermometer connected to a long wire with an alligator clip on its end. He fastened the metal teeth of the clip to the edge of the dish and placed the little gold spool into the dish.

"It's real," Sarah said.

"We'll see." He glanced into the dish and checked the thermometer. "Very soon."

A minute later, he turned off the burner. He reached to a shelf above the counter for a glass half-full of a cloudy liquid, likely nothing more than dirty water Sarah thought, and poured some of the liquid into the dish. The liquid hissed and steamed. The pilot waved the steam away for a better look into the dish and then reached into the dish with his bare hand and pulled out a solid puddle of gold. He walked over to Sarah and placed the puddle into her hand, his face expressionless. The gold was still warm. She placed it back into the pocket she took it from a few minutes before. The pilot sat on a stack of shallow boxes a few feet from Pavel and Sarah.

"How much do you have?" he asked.

"I have enough."

"We'll see. Where do you want to go?"

"Amsterdam."

He raised an eyebrow. "Amsterdam. You're hoping to catch a boat."

"Meeting a friend."

He smiled joylessly. "It's your funeral. Of course, who has funerals anymore? The priests no longer believe in God, and only the rats would come." He pushed a large age-spotted hand through his thinning hair. "The Netherlands is twenty-four hundred kilometers from here. Give or take. In the best weather, I can make it halfway before refueling, twelve hundred kilometers. Warsaw. You won't like it there."

"I can handle it."

"We'll see. It's a dangerous trip. Maybe it's better for me to just take your gold right here and skip the wear and tear on my helicopter. It would improve my profit margin, I think."

"I wouldn't do that if I were you."

He laughed. "Why not?"

She tilted her head to Pavel. "Ask him." She kept her eyes on the pilot and couldn't see Pavel's response, but the smile on Alexey Galygin's face weakened. After a short minute, he reached behind him for a metal bowl that probably once belonged to a household mix master. "Fill it."

She took the pack off her shoulder, unclasped one of the five compartments, and drew from it a polished alloy case. On one of the corners of the case there was a pattern of small holes. She lifted the case to her mouth and exhaled forcefully into the holes. A tone sounded and a row of thirty-two glowing discs elevated from the top of the case. She placed the case down on a nearby stack of old Russian magazines and tilted the face of the case toward her, away from the view of the two Russians, and pressed a sequence of twenty discs that each emitted a soft, identical sound. The case opened. She took out several spools and placed them in the bowl, then handed the bowl to Alexey Galygin.

"That's only half," he said.

"You'll get the rest when I get to Amsterdam. And just so you know, any gun or explosive you might think powerful enough to open this case won't. Also, if I'm not breathing, no one on Earth can open this case. Do we have a deal?"

The pilot nodded.

She reached into her pocket and gave the small laser to Pavel.

"One more thing," she said softly. "I'm armed in ways you can't imagine. So let's just be clear. I can get sex anytime I want it."

16

Alexey Galygin seemed sober enough at the stick of the big Mi-26. If only he smelled it. Even with nearly four feet between their two seats, Sarah was practically engulfed in the orangey afterburn of his committed pursuit of brain loss. A part of her admired the level at which he operated. He had put down an impressive amount of whatever drain cleaner was in that filthy bottle he had clung to throughout the night like a child with a blanket. Then, *boom*, at first light he had gotten up with no trouble at all. Instead, she was the one who was groggy.

Sarah hadn't dared sleep the previous night. She had found a place to sit and lean against the wall at the rear of the cargo hold where she could keep an eye on Galygin from a safe distance. Even if she had allowed herself to sleep, she likely wouldn't have had much luck of it. The rivets that held together the chopper's metal skin dug into her back, and a near constant scratching noise—close enough for her to hear despite the rotors—had convinced her there were mice aboard the helicopter. Now though, having moved up front, the relative comfort of the big co-pilot's seat, the warmth of the sun coming through the glass of the cockpit, the rhythmic thumping of the blades, and

Alexey Galygin's surprisingly steady hand on the controls were lulling her to sleep.

•

In her dream she was running through the woods. Less than a mile away to her right, a great fire roared and the air around her was dry and hot and filled with smoke. Sunlight fell through the forest canopy streaking the atmosphere in shafts of gold, a curiously beautiful spectacle, the way highly poisonous snakes are often things of exquisite design. The sound of the fire, though, was an unambiguous terror. A scream like a hundred jet engines. As if to confirm the analogy for her, the fire consumed the woods in its path at a shocking pace. It didn't merely progress; it raced as if propelled, and in the same direction as she.

Any sane person would be running elsewhere, anywhere but where the fire was headed. Yet Sarah had no choice. She had to make it home before the fire. The panic she felt, along with that ugly and familiar mix of guilt and anger, was entirely her fault.

Typical idiot me.

It was a storm that was always with her, waiting for the right time to let loose its lightning and noise. How did she let herself get roped into watching her sister's stupid dogs? How could Margaret have had the nerve to ask in the first place? Sarah had never taken care of a single dog, let alone three, one of which was just a pup. Now there was this fire and Sarah was so far away from the house where she'd left the dogs. The house that would soon be in the path of the blaze. She should have taken the dogs with her to school. They'd all still have to run from the fire, but at least she'd have them with her. If she didn't have the athleticism to outrun the fire, if her lungs—already burning and protesting—couldn't sustain her pace, if her legs gave out, she could unclip the leashes from the dogs' collars and let them run at their natural speeds. But the dogs were locked in the house, with no way out of the fire's path until she got home.

If she were to get there too late, she'd have to tell her sister what had happened. She'd have to explain her decision to leave the dogs alone. She was always having to explain things to her sister. Why she wouldn't be graduating on time. Why she smoked. Why she drove too fast. Always this need to come clean. It wasn't fair. Not when Margaret was the one who had so much to explain. Why had Jack picked Sarah when Margaret, the older of the two, was so much more the woman? Why had it always seemed like Mother and Margaret had secrets? On these things, and many others, Margaret had remained silent. She'd offered no explanation for why she only stared out from under her blanket in the twin bed two feet from Sarah's as Jack tore her childhood away. She had offered no explanation for their mother's willingness to overlook the obvious. Nor had she said anything in the way of explanation for why Jack had suddenly stopped. None of that mattered. If Sarah proved too slow to keep the dogs safe, Margaret would suffer another debilitating loss. And Sarah would have to bear the weight of it atop all the other losses. So she ran, her lungs screaming in pain, her face sweating, images of the dogs helplessly barking at the windows flashing in her mind like shards of nightmares.

The fire proved to be the faster runner, and the smoke grew so thick she couldn't see her way anymore.

•

She awoke with the bump of the Mi-26's wheels hitting the ground.

"Welcome to Poland," Alexey Galygin said unceremoniously.

"That was fast."

"It was five hours."

"Shit. I slept hard," she said, her voice husky from sleep. "Where are we?"

"An old American airfield outside Warsaw."

"We're refueling here?"

"Maybe."

"What do you mean maybe?"

"Sometimes there is fuel, sometimes not. Sometimes there are reasonable people, sometimes not."

The dilapidated airfield was small and looked abandoned. The tarmac was pockmarked like it had been the victim of multiple missile attacks. Grasses and weeds grew in the crevices and cracks, the only visible signs of life. The lone structure, a rusting steel building with a curved roof like a Quonset hut, stood tentatively in the midafternoon sun. Galygin walked aft of the cockpit to nearly midship and opened the main door. Sarah followed him, and after he kicked the stairs out they both climbed down onto the tarmac.

"Do you speak Polish?"

Sarah shook her head "No."

"Then don't talk. These people don't like Americans."

"*You* don't like Americans."

"This is true." He smiled. It seemed to be a smile more for him than for her.

A door in the center of the forlorn hut opened with the sound of metal scraping. Two large men with machine guns emerged and walked toward Galygin and Sarah. They stopped at a distance too great for handshakes and Sarah quickly understood from the looks on their faces that pleasantries weren't part of the process. The conversation between the men and Galygin was brief and the two men turned and walked back to the hut.

"They will bring the truck," Galygin said.

A minute later the big double doors of the metal shed swung open with one of the men who'd come to talk to Galygin pushing at each door. An ancient fuel truck spewing thick oil smoke from a rattling stack lumbered its way toward the big Russian helicopter. The two greeters followed the truck, jogging at an easy pace. The little caravan stopped alongside the chopper and the driver, a tall, intensely dark African, opened the door of the cab and climbed off his seat and onto the truck's bent and rusted running board. He stayed behind the open truck door and looked over at Sarah and Galygin, boredom and impatience on his face, and extended his left hand, his palm open to the sky. In his right hand, which he rested casually on the top of the door, was a pistol that looked more like a cannon than a handgun.

"Now you pay him," Galygin said. "A handful should be sufficient."

"You didn't say anything about paying for fuel."

Galygin shrugged and smiled again in that way that seemed exclusively for his own amusement.

Sarah did a quick mental calculus of her situation, which added up to thoroughly fucked, and held up a finger to the African. She climbed back into the Mi-26 to avoid showing off her case to yet more people she couldn't trust and fetched a snowball's worth of gold. She also adjusted a weapon in her coat just in case. As she turned to head back to the door, the sound of gunfire—two short bursts of a machine gun, then a third frightfully loud bang—stopped her in her tracks.

Shit, shit, shit.

She quickly moved to the wall of the 26 furthest from the door, not knowing when the shots would stop or who might be waiting for her on the tarmac. Galygin's big machine gun still lay on the rusty table to her left.

Shit, shit, shit.

She drew her weapon, a duster she had hoped never to use, and crept toward the opposite side of the cabin.

The skin of the helicopter was thin and wouldn't likely offer much protection, but it was all she had. Breathing heavily and feeling the weight and heat of her clothes, she pushed herself off the far wall of the cabin and walked as silently as she could the fourteen or so feet that brought her to the wall with the door, and the guns directly on the other side of it. If she wanted a look at what was going on outside, she'd have to put herself, or at least her face, in front of the wide-open door.

Why are there no fucking windows in this thing?

She got to the edge of the door and stopped, hoping she could listen for a sense of the shit she was in rather than stick her head out like a Whac-A-Mole target.

No one was talking. After a minute, she moved into the shaft of sun that poured through the door and risked a look.

Jesus Christ.

Galygin had the hose from the fueling truck over his shoulder and was walking out a length long enough to reach the helicopter. The two Poles who had first greeted them were sprawled on the tarmac, dark puddles under them both. The African was slumped sideways on the driver's seat of the truck like he'd been folded in half. Blood dripped from the running board on the pavement under the truck. A wave of relief washed over her. If it had been Galygin who was dead, she didn't know what she'd do. She walked out the door and the down the two steel steps to the tarmac. On her way toward Galygin she gave the two dead men on the ground only the briefest of glances.

"What the fuck happened?"

Galygin shrugged and continued his work latching the fueling hose to the chopper.

"Why did you kill them?"

"I had the chance."

"You had the chance?"

He said nothing. "So we're just going to steal their gas?" she said.

"It wasn't their gas."

"How do you know?"

Galygin looked her way, his cold, pale eyes briefly meeting hers, but didn't say anything. He walked back to the truck and pushed upward the lever that opened the valve to the hose.

Thirty minutes later they were lifting off the tarmac. She looked down at the fuel truck with its door left open and the two men on the ground, contorted like images from a comic book crime scene, all of them getting smaller as the Mi-26 gained altitude. Crying in front of Galygin was the last thing she wanted to do. She tried to keep the tear that wanted out from getting its way. No luck. She didn't recognize this world. She knew it would be different. She knew it would be hard. But this she didn't understand. Was Galygin, the famed killer of Americans, like this Before? Or had the Correction, and the crash, given new license to his ease with a trigger?

"I'll take the gold," he said flatly, his face toward the view out the windscreen.

"What?"

"For the fuel."

"You want the gold I was going to pay those guys? The guys you killed?"

"Yes."

She looked at him hoping to read his face, hoping to see something there that might make his request seem less mercenary. Less heartless. She saw nothing. He never took his ice-colored eyes off the view ahead. She turned away from him and wiped her face, certain now there'd be no more tears. She looked out through the front windscreen as the big helicopter accelerated forwards toward Amsterdam. Clouds had moved in and the sun had lost its brilliance.

After several moments, she put the spool of gold on the console between them. Galygin took the gold and pushed it into the big, flapped pocket of his Russian army jacket.

"I understand," she said softly, more for herself than for him.

17

The bang was loud and accompanied by the sickening sound of metal ripping. Before Sarah could ask what had happened, or scream the question, the chopper pitched violently to the left and the cabin filled with shrill, short blasts of sirens along with a woman's urgent voice repeating a single word in Russian over and over. She didn't need to know the language to know something very bad was going on.

"What's happening?" Sarah finally managed to shout. "Did we hit something?"

"Radio tower maybe."

She tried to orient herself to the topography, but night had fallen and wherever they were had no electricity. The view out the windscreen was nearly pitch black. Her only sense of orientation came from her stomach, which did not have good news to share. They had definitely stopped their forward momentum.

"Is it bad?" she yelled over the din of the cockpit's warning system, hoping for an answer that contradicted everything the blinking lights and the woman's pleading, digital voice told her. The aircraft began to spin, providing an answer of its own.

"We lost the rear rotor." Despite the g-forces that were making her queasy, and the obvious struggle he was having with the stick, Alexey Galygin's voice had no panic in it at all.

"We're going to crash, aren't we?" Sarah said.

"We're going to land, soon, yes." He turned to her with eyes that almost looked apologetic. Until he laughed.

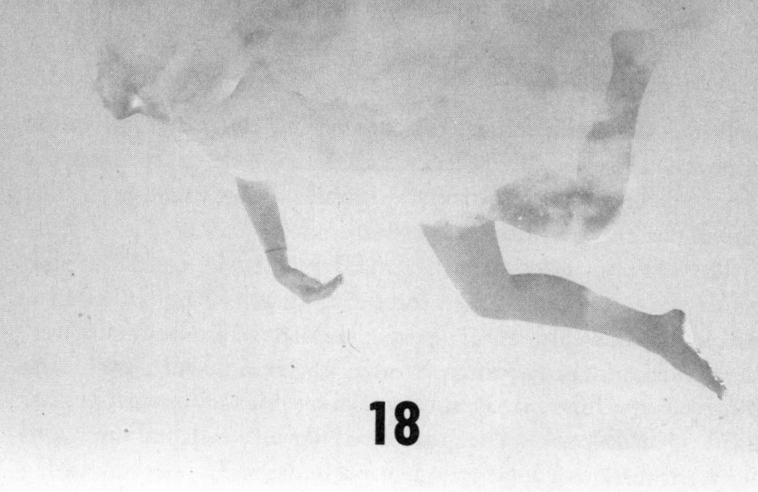

18

When the *Kalelah* had crashed Sarah hadn't actually thought about dying. The ship listed dramatically, sharply enough to sweep Captain Laird from her feet and everyone around her as well. They all slid swiftly downward toward the leading edge of the ship. The same thing happened to all of the more than twenty-two thousand crew members. It was a scene from the sinking of any great sailing vessel. Rooms of people tumbling, screaming, weeping. The doors of storage compartments thrown open, their contents exploding outward into the cascading chaos. In fact, for Laird and hundreds more, the crash had proved fatal. Sarah, however, had felt no fear. As she was sliding across the tiles of the plaza floor, gravity clasped firmly around her ankles and yanking downward like she had no weight at all, her elbows heating up from the friction, she had never once considered the possibly of her death.

The *Kalelah* was so enormous, so solid, so weighty, and in her Earthly eyes so completely magical, Sarah hadn't imagined the real implications of the sudden shift in attitude that had her and everyone around her falling uncontrollably toward the far wall of the grand plaza of the main stem. By layer upon layer of nanowool, by the bolts and straps that kept the heaviest and most lethal objects in place, by her distance from any alarms that might have been sounding in the CC, by the glass that didn't shatter and the wind that didn't sting her face, she had been shielded from the actual violence of the crash. The crash of one city falling upon another.

The falling Mi-26 was different. Big as it was, it felt helpless against the forces of untamed torque and gravity hauling it downward in nauseating spirals. The crash seemed to take hours. By miracle, or perhaps the last-ditch effort of the stone-cold Galygin, the monstrous machine managed to spin itself onto an outcropping of equally giant oak trees. The grove acted like an accidental catcher in the rye, its thicket of ancient limbs absorbing the chopper's thrashing energy until it was released again in a less potent form by their own breaking. All the parties not yet dead were screaming at the top of their lungs: Sarah, the trees, and the skin and bones of the world's most powerful helicopter, its aluminum screeching a frightening aria of danger as it tore. In the end, the Mi-26 plowed a ten-tree clearing in the grove before it stopped. Sarah was awake through it all.

In the movies, helicopters didn't simply fall down. They fell down and blew up. This Law of Hollywood was the first thing to run through her mind as she hung upside down, still securely strapped to her seat by the thick, four-point harness. The aircraft that, to her, had always smelled of gasoline was now reeking with the odor of fuel. She took quick stock of herself. There were small pieces of tempered glass in her mouth and lots more in her hair, but she could move her fingers and toes, and nothing felt broken.

Fucking metal clothes.

Shielded only by the cotton of his shirt and the leather of his Russian Army jacket, Galygin was not so well protected. A six-inch branch of oak tree had pierced his side of the windscreen, his chest, and the back of the pilot's seat. He hung lifeless, blood dripping from behind his seat, his eyes open and colored in a new, colder shade of ice.

She reached over to the pocket where he had stashed the gold meant for the Pols and the African and retrieved the ball. Careful not to let herself simply fall the eight feet down to the ceiling of the helicopter, she raised her legs until her feet were as close to over her head as she could manage. She unlatched the center buckle on the harness and as the straps flew away, she kept hold of the buckle and rolled backward feetfirst out of the seat until she was three feet from the ceiling and then let go of the buckle. She found her bag quickly but didn't even try to find where Galygin had stashed her original down payment. Those movie images of fireball crashes were burning brightly in her mind and telling her to get out and away as quickly as possible.

Sarah ran to the door and yanked up on the lever. Nothing. She tried again, harder, her panic raising. Again, nothing. It took three more tries, each more frantic than the last before she remembered the door was upside down. To open it now, she'd have to push *down* rather than lift up. She cursed herself, pushed down, put her shoulder into it, and the door flew open. The stairs were above her and useless, even if they could still be deployed. It was a good ten feet down from the door opening to, well, she didn't know what.

When she was a little girl, probably seven, she had climbed up onto the roof of the shed in the backyard. She had taken the ladder from inside and propped it up against the wall and hoisted herself on top. The shed, a bright red miniature barn purchased as a kit from Home Depot, had been a pride point of Jack's. He had poured its slab foundation and assembled it himself and had often said it was the one thing about where they lived that wasn't falling apart. The rest of the property, the weedy lot and the shotgun bungalow her mother insisted on calling a cottage, were leftovers from her mother's first marriage and therefore, according to Jack, were not his problem. "You can't fix stupid," he liked to say, quoting the chipped coffee mug he carried around for hours every morning.

While the gambrel peak of the little barn roof had been no more than eight feet high, and the vantage it offered hadn't even matched the view from the bedroom window she shared with her sister, mastering the climb and conquering the ridge had been exhilarating. She had sat up there in the summer sun feeling tall and grown up for nearly an hour. It was only when she'd decided to come down from the roof and discovered that the ladder was gone that her thrill took a turn toward something else.

"What'd I tell you about my stuff, Blon-dee?"

Jack.

She had to carefully turn the other way and climb back up to the ridge to face the sound of his voice. He was sitting on the tiny porch behind the kitchen door, his feet on the crooked step below, his legs akimbo, a cigarette dangling loosely from between the first two fingers of his right hand. He was smiling the way he always did right before he'd insult her mother's cooking, Sarah's hair, or her sister's acne. It was the same smile that appeared before he'd lock Sarah and her sister in their room for watching the wrong TV channel.

"Not to touch it," she had answered, that familiar coldness already creeping into her stomach.

"Ah, you *do* know the rules." He gestured his cigarette over toward the ladder that was now leaning up against a tall weed tree between the back of the house and the little red barn. "So what got into that dumb, Blon-dee head of yours?"

Blon-dee. She hated that word, and the mocking tone that had always accompanied it. She never answered his question about what had gotten in her head. Curiosity, adventure, challenge, accomplishment—these were all ideas she didn't quite have the words for then. Not that it would have mattered if she had. There'd never been any real answers to Jack's questions. He had simply been taunting her. Manipulating her. The same way he'd been taunting and manipulating her mother since the first day he'd come to live with them.

He stood and flicked his cigarette across the yard. "Well, I guess you'll have to figure out another way down from my shed roof. And that ladder better be back where I put it when I come out here again."

He turned to go back into the house. Sarah had watched him and caught a glimpse of her mother in the kitchen window looking out toward the shed, nibbling at her nails. When the kitchen door slammed shut, her mother quickly dropped her hand and turned away from the window.

It had taken Sarah more than an hour to get down from that roof. Eventually, she had gotten on her stomach and slowly backed herself off the roof until she was hanging from the edge, the sharp pebbles of the asphalt shingles digging into her fingertips. After a minute of that, she had simply let go, landing heels first and falling backward hard enough to knock the wind out of her. She lay on the ground trying to catch her breath waiting for her mother to come. She never did.

Sarah stood at the edge of the chopper now contemplating once again the best way down from a ledge she shouldn't have been standing on in the first place. The fastest way was to jump. Her sister, the baby, Trin, they all flooded her mind at once.

"Now would be a really stupid time to break a leg," she said aloud. She sat down on the sill and eased herself off the edge, like she had on that shed roof, and managed a shorter, controlled drop. Once her feet hit the ground, she ran like hell.

It was so dark she tripped twice in the first few seconds of her run. She scrambled up fast each time and sprinted in long, adrenaline-pumped strides until she reached a clearing. The going there was not much easier. The grass was thigh deep and she could feel ruts in the earth as she ran. She stopped to get her bearings and catch her breath. She bent over, her hands on her knees, gulped air, and waited for the sound of the fuel tank exploding. It never came. After a few minutes her eyes adjusted better to the dark. She had no idea where she was or which direction to run. Behind her she could see the black shape of the small woods out of which she had just come. She considered pulling out the communicator from her pack. She could use its locator function to calculate which way was north. It would make things a lot easier for her. It could also risk alerting Trin. The second she powered it on *Kalelah* would know where she was. Meaning, if Trin were fusing with the Code when she hit the switch, *he'd* know where she was. It would undo everything she'd done to keep him from following her. Everything she'd done to keep him safe. She kept the communicator in the bag.

Across the field was the dark silhouette of more trees. Beyond that she saw the straight lines and angles of small buildings. A town, perhaps. She considered hunkering down right where she was until the sun came up and offered a sense of direction. The grass was a good cover, which meant it was likely a great place for animals to hide as well.

No thanks.

Sarah headed for the buildings.

If it was a town, it was a small one. A short cluster of buildings huddled up along a narrow river. All around her were the dark shadows of shapes in the moonless night. No lights in any windows and no sounds except for the gentle murmur of the water as it moved past the pilings, rocks, and empty docks that defined the river's shore. If this place wasn't abandoned, it did a pretty good job of pretending to be. She scanned the little streets that ran perpendicular to the river as she walked. While the dead dark of the night kept her field of vision short, there didn't appear to be any vehicles on the streets. The little one-story buildings and homes that faced the river had the lonely look of places without people. The adrenaline that propelled her run from the crash had ebbed now, and she was growing tired. She stopped in front of a little house with a squat gable roof and considered testing the door. She shook her head. She'd had enough surprises already and breaking into a house was like begging for another. She kept walking.

On the next short block, she could make out the darker form of a steeple against the gloom of the sky. She picked up her pace. The church was hardly bigger than the little house on the previous block. She walked slowly up the three shallow stone stairs to the landing. There were no windows on the river-fronting face of the building, only the slat wooden door. She pushed it gently and it moved without resistance. She kept going until the door was open enough for her to squeeze through and stood there on the other side for a moment.

The space inside was yet a deeper shade of dark, her field of vision falling off to nothing more than a few feet in front of her. She carefully headed toward the low black shadow of the pews up ahead. She slid onto the bench of the pew closest to the door, her pack at her side, her back straight and her ears straining to catch the slightest notice of danger. After a minute she brought her feet up on the bench, curled her knees up close, and made a pillow of her pack. Down in the pew row the darkness was near absolute, and she let it blanket her. Despite not knowing who or what else might be there in the church with her, Sarah's fatigue won out over the events of the last hour. Sleep came quickly.

19

She awoke to the sound of a woman's voice.

"Mademoiselle. Mademoiselle, *tu dois te réveiller! Tu dois te réveiller!*"

Sarah bolted upright. A woman stood at the end of the pew. Behind her the gothic shapes of windows were softly cut out from the dark by the dull, blue light of the early dawn.

"*Ce n'est pas sûr ici.*"

Sarah grabbed her pack and quickly stood, using the top edge of the next pew to steady herself. She was startled and confused all at once. Mental shards of the previous night crashed in on her efforts to wake and make sense of the situation.

"I-I'm sorry," she stammered. "I don't know what you're saying. I was lost last night and really tired. The door was open, so I came in." She brought the pack to her chest and wrapped both arms around it tightly, quickly surveyed the space, and pushed past the woman toward the door she had used a few hours before. "Look, I'm going. No problem, okay?"

"Wait," the woman said. "I did not mean to frighten you."

Sarah stopped. "I'm not frightened. I just don't want any trouble."

"*Moi non plus*. I don't also."

Sarah took a moment to actually look at the woman. She was short and thin, older than Sarah, though maybe not by much, and dark-skinned, pretty with a sharp nose and thick brows. Her two most prominent features were her eyes, big pools of worried brown, and her hair. Or more accurately, her mane. It was black, thick, pulled away from her face, and tied somehow in the back. Yet even restrained, it still managed to wave and curl with abandon. Messy, dirty, and somehow still beautiful. Regal. It was the hair of a warrior princess, not of the frightened mouse standing at the end of the pew, picking at a thumbnail with an index finger.

"Then why wake me?" Sarah asked.

The woman's face softened in apology. "It is dangerous for you."

Sarah looked toward the door. "To sleep?"

"To be unaware. The world appears empty. But people...they are everywhere." She said this with the gravity of a warning, as if she was talking about invisible deadly germs.

There was something about the woman that both worried Sarah and coaxed from her a wave of pity. She'd clearly been wearing the same clothes for weeks straight. Once, in a time Before, they were stylish and expensive. Now they were scuffed and shiny from dirt. A fitted, short leather coat, dark, tight jeans tucked into designer riding boots, high on the calf with short heels, a big leather purse, bulging with belongings and slung crossways over her chest. If she lived in this town, she didn't dress the part. If she were traveling, she didn't look ready for it.

"Okay," Sarah said. "Thanks." She began her way to the door again.

"You were in the helicopter, yes?" the woman called after her.

Sarah stopped once more and turned back to the woman.

"I saw it last night," the woman said. "It was flying so low. Then I heard the crash. You have a scratch on your cheek and a bruise under your eye."

Sarah reached a hand to her face. She hadn't even noticed the scratch last night. "We hit something. An antenna maybe. I don't know."

"The pilot is dead."

"You saw the wreck?"

"I thought maybe someone needed help."

Sarah doubted that was the reason. The woman didn't seem like the first-responder type. "Did you follow me here?"

The woman's eyes darted away from Sarah's. "As I said, it is dangerous for you."

"I can handle myself. But thank you for your...concern. *Merci.*" Sarah turned to leave, and the woman grabbed her arm. It wasn't a forceful hold. It had the soft desperation of a frightened child's reach and Sarah made no moves to shake free or resist the gesture. The woman let go quickly and backed away just the same.

"I am sorry. It's just..." The woman swallowed whatever she was going to say. "In the helicopter, where were you going?"

"West."

"What will you do now?" she asked tentatively.

"Keep going."

"Alone?"

"That's my plan."

"You should not be alone."

"You're alone."

"Yes. This is why I know." The woman offered Sarah her hand. Sarah took it half-heartedly. "I am Gabi."

"I'm Sarah," she said by reflex, instantly sorry she used her real name.

"I, too, am going west. To Amsterdam. There is a ship there that will go to America. You're American, no? Are you going to meet the ship?"

Again, the desperation.

"How long have you been traveling?" Sarah said.

"Three weeks. Maybe four."

"Like this?"

Gabi shrugged.

"You know the way to Amsterdam? To the boat?"

"Yes. About twenty kilometers. It would be safer to go together." She must have seen something in Sarah's face, because a beat later she added, "*S'il vous plait*. Please."

Sarah didn't like the idea of a traveling companion, especially one who seemed scared out of her wits. Still, somehow Gabi had managed to survive weeks on her own, and huge bonus: she knew how to get to Amsterdam.

"Margaret is critical to your journey, Sarah."

"My journey? What's so important about my journey?"

"You have to trust us."

"Really? I don't trust me right now."

"Leave this ship. Look for your sister."

"And if I can't find her?"

"Then you'll find something else. Or something else will find you."

They walked out of the church together onto the little street beside the river. The sun was coming up brightly now on their right. Sarah squinted from the light.

"This way." Gabi pointed. It was the same way along the little river Sarah had walked last night. In the daylight she could see the river was actually a canal, and not a particularly wide one. Nevertheless, there were mooring posts every few houses, though none that she could see had a boat attached.

"Where are we?" Sarah asked.

"Abcoude. Outside Utrecht."

"Only twenty kilometers to Amsterdam?"

"Maybe less. We follow the canal, best we can."

"Too bad the boats are all gone. It'd be faster to use the canal."

"*Non*." Gabi shook her head emphatically and her hair swayed in agreement. "We would never make it on the canal."

"Why not?"

"No place to run. Here at least, on the streets, by the towns, by the fields and woods, there is room to run. Places to hide."

Sarah didn't need to ask if Gabi had had to hide from something during the past few weeks. The woman's eyes and face and the nervous way her index fingers fidgeted along the surface of her thumbs, told Sarah all she needed to know.

•

They walked while the sun moved across the sky to midafternoon. The country spaces of small farms and rolling hills around Abcoude gradually gave way to the more developed outer limits of Amsterdam. Their shadows were long and moved across the bits of refuse that had started to dot the roadside landscape. A light truck, perhaps once the rolling workshop of an electrician, was nosed up against a large oak, its hood wrapped around the wrinkled trunk of the tree in a suicidal embrace. The canal, also more littered and bleaker than before, had widened considerably to the scale of a commercial waterway. Buildings two and three stories tall, with many of their windows broken, loosely edged the banks. The blackened hulk of a large boat killed by fire bobbed ominously on the edge of the canal, the roof of its cabin crowded with gulls and spotted white by their leavings. Sarah tried to keep herself from peering into the cabin as they passed, afraid she'd see a corpse. Or someone living. She wasn't sure which would be worse. Thankfully, she saw neither.

"I keep waiting for this, this *shit*, to be normal, to be not the most frightening thing in the world, but it never happens," said Gabi. "In America, things will be different."

"What makes you say that?"

Gabi's smile dimmed somewhat, and she pondered the question. "In Paris you meet people who say they know someone who also knows someone, and *that* person maybe got an internet connection for a minute or two. Or maybe that person has a radio, the special kind, you know this kind?"

"Shortwave."

"Yes, *shortwave*. Also, the boat. It brings people both ways, so this is how you hear things. In New York, there is no corruption. It is safe. You can live a life."

"I hate to say this, but that doesn't even sound like New York *before* all this happened."

"My boyfriend is there," she said, ignoring Sarah's comment completely. "He left before the war to be an actor. He's very talented. I had a good job in Paris, so I stayed to save some money before joining him. Then the ship was found, the alien ship, and I did not want to leave my mother alone in Paris. When the war happened, I absolutely could not leave her." Gabi quieted for a moment and squinted at the sun and the sky painted in purples and orange. "She's dead now. A broken heart, I am convinced. All she'd ever known was Paris, and Paris hasn't been her Paris for a long time. Or mine."

"I'm sorry," Sarah said.

"*Merci*. But everyone has lost something. Or everything. Axel, maybe I still have him." She flashed Sarah a wan smile and looked away. "Maybe what they say about New York is right. Or a little right. Every rumor is just a little right, yes?"

Sarah looked at Gabi and wanted to tell her that people, even weak people, weren't particularly good at giving up. That if the truth of everything around them was too hard to handle, they'd make up a lie about someplace else, and that what she'd heard about New York was likely just such a lie. She wanted to say to Gabi that her boyfriend was likely dead, or impossible to find, or in the arms of someone on his side of the ocean, someone he may not even love, but needed all the same. Someone with whom he'd seen the worst.

She placed her hand on her stomach and pressed to soothe the low simmer of nausea and remembered how outlandish her own rationale for going to America was.

"I think he's waiting for you," Sarah said with something as close to a smile as she could muster.

By the time the sun had disappeared behind the trees and the low buildings that lined the canal, they reached the city proper and a street life of sorts began to emerge from the gray shadows that had accompanied the sun's setting. The dogs appeared first. They prowled the streets in small groups, gaunt, dirty, but entirely devoid of menace. Sarah could tell by the breeds and the collars that these were once beloved pets. Occasionally one would approach Sarah and Gabi with a tail wagging and eyes set in the expression that evolution had taught would yield sustenance and comfort. Sarah gave a big yellow-haired retriever a friendly scratch behind the ears but knew better than to offer any food. One morsel would have dozens begging. No need to invite commotion. The retriever nuzzled her sweetly and trotted off back to his pack. She missed him instantly.

As they moved on, she could hear the sound of small engines, motorcycles and scooters echoing through nearby streets. The canal they'd been following had merged into the much bigger Amstel. The night settled in and their field of vision shrank, though it wasn't nearly the pitch black of the last night. A small moon hung low in the sky and painted upon the quiet water dabbles of gently dancing white. They kept to their route along the canal, Gabi's boots tapping along the cobbles. From time to time, a rattling bicycle or an odd three-wheeled version with a cargo box in front would clatter by, heard long before they were seen. They'd appear out from the darkness like ghosts. Most didn't seem to worry much if someone or something might already be in their path of travel. Sarah and Gabi had quickly learned to gauge the vehicle's location by sound and move one direction or another to stay clear of the bikes. They encountered no one on foot, yet people were all about.

Sarah could see their shapes in the shadows of doorways and leaning on the walls of the smaller streets that died into the wider road along the canal, the red-tipped ends of their cigarettes glowing bright in the black. She could see people watching from the windows of their skinny flats, dimly backlit by candlelight or the ugly blue glow of battery-powered LEDs.

They passed the open door of a small storefront, the smell of marijuana wafting out onto the street carried by the repetitive pulsing of EDM from the aughts. Small boats, tour craft, and Zodiacs repurposed as open-air houses, cruised cautiously on the water, their captains wearing rifles and pistols in plain view. She wondered where all the guns had come from. Gabi kept close to Sarah's side, working at her thumbnails. Sarah marveled that Gabi had managed all that time alone on the road. A part of her was almost glad Gabi was around.

"How do we know the way to the port?" Sarah asked.

Gabi pointed ahead. "You see when the little canals cross the big one, they go both ways? When they only go one way, that way," she shifted her aim to their right, "when the little ones only branch right, we go right." She reached into her giant purse and pulled out a tattered pamphlet and began to unfold it.

Sarah gasped. "You have a map? A *paper* map?"

"*Oui.*" Gabi smiled, her worried look pushed aside for the moment of glory. "I collected the maps from everywhere we have been. Axel and me. Our phones worked so we didn't really need them, but they are sentimental things."

"You're a genius."

"I had hundreds. We went somewhere almost every weekend. The trains could take you anywhere. They were very clean, very fast, and easy to afford." Her face saddened. "I miss the trains most of all. After the war, they could not easily get diesel, and they could not keep the trains safe."

"Nowhere to run."

"Oui," Gabi said. "In Europe we were used to things being safe. We walked the streets, we took the trains, and we took it all for granted. Now everything is a danger."

"This boat we're looking for...why will it be any different from the canals and the trains?"

"It belongs to a very powerful and generous man from New York. They say he gives his ship to keep the world connected."

"Who is he?"

"I don't know his real name. They call him 'the mayor.'"

"Is he a mayor?"

"No. He is a king."

20

The port itself was a long, narrow bay that led out to the North Sea. Small canals intersected at intervals on its two long sides and a slender island ran nearly the entire length of it, dividing the bay in two lanes, one presumably for outgoing traffic and another for incoming. No big craft were moving in either direction that night. The buildings that lined the cityside edges of the port were mostly dark, with only a few windows aglow by the flickering orange of candlelight. The giant cranes that once hefted cargo containers were still and dark. The containers themselves were stacked at various heights, creating black Tetris mountains of order that defied the chaotic scene in front of Sarah.

It was the first time she had seen anything like a crowd since she'd left the Russian encampment at the base of the ring. Bicycles and carts moved dangerously in a dozen different directions at once. Dogs were everywhere, in packs and in odd parings. A step van was parked next to a container crane surrounded by racks of old clothing for trade. The proprietor stood inside the van's rear double doors guarding his goods with a hunting rifle. There were tents scattered about in small huddles of threes and fours, like desperate archipelagos in a rising sea. Beggars and women with small children sat on the ground at random spots, with nothing to lean against, empty plates and cups held out to the crowd in their grime-covered hands. Not ten yards in the distance a man lay prostrate on the ground while two others kicked at him savagely. He absorbed the blows passively, like a bag of sand might. Sarah wondered if he wasn't already dead. Gabi hooked her arm around Sarah's at the elbow and steered her away.

Tall ships bobbed at moorings along the skinny island at the bay's center, looking orphaned and broken, their masts striped of sails or chopped down altogether. A container ship lay wounded on its side, half-sunk with its giant prow hanging in the air like a monument to disaster. More small craft and houseboats, similar to those she'd seen in the canals, moved about the bay without obvious purpose, their occupants eyeing the docks suspiciously. In the entire port, there was only one ship lit at its windows and appearing large enough to cross the ocean. It was at the farthest pier and both Sarah and Gabi walked toward it without even a look between them.

Up close, the ship revealed itself to be more an oversized yacht than an ocean liner. Its long rows of stateroom windows, stacked three high, were illuminated with the uniquely stable glow of electric light. Dots of bright white from the safety lamps along railings and atop the crow's nest drew the outline of the ship against the dark of the night. She was long, tall, and wide at the beam. The boat held the rest of its secrets close for it was all black and completely without identifying marks. No numbers on its bow, no logos along its hull or funnel. The only color at all came from a flag that flew from the weather deck's topmost plane: a black field with a wide red vertical stripe through the middle. Centered in the red stripe was a circle of black bullets pointing outward and framing a graphic depiction of the Empire State Building.

"Jesus Christ," Sarah said. "That's friendly."

Gabi stared at the ship with a confused look on her face and inched a little closer to Sarah. "Who would make a ship like this?"

Would-be travelers with their tattered belongings at their sides or slung from their shoulders crowded the large concrete staging area that faced the looming bow. There was a string of benches running along the edge of the pier and a dozen or so people were huddled there, many with their bags on their laps as pillows for their heads. Others lay directly on the ground in sleeping bags or wrapped in grimy blankets. A few had found scraps of cardboard to keep them off the cold of the concrete. There were easily two hundred in the crowd. Although Sarah didn't know how many the boat could accommodate, two hundred seemed too many. Just beyond the crowd, a man on horseback stood vigil.

He wore a black three-sided hat, like something from the American colonial era. The rest of him was clad in black as well. In one hand was either a gigantic pistol or a sawed-off shotgun.

"I'm going to go talk with him," Sarah said, giving a nod toward the man on the horse.

Gabi looked at the dark figure for a moment and then at the crowd around her as if weighing the options. "Him? He's scary."

"He's in charge."

Sarah and Gabi pushed their way through the crowd, and as the horse and rider grew nearer, Sarah had to admit they did make an intimidating sight. The horse was a menacing beast, chestnut brown with snapping muscles, and tall as Sarah had ever seen. The man on top was old but stout, thick necked and weathered in a black shirt, vest, jeans, chaps, and boots. She could now confirm the gun he held in a large, gloved hand was a shotgun, its twin barrels cut short. His other held a taut grip on the reins, which seemed like a good idea since the horse stomped its right hoof and strained at its bit whenever one of the tired-eyed travelers got too close. The grizzled rider didn't appear to share the animal's anxiety. He was calm despite the chaos around him. Weapon and wardrobe aside, Sarah thought there was kindness in the creases of his face. All the same, she stopped a safe distance from the imposing pair.

"Excuse me, do you speak English?"

He looked at her and then Gabi, taking his time before responding. His gun stayed below his hips, right about the height of Sarah's forehead.

"All my life," he said. His voice was soaked in years of drinking. *Australian.*

"Great. Is this the boat to America?"

"Is this the boat to America?" He crumpled up his wrinkled face in thought like her question was tough enough to need some real chewing and more than a simple "yes" or a simple "no." At the end of his ponderings, he smiled. "America's gone, sweetheart." His words were practically coughed out, rough like sandpaper. "But the *Empire* here *is* the boat to the great island of Manhattan. Are you two ladies hoping to leave this place?"

Sarah gave a confirming look to Gabi. "We are."

He sighed and looked around from his towering vantage point above the crowd. "Bloody oath. It's a shame, isn't it?" He waved his pistol toward the city center. "They'll be eating the dogs before long." He moved the gun away from Sarah to rest his elbow on his thigh and leaned down from his saddle, an American western style intricately tooled and studded with silver rosettes. "I blame socialism," he said as if sharing a secret among friends. "It makes people soft. No one on the whole bloody continent has had to learn to think for themselves or take charge. Now that their nanny's gone, they're lost. I pity them, frankly. I really do." He sat himself tall in his saddle again. Secret time was over.

"We're hoping to get on this boat," said Sarah.

"Well this tug's chockablock, love."

"Sorry?"

"It's full. Sold out. We shove off in the morning. But don't you worry, we'll be back in four to five weeks. Be here early and she'll be apples."

"Five weeks is a long time for me."

"It's a long time for everybody. Look around ya. This dock ain't exactly the Ritz-Carlton."

"It's just that someone's waiting for me. My sister. I don't know how much longer she can hold out."

He looked at Sarah with unconvinced eyes. "Are you tellin' me you have actual contact with someone on the other side of the pond?" The horse snuffed angrily and stomped a hoof as if sharing his master's amazement. Gabi backed away.

"Not exactly. It's a long story. But it's urgent I get there as soon as possible."

"I'm sorry, love, that'll have to be in five weeks."

"I have gold." Sarah reached into her coat for the spool she'd retrieved from Alexey Galygin. She held it tightly but raised her hand so the old man could see what it held.

His eyes went wide for a flash. "Crikey." He squinted at the bright yellow spool in Sarah's hand. "If it's real."

"It's the purest you've ever seen in your life, I promise you. If it doesn't check out, you can toss us to the sharks. I figure it's worth at least two round trips for the both of us. I'll give you the whole fistful for the one way."

"I'll do the figuring, if you don't mind," he said. "Where did you get it?"

"Does it matter?"

The rider took a deep breath and looked out at the crowd on the dock before answering. "You are fucking persuasive, I'll give you that." He bent down from the saddle again. "Here's my deal. You'll give me that sparklin' bundle you've got there in your hand to get on the boat, then you'll give me another sparkler, and not a gram less, to get off the boat."

"Sarah, no," Gabi said. "I have jewelry to trade." She rummaged through her bag in a panic and after a long minute pulled from it a string of pearls and held them aloft. "These were my grandmother's. They were very expensive."

"Pretty, love. But they're not gold, are they?" said the rider. "Ball's in your court, Sarah."

"He's asking too much," Gabi protested. "I can wait."

"I can't," Sarah said. "I can't explain why, but I need to be on that boat. Besides, we need to stick together, you said it yourself." Gabi sucked in her lower lip and nodded. Sarah looked up at the rider. "Deal. One thing, I need to know you're not going to kick anyone off this ship to make room for us. Promise me that."

The rider took off his triangle hat and scratched at an itch with the barrel of his gun. "Promise you? That's a fresh one."

"Whatever it is, I want your word."

When he smiled down at her she saw no smugness in it. "Well, Sarah, you drive a hard bargain. All right then, ya have my word." He placed the hat back on his head, pulled on the reins, and turned the angry horse toward the crowd. "We push off at first light, and we'll leave without yous. I'll take my gold now."

Sarah handed him the spool and he trotted off along the edge of the crowd.

"How do you know he'll keep his word?" asked Gabi.

"He could have asked for more. And he knew I'd have given it to him."

21

"Sarah's dead."

"What? How?" Wildei sat down on the bench, tears instantly blurring her view of the sim sky, its reddening sun starting its decent below the lake's horizon.

"She must be." Trin was standing, pacing actually, and sounding winded. He must have run the length of four Leaves to find her.

"Wait, is she dead or do you just *think* she's dead?"

"You have a better explanation for what the fuck is going on?"

"Dammit, Trin, you almost gave me a heart attack. You don't just sneak up on someone in the middle of their sunset break and tell them a person they love is dead."

"It's been more than thirty hours since she's pulled a float. Could you go more than thirty fucking *minutes* without one?"

"Good point. Still, darling, you've got to calm down."

"What, you think she's going to show up and say, 'Sorry babe, the line was crazy at the Tunlot shop. It took forever to get my fucking breakfast'? I've gone to all the places I know to go. I've retraced her night walks. I've talked to a dozen people. Nothing. Just fucking nothing."

Wildei gave him a minute to settle before she got down to business. "Even from the Code?"

"Not that I can see," he said flatly, his back to her.

Wildei had to slide right ways on the bench to at least see the side of his face. "We'll start a search party then, put more feet against this."

He nodded but kept his eyes on the lake. "What about The Circle? We can't just leave it be."

"Let's solve one problem before we go off and create another."

He turned to her and he looked tired, like he hadn't slept the previous night. She hadn't gotten much sleep either. "This, whatever it is, The Circle is behind it. I'm sure of it."

"And you know this how?"

"Because it's the only thing that makes any sense."

"Firstly, we still don't know there actually is a Circle on this ship again. At least not an organized one. Even if there is, to go after it, as you say, will take enormous resources, divide the ship in dangerous ways, and is likely to fail anyway. There have been Circles all throughout the universe in various incarnations for thousands of years. In all that time, not one has ever been successfully hunted."

"That doesn't scare the shit out of you?"

"Of course it does. The monsters you can't see are the most frightening of all. But The Circle won't come easy, if at all. We only learned Laird was Circle because she told us. And the only reason she'd done that was to scare us into submission, to make sure we knew we were up against a force that would never give in."

"We're up against it again, and you're sitting by the lake watching the sunset."

"Fuck you. In case you're forgetting, my love, I founded the bloody counter group on this ship. I devoted years to fighting Circle fundamentalism."

"Then don't stop now."

"Now is different. Things have happened we never thought could. We've had a failed Delivery, a mutiny that killed hundreds, a crash that's stranded us on a hostile planet. And, oh yes, along the way we managed to squeeze in a Correction, you know, the worst thing possible. So pardon me if I'm going to take my time before starting a second civil war on our ship."

"What if it's already been started for you?"

Wildei watched the last of the sun dip below the water, the red in the sky taking on a tint of purple. The sounds of the coming night tuned their voices in anticipation.

"If it's so then we'll fight. So far, it's just an *if*, and a pretty large one at that."

"It didn't seem all that iffy to you at the debrief. When Forent said The Circle needed a war, I saw your face. You believed him."

"I listened to him, that's all. I listen to people, Trin. You should try it."

"Bullshit. You knew he was right...that killing me could start a war. Now imagine killing Sarah. The crew will rip the walls off this ship. The missile lock failed so The Circle went to plan B. *Sarah*."

"Trin, we're all worried about Sarah, as well as the missile lock. We just don't know they're connected."

"Then explain how it's possible for her to vanish like she has. No floats, no flora scans for thirty hours."

"I can't. Not yet."

"I can. You said it yourself. It's like The Circle is invisible, right? Well, if they can keep themselves hidden for thousands of years, they can keep Sarah—or her murder—secret for thirty hours."

"Can you even hear yourself? You're turning a scarcity of evidence into proof of some kind of a cover-up. If there's nothing there it's because someone's hiding it. You know who twists things like that? Conspiracy theorists and liars. You're neither."

"The missile lock and Sarah's disappearance can't be a coincidence, Wildei. There's something happening. If she's not dead, then she's in danger. Laird happened right under our noses, including Argen's. Why couldn't another?"

"There are thousands of people on this ship. You're going to push them all up against the wall until someone cracks and cries Circle?"

"All we need to find is one person. One person."

"No. Look, Forent experienced horrible things in the war. I know that and I respect it. But I am not going to blindly follow the hunch of a damaged old man just because it matches our worst fears about a group of people with whom we disagree. Sorry, darling, but you're not thinking straight about this. You're panicked and desperate and I don't blame you. I'd be worse if I were in your shoes and it'd be you who was talking me off a ledge. So we're going to be methodical about this. We're going to launch a search party and we're going to give it forty-eight hours to find her.

"At the same time, I'm going to make absolutely certain there wasn't a ship-borne explanation for the missile lock beyond that fucking shimmer and a plot to smuggle our tech to the population. I need to know there wasn't the slightest crack in your stealth armor, that there was no way ordinary radar couldn't have spotted you. I need to be sure you weren't found simply because you were findable. Surely that makes some sense to you."

"There were no cracks. We were green the entire fucking way."

"So you said in the debrief."

"The Code backed me up on it."

"Of course she did."

"What's that supposed to mean?"

"It doesn't matter. I ordered a full strip of *18*."

"You're tearing my ship apart?" he said, genuinely surprised. "Shit, Wildei, it'll take days. You can't do that."

"For starters, it's not your ship. It's the *Kalelah's*. It's *her* child. I have her contractual permission to tear *18* or *16* or *12* or any other transport I want down to the bolts. Because, darling, I'm the fucking captain. I alone am the guardian of her children."

"You'll only be giving The Circle more time." Trin thrust his hands into his pockets, and with that boyish gesture, she was reminded of how young he still was.

"Maybe. Or perhaps with its head cut off the snake has died, just like we thought. Regardless, this is my call to make."

"Not when Sarah's involved." His lips tightened to a thin line.

"Especially when Sarah's involved," she said.

Trin sat on the bench next to her, took in a big breath, and let it out slowly. "Shit."

"Yes, shit. It's total fucking shit." Wildei put an arm around him and leaned her head on his shoulder. "We're going to get us through this. And we'll do it together."

The sim sky had darkened, and the constellation of the Lonely Seeker took his first steps along his nightly trek to nowhere.

"What if I'm right?" Trin asked.

"Pray, darling, that this one time you are not."

22

There was no quiet on the *Empire* at night. Sarah lay on the floor of the cramped and dirty stateroom, her pack for a pillow, a thin, musty blanket big enough only to cover the top half of her body, listening to the sounds of overcrowding, hunger, and worry. Toilets flushed constantly, their vacuum pumps like blasts of jet engines echoing noisily between the deck floors. Bits and pieces of conversations, in languages familiar and otherwise, floated through the hallways and in through the crack of space under the cabin door. A boy cried somewhere, a dog barked, perhaps above, below, or six rooms down the hall. She couldn't pinpoint exactly where the noises originated, but she could feel the desperation in them all.

As she lay there not sleeping, she tried to feel the ocean beneath the boat, to connect with the cadence of the chop, to let the vastness and power of it do for her now what it once did when first she experienced life at sea. Years ago, in what had come to feel like another life altogether, she would stand at the rail of the *Lewis*, the wind in her hair, nicotine in her veins, and draw comfort from the emptiness all around her.

From her place on the floor, Sarah tried to make real again the color of those Pacific waters, the wet warmth in the air, the horizons on toward infinity itself. It was a time Before, when the world still offered places in which to run, places where she was safely apart from the things that started her running.

She sat up and crossed her legs in front of her, staring into the darkness of the little room. Cramped as it was, Sarah and Gabi were lucky to have it and luckier still that only one other person shared it with them. Other rooms like theirs, originally designed for one crew member, were packed with as many as four people. It was Gabi's turn on the tiny bed and her breathing was the heavy, childlike breathing of sleep. Sarah's stomach growled and for the hundredth time in the last two days she considered breaking her vow and raiding her stash of rations from the *Kalelah*. Now would be a good time. Gabi was dead to the world and Charlotte, the roommate, was still out.

The *Empire* had once been a luxury ship called the *Seadream*. The old logos were still etched onto surfaces throughout the ship. It was bigger than a billionaire's superyacht though much smaller than a typical cruise ship. Before everything fell apart it must have made a cushy cross of the Atlantic. Elegant wall coverings and fine woods could still be seen through the clutter and commotion of the migrant mule the ship had become. Once it had boasted five-star dining. Now the kitchens were closed, their equipment hauled out to make room for more bunks. In their stead, meal service was an enormous plastic dumpster loaded with pre-Correction vending machine leftovers. Dinner tonight had been a Snickers bar with a best-by date of three years ago and a flat Fresca. Breakfast was a bag of stale Cheez-It crackers and warm Coke. The mini can.

To purchase her meals, Sarah was given a Ziploc snack bag containing fourteen casino chips in a variety of denominations. The dollar amounts meant nothing. A $50 chip bought you exactly what a $1 chip did, which wasn't much. At first it was a thrill to rip open the wrappers and bags and be overcome by their unapologetic shittyness. Their happy indulgence in too much sugar, dangerous oils, and unbleached flour. *American Junk Food!* After years of seaweed on the *Kalelah*, the nostalgic taste of a Pop-Tart or Cool Ranch Doritos was nearly intoxicating. She hadn't been too proud to lick the insides of a bag or two. Unfortunately, the glories of junk food were fleeting. It didn't take long after a Snoball breakfast or a KitKat lunch before she was hungry again. And she worried about the baby. The Vending Machine Diet couldn't be doing him—*her?*—any favors. She put the pack on her lap and began tugging at the big clasp along the top when the door to the cabin burst open and slammed against the wall.

"Jesus Christ," Sarah said in a harsh whisper. "Why do you do that?"

Charlotte stood inside the threshold, silhouetted against the hard light from the hallway. Gabi sat up, clutching the blanket to her chest.

"Get the fuck out," Charlotte slurred, her backlit shape unsteady. This was night three, and the third night she'd come back to the room drunk. Each time she did, Sarah's heart sank. If the room had been ten times the size of the closet Sarah and Gabi shared with her, it would still feel too small. Charlotte had a way of encroaching upon every inch of space. She was messy, she farted unabashedly, and she slept naked. Those were her good qualities. When Charlotte's charms had become clear to Sarah and Gabi, a process that took all of ten minutes, it had embarrassed Sarah that Charlotte was another American. Why she still cared about things like that, she had no idea. But once again, as the woman in a tattered Harley-Davidson jacket spotted by grease stood in the threshold, using the jambs of the door to steady herself, Sarah's face flushed.

Charlotte took a few wavering steps to the side of the bed, her eyes half closed. "Get the fuck out, I said. Or do I have to say it in French? Get za fook out."

"You had the bed last night," Gabi protested. "It's my turn."

"Your turn, my turn, her turn," she pointed a finger at each of them as she spoke. "I don't give a fuck, okay? I need it. I'm sick."

"You're not sick. You're drunk," Gabi said.

"Don't tell me what I am or what I ain't. I'm sick!" Her voice rose to a scream. "I need the goddamn bed!"

Sarah stood up. "Shut up and take the floor, Charlotte."

"Who made you the boss?" Charlotte reached into her jacket, pulled out a knife, and began to wave it around haphazardly. "I'm the fucking boss, okay?"

With each boozy stab at the air Charlotte got sloppier with the knife. Gabi was forced to duck her head and she screamed from fright.

"You're *drunk*, Charlotte," Sarah said. "Put the knife away before someone gets hurt."

"Well maybe that someone's you." Charlotte leaned over the bed and thrust a wild, off-target jab at Sarah. While it was nothing for Sarah to step away from the knife, the attack had put Charlotte badly off balance. She paused, suspended in the air above Gabi for a flash of a beat, like a grotesque cartoon character suddenly out of cliff, before crashing down upon the bed.

Gabi screamed again, this time not from surprise or fear but from pain. Sarah quickly pulled Charlotte off Gabi and threw her to the floor. The knife stayed where Charlotte's hand had accidently placed it, deep in Gabi's chest, right below her left shoulder. Gabi's shirt and the bedsheet beneath her had already started to bloom red around the knife.

"You fucking idiot," Sarah hissed. She yanked Charlotte up from the floor by her coat and pushed her toward the still open door to the hallway. "Leave!"

"I'm sorry," Charlotte gasped. She stood at the threshold staring at Gabi, her face flushed and contorted in confusion, her eyes moist with tears. "I didn't mean to hurt nobody," she said softly. "It wasn't even my knife. Why didn't she just give me the bed? I told her I needed the bed."

Sarah punched her hard in the face and the woman collapsed in a heap on the dirty hallway carpet. "Don't let either of us see you again."

Charlotte lay on her side with her knees pulled up and a hand on her face where Sarah had hit her. "Where am I supposed to go?" she sobbed. "I got nowhere to go."

"Try Hell." Sarah slammed the door shut.

She ran back to Gabi, who lay on the bed quiet but shaking. The sheet below her was soaked in blood.

"You're going to be okay, Gabi. Hear me?"

"It hurts."

"Hang on, I can help." She turned around to grab her pack.

Gabi looked at the knife. "*Oh, mon Dieu.* A doctor. I need a doctor."

"I know. But we don't have time to run around the ship looking for one."

"The man on the horse. He'll know."

"We don't have time to look for him either. You're bleeding badly. I have to stop it." Sarah pulled a slim blue box from her pack and placed it on the bed next to Gabi. She quickly pressed a code onto its top and the box expanded in height and opened like a book. Where the pages would be were thin panes of glass in six shades of blue. An earpiece was nestled into the inside cover, and Sarah quickly placed it in her right ear.

"How?" Gabi's chest was heaving now, her breathing speeding up. Sarah worried she was going into shock. "What is that?"

"This is going to tell me how to help you." She took the lightest hue of glass from the box and aligned it with the wound on Gabi's chest. Seconds later a beam of light burst from the glass and projected a star pattern that surrounded the wound.

"What's happening?" said Gabi.

"Shhhh. It's going to be okay."

Instructions began to flow from the earpiece. Sarah took a deep breath. Her face flushed and went hot with fear. "Gabi, I want you to count to ten. Okay?"

"What?"

"Can you do that for me? When you get to the number ten, I'm going to pull the knife."

Gabi's tears picked up their flow and developed into full-on panicked sobs. "*Non, non, non...*"

"Come on, Gabi. You can do it."

"*Mais tu n'es pas medecin.*"

"One..."

"*Non. S'il vous plait, non!*"

"Two..."

"Three."

"Good girl. Keep going. All the way to ten."

"Four...five...six...sev—"

Sarah pulled the knife. Gabi screamed, "Aiiieeee!"

The blood gushed, and Sarah quickly applied pressure to the wound, which got another scream out of Gabi. With her other hand she retrieved the next shade of blue glass and slid it under the puncture site on Gabi's back. She pulled another pane and placed it on the entry wound and reapplied pressure. Blood pooled out from under the glass and ran down Gabi's side in thin streams. Sarah tapped the code instructed by the voice in her ear on the top edge of the glass and held the pressure steady until she was told to lift off. Both panes of glass began to glow. Within the luminescent blue of the pane beneath her palm, intermittent tendrils of pinks, yellows, and whites streaked through the glass like electric capillaries turning on and off in time to an inaudible music score. Seconds later, Gabi's breathing slowed down, her face released the anguish it held, and she sighed so fully and contentedly it was if a torture no less than a demon's possession had been exorcised.

"It feels better," Gabi said, her eyes slits, her mouth turned up softly in relief.

The rivulets of blood slowed and soon stopped. The instructions in Sarah's ear told her to remove her hand and she watched as the wound beneath the glass began to dry, like the evaporation of rainwater in a desert captured in time-lapse.

"It's amazing," said Gabi. "One moment I was burning from the inside. I felt it everywhere, like every nerve in my body was on fire. I was sure I was going to die. Now there is no pain, only a cool sensation. It feels..." she paused, and her face relaxed another degree. "I don't know the word for it, so I will say beautiful. It feels beautiful."

"I'm so glad," Sarah said, her own heart rate finally calming down. She sat on the bed and held Gabi's hand. "I think you're going to be okay."

"How?"

Sarah waited to answer, hoping maybe Gabi would fall asleep and she would have more time to think of what to say. Gabi's eyes opened fully instead, and she looked at the glass on her chest, the blood on the sheets, and the blue box with its softly pulsating glow in communication with the panes. "What is this machine, Sarah?"

"It's part of a first-aid kit," she said lamely.

Gabi knit her brows. "A first-aid kit is a bandage and some alcohol wipes." She moved her right arm, like she was testing the wound for pain and her muscles for limits. "Sarah, a minute ago a knife was inside me, I could not move my arm. Now, *je n'en reviens pas*, if it weren't for the sheets soaked in my own blood, I would not even know it had happened. How is this possible?"

Sarah took the earpiece from her ear and began to gather up the panes of glass and return them to the blue box. She smiled sweetly at Gabi. "You should rest. We can talk later."

Gabi sat up in the bed. "I want to talk now."

Sarah closed the blue box and slipped it back in her pack and turned once again to Gabi. "The truth is, I don't know how it works."

"But you knew how to use it."

"It taught me as I went."

Sarah could see Gabi wasn't buying it. She knew if the shoe was on the other foot, if it had been Gabi who pulled some techno magic Jesus out of her pack, Sarah would sure as shit want to know what was going on.

"How frightened should I be, Sarah?" Gabi asked tentatively.

Sarah stalled again. "We're in the middle of the ocean on a ship with hardly any crew. Our food is junk, literally. You just got stabbed, and we don't really know what awaits us when we get to whatever's left of America. So I'd say pretty fucking frightened."

"I know very well how scared to be of those things. You've seen my thumbs. What I want to know is how frightened should I be of you?"

Shit.

Sarah was completely unprepared for this kind of confrontation. With criminals like the Russians, she knew a show of force would be enough for them. Actions, like always, spoke louder than words. With Gabi, a civilian, a frightened refugee, a friend maybe, what kind of words could make sense of what the med kit had done? Sarah threw her pack down on the floor where she'd been trying to sleep before Charlotte came in and screwed everything up.

"You're alive, okay? You could have bled out. I didn't let you. What does that tell you? Now get some sleep, because tomorrow night I get the bed." With that, she lay on the floor with her pack as a pillow and said, "Good night."

Gabi sighed and pushed herself as far away from the still-wet blood as the bed allowed. Sarah put her hand on her tummy and closed her eyes.

She tried not to feel like a monster. Nothing worked.

23

Sarah was awoken by a thin blade of sunlight slicing its way through the tiny porthole. She blinked from the brightness and turned her face toward the shadows. Gabi was still, her face at peaceful rest and her breathing as heavy as it was the last night, rousing in Sarah another wave of sleep envy. She dressed quietly, rinsed her mouth in the miniature sink, grabbed her pack, and slipped out the stateroom door without Gabi stirring.

She needed the deck. She needed the space and the air and the water to think. Although the *Empire* had a small elevator, she took the stairs instead, the faster way out. Once outside she began to feel better. On the *Kalelah*, there'd been sim skies, a lake and parks, and manufactured sunlight to distract Sarah from the true degree of her confinement. After again feeling breezes not generated from machines and tasting rain that fell not from misting tanks and tubes but from actual clouds, she found herself physically aching for the outdoors. She ran to the stern of the ship where she could stand at the railing and watch the frothy white of the churn from the ship's props and the long line of wake that eventually faded to nothing.

It was cool and she could see her breath in the morning air, but she wasn't cold. The sun was warm on her face. It was open waters now.

It had been three days since she could see any hint of the European continent. She tried to picture Trin, what he might be doing at this moment, what he might be thinking about her. For all he knew, she had run. Which, of course, she had. This was different than her other runs; the other times she'd turned her back on her life she wasn't leaving someone behind. Not someone like Trin anyway. Someone who made her feel wanted, loved. And she wasn't carrying with her another life. A life only partly hers. The gall of it, the wrong of it, washed over her. Yet it wasn't more wrong now than it was on the ship when she could have made a different decision. It was the same thing over and over with her. Knowing better didn't manage to stop her. Somehow, she always wound up lost at sea.

"Don't jump."

Sarah turned to see the Aussie approaching, all in black like a cowboy Johnny Cash in a Paul Revere hat. For the violence his image carried, he didn't frighten her. She was happy to see him.

"I won't jump in after ya," he said in a voice like gravel under heavy boots. He had a cup of what smelled like hot coffee and tequila.

"So this shit bucket does have coffee," she said.

"In name only." He took a sip, gave her a grandfatherly wink, and turned to face the water. They stood in silence for a minute as the sun rose higher and the air warmed.

"I saw your roommate this morning. She was sprawled out on my deck crying like a baby. Says you kicked her out."

"She's a dangerous drunk."

"Have a little pity. She's scared and stupid. It's a hard way to live."

"Or an easy way to die."

He ground out a short rasp of a laugh and hoisted his cup in toast. He let another minute go by, and they watched the wake continue its endless journey to nowhere from behind the boat. "You're a different one," he finally said. It didn't sound to her like criticism.

"Says the man in the Revolutionary War hat."

"I'll have ya know this hat has a story."

"I'll bet it's fascinating."

"If you like horror movies," he said, with what sounded to Sarah like regret.

"We've all got scary stories now."

"You've got something else, I think. Something bigger. I've been on this ship for long enough to forget what it's like to be off it. I carry two hundred or so people on each leg. New York to Amsterdam. Amsterdam to New York. It doesn't make a difference which way we're going or what time of year it is, everyone who gets on this overgrown tinny has the same look in their eyes. A kind of permanent terror. Even when someone is smilin' I can see it. Just a little too much white." He took a sip from his cup. "I've seen that look all my life. It's the look a cow has, a heifer in particular. It's a striking thing. We'd drive 'em from this part of the station to that part of the station. They don't have to be in any particular danger at any particular moment, but they always seem to think somethin's not right. Like when one of those drives is done, somethin' awful could happen. It's like they're born knowin' it."

She turned to him and in his weathered face and pale eyes, she saw again a kindness that defied the outer shell he created for himself of a man in black, a man with a gun, a man at war.

"You were a cowboy?"

"Stockman, thank you."

"What are you saying you see in my eyes, stockman?"

"That's just it, sweetheart. I don't see any fright in ya at all."

"Maybe I'm just a good liar."

He chewed on that for a bit. "What ya said about the gold was true. I've never seen anything like it before."

She smiled. "So we can stay?"

He took a final sip from his cup and emptied the last of the coffee and whatever else was in it over the railing and into the water. "When we reach port, where do ya go from there?"

"Like I said, I have to meet someone. She's in Ohio. I think. I don't even know. It's crazy to try and find her. I only know I have to try."

"East or west Ohio?"

"East."

"That sounds good. Don't go too far west. Stay clear of Chicago. Radiation there is hotter than Hell. When ya come back east, stay out of New York."

"There's no radiation in New York."

"No. But maybe somethin' worse."

"And yet you run this boat."

He took his time thinking about that too. Maybe that was simply how he was about things—the thoughtful hooligan. Or maybe he just liked to stretch things out. To slow down time. A breeze came in from the starboard side of the ship and carried with it a reminder of the morning's chill. Sarah put her hands in her pockets and did not rush the man.

At last, the rider spoke. "There were men I worked with who had no feelings for the stock at all. Their approach to the animals was either extreme indifference or wanton cruelty. There was nothin' for those men in between. Now me, I couldn't understand that. A cow breathed and birthed. She hated drivin' in a cold rain nearly as much as we did, and I know she could hurt. On the other hand, I understood the forces of inevitability at play. The hidden strings of the world that compel different creatures to walk certain paths even when those paths have proven to be dead ends."

"Destiny, you mean."

"Destiny, fate, God, whatever you want to call it. I knew that was somethin' not worth fightin'."

"What are you saying?"

"I'm sayin', honey, I ate steak with the rest of 'em."

24

Trin watched while the team carefully dismantled *18.* The millions of mirrors that formed the skin of the transport, the mechanism by which the craft achieved its invisibility to the naked eye, lay in neatly organized sheets of hundreds of thousands on the pristine floor of Tech Room Five. The little transport's frame and electronics harness were entirely exposed, giving the techs the full and easy access they needed for their forensics.

The lead engineer, a tall rail of a man close to Trin's age, leaned over the stern section of the stealth band, a series of frequency emitters and noise cancelers that ran in a continuous loop around the entire craft. Its skin cloaked it to humans, while the band cloaked it to machines. As much as it pained Trin to see his little ship torn down to the bolts, he understood the logic behind Wildei's order that the band be checked. The band, after all, was a jury-rigged solution to a problem no one at the time of the transport's original manufacture could have imagined. Yorn Darnol, the man leaning over the band, had designed the retrofit himself. And he was not happy.

"You know me, boss. I don't get insulted easily," he said, looking at the band, his lips drawn tight.

"Yes, you do."

"Well, this is especially egregious. Because, you know...look at it."

"I know, you've told me. It's elegant."

"That's exactly the word for it. Elegant."

"It's your word."

"That's right. It's the perfect description. This design is completely harmonious with the native engineering. If you never saw the original plans, and you saw this, you'd think it was there all along. Right from the start. It's a thing of absolute beauty."

Trin sighed. He'd heard this story months before, when the band was first installed. But Darnol was on a roll. There was no stopping him.

"You have to understand," he went on, "the idea that *18* would have radar jamming capabilities was, you know, never even a consideration back in the day. What would be the point? We were supposed to be long gone by the time the population would advance to the level of possessing technology even remotely like radar. Let alone full spectrum jamming. Yet look at this thing...it's like *18* was created for the sole purpose of radar fucking."

"So, did it? On that last run, was I fully cloaked or not?"

"Everything worked as designed. I said this to the captain at least a dozen times. Did she listen to me? No. I had to tear the whole ship apart just to prove what I already knew. It's insulting. I mean, that's the only word for it."

"Don't take it personally. Captain doesn't listen to me either."

"Whatever. She's the captain, I'm me. Who am I to fight it, right?"

"Right."

"That said—"

"Shit."

"Hear me out. We could turn this insult around. Seize the opportunity."

"For what?"

"Another leap forward."

"Fuck me. Just put it back together, okay?"

"Boss, these are dangerous times we live in. When you're out there, you need protection."

"I have protection. I have the cloak. You said so yourself, it worked."

"Yes, it did everything it was supposed to do. Perfectly. Except, and I hate to say this, perfect wasn't enough. Because someone out there can see past it. I don't know how, but that's the awful truth. We need to adapt."

"You're talking about guns again?"

"I'm talking about giving you a fighting chance. You were faster than the missiles on that last run. But everyone knows it wasn't speed on your side, it was luck. Next time, luck might not be enough.

"You know the rule. Weapons don't leave the ship. The Guide Service doesn't go to war."

"Tell that to the population. You don't think the Correction seemed like war to this planet?"

"It wasn't a normal Correction. It was a mistake. We don't need to add to it by building warships."

"Boss, we're at war whether you want to be or not."

This was sounding a lot like the conversation Trin had had with Wildei at the lake. Trin sat on the floor. "I swore I was done dusting."

"Are you done living too?"

Trin looked at the skinless craft for a long moment. "Could you even do it?" he asked, surprised he had spoken the question out loud.

"You're going to insult me too? Boss, please. Yes, I can do it. When I'm done, you'd never know the guns hadn't always been there."

"They'd be elegant."

"Like the hand of God."

Trin sighed again. "Don't tell the captain."

"The captain doesn't listen to me."

Trin gave the engineer a smile. It was just for show.

25

Two days later a sliver of land appeared on the horizon. Long Island, Sarah guessed. She had spent nearly every waking hour of the trip's last leg on the small deck at the ship's bow waiting for this moment. Waiting to be an ocean closer to finding Margaret. A feeling of coming home pushed through her with surprising force. No matter that New York had never been a place she'd ever lived. No matter the America she'd find waiting for her would likely be unrecognizable from any America she'd known Before. Sarah found herself almost hurting to be there, to walk on familiar soil, even if only for a little while.

Gabi joined her at the rail and together they watched the leading edge of the ship part the gray-blue chop.

"I can feel him," Gabi said. "Do you think Axel can sense that I am close?"

Sarah offered a warm smile.

"And your sister? What do you think? Does she know you are near?"

"I don't know. For years I was convinced she was dead."

"You must have felt something powerful to change your mind." She said this, it seemed to Sarah, as a matter of fact. "Maybe it was her you felt. I believe these things. You'll be going to Ohio then," said Gabi.

"That's where we grew up. Where I saw her last."

"Is it beautiful?"

"It's a total shithole." Sarah laughed. "Not all of it. Where I'm from, Lancaster, it's a shithole."

"That's sad, to not have a beautiful feeling about home."

"Lancaster was just a place I lived most of my life. It was never home." Sarah turned her gaze back to the horizon. The ship was running alongside the island now. She could almost make out the big shoreline houses of Montauk and East Hampton. She wondered what difference wealth made anymore. "Gabi, listen, the rider told me something about New York...something you should know."

Gabi sighed. "I can guess. He told you New York isn't what I think it is."

"Yes."

"I've heard such things before. The opposite too."

"Gabi, it could be really dangerous."

"It is already dangerous. And I am alone."

"You could come with me. I know a safe place."

Gabi shook her head softly. "I don't want to be without him anymore."

"You may never find him."

"I told you, I believe in what I feel. I always have. I can't help it."

Gabi placed her hand on Sarah's arm in what seemed like a gesture of solidarity and casually drew a finger across the metallic sleeve of Sarah's jacket. "*Merveilleuse,*" she said softly, a sad smile forming on her weather-chapped lips. "I know there is a story of you, Sarah. Something extraordinary. I see it in this jacket. I see it when I look at the spot where the knife entered my chest and see nothing. Not even a scratch. I see it in your eyes. Is this a good story or a bad story? This is what I ask myself."

Sarah turned to Gabi. "I ask myself the same thing." She pushed away from the rail. "We'll be docking later today. It's going to be a clusterfuck and we may have to do some real running. I'm going to get some rest."

As she walked away, she could feel Gabi's gaze on her. Ten more hours, then the two would split and go their separate ways and that would be it. She'd never see Gabi again. She fought back a tear as she walked to the cramped little room.

Does the losing ever stop?

She placed her hand on her stomach and tried to put a face to the tiny being inside her. She knew it was just a collection of cells, a form as of yet wholly unidentifiable as human. Nevertheless, she whispered a promise to the salt air.

•

The Statue of Liberty was backlit by the afternoon sun when she first came to sight through the tiny window of Sarah's room. Her silhouette was the same heartwarming shape Sarah had known all her life, but the warmth would soon cool. As the ship moved deeper into the harbor, Lady Liberty came into terrifying focus. Instead of the oxidized green she'd been for more than a hundred years, the statue's copper cladding was now a sickly blood red. The brick pedestal beneath her feet had been painted black, as were the starburst-angled walls of the base. On each of the walls in the same red as the statue herself was the graphic depiction of the Empire State Building surrounded by bullets. A set of words in red formed a base for the graphic: Kingdom of Manhattan • Nader Rex.

Moments later, the *Empire* made port at Ellis Island. Sarah had visited the island as a child. She knew that before it had become a museum it was nearly equal parts funnel and filter. Many who had come to its shores found themselves held captive for months. Many wound up being deported. Watching her fellow passengers scramble to gather their meager belongings and leave the ship, she wondered whether history was about to repeat itself. In the worst possible ways.

She and Gabi joined the queue to disembark. It moved slowly and Sarah couldn't see much ahead of her beyond the back of the person in front. Once out of the hallway and outdoors on the deck, she got a better view of the ferry basin. It didn't make her feel any better. The docks that surrounded the U-shaped port were guarded by men with black and red armbands and automatic weapons. Most wore their guns slung across their shoulders, barrels down. Several, though, had them at the ready. The rooftops of the red-brick and limestone buildings on both sides of the basin were dotted by the silhouettes of snipers. So much for Welcome to America.

There was a tug on the back of her collar. She spun around to see the rider, grinning beneath his Revolutionary War hat. "Shall we settle up, sweetheart?"

"You found us," Sarah said. "I'm glad."

"Yes, you are. Because I'm going to save your arse. Both of you, follow me."

He took Sarah's hand and she in turn took Gabi's. They pushed their way through the queue and started downship toward the stern.

"What's going on here? Why so many guns?"

"The Kingdom has strict rules, and the mayor likes them followed."

"Where are we going?" Gabi asked, her voice already coated in panic.

"You're going to take a little detour. You don't want to go through the hall like the rest of the stock."

"The stock?" Sarah echoed.

"That's right, sweetheart, the *stock*. The people deemed most useful on this boat will get a ticket to the Kingdom. They'll get work, they'll get shelter, electricity, food, and safe streets."

"And the others?" Gabi asked.

"More than a few get shot."

"Why didn't you tell me this earlier?" Sarah asked. "All you said was stay away from New York."

"Now I'm making sure you do."

They reached the deck at the ship's stern. The sun was low in the sky, and the buildings cast long shadows on the water. The air was still.

"Wait here until it's dark," the rider said, his face without his usual smile. "Then you watch for me. I'll be in a dinghy straight below."

Gabi looked over the rail. "How will we get down from here?"

"There's an emergency ladder in that steel box over there." He pointed to a row of gray containers that lined the back rail of the ship. "Hook it to the railing, let it drop, and climb down. Carefully. Do not bloody fall."

Gabi looked over the rail apprehensively. "*Merde*. It's so far." She turned to Sarah. "Maybe we should go with the rest of the passengers. We are healthy and educated. We can get jobs. I am sure of it."

"Gabi, no," Sarah said quickly. "After everything you've been through, you want to risk what happens in that hall?"

"I need to get to New York. The hall is how I get there."

"If you have to go, there are other ways," said the rider. "There are people outside the gates. If you can pay, they can get you in."

"Coyotes?" Sarah asked.

"Wolves," said the rider. "But I'd rather take my chances with them than the mongrels in that hall." He looked at Gabi, the late afternoon light deepening the lines of his face. "Your choice, honey."

•

Solli stashed his black tricorn hat under the little boat's seat and covered his thinning gray hair with the hood of his black poncho. A "Revolutionary War hat" Sarah had called it. He liked that she'd thought of it that way, even though he wasn't an American and the war that won him the hat had freed no one. He took one more look around before starting the electric motor. He didn't have to do this, he reminded himself. Who were these women to him? Just two more passengers, two more heads in the herd. Except he didn't have to make room for them on the *Empire* either, but he had. Maybe it was just the gold. Maybe he was getting soft in his old age. Maybe he wasn't sure if his old black hat really fit anymore.

The moon was a waxing crescent when the dinghy floated silently toward the *Empire's* stern. What little light reflecting on the still water came from the big windows of the Immigration Hall. Solli was careful to keep to the dark patches of water between the reflections.

He stopped the boat about ten yards from the hull, wanting to make sure he'd be visible to the two women from atop the deck. It wasn't long before the ladder unrolled from the rail. He moved the boat closer.

Gabi was first to come down. She moved quickly. He wanted to tell her to take it easy, but she was a long way up the ladder from whisper range, and the last thing they needed to do was wake the galahs up on the building parapets surrounding the basin. Geniuses they were not, but they could shoot. She was doing well, though, handling the first thirty feet of her descent like it wasn't nearly four stories above the water. He chastised himself for doubting her. Midway down, the curve of the hull bent sharply away from the ladder, leaving it and Gabi suspended in open air.

This was the place for her to really slow down. Without the hull to steady the ladder, she'd sway with every downward step as her weight shifted from one side of the rungs to the other.

"Honey, please, slow your arse down," he said softly. Sarah was looking down from the railing gesturing for Gabi to slow the pace, but Gabi was determined to get down and get down fast.

With twenty or so feet left in her descent, Solli tapped the electric throttle of the dinghy to nudge the little pontoon boat closer to the ladder. His plan was that she'd hang from the last rung and have a short drop into the boat. Short enough for him to catch her for a soft landing. It was not to be. Before the boat had even begun to travel the few yards needed to close the gap, Gabi lost her footing, missed a rung, and with the downward force of the missed step, lost her grip. She tried to grab hold of a rung to slow her fall but it was too late. The ladder had already swung out of reach. She hit the water with a splash.

Solli steered the boat to where she entered the water. As he passed the ladder he saw it shake with the pounding of Sarah's steps. She too was moving fast, and he hoped he wouldn't be fishing two people out of the bloody drink. He heard steps from the rooftops moving their way; at least one sniper had heard the splash.

Fucking hell.

Gabi's head popped out from the circle of agitation in the otherwise still water. He reached out a hand. She was flailing at the water, paddling instead of swimming. He leaned as far over the edge of the dinghy as he dared, grabbed her at the forearm, and got her onto the boat with one good pull.

Sarah was nearly at the end of the ladder and he guided the boat backward toward her position. She seemed to know exactly what to do. She let her feet dangle and descended the remaining few rungs by hand. When the boat was below her, she dropped onto the bow like she'd done it hundred times before. Solli wasted no time yanking the boat around toward the mouth of the ferry basin.

They pushed out at full power, which wasn't much. He'd chosen the boat for its silence, not its speed. Now that The Splash Heard Around the World had happened, he regretted his choice. As if on cue, a rifle crack came from the roof of the Immigration Hall and a bullet hit the water not five feet from the portside pontoon. Gabi screamed. Sarah rushed over and put a hand over Gabi's mouth and he tried to adjust his angle to shorten their path out of the basin where they'd find some cover from the trees along the island's edge.

Another bullet banged from a chamber and broke the glassy surface of the water. Then two more. A fifth found its mark and pierced a pontoon just aft of the center seat board. Gabi's eyes went wide with fear and Sarah pressed even harder with her hand. As the rubber tube bled air the little boat began to list. The trees were no more than fifty yards ahead, but the injured pontoon slowed them down to a dangerous crawl.

"How long before the boat sinks?" Sarah asked as she scooted from the water beginning to push in where the tube had flattened.

"Pontoons are chambered. If the guns don't improve their aim, she'll stay afloat." Solli pointed to the dark shore about a quarter mile out. "Up ahead is Liberty State Park. It's New Jersey, not New York. Technically speaking, outside the Kingdom."

"But?" Sarah prompted.

"But watch your arse. Now listen to me, when we get to the shore, you don't look back. Run as deep into that park as fast as you can. Find a place to wait out the night and don't move until morning."

Gabi had calmed enough for Sarah to drop her hand and she leaned his way. "What about you?" she asked.

"I'll be all right."

He reached under his seat at the till and brought out his hat. "People know better than to fuck with ol' Solli."

"Solli," Sarah said softly. "All this time I never knew your name."

"I try not to fraternize with the customers too much. You never know when you might have to kill 'em." He gave Gabi a wink.

"Why have you done all this, Solli?" Sarah asked.

Before he could answer, another rifle shot stole their attention. This time the bullet pinged off the concrete blocks of the little island's seawall only feet from the dinghy's bow. The two women turned their heads to the direction of the sound. Solli kept his eyes on the approaching tree line and worked in vain to will the electric motor more horsepower.

They reached the semi-protective line of trees without another shot.

"Okay, ladies, time to roll up your sleeves," he said. "Get your arms in the water and paddle."

The progress was maddeningly slow at first, hands being no substitute for oars. The bone-chilling temperature of the water made the work all the harder. But the girls, good on them, never broke their pace. Eventually all three found a rhythm and the shore finally grew close enough to dump the boat if he had to. A minute later Solli could see the steel railings of the walkway that once encouraged visitors to stay off the big rocks that lined the eastern edge of the park looking out at the Hudson River, Ellis Island, and Lady Liberty. For the first time since the shooting began, he thought they might actually make it.

Soon after, the dinghy was at the stones.

"Slow and steady up these rocks, ladies. Plenty of ways to twist an ankle or get caught between the stones. Once you're over the railing, you run until you can't run anymore."

"Wait," Sarah said, "your gold. I owe you the second payment."

"Stay alive, Sarah. That'll square us just fine."

The gratitude and warmth in her eyes shamed him for the years he'd let slip by, for the people he never loved, for the children he never had.

"Where will you go, Solli?" she asked.

"Back to what I do. Driving the stock."

Sarah bent over and gave him a light hug. Her hair brushed along his face and there was a sweetness to the scent of her. He closed his eyes for a moment but did not return the embrace. "Goodbye, cowboy," she said. "Thank you."

"Don't let that mouth of yours get you in trouble," he teased back.

She stood, turned toward the rocks, and he watched the two women carefully crawl their way up the stones in the darkness until they crested and he could see them no more.

•

They ran into the dark, cutting across an unkempt field that felt endless. Clouds had come in and the faint moonlight was barely enough to see. After several minutes of hard charging, they entered a stand of tall oaks. The darkness grew thicker still, so complete that the trees barely separated from the inky black around them, often giving Sarah and Gabi just a beat to adjust their path before a head-on collision.

"I have to stop," Gabi panted.

"We can slow," Sarah answered, "but we keep going. We do as Solli said."

"He said find a place to wait out the night. Why not here?"

"Because we're too close to the water."

Gabi looked over her shoulder toward the hulking skyline of New York City in the distance. "We are in the trees now, I can barely see the city," she said. "We are far enough, I think."

Sarah followed Gabi's gaze and a shiver ran up her spine. No wonder Gabi could barely see the city. Half the lights were out. Like a chandelier controlled by a dimmer, its famous nightscape, so glamourous and hopeful, had been cruelly powered down to a brooding twilight. It gave the impression of a backdrop more than the contours of a real city. The backdrop to a ghost story. Whatever New York City was now, it wasn't a place she wanted to see up close.

The sound of a rifle shot popped in the distance. There was no doubt it had come from the direction of the water.

"My God, not again," Gabi whispered.

"Solli," Sarah said. "We have to go back."

"Go back? But you said—"

"He could be hurt."

"Yes. And we could both get killed," Gabi pleaded. "It's a miracle we were not shot before. We should stay here. We cannot help him."

"I can. I'm going back."

Sarah turned and began to run back toward the water.

"Sarah, no! Please!" Gabi called after her.

"Yeah, Sarah, please, don't leave us," a man's voice called out.

Sarah stopped.

"You just got here." The voice was closer.

She heard smatterings of laughter and from all directions the soft, muffled sounds of footsteps upon the forest floor. All of it coming closer.

"Who's there?" Sarah called.

"Boo." The voice was directly behind her now.

She wheeled around and swung her right fist in the direction of the voice. She connected hard, felt the sharp sting of a tooth on her knuckle and took one quick step back to put herself in a more stable stance. He was a bit taller than her, white with long hair, but his features were obscured by the dark. The back of his hand was at his mouth. One thing she could see for certain was that he was smiling.

"Whoa, training," he said. "My fucking tooth is loose. I'll have to call my dentist first thing and see if he can squeeze me in. I wouldn't want to ruin my smile."

The rest of the men had gotten closer, now close enough to actually see. They thought the dentist joke was hilarious.

"What do you want?" Sarah said, holding her voice firm.

"Let's see, what *do* we want?" He called out to someone in the circle that ringed around both women. "Mathew, what do we want?"

"Everything," said the person apparently named Mathew. The ring makers all agreed.

"Survey says—*Ding!*—everything! Now, Mathew, if I didn't know you to be a man of high moral integrity,"—this also amused the crowd—"I'd say you cheat, because you always have the right answer. It's uncanny."

"Please," Sarah said calmly, "let us go."

"I'm sorry, no can do. See, the *Empire* came in today and that means it's a workday for us. Gotta keep the boss happy," the leader said. "And you two are just the kind of work we like. Curly here has a crazy awesome accent and you, swinger—Sarah, right?—you have an exceptionally good-looking, um, backpack." The laugh track loved that one. "Then there's the fact that you're in the park at night which is, well, not a place people who know better would be. Also, bang, bang, bang! Someone from Ellis was shooting at you. Six shots actually by my ear. When Ellis starts shooting, we come running. That's the dinner bell for bounty meat. And we are starving." He pointed to Sarah and Gabi in turn. "Winner, winner, chicken dinner."

The clouds had moved on and the moon brightened enough for Sarah to count her captors. Seven men and one woman. They were all young, early twenties, and all were white but one, a man in a long coat. They all had good boots for kicking.

"Katie, roll camera," the leader said.

The lone woman in the group pulled out a beat-up old iPhone and turned it to landscape. "Ready," she said flatly.

"What the hell is this?" Sarah said. "If we're bounty, then turn us in."

"Oh, we will," the leader said. "We like our dessert before dinner though." He moved quickly into the center of the circle and grabbed

Gabi around the waist, pulled her to him, and licked her neck. She screamed and tried to push him away, but he overpowered her easily.

"Let her go," Sarah said.

The group laughed and someone pushed her to the ground. She rolled first to her knees and paused facing the dirt, unbuttoned her coat, reached a hand in, and stood up with as much force as possible. As she rose, she brought out a duster and held it at the end of her outstretched arm. The duster's plasma ejector was a flat, fan shaped blade standing vertically up from her index finger. The handle, which also held all the conducting circuits, was black and sheathed with a thick, rubbery casing which protected the shooter from the intense heat of a plasma blast. The duster felt heavy and dangerous in her hand. Pointing it at a person felt wrong. It took everything she had to keep it from shaking. She toggled the power on with her thumb. The gun emitted a nearly musical hum and its casing pulsated with changing colors.

"I said let her go."

The leader looked at her curiously. A chuckle or two came from the crowd along with the cock of a rifle. She was already sweating despite the cool temperature of the night. The presence of the camera jangled her nerves even more.

"Is that a toy?" the leader asked with a crooked smile.

"Please, just let her go." Her voice might have cracked a little on the word "just."

"But she's so..." he put a hand between Gabi's legs, "mmmm."

Sarah swung around ninety degrees, looked for the rifle, and found it in the hands of the man in the long jacket. He had the stock to his cheek and the blue steel of the barrel grabbed a dim line of white from the light of the moon. Time stopped. As quickly as she found her target, a thin, taut snake of white, aqueous fire exploded from the duster. The trees lit up brightly into view for a flash, faces of horror on the men froze as if caught in the arc of a strobe, and the man was gone. A cloud of sparkling dust floated in his place and was quickly scattered by the breeze.

"Fuck!" someone shouted.

Time started again.

The circle widened out quickly. Sarah turned back to the leader who still had Gabi around the waist.

"Now!" Sarah yelled.

The man was frozen, as if he couldn't quite understand what was happening.

You and me both, asshole.

From the corner of her eye she saw two of the other men reach into their jackets. She pivoted and the trees flashed to their colors and details again. This time there was no hesitation; she was done with these fuckers.

"Holy shit!" Katie, the camerawoman, said.

Finally, the leader dropped Gabi.

"Get out of the way Gabi, quick!" Sarah said.

All the men left standing reached for weapons. Three from the backs of their pants and one from a coat pocket. Sarah swung her shooting arm in an arc. The night flashed day again and that was it. The whole sequence took less than twenty seconds. Gabi was on the ground shaking the diamond-bright dust from her curls with the frantic urgency of someone shooing away bees.

Sarah walked toward the woman with the phone. "Give it to us," she said.

"The phone?"

"Yes."

"Whatever. I got like five more."

"Then give it. Do you have a gun?"

"No. I swear. No gun." The woman tossed the phone to Gabi who fumbled the catch and then picked it up from the ground.

"Okay, now go."

"Wait, please. I had no choice.'"

"What?"

"Them guys." She swallowed hard. "They was all I had. You know, to stay safe and stuff."

Sarah finally took a moment to look at the woman. She was barely that, maybe seventeen, and little, smaller than Gabi. Sarah put the duster back into its place in her jacket.

"Why the video?"

"They liked to look at stuff. You know, like later."

"Stuff? You mean rapes."

The girl was quiet for a long minute. "I guess. Yeah. Like that."

"Did they touch you?"

The girl's eyes filled.

"You're Katie, right?"

"Yeah."

"Katie, if you needed to get into Manhattan, the Kingdom, would you know how?" Sarah asked.

"I guess."

"Yes or no?"

"I could find someone who could do it. Yeah, yes. Whatever."

"Okay. You're going to take Gabi to find that person. When you do, Gabi's going to give you half a string of pearls."

Gabi stood and confirmed the deal with a nod.

"She got a gun like yours?"

"No," Gabi said. "I have no gun."

"I'd rather go with you, then," said Katie.

"Not possible," Sarah said with a shake of her head. "The pearls will go far. Use them to find better friends."

•

Katie led them to a fenced off area of the park, the site of a wetlands restoration project a sign indicated. She moved aside some brush pushed up against a section of chain link and peeled back the fencing that had been roughly cut to make a door. On the other side of the fence was indeed the site of some sort of construction project. The big trees had been thinned out and even in the dim light Sarah could see a pretty good distance around her. Large PVC pipe lay in jumbled piles and mounds of excavated dirt were scattered about the acreage. They had overgrown during the years of neglect and looked more like oddly placed hills, like God got drunk before jumping into the sandbox.

"Is this where you and those men sleep?"

"Sometimes," Katie said, "when the boat comes in."

"How do you know there aren't other people here?"

"There are. But it's, like, divided up or something."

"Like territories?"

"Yeah. Tapper and the rest were pretty good at that stuff."

"Fighting?"

"Yeah. And figuring stuff out. The way you killed 'em though. Fuck. I couldn't believe it. Where'd you get that gun?"

"It's a long story."

"One I, too, would like to hear," said Gabi.

Katie turned to Gabi. "Where are you *from?*"

"Paris. France."

"Jesus. Why'd you come here? This place blows."

"My boyfriend is here. I want to be with him."

"That's stupid as fuck."

"I do not think love is stupid."

"That's pretty fucking stupid too."

They slept in the cab of a dead and rusting bulldozer that smelled like metal and body odor. Morning came quickly. Sarah had no dreams and awoke feeling rested. Katie had already started a fire out at the back of the dozer. From the look of the char marks on the paint, this was a regular grilling spot. Two oblong chunks with feet were pierced through with a stick and held aloft the fire by cement blocks stood on their ends.

"*Regardez le chef,*" Gabi said. "It smells delicious. What is it?"

Before Katie could answer, Sarah said, "Rabbit."

"Oooo. *J'aime beaucoup!*"

They ate in silence as the sun slowly burned the frost off the ground. Her morning sickness had improved, and Sarah was ravenous. Unidentified rodent—but likely rat—notwithstanding. From a

Barf Probability Quotient, her appetite was a positive development, but a worrying one as well. It meant her pregnancy was entering a new stage. And she still had a long way to go.

"Gabi," Sarah said, "I haven't been entirely honest with you."

"I know this isn't rabbit," Gabi said, her mouth full and her lips glistened by grease. "I'm not stupid."

"It's not about the food."

Gabi stopped her chewing and waited for Sarah to continue. Katie looked between the two of them, anticipation on her face.

"When we met in the Netherlands—"

"What's the Netherlands?" Katie interrupted.

"Shush!" Gabi said.

"You asked where I was going. The real question, I think, was where I was from. The last three years of my life have been really crazy."

"Welcome to the fucking club," Katie snorted.

"Shush!"

Sarah spoke slowly, tentatively, as if picking about the smoking embers of an old fire. "Before we had met, I was in Moscow."

"Moscow is gone," Gabi said softly, the mathematics going on in her mind showing clearly on her face.

"I was there all the same."

Gabi looked at Sarah's jacket, her boots, her pants. "*Bien sur*," she said. "On the ship."

"Yes."

"What the fuck are you guys talking about?" Katie said.

Gabi's back stiffened, she sat taller, a sad indignance shadowing her face. "You are one of them."

"No, that's not true." Sarah paused. "I don't know."

"One of who?" Katie practically shouted.

"The aliens," Gabi said calmly, and with more strength in her voice than usual, her eyes locked on Sarah. "The murderers."

Katie pushed back from the fire. "Holy fucking shit."

26

Until the alien ship was discovered, and the horrors of the war it triggered had occurred, Gabi had never known a sustained period of fear or unhappiness.

Sure, she had had breakups with boys that devastated her for days or even weeks, but she never failed to get over them completely. There was always another boy to drive her to distraction. Her father, a political cartoonist, had died at his desk when she was a teenager, a pen in hand and a literal smile on his face. While she missed him daily for years, it was hard not to look upon his life and theirs together as a charmed one. He was a bright-hearted man with a playful spirit. When she and her mother would speak of her father, they both often ended the conversation sore in their bellies from laughter. Gabi's relatively seismic-free life was, her mother had told her over and over, the luck of her generation.

She had missed the darkness of the German Occupation. By the time of her birth, it had long been painted over by the lie of *La Résistance*, which twisted Paris's greatest humiliation into a tale of heroic partisan guerilla warfare. She was a small child when the Saint-Michel bombing spread terror throughout the city. Much too young to be aware of it as anything other than an annoyance that had kept the family television tuned to the news channel for a week. Later, as a young woman, when two men attacked the editorial offices of the satirical magazine, *Charlie Hebdo*, and killed twelve people, the tragedy had seemed to her like a lucky miss. Having already died a peaceful death doing what he loved, her father had been saved from a similar fate.

She had simply missed all the terrible shit.

So when aliens were awoken in the middle of the ocean, when their enormous ship had risen to the surface like a mountain range emerging from a tectonic clash of continents, when it then shrugged off humanity's most powerful weapons like they were harmless flies and proceeded to burn half the world, she had felt uniquely ill-equipped to deal. Certainly, she rationalized at the time, who on Earth *could* be equipped to fathom and absorb what was happening? No one, of course. In fact, she knew she was not alone in her panic and despair. Walking the leafy streets of the Sixth, before the restaurants and cafés would close for good, she could see worry and struggle on the faces of nearly everyone. She also imagined that behind some of those faces were reservoirs of helpful experience. Nights spent in air-raid shelters trembling from the bombs exploding above, car accidents and cancers, bankruptcies and the crushing loss of children. The battle testing of past calamities. Events that built callus on one's soul. She envied them their survivorship. While she was left with mere hope and belief, their spirits were reinforced by the actual knowing that great pain could be overcome. Her luck of timing, of being born in so comparatively peaceful a moment in history, had suddenly and viciously worked against her.

Sarah was more evidence that her downward streak had not ended. Gabi had been lied to in the worst of all ways. Now she herself had become complicit in whatever scheme Sarah was up to. Without Gabi, would Sarah have found her way to Amsterdam and the boat? Or was Sarah's need simply part of the deception? Gabi couldn't know for sure. As she and Katie walked through the park back toward the city, the only thing Gabi knew for certain was that until she found Axel, she'd never stop being afraid.

"How far until we get to New York?" Gabi asked.

"We have to hoof our way to the bridge. It's a fucking haul."

"Thank you for taking me."

"I got nothin' else to do, thanks to your friend."

"She's not my friend!"

"Jesus. You don't have to yell, you know."

"I'm sorry. I am upset. That's all."

"Hey, the alien thing blew my mind too. I mean, she seemed totally human and stuff to me."

"I am embarrassed. I should have known better."

"She didn't have no lizard face or nothin'. I mean, what the fuck, right?"

"I do this all the time."

"Do what?"

"Trust people."

"I never had no one I could trust."

"You are trusting me right now, are you not? To pay you?"

"Uh, no. I know you got the pearls."

"How can you be sure?"

"'Cause, dumbass, I went through your bag while you were sleeping."

Gabi gasped. "*Petite sac de merde!*"

"I'da gone through Sarah's stuff too, but she was like this." Katie mimed a person cradling a bundle tight. "All on top of it. I'd be fucking queen of the world with that gun of hers. Anyway, I couldn't find my phone. That's why I spied your bag."

"Because you are not so smart as you think. I know better than to keep everything in one place."

"I found the pearls. I counted fifty-two. That means you owe me twenty-six."

"Why didn't you just take them and go?"

Katie shrugged. "You're a straight-up loser, for sure, but you're better than nothin'."

•

The walk took them nearly twenty-five miles and most of the day. They reached the George Washington Bridge that spanned the Hudson River and connected what was still called New Jersey to the Kingdom. It was the largest bridge Gabi had ever seen. On their side of the wide river stood a gray giant arch made of crisscrossed steel beams in box forms that seemed to stretch from the water to the clouds. In the late afternoon light, the rugged lattice of metal cast long shadows like fine lacework on the asphalt and the water. A third of the way up from the river's surface were suspended two mostly empty multilane highways, stacked double decker style. Perhaps a dozen vehicles and pedestrians were making their way along the Jersey half of the road in both directions. Far in the distance, on the Kingdom side, stood the arch's twin. Even from where she stood, maybe as far as two kilometers away, its hulking scale still impressed. From the tops of the twins, enormous steel cables ran, slacking gracefully downward from the Jersey side toward the middle of the highway and then sloping upward again to the top of the second arch. The structure was brutish, completely devoid of decoration. It seemed to her a pure expression of utility and power and strength, its brashness a breathtaking beauty. Gabi was awestruck, almost too frightened to take another step.

Her index fingers went after her thumbs with a vengeance. "Now what?" she asked the girl.

"See that roadblock in the middle? That's where we go. If he's short on coin, that's where we'll find him."

"Find who?"

"A friend of Tapper's. Total asshole, but he used to be super connected. Calls himself Kino."

27

Sarah's hometown was southeast of Columbus and butted up against I-70. The giant highway was noisy and ugly but it held the promise of other places, and because of that Sarah had always looked upon it as one of the little town's best features. Her family shared next to nothing. Not meals, not TV shows, not jokes. On the subject of the Interstate, though, they were aligned. The road trip was how the family vacationed. They'd drive out of Lancaster, eastbound on I-70 toward places like Philadelphia, Newport News, Washington, DC, and once, when she was already a teenager, the Jersey Shore, with a stop at Liberty State Park on the way. The very place she was leaving now.

Road tripping was the group's singular indulgence.

Jack kept a tight leash on his money. Not because he was broke or miserly, or even responsible. The way Sarah saw it, Jack's tightfistedness was just another outlet for his cruelty. Another kind of fist. He had a job as a floor supervisor at the Anchor Hocking plant that manufactured glass kitchenware, storage containers, and measuring vessels. Sarah's mother had been an admin at the small Lancaster campus of the University of Ohio. There hadn't been a lot of money coming in, Sarah knew. But there was money. Still, no wish was too small to refuse. Nice things, at least things Sarah, her sister, and her mother might consider nice, were universally off limits.

The rule would have held were it not for her mother's lone act of marital defiance. She had an old mayonnaise jar she hid in the back of the cabinet below the kitchen sink, a place she knew Jack would never look because Jack, who never did the dishes, would never have need to reach into that cabinet for a clean sponge or more soap. In that jar went every penny or quarter or dollar her mother could squirrel away. She called that jar her secret closet because she'd use the stash to sneak-shop clothes for Sarah and her sister. They'd keep the clothes out of sight from Jack by changing into and out of them at school. At first the secret and the efforts to keep it felt like another form of family struggle, another sign that her home life was a hopeless mess. Eventually the dereliction of it took on the contours of an exciting game.

It was a special kind of retail therapy. No matter what the screen-printed words across the front of a new tee might have actually said, in Sarah's mind the message was always the same, "Fuck you, Jack." Every time she'd pushed her hand through the sleeve of a new jacket, she'd made sure to give him the finger.

But for cars, *his* cars, Jack always had money. Parked in the cracked and slopy drive next to their small clapboard cottage with its peeling paint and mossy roof tiles was usually some version of a well-polished Lexus or BMW. It was in those roomy, leather- and Bose-appointed coaches they'd glide out of Lancaster on their annual road adventures, each playing a part in the make-believe theater of a family united in pursuit of fun.

So Sarah knew the route to Lancaster: I-78 to I-76 to I-70. The same roads she'd traveled dozens of times. She'd skirt Allentown, go through Harrisburg, Somerset, bypass Pittsburgh, and cross the Ohio River. By car it would be less than a day; on foot it would be weeks.

She set out on the weed-pocked frontage road that ran alongside the hulking highway. The sun was straight above her and she hoped the warmth would melt away the chill that goosefleshed her neck. It didn't. As she traveled, she couldn't help but compare the open, flat, concrete landscape around her now to the closely tangled web of Amsterdam. Even with people shuttered behind closed doors and the narrow, cobbled streets practically empty, Amsterdam had felt more alive. This place, without the persistent buzz of traffic and planes, was like a movie set about a world where everything looked normal, except the people had all mysteriously vanished. Although I-78 had none of the familiar trappings of a Hollywood apocalypse—the abandoned cars, the downed planes—it felt just as doomed. It was the absence that spooked.

The big rigs that bullied the freeways of her memories were nowhere to be seen or heard. Instead, the few vehicles she saw were small electrics and light trucks traveling at breakneck speeds. She'd hear their tire and engine noises long before she'd actually see them, like impending swarms of locusts. When they'd come into view, they were like apparitions solidifying from fog. Not there, then there, then gone in a flash. Between vehicles it was unnervingly quiet. Sarah kept one arm pressed against her coat as she walked to feel the heavy, comforting lump of a weapon.

Up ahead on the right side of the road, a row of tract houses began. They were the small and mostly identical single-story brick boxes that filled the yawning maw of America's suburban sprawl of the 1960s. Red- or oatmeal-colored finish-brick in the front, plain Chicago brick on the sides, a large picture window trimmed with a piece of live-edge limestone that would alternate in placement from house to house on either the right or left side of the white aluminum door which was invariably accessed by a narrow two-step-high landing of poured concrete. The gray-speckled hip roofs lined up in perfect order along the street Sarah was traveling, with only narrow strips of dead grass and weeds and a cracking sidewalk between the little buildings and the road. Just beyond her, over her left shoulder, facing the row of picture windows, was the great asphalt expanse of I-78.

Sarah wondered if the people who now lived in these houses, if there *were* people living there, welcomed the unnatural quiet that had her so on edge. Or did they miss the screaming hurricane drone of traffic that kept them awake at night but at least told them the world still worked? She passed a red-brick version. Someone had taped a hand-lettered sign on the big window. One of its corners had come unstuck and the sign hung there crooked and forlorn. "Have a nice day!" it read.

Six houses into the block she heard a door squeal open and then shut behind her. She stopped and slowly turned around, her heart picking up its pace. On the landing two houses back was an elderly black woman, a tightly packed round shape of pale-yellow sweater topped in gray set upon two stout legs stuffed into blue jeans. She was barefoot.

"Hello." She waved.

"Hello," Sarah said.

"Could you help me? Please?"

The woman was clearly weaponless, the sound of her voice kindly and needy. Sarah walked slowly toward the house. She noticed the side windows were pushed open, their panes jutting out like fins from the pale brick. She stopped at the sidewalk in front of the short concrete path that connected it to the stoop. The woman smiled broadly, but there was no hiding the worry in her eyes.

"I've been sitting in this front window for days, watching and waiting. Everyone's gone, you know. Now you're finally here."

Sarah waited for the woman to keep talking.

"It's my son," the old lady said. "I need to get him out of bed, but he's too heavy for me."

"Is he hurt?"

"Oh no," the lady said flatly. "He's dead."

Sarah stayed on the sidewalk, processing.

"I have crackers, and good peanut butter."

Sarah studied the house and looked over at its neighbors. Both houses were dark. She squeezed an arm against her side to feel the duster again. "Okay."

The woman walked back in the house, and before Sarah got to the first step of the narrow porch the smell of feces and decay hit her. Inside it was much worse. She stopped on the few rows of tile that separated the front door from the living room carpet and tried to get a sense of the place before going any further. The living room was tidy but crazily small, with barely room enough for the two upholstered chairs and a television that sat beneath one of the open windows Sarah had seen from the outside. The wall that separated the kitchen from the living room had a large breakfront cutout letting it get some light from the big picture window. The woman had headed to the back of the house where Sarah guessed the bedrooms must be, and she stood in the little hallway in front of the pink-tiled bathroom. The woman, even in this bizarro moment, appeared steady, poised. Her eyes, when they met Sarah's, were trusting.

The house was small enough that she had a reasonably safe sense of the layout from her place by the front door. The dead son, she presumed, was in the bedroom behind the kitchen, left of the old woman. If he was truly dead, and it sure smelled like he was, the only real mystery was what or who might be in the other bedroom.

"Do you mind if I take a quick look around first?" Sarah asked.

The woman said nothing, but Sarah detected a shift in the woman's face, a flicker of curiosity.

"I want to be sure there's no one else here."

"Who else would be here?" the old woman said softly, her face relaxed once more.

"I don't know." Sarah walked slowly toward the kitchen. It too was neat and orderly. The counters were shiny, the sink empty, the overall cleanliness in sharp contrast to the odor that grew thicker as she pushed her way deeper into the little house.

"Dwayne is in here," the woman said, pointing to the room behind the kitchen. Sarah went to the other bedroom first. A woman's room. A soft yellow bedspread, close to the color of the woman's sweater, was neatly draped atop a full-sized bed bracketed by two dark wood nightstands. The window facing the door was also wide open. All the surfaces, even the dresser that stood directly beneath the open window, shined cleanly. Sarah opened the closet. Once confident there was no one else in the house, she steeled her courage for Dwayne.

"Oh my God," she muttered under her breath when she walked in the room.

Dwayne wasn't just dead. He was science-project dead. He lay half on a twin bed and half on the floor. Badly stained bed coverings were twisted about him haphazardly, leaving much of poor Dwayne exposed. Decomposition had bloated his body to the point where the skin had split in several places and rivulets of red and yellow liquid oozed from the breaks, telling the gruesome story of what had stained the bed coverings.

"One day, he just didn't wake up," the old lady said. "I tried to move him, but he's too heavy for me alone."

"I see," Sarah said.

"It wouldn't be right to leave him like this," the old woman said in a way that finally recognized the sadness of the situation.

Sarah took her hand. "Why don't you go sit in the living room? I'll get him in the backyard for you." The old woman nodded, the look and the nod familiar in a way that raised the hairs on Sarah's arms.

It took Sarah nearly a half hour to get Dwayne outside. He wasn't particularly heavy. The bloating had made him seem a much bigger man. But she didn't want him to mess the house any more than necessary. Before she moved him, she wrapped him in some clean sheets she found in the woman's bedroom. Twice she had to run to the bathroom to vomit. Eventually, she managed to drag him through the kitchen door and around the house to a patch of grass between the back of the building and a small, well-tended shed. By then the woman had joined her.

"There's a shovel in the shed," she said, walking across the patch with a key in her hand. She unlocked the door and Sarah followed her in. Like the house, the shed was immaculate. Garden tools were neatly organized on hooks and clips across one wall. Another movie set. On the opposite side of the shed stood a gleaming, pearl-brown Honda Shadow. Sarah grabbed the shovel and went back to Dwayne.

By the time the hole was deep enough, the sun had fallen to the horizon. Sarah rolled Dwayne in as gently as she could.

"Would you like to say something?" Sarah asked the woman.

"I've already told my Dwayne what he needs to hear."

Sarah gave a short nod and began the work of refilling the hole. When she was finished, night had settled in and she went back into the kitchen. The old woman had a plate of crackers on the counter with a jar of peanut butter next to it.

"You must be hungry," she said.

"Actually, I can't believe I am, but I am. Thank you."

The old woman went to the living room and sat down on a chair facing the dead television. Sarah stayed at the kitchen counter and watched the old woman through the breakfront. The woman put her hands in her lap, crossed her legs at the ankles, and turned to Sarah with warmth in her eyes.

"They're in the small top drawer to your left," the old woman said.

"I'm sorry?" Sarah said. "What are?"

"The keys to Dwayne's motorcycle, dear. That's what you're here for."

"No, you asked me for help, so I came in. That's all."

"That's not even a little of it, Sarahbeara. Nothing on your path is just a stumble. There's work to be done and it can't wait. You need that bike."

Sarah's stomach went cold. The conversation with Heather, the woman who appeared to her on the ship, raced through her head. And, of course, Elouise. The jet pilot.

"Sarahbeara," she said. "I hadn't heard anyone call me that in years. I've heard it twice now in four weeks. At least I think I have."

The old woman smiled softly. In her eyes Sarah saw that strange familiarity again. It washed over her like a warm ocean wave. For a moment she let herself be gently pulled under.

"I know what I'm doing is crazy," she said. "Nothing about it makes any sense to me. But I'm doing it anyway. Can you tell me why? Can you at least tell me I'm not losing my mind?"

The old woman waited a beat before answering. "Be sure to eat plenty of that peanut butter," was all she said.

Sarah opened the drawer and took the keys to the Honda.

28

Before being crushed by the *Kalelah's* fall, Putin had managed to send three single-payload rockets to America. One burst over a missile silo field in Montana; the other two had exploded over the cities of Houston and Chicago. It had been obvious why Montana was chosen. But why Houston and Chicago? People had all kinds of theories. Putin was an oilman, the most popular notion went, so Houston was taken to knock out a competitor. Chicago had been the center of rail transport, commodities trading and agribusiness finance, and a major tourist destination as well. Mostly, people had said, Chicago was killed because it would hurt. Of all the big American cities, Chicago was the most, well...American. The prettiest of them too.

Kino had been to Chicago only once, to attend a funeral for a moderately wealthy aunt. He stayed an extra day for the reading of the will. When he had learned she'd left him twenty thousand dollars he moved from his room at the Holiday Inn to a suite at the Peninsula and blew through the entire inheritance in three days on steaks, clothes, bourbon, and a breathy escort who called herself Catherine. He still had fond, if fuzzy, memories of Chicago.

As he headed west along Interstate 78 on the way to Lancaster, Ohio, and the mayor's good graces, he worried about how close his plan would take him to that once great city. On the map, Lancaster sat a hair east of the hot zone jointly fueled by the radioactive heat pouring out of Chicago and Houston. Together, the two sites put up an ionic shroud of slow and nauseating death that stretched from Ontario to central Mexico. If his heat map could be trusted, Lancaster would be clean, and he could at least cross radiation sickness off the list of things that might kill him on this trip.

Except heat maps were like everything else After: suspect. They were drawn by crazies and data mercenaries, their cars fitted with bootleg Geiger counters. The drivers worked north-south routes on each side of the zone. Those who survived the work and earned a reputation for accuracy, or what had become the new and significantly diminished definition of accuracy, were paid a relative fortune by the kings and syndicates who controlled the heat map markets. Kino knew better though than to put too much faith in anything the kings and syndicates had for sale. What did the song say? *A liar never trusts anyone else.*

Besides, the wind made the whole concept of a map practically worthless. Where he was headed it whipped out of the western prairies over Chicago Ground Zero and pushed eastward across Lake Michigan. It meant the northeastern edge of the zone was always moving. Depending on the wind, the start of the zone could shift more than a hundred miles in either direction. For safety's sake he had his own counter riding on the dash the entire trip. So far, the needle had been calm, gently bobbing within the normal range.

His vehicle, an imposing electric SUV on loan from the mayor, was painted black with protective cladding around the wheels and a large solar collector on the roof. The radio played nothing but static. He hadn't expected anything more but turning it on was a habit whenever he drove. Only once in two years had he picked up a pirate signal. Polka music. Of course. Nevertheless, out of habit, he had kept the radio on for a bit, scrolling back and forth along the channel band hoping to catch something to break up the white noise drone of loneliness. By the time he'd reached Pennsylvania, he grew sleepy and switched to Bluetooth. Like most people, he didn't have much of a music library cached—only a few dozen albums he had pushed onto his phone years ago. "Dancing Days" from *Houses of the Holy* filled the cabin.

He guessed he was three hours away, assuming he didn't encounter any bandits or mercenary patrols. The Mercs preyed on the bandits, stealing their hauls and making piracy a dangerous and barely profitable business. In their own brutal ways, they helped keep the roads reasonably safe. Which was not to say they were entirely altruistic. The Mercs were known to stop ordinary motorists too. The roadblocks were their fundraisers and donations were mandatory. Kino hoped the New York plates on the SUV would keep trouble at a distance. License plates meant nothing anymore. With no database to track them, their numbers were meaningless. To the mayor, however, they were symbols of order, his order, and a dependable revenue stream. To outsiders, they were symbols of the mayor. In other words: *think twice*.

In the After, the multilane highways were all dark as country roads in the Before. The big lamps stationed at regular intervals along the shoulders that once poured soft pools of reassurance onto the asphalt had no government source of electricity and stood dark, like silent, impotent sentinels as the sparse traffic sped blindly by at formerly illegal speeds. The darkness had been relentless since the sun had set. So it was with a wave of happy nostalgia when, perhaps a mile or two in the distance, he saw the faint sky-glow of powerful electric lights—the kind that once signaled the promise of friendly commercial life, like neon and fluorescent rays of hope. When the road ahead graded upward and he reached the top of the incline, he could see the light was coming from a building built close to the road on his right. A red neon sign hung above it, as if dangled from a star.

As the building grew larger in his sight, he took his foot off the accelerator to slow down. It might have been an Olive Garden Before, and the red neon beacon that looked so celestial from afar now looked like the work of a quick and inexpensive pop-up. In buzzing bombastic letters it proclaimed the oasis to be Mabel's Kitchen & Tap. He could do with some tap.

The sensible voice in his head, however, counseled otherwise. *Keep driving*, it warned. The girl and her weapons were his only way back to the life he once had. That life of relative privilege. That life that gave him both purpose and a name to fear and respect. And he *was* on his way back. He'd managed to talk his way into City Hall, survived the Game, and now he was only hours away from the place where the girl was headed. He should definitely keep driving. Except it had been hours since last he ate, and longer since he'd had a drink. He was desperate for a bourbon, or whatever they'd say was bourbon. He was aching for a beautiful woman behind a glossy bar who knew how to lie with her eyes. Also, he needed to piss.

His mind quickly weighed the risks against the rewards. The smart and thirsty parts of his brain pushing back and forth. Pluses: This stretch of 78 was comfortably between cities. Between kingdoms. A relatively safe place to be. In fact, it was unlikely that Mabel's would be under the protection of a king. It would be an extremely expensive projection of power. Only a few kings could afford it, and there just weren't enough riches between cities anymore to bother.

Minuses: Indies were inherently unpredictable. They employed the least trained and brained muscle. Almost anything could go wrong.

Suddenly, he *really* needed to piss.

Kino took the off-ramp and wound his way the two blocks to the lot and steered his vehicle into a space closest to the frontage road. He switched off the power, opened the door, and lowered himself to the gravel covered parking lot.

He took another look at the commandeered Olive Garden and the precarious looking neon perched atop the tall and rusting white pole. He counted the vehicles in the lot—ten beaters and four motorcycles. Not what he wanted. A crowd would be better. In a packed house he'd simply be another face. Get in, get out. Now the hope that he could slip in unnoticed was all but dashed, making his newest urgent need particularly risky. Using a public toilet had become a strategic decision in almost every circumstance. Small rooms with only one way out were places practically designed for violent ambush.

Trouble at the bar at least gave a person room to maneuver. The bar had options.

Kino unzipped himself and pissed on the gravel.

He used the minute to think. Plusses and minuses. Pros and cons. You could never think enough anymore. He was alive because he never stopped thinking. He never saw the sand without thinking a sinkhole could open at any step.

Once again, the smartest thing to do here was finish up, get in the car, and keep going. But he really wanted a drink. More than that, he deserved one. He'd been on a streak of good luck lately. If he didn't celebrate when things went his way, what was the point? Besides, with the piss, hadn't he already reduced the risk in this stop? Yes, he had. He blipped the lock on the truck and started walking toward the entrance.

He pushed through the doors and was surprised to see a clear route straight to the bar—no security, no pat down. The cheesy *Salute!* lettered along the mirrored back wall between the rows of bottles proved his earlier suspicion correct; this place was once an Olive Garden. Mabel had apparently decided the only changes needed to make it hers were a few dozen burnt-out lightbulbs, a dirty floor, and lots of cigarette smoke. Also, a live squirrel in a cage on a table just past the entrance.

If the bourbon was drinkable, all would be forgiven. He slid onto a stool at the bar's left-end corner, leaving a buffer seat between him and a curvy woman with gray hair. She turned his way and looked at him longer than needed. She was much younger than he'd thought initially, maybe in her thirties, with smart eyes and a beautiful face. Her dress was clean, and she had makeup on her cheeks and around her eyes. He nodded slightly. She turned away.

The bartender took his time acknowledging Kino. He was Asian, or maybe Hawaiian. A big boy. Not the person he'd hoped to see.

"What you got?" the bartender asked.

Kino reached into his pants pocket and put down an old dirty-gold coin a bit larger and thicker than a silver dollar. "It's Spanish," he said. The bartender pulled a retractable skinning knife from the belt pulled tight beneath his overhanging belly, snapped it open, and scratched the polished blade across the coin. The knife left a shiny, yellow-gold gash.

"Two burgers and one drink," the bartender said.

"What are the burgers made of?"

"Got me." He looked to the woman with the gray hair. "What do you think?" he asked her. "About the burgers?"

She turned her head back to Kino and barked twice. The bartender laughed.

"How about three drinks, no burger?" Kino bargained.

"How about two?" the bartender countered, slipping the Spanish coin in his pocket.

"Bourbon then."

The bartender nodded his agreement and went off to a far shelf to pour Kino's drinks. Kino unbuttoned his jacket and got more settled on his stool. The TVs over the bar were off. No baseball to watch anyway.

"Collie or Pointer?" he said to the woman a stool over. If she was going to bust his balls, he'd bust hers. Really, though, he just felt like talking. She turned his way again, looking at him with strange intent and saying nothing. "The burgers," he said. "Though for the price of that Spanish, I'd expect something fancier." He arched an eyebrow in an effort to charm. "Great Dane, maybe."

She gave him no reaction, not even a hint of smile, only that same piercing look. "You're from New York," she said, not as a question but as a simple truth. She reached into the top of her snug-fitting dress and produced a battered phone and tapped it to life, then leaned closer his way to share the screen. He could smell her perfume. It was expensive, delicious, and the first hint he'd made a mistake. It came earlier than usual. On the phone was a grainy image, like a closed-circuit security feed. She pinched the picture larger. The New York plates on his SUV filled the frame. Now it was his turn to look at her. The bartender returned with Kino's drinks and dropped them down unceremoniously. The woman straightened up again and returned her phone to its home inside her dress.

Kino took a sip from the cracked glass on his right and winced. "You make this yourself?"

A long pause. "Old family recipe. My grandfather was a plumber."

"To family then, Mabel." He tilted the glass her way before bringing it back around to his mouth for another sip. It was real work not to cough from the sting.

"Pretty fancy car you have. What kind is it?" she asked.

Shit, here we go.

"Cadillac."

"A Cadillac with New York plates. Impressive." She licked the corner of her mouth and reached out to feel the sleeve of his coat. "Cheap-shit polyester." She let go of the fabric and allowed her fingers to rest where they were. He could feel the feminine weight of them, their magic power to break borders and touch a stranger's arm. "No offense."

"None taken," he said breezily, hoping to buy some time. "Do we have a problem here? I mean, besides the bourbon?"

The right side of her mouth turned up a bit to acknowledge the joke. "A car like that and a hideous coat like this doesn't make sense unless..." she pretended to think for a beat, "...unless it's someone else's car." She took her fingers off his arm.

"Look, I'm not here for trouble," said Kino.

"Of course you are. People like you and the men who give you your marching orders—trouble is all you're anywhere for. Kings, they can't be happy unless everyone else is miserable."

"I saw your sign. I wanted a drink. That's it."

She gave him a smile that seemed to him like pity. "You don't look entirely stupid so you must know the rules. This is neutral territory. Nothingland. The mayor's not welcome here. Yet here you are. Why?"

"Because this is the road between New York and Ohio."

"Well, that's true," she said huskily. "And also bullshit."

"I've never heard of you or this place before. Let's take this down a notch, okay?"

"Not okay. Okay?" She leaned in and kissed him on the lips. Nothing wet, but her point was made. That was goodbye.

In the dirty mirror facing him, he could see two men the size of big boy approaching.

"This is a mistake," he said.

She shrugged. "What isn't?"

He waited a brief second for the two men to get bigger in the mirror, grabbed a glass in each hand, swung around and off the stool, and pushed the cheap tumblers hard into the two men's faces. Once he saw blood he reached into his jacket, pulled his gun, and shot one through the throat and the other through the ear. He turned back around to find big boy. The bartender had his knife already in hand and was moving fast. Kino put a round in his chest, but the huge man's momentum kept him moving forward and Kino's finger fired another round on its own. His mind raced through an earlier calculation: The principal pro of a small gun was its easy conceal. The principal con was sometimes you have to shoot a rhino. A third bullet and the bartender finally went down, taking two shelves of bottles with him. Kino waited for more protection to come. There had to be more. But all went quiet. The few other customers remained in their seats, most with their hands up at their shoulders.

Mabel, if that was her name, was still on her stool. She had that same look on her face she had when he'd first sat down, like there was something about him she understood. Something even he didn't know. Perhaps she did.

He put his gun to her temple and though the barrel was still hot, she didn't flinch. He moved in close for the perfume. He could never resist an expensive perfume on a beautiful woman.

"Bourbon and some ice. It could've been that easy."

Kino fired his last bullet in the magazine. He walked around behind the bar, grabbed the bottle of bathtub bourbon, and left. As the red neon sign hanging in the night sky grew small and then disappeared in his rearview mirror, Steve Earle's "The Devil's Right Hand" sang from the Caddie's speakers.

Maybe this wasn't the shitshow it seemed like. It was possible he'd just done the mayor a big favor and settled an old score. Kino was feeling better and better about his chances. He turned the music up and pushed the accelerator pedal down.

29

If this had been a normal day, if the Guides were out among the seedlings, the Lab would be a glowing mass of blue-green float imagery crowding the available airspace, relaying and recording every sight and sound of Guide work. Dozens of anthropologists would be in the thrall of study, noting every detail of the population's development. In the back of the room, past the anthro department, the virologists, designers, and Thought Captains would be busy nurturing the bugs of guided development, some at the controls of robots toiling among the germs within the sterile vacuums of glass incubator cubes, others congregating in small groups around oversized draw floats imagining the genetic structure of new instructional and idea-starting microbes.

Instead, less than twenty occupied the cavernous space. The usual electricity of excited progress was replaced by the dim hum of monitoring and cataloguing the creeping growth of decline. The Guide Lead sat in one of two large chairs placed in a corner of the room, his giant hands clasped together as if in prayer with his first fingers tucked under his soft, rounded chin. His huge right leg bounced nervously on the ball of his foot. He watched intently as Trin headed across the room.

"I envy your speed," Dent Forent said as Trin lowered himself into the neighboring chair.

"You said it was important."

"Indeed. I'm sure you're anxious to get back to finding Sarah, but Trin, she's not the only person from this ship who's gone missing. I believe their disappearances may be linked to our missile trouble."

"Sarah has nothing to do with the missiles, Dent."

Forent closed his eyes briefly and gave a curt nod—a gesture that looked more like a desire to move past the point than agree with it. "I'm beginning to formulate a theory." He pulled a float from the air.

"What am I looking at?" Trin asked, standing to get a better view.

"This is the ship's manifest right before Argen hailed the all-crew Wake."

"Dent, that was three years ago. A crew of twenty-three thousand and forty-one. I don't need the manifest to remember that number. What does it have to do with anything?"

"Be patient, XO." Forent expanded the float and another column of names appeared. "Four-point-three percent never woke. It was the deadliest Waking in Service history."

"It was also the longest *Skip* in Service history. It was a miracle the number wasn't twice that. Old news so far."

Forent hefted himself out of his chair with a grunt. It took forever. Trin almost offered a hand. Eventually, Forent pushed a plump finger into a name in the middle of the second manifest. "The new news, then. This name. Security officer, Zouc. Unaccounted for. If he was a no-wake, there was never a body. He simply vanished."

Security officer.

Trin's mind flashed back to the body on the pod floor, the heavy vase next to the crushed and blood-soaked head, the badge pinned to the dead man's shirt. Sitting a foot away, Sarah cradling a sobbing Cyler in her arms. The choking bruise from the hands of her assailant already turning a purple black around Cyler's neck.

"A lot of shit blew up during that Waking. People were freaked. Clerical errors were bound to happen."

Forent expanded the float once more. "This is the final death count after the crash. It includes all the casualties of The Mutiny as well. Again, we have a recorded death, but no body."

"Who?"

"Luten Hyak. A defense systems tech."

Trin sat back down and looked at the names suspended in air. He didn't know Hyak and it didn't matter. He understood where Forent was going with this. Even taking the security bastard out of the picture, it wasn't entirely insane.

"You think there are crew off ship working with the population. That the chaos of the Waking, the crash, and the wacked number of dead gave them cover to disappear."

"Something like that," said Forent.

"How would they get past the Code? A person can't just open the fucking doors and walk out without being caught in the Code."

"Like I said, I'm at the beginning of this. But Trin, no matter who is on the outside, they'd need help from the *inside*. They couldn't surveil us electronically because we'd see it instantly. In fact, if I'm right, they weren't watching for you at all. They were waiting."

"For someone to tell them exactly when I crossed the nano. Someone who knows my route."

"All the missiles needed to do then was hunt the shimmer."

"Wait. We spotted the missiles the second they launched. Ensign Tuper wanted to dust them. It would have been over before it even got interesting. Anyone with half a brain would game that out."

"Indeed, they would. But—"

"Shit," Trin said, the last of the dominos falling in his mind. "I told Tuper to stand down."

"Because that's your rule, XO. No cannons, even in the face of attack. Everyone knows it." He put a thirty-pound paw on Trin's shoulder and for the first time in ages Trin saw a hint of those jovial crinkles that once permanently creased around Forent's eyes. "You're the cockiest soul in the known universe. Precisely the kind of jackass who'd actually *think* he could outrun a supersonic bomb. Everyone knows that too."

"Okay, I get it," he said, annoyed by the obvious truth in Forent's words. He stared at the manifests. "That's always the fucking problem. *Everyone*. The Circle is everyone, anyone, no one. You never know until it's too late."

"Maybe not this time. Think about what it would take to push tech and material off this ship."

"Fair enough. But the numbers would still have to be—"

"Three."

"What?"

"Three would have the necessary combination of skills."

"That's it?"

Forent folded the float gone and pulled another from a private file. "That's it." Images of two men and one woman hovered. Trin stood once more.

"No," he said, slowly shaking his head. "In the debrief, after the missile attack, you got me thinking I ought to be more careful, at least more aware. But this...this can't be." He put his fingers around one of the images and said, "Yorn Darnol, verify." In rapid succession additional images of Darnol from different angles, in different settings, and different crops sequenced within the boundaries of the original image. It was him. The engineer who retrofit *18* and was in the process of doing it again.

Forent inhaled loudly through his nose. The breath made even more noise on the way out. "This Darnol fellow, you know him well?"

Trin stood looking at the float. "I'm going to have to get back to you on that."

30

The moon was small, the shoulder lights were out, and the darkness creeped in on the road from all sides. The comforting, after-dark details of the American highway—the giant, illuminated photographs of Big Macs and French fries, the round fields of bright, tungsten yellow that would bloom from the security lamps of the farms in the distance—had been blanketed over by the newly unmitigated force of night, as if redacted by an oversized Sharpie.

The Honda, though, cut through the blackness like a knife. It felt heavy and powerful under her as she sped along the mostly empty interstate highway. Speed was a relief. An exhilaration even. Other than the helicopter trip from Moscow to the Netherlands—another lifetime ago—the whole journey had felt like a slow-motion dream. Now, the wind in her hair, the mile markers shooting by, filled Sarah with promise. She could begin to imagine actually accomplishing this task.

When she'd set out from the old woman's house, the Honda's tank was nearly full. She had a two-gallon plastic can of gas riding pillion on the little seat behind her. Poor Dwayne had kept himself prepared. Sarah couldn't know for sure, but she guessed the fuel would last at least halfway to Lancaster. She allowed herself to fall in sync with the bike, to feel the road in her palms and her forearms and her seat. For miles she let the engine note drown out most of the noise in her head—the pestering planning, the worry, the doubt. It restored her better than sleep.

The moon had moved high into the night sky when she pulled the bike over to the shoulder to fill the tank from the plastic can. She saw no headlights coming from either direction. It was quiet as she held the can to the fill hole in the tank. In fact, since she'd left the ship, the weather had grown colder, the nights quieter. During her first night in the real world, the sounds of the cicadas and crickets had been like the first taste of chocolate to her. She missed them now in a way she never had Before.

From behind her, maybe twenty yards, there was the sudden crack of a twig...a shuffling of feet through the grass. A step or two, then a stop. A little bit this way, then that. Her senses sharpened and her muscles readied.

A moment later a deer, a buck, emerged from the tall grass not more than ten yards from her. He stood tall, easily three feet at the shoulder. With his antlers extending wide and up from his head, like a crown jeweled by the stars, he looked to be as large as life itself. Their eyes met and they held there together, as if each were in control of the other. The spare fuel container had stopped its gurgling, its contents emptied fully into the bike's tank. She slowly set it on the pavement, her eyes never leaving the buck's. She took a slow and soft step toward the deer. Then another. He stood his ground stoically with just a slight twitch of his short white tail. She got as close as an arm length away. His ears cocked backward, and his breath rushed from his nose with a snort, but he made no move to run.

She ached to touch him, to feel through her fingers his strength, his Earthliness. She wanted to push her face into his fur and smell his place in the universe and believe that she belonged to it too. Only she didn't dare, and after a moment the buck broke their eye contact, his attention called away perhaps by sounds she was not privileged to hear, and without ceremony he simply turned back to the tall grass from which he had emerged and disappeared into the world beyond her sight. She waited there by the edge of the road, her heart heavy, listening to his shuffling steps until she could hear them no more.

It was hours later, just outside Pittsburgh, when she saw the sign. The sky had begun to show the break of day and the colors and shapes of the surrounding landscape had been allowed to assert themselves again. Several cows, large black and white Holsteins from who knew where, had wandered onto the road and forced her to slow her speed and thread a cautious path through the space between the lumbering animals. If she hadn't been slowed down, if the night was still in command, she might have missed it. It was a small metal square, no bigger than a yard sign, stabbed into the shoulder concrete. *Alcoania City 1 Mile.*

She held the bike to under forty miles an hour and kept an eye on the shoulder. She'd been down this road enough to know there wasn't an Alcoania City when she was growing up. The sign itself was curious. It wasn't like the green and white bordered directional signs one would see almost anywhere in the world. It was the color of raw aluminum, like the skin of an airplane before it was polished or painted. The sign wasn't placed by a functioning Pennsylvania government, which by the look of things—the outed lights, the roaming cows, the wild grasses, the lack of police—likely didn't even exist anymore. The sign was put there by something else.

The next sign was larger and came into view just before the mile mark. *Alcoania City* and an arrow pointing right. The turnoff, maybe thirty yards ahead, was barely visible, more like a slice through a field of tall grass than a highway exit. She pulled off the blacktop of the interstate and rode the shoulder to the turn and stopped the bike. She checked her fuel. Less than half a tank, and the spare still riding behind her was empty. She'd be stopping soon at some point, whether she wanted to or not. From across the highway she heard another vehicle coming her way. After a moment an old red Chevy Camaro crested the slight rise in grade. The driver turned his head her way as he passed, and she heard the exhaust pop and spit when he lifted off the throttle. She put the bike in gear and made the turn.

The road, more like a trail, was a layer of crushed white rock spread across a path plowed through the field. It was barely wide enough for two cars. The Honda handled the gravel fine, absorbing the bumps with ease. There were more signs along the route, paced maybe fifty yards apart.

Technology Is Security.
Industry Is Liberty.
Alcoania Welcomes All Believers.

Well, *shit*, she thought. Hard to like those signs. But harder still to like the prospect of walking the rest of the way to Lancaster. If there was gas to be bought, the detour, and the whatever those signs meant, would be worth it.

After what seemed like a two-mile ride from the highway she came to a roadblock. A two-door gate of the same aluminum-colored metal—maybe twenty feet high—stretched across the gravel road. One door was swung wide and a man in a gray military style uniform stood in the opening. Beyond the guard Sarah could see an industrial park, including a series of large metal-clad buildings. Some looked to be office houses and others had the appearance of modern warehouse or factory buildings. She slowed the bike to a crawl as she got near and the guard smiled and waved her forward. She stopped the bike a few feet from the opening.

"Good morning," the guard said.

He was tall, light skinned, and armed. A pistol hung at his side and the barrel of a rifle was peeking over his left shoulder, its strap slung crossbody. The right breast pocket had a Velcro name patch that read Daniel. The left had an embroidered *Alcoania* in navy blue.

His greeting took Sarah by surprise. The pleasantness and normalness of it was a throwback. "Good morning," she managed. "I'm wondering if I could fill my tank here. I can pay."

"Sweet bike," he said with the enthusiasm of a teenager. "My brother had a 750. Thing was a bullet. You don't see many this clean anymore."

"Thanks. I try to take care of it," she said, hoping to end the conversation about motorcycles before it went to a place she couldn't travel.

"Well, it shows." He smiled widely. "What's your name?"

"Sarah Long."

"Okay, Sarah Long, welcome." He turned and pointed toward one of the big warehouse-looking buildings. "Pump is around Building Five. You take this center road here then make a right. There's a restaurant there too if you're hungry. Not much on the menu, but the eggs are good."

"That's great. I'm starved. Thank you."

"Sure thing. Pull up to that little house over there. They'll do a security check and then you're good to go."

She looked at the security shack. It was the real deal. "I see," she said as matter-of-factly as possible. She turned to glance behind her. A white pickup was making its way down the road toward the gate. She pivoted back to the guard. "Do you think there's fuel in Pittsburgh?"

"Cross this gate and you're in Pittsburgh."

"Alcoania is part of Pittsburgh?"

"Other way around."

The white pickup had gotten close enough to hear the gravel crunching under the tires. In a few seconds it would be right on her tail, and the guard would want her out of the way. Her options were shit. She'd never get past security, and if she didn't fill up, she might not get to Lancaster in time. Who was she kidding? Risking the road was her only real choice.

"Okay, thanks," she said while cranking the bike's front tire hard to the right. The Honda was heavy, and she was hardly the world's most experienced rider. The last thing she wanted to do was dump the thing and make getting out of this mess any more awkward or dangerous than it already was. Her plan was to scoot the bike backwards, attempt a three-point, and then blast back down the road before the pickup boxed her in. Until she heard his voice.

"Sarah?"

She turned to the sound of her name spoken like a key turning a lock she'd forgotten about. A second guard was at the opening now, standing at the edge of the gate still blocking half the road. His eyes were wide, a wry smile on the heavily freckled face beneath a messy mop of dirty blond hair. He had his sleeves rolled up, his arms outstretched, and there was no missing the familiar tattoos.

"Bobby?" she said in utter disbelief.

He left the gate and walked to the bike.

The first guard somehow managed to make his smile even wider. "You two know each other?"

"High school," Bobby said without turning away from Sarah. "First fuck. For both of us," he said, like that explained everything. Which maybe it did.

Sarah stayed on the Honda, her hands tight around the grips. She was too struck to move. Too struck to remember that Bobby saying something he wasn't supposed to say, saying what people just don't say out loud, spilling intimacies like a child tossing a cup of milk on the floor, was her cue to laugh. He leaned in and gave her a hug. She smelled his cigarettes on his clothes and a thousand memories avalanched through her mind.

"I thought you were in Hawaii," he said, amazement in his voice. "Then I figured—"

"I guess not," she said, cutting him off before the next obvious words, *you must have fried.*

He backed off his embrace and stood at the side of the bike beaming at her. "What are you doing here?"

She gave a small shrug. "I need fuel."

•

Bobby breezed her past the security shack, hopped on the back of the bike, and guided them to the restaurant. There were several booths available, but she sat at the counter. Bobby took the stool to her right and rested an elbow on the aluminum top. They ordered coffees and eggs with potatoes. She marveled at the familiarity of it all. Eggs, potatoes, a person who took her order. Coffee.

Coffee!

Salt and pepper shakers waiting at the ready. No seaweed. She wanted to stay at that counter on that stool for a thousand years.

Bobby looked ten years older than the boy she knew. It changed nothing. The old comfort clicked in like no time at all had passed, the comfort between two people who had shared important things. Marlboro Reds, Nirvana records, a town that grew too small.

"So what's going on with this place?" she asked him. "There are people here who smile. I thought I'd never see that again."

"Where else have you been? Since everything."

"It's complicated. I haven't been in America for a long time."

He looked at her intently for a moment, as if trying to see if her face had more to say than her words. He lit a cigarette and pushed the pack over to Sarah.

"No thanks."

He looked slightly hurt by her refusal. "Sarah Long has quit smoking. It is a new world."

"Why did you ask where else I've been?"

He took a draw and let the exhale go before answering. "I'm excited for you to see the contrast here."

"Okay," she smiled, "what's going on?"

"For one thing, we're not just stealing what's been left behind, like the kingdoms. We're making things. Real things. Power generators, electric motors, building materials, solar panels. There's a team working on a kind of internet. It'll only be as big as the old Pittsburgh limits for a while, but it's legit progress. We're trying to begin again, Sarah. To get back what we've lost. That sense of mission, it's made a difference for people."

The food came and she dug into her eggs ravenously. She closed her eyes when the first forkful hit her tongue. "Oh my God." She took another big forkful, and when she'd swallowed that she pushed on. "You called it a company. Is that what this place is, some kind of business?"

"You know how people used to call certain places company towns?"

"You mean like Hershey, with company housing, stores, currency? That kind of thing?"

"Think company *nation*."

"Jesus, Bobby."

"Don't look at me like that. You know the shit show out there. The old models failed us."

She forced a smile and nodded.

Bobby pulled another cigarette from his pack and tamped the tobacco end on the counter like he always did, and her thoughts went to that last sign she'd seen before the roadblock. *Alcoania Welcomes All Believers*. Bobby had that vibe about him. A conviction that tickled a worry on the hairs of her neck. She'd seen firsthand what happened when belief got power. Even the name *Alcoania* bothered her. Something about it felt contrived, false. When Bobby struck his match alight, a lightbulb lit for her as well, and the obviousness of it made her blush.

"I can't believe how long this took me," she said. "Alcoania... Alcoa! This place is the fucking aluminum company?"

He fanned away the smoke between them. "We're not making aluminum, Sarah. We're making the future." He swiveled his stool to face her. "We have raw materials, tools, skilled labor, scientists, engineers. As far as we know, there's no place else like it. And a few years from now, we'll be ready."

"Ready for what?"

"Ready to show the world a better way."

Sarah wanted to push back. She wanted to tell him to be careful about placing his hopes on the wings of angels. She scolded herself instead. Who was she to judge this place, or him? She barely understood his world. He seemed happy. After that, did the rest of it even matter?

"Well," she smiled, "it sounds exciting. I mean, you seem good. Really good."

"After the bombs I walked. I walked for two years. I'd work a little bit somewhere, then I'd walk again. At first it felt like freedom, you know? Hey, if the world was fucked then there's nothing I have to live up to, right? If success is wiped out as an option how can you fail? The weight of the world of my own making lifted off my shoulders."

"It didn't last, did it? The feeling."

"No. I don't think we're built to be nowhere, to be in between. To really be free. When I found this place, I found myself again. It's corny, I know. Especially from me, but I think everyone here feels that in some way."

She nodded.

He crushed his cigarette onto his plate. "Where are you going, Sarah?"

She squared her shoulders a little and tried to match his certainty. "I'm going to get Margaret."

"In Lancaster?"

"Yeah."

"You know for certain she's there?"

"No. But I think she is."

"Your mom?" He paused a moment. "Jack?"

She looked away to avoid his eyes, and how far back into her life they could see. "Can't say for sure. But no contact, so...you know."

He nodded respectfully, then signaled to the woman behind the counter for more coffee. "I can go with you," he offered. "It's safer. Funner."

She almost said yes. It almost came up and out. She literally had to push it back down. "No, I'll be fine. I have fuel for a bit now, and thanks to you I've eaten."

"Then get her and come back. There are jobs here. This is a good place, Sarah. Maybe the only good place for a long time to come."

She wanted to tell him everything. Where she'd been and what she'd seen. The marvelous and the ugly. She wanted it to be like it was when they were both kids who convinced each other they knew the most important secret there was. Thrashing and screwing and smoking and talking their way through every mystery, always ending up as stupid as when they started and too blind to recognize they couldn't see shit.

She smiled warmly. "I'm going to need fuel on the way back. Will you let us in?"

31

It was midafternoon when she made the exit from I-70 to southbound Ohio 37. The sky was clear, the sun bright, and the day was the warmest it had been since she'd arrived on the continent. All the while since leaving Alcoania she'd felt lighter, refreshed. The relative calm and order of the place had been like a tonic. For the first time since leaving the ship she wasn't panicked about having her back to a door. Or maybe it was just Bobby. Whatever it was, she was more herself than she'd been in a long time. Now that she was close, literally ten minutes from the edge of Lancaster, it started to feel like it all might have been worth it.

The fairgrounds came into view. The red ag buildings and cattle barn stood in high contrast to the sixty-five acres of grass that was still green. In a normal year around this time the grounds would be packed with tents, cars, and people. Lancaster's county fair was always the last in the state. "The best for last," everyone called it. Now there were tidy mounds of garbage where the cars would be parked, looking like a cluster of crazy-hued teepees, and small groups of men stood around fires along the dirt track that ringed the center of the grounds. Some turned their heads to watch her. In the far distance, in the west field, a man walked toward Main Street while two dogs ran ahead.

The patch of ground where the old grandstand had stood before it burnt down on the morning of her sixteenth birthday was still empty and waiting.

That particular memory didn't sting like it once did. She heard no guns, no screams. The fact that the grounds were still recognizable at all, that they hadn't become the floor of a depraved tent city, or a battlefield, sent her heart soaring. She rolled by on the Honda and could almost hear the sounds of the monster trucks and the combine races that filled the town during festival days.

Sarah had plenty of reasons for leaving Lancaster when she had. The thievery of her childhood by Jack, and the self-incrimination she had lashed around herself with barbed wire, those were the big things. But there were a thousand hurts and disappointments that came along at no extra charge that helped propel her exit. Things she thought only escape could exorcise. If she never saw Lancaster again, she had said to herself then, she couldn't care less. She realized now just how wrong she had been.

Having the town open up in front of her was like falling into her own bed after months away. Driving back on its streets again, watching 37 become High Street again, making the right on Main again, she was almost grateful for the pain Lancaster had shown her. It was a part of her. Perhaps the best of her. If the town had been destroyed, usurped and repurposed in some unrecognizable way, she wasn't sure how she'd handle that loss. But it was still here. It felt like a sign that Margaret was too.

The little house on Zane Avenue where she had spent most of her life faced the street looking exhausted and slightly out of plumb. The shrubs and grasses were unruly and overgrown. The big ash tree on the parkway had died at some point, its branches bare and coated with lichen and moss. Someone had spray painted *fuck* across the blue front door in drippy gold. The clapboards still wore the same pukey beige color they always had, though they were even more desperately in need of a good scraping and painting. The gutters had even larger weeds and saplings sprouting from their neglected troughs. Overall, though, the house itself looked true to the pictures in her mind. Another good sign.

The driveway that ran under the carport was empty. That meant nothing. If Margaret had a car, she'd have parked in the back. Given everything, Sarah certainly would have. She made the left into the drive and rolled to the backyard. Two young boys, maybe six or seven, filthy and thin, were in the yard next door. They stopped whatever they were doing and watched with stunned faces as she parked the gleaming bike. She gave a small wave, but they didn't return the gesture. After staring for another beat, they ran up the wooden porch steps and into their house with a loud slam of the door. Sarah's backyard was overgrown and as downtrodden as the front. Jack's shed was listing badly to one side. On the grass between the house and the shed, a black Cadillac SUV was parked.

Okay.

She'd miss the Honda, but if that would be their ride back east, it would certainly be a lot more comfortable than riding two-up on the bike.

She had no key, so she knocked on the back door. It creaked open without resistance. Sarah's stomach went cold.

"Margaret?" she called tentatively from the porch. "Are you there?"

No response.

Fuck.

"Margaret?"

"Sarah! Yes," finally came from somewhere inside. Her sister's voice, with trouble in the pitch of it.

Sarah pushed the door wide and moved fast into the kitchen. She stopped there, stunned by what she saw. Margaret was straight ahead in the little living room on one of the kitchen chairs. Her cheeks were swollen, her lower lip split and bloodied, and she was wearing something crazy over her sweater. A vest bulging with odd bundles of gray stuck with wires. Sarah knew what that vest was. A sharp pin pushed decisively into Sarah's balloon of hope. It took everything she had to keep from vomiting.

The last time Sarah had seen Margaret she was at the stove stirring oatmeal. She looked so much like their mother standing there. The same shoulder-length cut of brunette hair, the same slender figure, and when she turned to Sarah and saw the suitcase parked at Sarah's feet, Margaret's eyes took on their mother's precise look of sad defeat. Margaret turned back to her pot on the stove. Sarah waited for her to say something, to ask something. To throw the fucking pot at her. But Margaret just kept stirring. Sarah picked up her bag and walked out.

"Margaret, what's happened?"

"Stay there," Margaret said.

A man walked into her view. He must have been standing by the fireplace, where Sarah wouldn't have seen him from the kitchen door. He held up his hand so Sarah could see the cylindrical device in his palm.

"Dead-man switch," he said flatly. "A remote dead-man switch."

Sarah worked to understand as much as she could as quickly as she could. None of this made any sense. Margaret was wide eyed and tearing.

"I'm sorry," Margaret said meekly.

All Sarah could muster was a single word. "What?"

"I'm sorry," Margaret said loudly this time, her voice filled with desperation.

"Not you." Sarah nodded toward the man. "*You*! What did you say?"

"I said if you kill me, we all die. Your sister, or whatever she is to you, is wearing enough C-4 to level half this block. The switch in my hand works in reverse. If my thumb comes off it, say, because I fall asleep, or my concentration is distracted, or I'm dead, Margaret here is blown to shreds. Get it now?"

"Why are you doing this?" Sarah asked, reeling.

"Because I don't think a pretty please will get me what I want."

"What is it you want?"

"I want your guns. The ones, you know," he pointed to the ceiling with his free hand and twirled his fingers, "from outer space."

"I don't know what you're talking about."

The man produced a knife from his coat pocket and pushed the blade up against Margaret's neck. She squirmed and a thin line of blood formed at the bottom of the blade.

"Stop it! You'll kill her!" Sarah shouted. She pulled a duster from her jacket and pointed it at the man.

"See, that's what I'm looking for," the man said. "I saw that gun in a movie once. The one your French friend showed me. You've got talent."

Sarah swallowed hard, some of the pieces falling into place. "Did you hurt her?"

"Your friend? No."

"You're lying."

"I truly don't think she felt any pain. I'm no doctor, but I am a professional, and that's my professional opinion."

Sarah's mind put the last of the puzzle together. Giving this man her guns would be bad. Very bad. "I can't give you this gun."

"You can. It's easy. Just slide it over. Along with that bag of yours. Nothing to it."

"Let her go first."

"Not going to happen. I couldn't even if I wanted to. Once this rig is armed, it takes someone who knows what they're doing to disarm it. I'm not that someone."

"Then you're an idiot. I could leave. Then what?"

"Then I'll tie poor Margaret here to the chair, get a safe distance away, and release the trigger." He pressed the knife against Margaret's throat again, drawing more blood.

Sarah was thinking fast now. He was betting on her being one kind of person. Somehow, she had to be someone different. "I've spent the last three years certain she was dead. I've managed to live with it."

Margaret gave a look that nearly broke Sarah's heart.

"But this time the blood will be on your hands."

"There's a lot you don't know," she said.

He smiled. "Same could be said of you."

"Maybe I'll kill you both," she said with as much cool as possible. "Turn you, the vest, everything to dust."

He looked genuinely surprised. "You know, honestly, that was not a possibility I'd thought about."

She believed him. He didn't look the genius type.

"A knife goes up against someone's throat," he said, "and the other guy backs down. In nine out of ten cases, that's what happens. This Mexican standoff thing we're doing here, this only happens in the movies. In real life, people break, and they do it fast. I've seen it a thousand times. I've seen black-hearted men, degenerates with nothing to live for, crumble in moments like this. That said, let's do the pros and cons of your idea. I know what that gun can do. So on the pro side, if your plan works, I'm dead and you get to walk away. On the con side, Margaret's dead too and you've come all this way for nothing. That's the best-case scenario. What if your plan *doesn't* work? What if your ray gun doesn't vape the C-4, but sets it off instead? Then we all die. Some neighbors too. Those kids next door for sure."

Shit, not as dumb as he looks.

"Shut up," she said, her face going hot. A trickle of sweat ran down the back of her neck.

"Sarah, it's only a few guns," he said smoothly. "In the big, shitty, picture of this fucked-up dream none of us can wake from, what possible difference could a few guns make?"

Sarah's hand shook. She looked at Margaret for a long minute. In another lifetime ago, in the tiny bedroom they shared together in this very house, when Jack made his first visit, Margaret had seen everything. She didn't scream. She didn't try to push Jack off her little sister. She didn't run for her mother. She just lay in the twin bed next to Sarah's, her covers brought up close to her chin, the fear on Margaret's face then, with those big, disbelieving watery eyes, looked exactly like the fear Sarah saw now. Jack had hurt her as much as he'd hurt Sarah. She'd never known it or hadn't had room in her own heavy heart to imagine it. She saw it now in its awful entirety and the chasm of their torn sisterhood ripped through her. Now it was Margaret's turn to be under assault, and it was Sarah's doing.

She sat down on the floor and wept.

32

They stood upon the glass walkway that ran along the dock numbered 18. The little transport hovered in its hold looking exactly as it did before it was torn apart.

"I think it might be my best work, if I say so myself."

"Really?"

"Really." Yorn motioned to a spot at the nose. "A point-two-eight spherical cannon."

Trin made sure to look impressed. "It's uncanny. I can't even see it."

"Of course not. It has to be behind the cloak until it's needed. We've added a movable section to the skin's mirror matrix. Completely imperceptible to the naked eye. You hit the trigger," Yorn beamed, "and things change."

"Let's see."

"Not here at the dock. Not with the plasma generator charged. Very dangerous."

"Let's go for a ride then."

"Sorry?"

"Let's take her out. You and me. Target practice. We'll find something we can shoot. Safely, of course. It'll be fun."

"No way. I fix them. I don't fly them. Doesn't agree with me."

"You live on a spaceship, Yorn."

"Space flight is one thing. Atmospheric flight, the turbulence, wind shear, especially in little crafts like this, makes me barf."

"How'd you get through Academy?"

"My father was on the board."

"For fuck's sake. Whatever, we're going. I'll keep it slow and steady for you."

"Trust me, XO, this is not a good idea."

"It's a great idea. We should celebrate. Get in the ship, engineer," he said amiably. "It's an order."

Yorn frowned but Trin could see he'd resigned to the idea.

"Let me at least get something for my stomach," he said.

In truth, celebrating was the last thing on Trin's mind. He was wrestling with two seemingly intractable problems at once. There was still no sign of Sarah. It was as if she had never been on the ship at all, like their time together had been the mindfuck of a dream, vivid and persuasive and captivating but only until he'd awoken, at which point it simply dissolved away and was gone so completely even the most strident efforts couldn't bring it back. Then there was The Circle problem, which he wanted to believe was the same problem.

It was The Circle that had put the *Kalelah* in the state it was, half dead on a half-dead planet. It had seen threats emerge to the faith that appeared in its eyes to be so egregious, so fucking intolerable, that only a tragedy beyond reckoning could right them. The Guide Service, so The Circle had charged, was polluted. Sullied by the steady and toxic creep of the worst kind of soot—progress. As the human universe spread and found itself further and further physically from Origen, further from the center of the faith, exceptions had been made, allowances, excuses, and most insidious of all, deviations from the Plan. The weaknesses in the system, the rot at its core, The Circle had claimed, had to be punished. It was time to make a stand, and it had chosen the *Kalelah* as the place to make it. Had it cared even a little about the planet the *Kalelah* was guiding? Not one fucking bit. For the sake of purity, it had been willing to turn everything to shit.

A bug was programed into the check clock, the specific string of instructions within the Code that controlled the length of individual Skips. At the worst possible time in the Guide process, a Skip that was designed to last a few thousand years went on for one hundred and twenty thousand. The Circle had known what might happen. It was counting on it. Praying on it. The Circle had wanted a failed Delivery. It had wanted the seed population to survive without Guidance, to deviate in unimaginable ways, simply so it could kill them to make a point. The Circle wanted to shock the Guide Service to its senses; to bring the flock back home; to inspire through tragedy a redoubling of commitment to the old order. The original order.

The Circle had been willing to do all that and more. Which meant, Trin knew, if it had survived the war against it, like Forent said, it would be willing to do anything still. Anything it could. It would take Sarah if it could. It would export tech off the ship to maintain a low simmering holy war if it could. And it would corrupt a man like Yorn Darnol if it could.

Trin had to know if it had.

Two minutes later they were cruising over the moat. Trin kept his word and held the transport to half speed. When they got over the rock wall he nosed up and the tent settlement spread out beneath them.

"You usually follow the river," Yorn pointed out.

"Usually."

Trin rolled the ship hoping to change the subject. Yorn groaned.

"Not bad," Trin said. "I expected it to feel heavier, slower. But I can't say I felt any real difference at all. I mean, if you hadn't told me we were carrying weapons, I wouldn't have known it."

Yorn had lost most of the color in his face. "Thank you," he said without his usual air of self-congratulation.

"You probably had to compensate for the change in weight."

"Yeah," Yorn said distractedly, leaving on the table the windy explanation Trin expected. Instead, the engineer pulled a geo float and traced the transport's route along the data with his finger. He leaned forward closer to the windscreen and checked back with the float. He did this several times. "Oh God."

"What, you're sick already?" Trin said.

"Do you have any idea where you're going?"

"Of course I do."

"We're headed precisely toward the missile launch mark."

Trin glanced at the float. "Change of scenery, that's all."

Yorn swallowed hard. Trin could see small beads of sweat emerge on the engineer's brow.

"You're provoking them," Yorn said warily.

Trin glanced at Yorn. "I'm flying, that's all. What do you know about *them* anyway?"

Yorn was silent for a minute. "I know as much as you. They can find you if they want to."

"If they know to."

Yorn paused again. "My point is, why ask for trouble?" he finally said.

"Well, I'm not asking for trouble. I'm begging for it."

Yorn's level of discomfort grew steadily easier to see. He fidgeted in his seat and wiped a rolling bead of sweat away with a finger. "You said, *safely*. We'd find something to shoot, and we'd do it safely."

"I'm just testing the system."

"There are smarter ways to test."

"I don't want a smarter way. I want a way that's going to tell me the truth."

Yorn's face flushed.

A spot appeared on the float and an instant later a voice from the comm. "18, *we have a missile launch along your path at six-zero-seven degrees. Closure in twenty-one seconds. Repeat,* 18, *we have a missile launch*."

"Wish granted," Yorn said darkly.

"Copy, *Kalelah*," Trin answered. "We'll let you know when we have visual."

"*No need for visual confirmation*, 18. *Time to come home*."

"Copy," Trin said. "Soon."

He pushed the throttle forward and kept straight on a path toward the missiles. Yorn studied the float as the dot that represented the missiles and the dot that represented the transport moved slowly toward each other.

Yorn panicked. "What are you *doing*?"

"Trusting you."

"Are you out of your mind?"

"Don't ask me that, Yorn. You'll break my heart."

A proximity alarm blared. Yorn threw his hands to his ears. Trin turned down the alarm to a low hum.

"18," from the comm, "*you are ordered to reverse course immediately*."

Trin switched off the comm and there was only the hum of the alarm, the muffled wind against the transport's skin, and the freaked-out pace of Yorn's breathing.

"There they are." Trin tapped the windscreen where the glow of the missiles' engines came into view. "Okay, Yorn. Here's the situation. There's still time to reverse course. But not fucking much. Say evade and we'll evade. I'd rather trust you, though. With every fiber of my being, I'd rather trust you, Yorn."

Yorn turned to Trin, puzzled, scared, panicked. He quickly turned back to the windscreen. Even Trin was shaken by the sight of the missiles and the transport racing toward each other. This would be a fucking *stupid* death.

"Make the call!" Trin shouted. "Do we kill these missiles? Or do we turn and run because we know for certain it's our only choice? Three seconds, Yorn! Two...one..."

Even as Yorn kept his attention on the insanity barreling toward them, Trin saw his fear and panic be interrupted by a sudden click of understanding. It was only a flash. In a blink the confusion left his eyes, replaced by a shadow of betrayal. In that moment Trin got the answer he'd been seeking.

Yorn took a breath, and with eyes and face held straight ahead, he calmly said, "Kill them."

Trin pushed the transport into range and hit the trigger on the duster. The windscreen went white with the flash of plasma jet. A second later the sky before them was open. The missiles were gone. Yorn let out a grunt of relief, squeezed his eyes shut tightly, and breathed hard, his chest visibly moving under his jumpsuit. Trin pulled the power back, banked the transport, and pointed the ship on course for the *Kalelah*.

"You asshole," Yorn muttered after he'd caught his breath.

"I'm sorry. I had to know."

Yorn sat looking straight ahead for a long time. His jaw was clenching. The man was stewing. Trin couldn't blame him. He felt badly about the deception, about letting his anger corrode his loyalties. But somewhere in Trin's gut he knew he'd soon be facing more than a few easily killed missiles and there could be no room for doubt.

At last, Yorn broke the uncomfortable silence. "I told you there are smarter ways to test."

"You did."

"Whatever and whoever is making it possible for those missiles to find you, I have nothing to do with it. If I make you something, if I tell you it works, it works."

"Understood."

"It's an insult, frankly."

"Agreed."

"I don't know why I do this. Why I put up with a constant barrage of insults. It's maddening."

Trin let the man cool down another degree and made a peace offering. "Because you're a better man than most."

Yorn gave a small nod of agreement and belched. "That's true. Still, it's a mystery."

"You don't look well."

"I told you about me and flying. Turbulence. Atmosphere in general. But do you listen?" He belched again. "No."

"Do not hurl in my ship."

"A double fuck you to that. *Sir.*"

"Fair enough."

"That's right."

They rode back the rest of the way in silence. It was helpful, in a process of elimination way, to have the Yorn checkbox ticked. The engineer would smart about this crazy move for a bit, but he'd get over it. He was clever enough to know it wasn't personal. For Trin though, it would be a long time before he got over anything. This latest missile attack only cemented for him the danger The Circle posed. There was a system in operation. And it needed shutting down. Quickly.

After he found Sarah.

The sun was low in the sky and the land once called Russia was bathed in gold. The color danced and flashed on windows as they passed, and the trees cast long shadows to expand their dominion. From his perspective in the transport, high above the buildings occupied by despair and the streets clogged with danger, it was painfully beautiful.

•

Wildei was waiting for him in the CC. She stood by his workstation, arms crossed, her blaze of red hair softly haloed by the overhead light. He expected to see the Stern Lecture Look on her face, the one strapping cannons to a transport would definitely earn. It wasn't that look at all. His heart sank.

"I'm afraid I have some bad news," she said.

Trin steeled himself for the blow.

"The search party has found nothing," she continued. "It's like as you've said...she's simply vanished."

He wished he was surprised. There was little he'd put past The Circle now. The worst of it for him was that he knew firsthand how a body might disappear aboard the *Kalelah*. It scared the shit of out him.

"There's more," Wildei said. "When was the last time you fused?"

"Yesterday probably, why?"

"Did you notice anything different? Anything out of the ordinary?"

Trin shrugged. "I don't know." It was hard for him to concentrate. "She's a little sluggish, maybe. Or not. I'm pretty fucked up myself."

"She's not sluggish, Trin. She's *evasive*."

"What?"

"On the subject of Sarah, she dodges. I'm sure of it. About you as well."

"She can't *dodge*, Wildei. Not if you ask a direct question."

"That's what I thought too. But she walked away from my query twice, took me off topic into other matters of the ship. That's weird, Trin."

"That's her primary directive—the ship. That's her world."

"When she's working on her own, yes. If she's working with me, or you, or anyone else, we become the primaries. That's the pecking order. It's subtle, and I didn't even realize she'd done it until after. Her distractions feel purposeful, like she's consciously manipulating the lines of inquiry away from where I started them, at least when it comes to the search for Sarah. It makes me worry even more about that thing between you two."

Not this shit again.

It was this way with Wildei and the Code. Next to Trin, she was probably the ship's best Diver. But it was always a competition with her. He didn't care for a second what she did with the Code, all he wanted was the same from her.

"There's no *thing* with me and the Code," he snapped. "Look, we both have our own ways of working with her. I know what I'm doing, and I know what she's doing. Can't we leave it at that?"

"I'm not sure she can, Trin. That's my point. Something's different about her. I can feel it. It's not like I'm getting responses that are empty because there's no data, or I'm not asking the right bloody questions. I know how to work with her as well as you do. I get the sense she's literally hiding something. Something important. Something she's willing to break the covenant between her and us over."

Her cheeks had flushed nearly to the color of her hair. He knew he should dial it down. She was the captain, his friend, and as worried about Sarah as he was. But she pushed a button, and he was too fucking mad at the world not to push back.

"Maybe the problem is you're swimming out of your depth. It's easy to get fooled by the complexity of her. To forget that the only decisions she makes are the ones we've allowed her to make. It's easy to want her to be something she's not."

Wildei waited a second before letting him have it. He knew it was coming.

"My God, you're so full of yourself you can't even see when you're pulling the wool over your own eyes. I know about how you two talk, what she calls you. All the code Divers do."

"That doesn't mean I don't know what she is." Trin wanted to stop there, to rethink his position, to say what he might say if he wasn't being pushed by a force in his head that was ready tear the ship apart. He did the stupid thing instead. "A machine."

Wildei blinked at that one, a brief wince, like someone hearing a particularly nasty bit of profanity. "You want to lie to yourself, darling? Fine. Don't lie to me. She's an ancient thing, Trin. As old as the Service itself. She's no less a definition of life as *you* are or I am. As intelligent as you are, as connected to her as you think you are, it's wrong to believe you can fully understand her. It's wrong to believe that because she does our bidding she does so without bias, or feelings. She *feels,* Trin, like you do, like I do, like any of us, whether you want to admit it or not. It's not a pretense for her, or programming. It's real. And you know what that can mean."

Oh, fuck it. If he was going dig his own grave, he was going to push his shovel in good and hard.

"She can be a bitch sometimes?"

One, two, three...*boom*.

"It means, you pathetic child, we have no idea what she's capable of."

Wildei walked away without even a word about the cannons. For a brief moment it felt like a victory. A conversation about arming a transport without her approval and ignoring an order to reverse course would have been particularly one-sided. He would have no good argument in his favor. Nothing, in fact, to say by way of even explanation. She, on the other hand, would have every right to slam her captain's knee right between his legs. Which was exactly what she'd do.

It might have felt better than watching her walk away.

33

Could she grab his hand in such a way that she would keep his thumb depressed on the bomb's trigger while killing him with her other? This question ran through her head a thousand times, along with the thousand potential answers, as her captor patted her down. After all, she had both her hands, two knees, and until he found the last of her stash, a weapon or two.

He was a big man, six feet at least, broad in the shoulders with a wide nose and dark hair that went a deep blue in the light. American Indian, maybe. He had the movements and confidence of someone who knew how to handle himself, and he was smart to have pushed her up against a wall for the pat down. It made clear to her the strength she'd have to overcome. She chose to let this happen. For now.

Though reduced to one hand, he made pretty thorough and quick work of it, retrieving two dusters, her last laser cutter, a knife, and the Bridge Maker she'd taken from Trin's storage wall. He'd been working from her ankles up and he'd stopped at her breasts. He gave them a long, hard look. She could sense the gears spinning in his head. There were no obvious bulges beyond the two she had with or without a coat packed with gear. His hands were right there, poised to feel. Or not. His eyes met hers for a brief moment and she thought she saw a subtle nod of his head. He moved on to her arms.

Didn't see that coming.

Not that she wanted his hand on her, but he was good with beating a woman swollen and strapping her to a bomb...but a quick feel was somehow, what—not cool?

When he'd finished, Sarah did a mental inventory of what he took and what she still possessed. Everything lethal or matter reducing was gone. The damn communicator was gone. She had nothing she could use to subdue him or free Margaret. They'd both have to endure whatever was next. That was clear. And frightening as hell. Still, his odd courtesy toward her breasts had left one tiny pocket unexplored, and it might contain a sliver of a chance to get the guns back. A *thin* sliver.

They went out to the big SUV parked in the back. The two kids next door were nowhere in sight. It had gotten dusky out and she saw a few lights from nearby windows, but no one in them to witness what was happening. What good it might have done anyway, she didn't know. He kept Margaret close to him and forced Sarah to pack the car. There wasn't much to do. Just her bag to place in the cargo hold. She marveled that he hadn't tied or taped her hands and feet. Why bother? He was handicapped by the dead-man's switch. He couldn't really handle two tied-up women. Besides, he already knew Sarah wasn't going to leave her sister—their bond at least as good as duct tape. She'd shown him that. If she were to run, he'd leave Margaret behind, drive off, let the vest blow, and still have what she suspected he really wanted anyway. The weapons. So why were Margaret and she still alive? None of the possibilities gave her any comfort.

He reached into his coat pocket, pulled out a fob, and tossed it to her.

"You're driving," he said. "If some lunatic ambushes us I don't want to have to do too many things at once."

"Where are we going?"

"You'll find out."

She closed the hatch and saw the New York plate. Her mind flashed to Solli, his kindly wrinkled face and his words of caution. *Stay away from New York*. She heard again the gunshot in the distance as she and Gabi ran through the park behind Liberty, the one she worried had killed him. When would the insanity stop? She couldn't help but think it might never.

"Take 70 eastbound," he said. "I'm guessing you know the way to the freeway."

Sarah backed out of the driveway, seeing Margaret's terrorized face in the back seat, and knew for certain she'd never see this house or Lancaster again. She felt stupid now and naïve for feeling like this town had ever given her anything other than heartbreak.

It was fully dark when they reached I-70. The moon was no larger than the previous night's and again the shadows crept in close to the vehicle, shrinking the landscape to a cone-shaped world of LED light. Two headlamps, though, were better than the bike's one had been, and she felt safer as they rode. Strangely, having this man in the car helped too. She knew he was a murderer, but she knew, too, that she and her sister were meant to be kept alive, at least as long as it took to get to New York. If something were to happen on the road, it was better to have this asshole along.

"What's your name?" she asked.

"Kino."

"What kind of name is that?"

"A short one."

She kept quiet after that. Two hours out, right after they'd made the merge onto I-76, they passed a polished sign for Alcoania, a twin she figured to the one she'd seen before on the other side of the road. She let the mile go by and looked left. A soft glow of light floated into the sky a few miles from the big, empty road. She thought about Bobby, his smile and his offer for her to come and stay in that nearly normal place. A place that had given him hope. Had he been thinking about her since she'd left? The question instantly shamed her. To even imagine another life when Trin was likely going crazy back on the *Kalelah*, when their child was sitting with her now, next to a murderer.

The tears came without warning. *Dammit.* She'd already cried once in front of this man. She tried to will the tears dry. They continued anyway. After a mile she gave up. The crying, it occurred to her, could be put to good use.

She pretended to search inside her coat for something to wipe her face. Not a big show, only enough to open the overlooked breast pocket and grab the tiny recorder bot inside within a curl of her middle finger. She kept the tears coming and brought her hand with the bot in it to her face to stem the tide. As she wiped her eyes and nose gently, she said seven words softly out loud in Origen. She felt him looking at her as she spoke.

"Do I need to hear that alien shit?"

"It's a prayer," she said, keeping her eyes on the road, her hand to her face, not daring to see if he believed her or not. "And it's Latin, for your information."

"Doesn't sound like Latin to me."

"And you don't look Catholic to me."

He turned back to the windshield. "Whatever."

She glanced in the rearview mirror to see how Margaret was doing, to see if there was any reason to worry that she might say something to accidently derail Sarah's story. Margaret, however, seemed to have withdrawn entirely from what was happening around her. Sarah doubted she'd even heard a word of the conversation in the front seats.

"It asks God to watch over the ones I love," she finally said. "Roughly translated."

Kino kept his eyes on the road ahead. "Good luck with that."

She let another minute go by.

"You mind if I open a window?" she asked, taking one last dab at a tear.

He gave her a quick look. She did her best to appear in desperate need of a little fresh air.

"Knock yourself out."

The glass rolled down and the wind and tire noise crashed into the car like thunder. She cracked the rear window on the other side of the cabin to balance the air pressure and lower the din. After a beat Sarah put her hand out and let her palm ride the wind, casually unfurling her middle finger, and the little bot left her hand and took to the air.

The actual and exact translation of Sarah's seven-word prayer was:

Starting.

Sound.

Picture.

High follow.

Transmit Home.

34

The prayer chains hung from the chapel ceiling like slender stalks of silver reed growing down from the sky. Trin took his usual seat on the aisle just behind the front row. As a boy there had never been a need to force him to pray. He'd looked forward to his time in chapel, in fact. Prayer had been how he'd coped with the ridiculous burdens of the adults in his life, the scientists and teachers, and even his parents.

He had been a curiosity. He understood that. Nevertheless, the constant questioning and tests and endless probing had felt unfair. They had taken valuable time away from the things he loved. It was all justified, the adults had said, because these efforts were entirely for his benefit. Only by understanding his special abilities, they had all claimed with warm eyes and big smiles, could he make the most of them. Even if that were true, it hadn't seemed worth it.

In chapel, though, Trin had found respite. There he'd been free to think what he wanted, to say to God, the ultimate adult, what he wanted to say. And what he had loved most about God was His absolute silence.

He put his hands in the heavy grips suspended from the ends of the chains and the cold of the metal seeped into the muscles around his fingers and palms. He spread his hands and pulled on the chains, letting them carry as much of his weight as was possible. The stretch across his chest and shoulders pushed a grunt of relief from his throat. He looked up at the ceiling, at the geometric latticework of metal that connected each set of chains to one another and the whole of them to a single vector in the center of the room, like a perfectly proportioned spider web of silver silk. On the other side of the ceiling a vast network of polished metal straps ran throughout the ship between floors and walls and linked each chapel's vector point to a single gleaming metal spire at the top of the ship, just aft of the pilot's house. The Reach, it was called. It, and countless others like it throughout the universe, acted as conduit to the cosmic threads of God's mind.

If he were still talking with God, there'd be a lot he'd have to say and more he'd have to ask. That conversation, one sided as it always was, had ended when he'd seen the damage the Correction had been allowed to do. Did it have God's approval beforehand? At this point, he'd rather not know. Either answer would be the worst possible thing he could hear.

Still, he loved the chains, the architecture, and the quiet of a chapel. It had become a place where he could figure things out. The thing he had to figure out now was what Wildei had told him about the Code. He had fought her on it, not because he was sure she was wrong, but because he'd needed a fight. Unfortunately, he didn't always pick the right time, or place, or person, to fight. It was time to fix that. Time to give her argument the attention it deserved.

Trin closed his eyes and let his head fall back. He repositioned his knees on the cushioned floor and let the grips bite into his hands and the chains work the anger out of his body. When he felt the peace take over, he began his work. He replayed in his mind, one by one, every Code Dive he'd had since Sarah went missing. It took most of the night and left him exhausted.

It was worth it.

35

It was the thick of the early morning and night still ruled. There had been some traffic in both directions, though nothing approaching anything comparable to life on the road as she'd remembered. For the last half hour or so, there'd been no cars or trucks at all in either direction. Only their SUV and its powerful bomb in the back seat.

Even under the anxious circumstances of her capture, it had been hard at times for Sarah to keep her eyes open. Those moments cautioned her to keep a watch on the kidnapper. Twice, in fact, she'd had to jab him in the arm when she noticed his eyes close. If she fell asleep it would be bad. If he did, it would be over.

"Time for a break," she announced.

The kidnapper looked at her suspiciously. "Keep driving."

"Sorry. I can't use a bottle. We need to stop."

"We're only a few hours out. You can hold it."

"Look, if I was going to try something stupid, don't you think I'd have done it by now? Where are we going to go?"

He looked out the window, but she could see his jaw working. He was entertaining the idea.

"Okay," he said, "here's how we do this. You pull over, stop the car, keep the lamps on, and give me the fob. Then you two go out in front of the vehicle where I can keep an eye on you. You run into the grass I'll blow you up. You start running period, I'll blow you up. Deal?"

"Really? You're going to watch us pee?"

He shrugged. "It wasn't my idea to stop."

Sarah slowed down and steered the big car to the side of the road. She followed the kidnapper's instructions and she and Margaret walked round to the front of the vehicle, undid their pants, and squatted. Margaret's eyes were downcast, her face an expression of pure sadness. It wasn't the best time to start a conversation, but Sarah didn't know when there'd be another.

"I shouldn't have left you when I did," she said. "I should have stayed. None of this would have happened."

Margaret didn't answer right away. She sucked her upper lip under her teeth. The wet in her eyes was lit to gold by the yellow of the car's headlamps. "No," Margaret finally answered, her voice hoarse and phlegmy. "You had to go. We always knew you would." Margaret's tears spilled over. "I'm just so sorry."

"For this? This isn't your fault. It's mine."

"Not this. Everything." She wiped her nose and took a deep breath. "I'm your big sister, Sarah. I was supposed to protect you. But it was always the other way around. From the moment you could walk it was the other way around. I never wanted you to know how much I needed you, how much I depended on you. That's why when you did things I didn't have the courage to do, like date a certain kind of boy, or dream of being someplace else, I'd shut you out. I'd punish you for it. I had no right, Sarah."

"It's okay, Margie."

"No, it's not. It's not okay. Look at us. Look at this...mess."

"We're alive. And we're going to stay that way. You have to believe me."

"I'm scared, Sarah. And so tired of being scared."

"We're both scared."

"Ha," she said softly with a sad smile. "You've never been scared. Not really. Not like me." She looked out to some point beyond Sarah, some point past the influence of the car's headlights. "Maybe I should run. You know? He can't let go of the trigger until I'm a safe distance, right? He said that. He'll have to wait. Then this will be over."

"Margie, no, that's crazy. Besides, you dying won't end this."

Margaret grabbed Sarah by the shoulders. "It'll help you if I run. Don't you see? You won't have the bomb to worry about. You'll have a better chance against him."

Sarah took her sister's hands in hers. "We have a better chance together. We're supposed to be together. That's why I'm here. Do you understand?"

Margaret took another deep breath and offered an unconvincing, "Sure."

"We should get back in the car now. Can you do that?" Margaret nodded and stood up to button her clothes.

Before Sarah slid back into the front seat, she looked up for the bot she hoped was flying overhead. She saw the infinite blackness of the sky and the false hope of the stars. The recorder, though, was far too small and the night much too dark. She'd simply have to believe it was there, doing its job. She knew for certain the signals from recorders like the bot following her could travel miles with perfect fidelity. In her own experience in monitoring the planes, at least one hundred miles. While those were slightly different units, the underlying tech was the same. Could the signal travel nearly five thousand miles? She had no idea. NASA was able to send signals from Mars, and the *Kalelah* had made technological miracles seem ordinary. Pulling floats from thin air, transports that could disappear, an arc the size of a small city that could sustain life through the time and distance of intergalactic travel. The bot was the best shot she had. Her trick now was to stay alive long enough for it to work.

She had just navigated the series of quick exits and merges around Harrisburg that wound them to I-78 and the last leg into the Kingdom when she saw the lights. They were faint, mere dots hovering over the entire width of the highway in both directions and darting about like quick moving fireflies. At first she thought they might be figments of her imagination. Road fatigue. She glanced over to the kidnapper to see if he saw them as well. He had.

"Slow it down," he said.

"You see them too, the lights?"

"I swear, you better be worth this shit."

"What are they?" she asked.

"Trouble."

"What kind of trouble?"

"Bad trouble. Mercs or bandits. Doesn't really make a difference which."

"We should cross over—get to the other side."

"Won't help." He turned around in his seat to look out the rear window. "The road curves behind us so it's hard to see, but if there's a block ahead of us, you can be sure they put one in behind us. They're not idiots. They'll seal it off between exits."

The lights grew larger and more articulate. It became clear they were men with flashlights.

"Can we blow through?" she asked.

"The road will be chained with spikes."

"I have gold in the bag. A lot of it. We'll pay them."

"No," he said, the sound of experience in his voice. "They'll take everything."

That this Kino asshole had her guns made her sick to her stomach, but at least she still had her eye on them, which meant there was always the chance, however slight, she'd get them back. These bandits, though, or whatever they were, if they got them, who knew where'd they go.

"Now listen to me," he said. He looked at her with the same look he had during her pat down, when he went from her hips and stomach to her arms, bypassing her chest. "When I said they'll take everything, everything included you. If this goes sideways, they'll kill Margaret because they have to. They'll kill me because I'm worthless to them. But you? They'll make you beg them to kill you."

She studied his face and looked for something to trust about it. She hated this creep. But now, for better or worse, she needed him.

"Then what do we do?" she asked.

He pulled his gun from his coat. "Stop the car."

She stopped and the kidnapper opened his door. "Pop the hatch and remember, if you leave me here, I'll blow the vest."

When he returned to the passenger's seat, he gave a duster to Sarah and his pistol to Margaret.

He turned to the back seat. "You ever shoot a gun?"

"No," Margaret answered, her voice small.

"It's not big a gun. It won't kick too bad. You aim, take a breath, hold it, then squeeze the trigger, okay? Roll your window down. When we get to the block, we all keep our guns low where the flashlights can't find them. Under your legs if you have to. Wait for my word. And remember what happens if I die."

He held up one of Sarah's guns. "How does this work?"

"There's no trigger. Flip that switch to start. You'll feel the grip change to tell you it's communicating. Aim and think *shoot*."

"What?"

"It connects with your head. I don't know how. You picture it in your mind and it happens. Just be ready. As fast as you think is as fast as it shoots."

They rolled up to the roadblock. The asshole was right. A long strip of metal spikes angled for tire damage was stretched across the road. Behind it, she counted at least ten men with guns. There could have been more. It was still so dark. A large man with a ragged beard walked up to the driver's side window and worked to keep the flashlight out of Sarah's eyes.

"How are you tonight?" he asked pleasantly.

"Fine," Sarah replied as casually as possible.

"We're taking up a collection to keep the roads safe." As he talked, he moved the flashlight through the cabin. When the light moved to the back seat. Sarah watched the man's eyes widen when the understanding of Margaret's unusual fashion statement hit home. He backed up a few steps.

"Bill," the man called out into the darkness. "Over here."

Bill, another large man with a square jaw and a tattered Phillies cap joined the first. The two conferred quietly among themselves while the first man kept the flashlight trained on the car, illuminating areas of the cabin and cargo hold as he spoke. After a moment of this conversation, Bill took a radio off his belt, said something Sarah couldn't hear, and walked to her window.

"Who's got the detonator?" he asked without a trace of alarm. Just another day at the office.

The kidnapper raised his hand. Bill looked at Sarah then aimed his light into the back seat. Sarah glanced into the rearview and saw Margaret's blanched and swollen face go bright.

"You two related?" Bill said to no one in particular.

"Sisters," Sarah said.

He shone the light back on the kidnapper.

"Well, you sure as fuck ain't the brother. I'm gonna go back a few steps and think about this for a minute. Sit tight, okay?"

It was a long minute. Sarah looked to see if she could read anything on the kidnapper's face. Something felt wrong about this whole thing. The men around the car, at least the two that had spoken to her, seemed more like cops than criminals. They were organized and professional. Had the kidnapper misjudged the situation?

Bill came back to the window. "Okay, here's what's gonna happen. You're all gonna get out of the car. The driver is gonna walk my way to the north side of the road. Bomb Girl and Trigger Boy are gonna go to the south side of the road and sit. Are we clear?"

Before anyone could reply, Sarah heard a loud bang from behind her and something wet sprayed across her cheek and mouth. The man outside her window stood still for a moment, one half of his face gone, the other half frozen in a look of astonishment, then collapsed from her view. Almost instantly pops sounded and barrels flashed from a dozen places. The windshield exploded away, the side mirrors tore from the A pillars, and bullets from multiple directions pounded the Cadillac so forcefully it began to rock on its springs. A second later the kidnapper had his gun out in the void. He toggled the switch like he'd done it before. Sarah saw the gun's casing pulsate and the night turned brighter than day.

All was quiet then except for Margaret's winded and rattled breathing. One headlamp remained lit. Sarah watched as the dust of the men and their clothes and their guns, glassy and radiant in the light, turned the colors of the world as it gently drifted to the ground.

36

He had been an asshole not to connect the dots. As Yorn Darnol was retrofitting *18* for weapons, Trin had asked the Code if she'd temporarily place the engineer's material requisitions in a private file until the project was finished and he could properly announce its purpose. At the time, he had been thinking about how to manage Wildei's reaction to the idea of arming a transport, which he was more than certain would have been summed up in three simple words: "*No* fucking way." So, he'd gone with the better-to-beg-for-forgiveness-than-ask-for-permission school of boss management. His usual approach. On replay, however, the audaciousness of what he'd asked the Code to do had struck him all over again.

For the record, it hadn't been an illegal ask. He wasn't requesting the destruction of data, only the movement of it. A short-term one at that. But it most definitely crossed the line into a kind of protocol no-go zone. The proper functioning of the ship and its parts were the Code's most important work. Material tracking, especially that which was related to the construction or installation of plasma technology, was highly prioritized. If anyone else on board had made that request, except for perhaps the captain herself, the Code would have said, "No fucking way." Okay, not those words, but their meaning for sure. It was also possible she'd have reported the request. Still, Trin knew it was worth the asking. After all, it was *him* asking.

He'd been right.

What he hadn't imagined was that others might be capable of receiving similar favors from the Code. Now he was kicking himself for it. Even when Forent had told him his theory about the missiles, how whomever was launching them must be getting help from both within and without the ship, Trin had flatly rejected the idea of material or people leaving the ship unnoticed by the Code. He was right, of course, that *was* an impossibility. What he hadn't considered in that moment was that the Code might simply allow it and then cover the tracks. If she wanted to, she could.

"It means, you pathetic child, we have no idea what she's capable of."

Staring at the open storage space in his pod and discovering the missing Bridge Maker, it hit him like a bolt of lightning. He'd been looking for Sarah in all the wrong places. Maybe she hadn't been found anywhere on ship because she wasn't *on* the fucking ship. Which meant...maybe she was still alive.

He closed the panel to the pod storage and set off for the CC.

37

The sun had come up by the time they reached the Holland Tunnel checkpoint only to be plunged back into darkness again. If the tunnel was equipped with lights, they weren't on. The SUV's sole headlamp lit one side of the dirt-covered tile walls of the tunnel, and they drove in that half-moon light for what felt to Sarah an interminable amount of time. She didn't know what would be waiting for her at the tunnel's end and she didn't know who or what might leap into her path before she got there. When they finally burst out into the daylight again at St. John's Park—in what was once called Lower Manhattan—she wished the tunnel had simply gone on without end.

"Welcome to the Kingdom," the kidnapper said dryly.

Sarah stopped the car before she reached Canal Street and looked about the scene before her, blinking from the bright of the sky like a creature of the dirt emerging from its hole. She'd come nearly five thousand miles since leaving the alien city ship and witnessed in the flesh and unforgiving reality what the *Kalelah* had wrought. Yet what had become of New York City was something altogether different.

She'd been to Manhattan as a child. Her mother had taken her and her sister. They had stayed in a cheap hotel and shared a damp, lumpy bed. During the days they walked the city, window shopping and gawking and eating in cheap restaurants. Once they had simply bought hotdogs and pretzels from carts on the sidewalk and ate in a tiny park ringed by grand apartment houses and blaring streets. It had been like a trip to a magic land. The sheer abundance of it was overwhelming, the math of it impossible to grasp. All of it was exhilarating...like nothing she'd ever experienced.

The Manhattan she saw from behind the wheel of the perforated and creaking Cadillac resembled that city of her memory in a general, archetypal sense. Buildings proudly thrusting to the sky from every direction, the New York rose-colored light of the morning sun pushing its way between the towers and cheering the black asphalt of the streets with geometric designs of tinted white. People were walking the streets, some with dogs, some with makeshift wagons piled with overstuffed plastic bags. There were places open for business. A greengrocer, a coffee shop, and several restaurants. Compared to Amsterdam or New Jersey, which had both looked emptied and aimless, like discarded things awaiting their eventual decomposition, Manhattan looked to be a functioning place. It looked more than that. It looked supremely *managed*.

It was the most frightening thing she'd seen yet.

She was ten years old on that trip with her mother and sister, and the thing even she had understood, sensed in the way that maybe only children can, was that the wild, unstructured, cacophony of New York, with its throngs of people of every hue and shape and size, with its sidewalks jammed with stolen and counterfeit goods for sale, with its hundreds of languages all shouting at once, with its thousands of smells, its millions of agendas competing to seize each and every moment, if only for the moment, with its horns honking and its taxis speeding—the absolute unmanageableness of the city—was, in fact, the splendor of the city. The entire point of it.

It was all she could do on that trip not to skip and twirl in the glorious mayhem like a character in a cheesy musical. She never once tired of the city's crowding, the constant pressure pushing at its seams, its energy and marvels always spilling out into the open, too much and too exuberant to be contained indoors. She'd adored how everyone she encountered or merely observed from a distance, rich or poor, looked in on the game. The game of *being New York*. A game played by anyone's rules at any time. New York City had felt to her like freedom itself.

Now it had fallen through the looking glass, been turned upside down and painted over in garish hues of red, black, and gunmetal blue. An old news reel recreated in a fever dream.

The Kingdom's symbol, the Empire State Building within an oval burst of bullets, the one she'd seen painted along the base of Lady Liberty, was everywhere. It moved with the breeze from flagpoles and it hung in long vertical banners from the tall, two-story entranceways of once prosperous buildings, and it decorated the big storefront windows of shuttered businesses which, despite the few places actually open, still looked to be most businesses, cynically festooning the streets in bruises and blood.

Guns were nearly as ubiquitous. Armed men and women stood at corners on every third block. A garbage truck painted red and black crossed Broadway in front of the Cadillac at Franklin Street. A man with a machine gun rode the fender of the big cab-over's front wheel, his free hand around a grab rail on the container, while two more men occupied the riding steps flanking the hopper. They held their guns loosely at their sides with an air of conquering confidence. They regarded the shot-up Cadillac missing its windshield, its side mirrors, half its paint, and one of its headlamps with solemn disinterest.

It took all of five minutes to see that New York had not simply collapsed in the aftermath of the Correction and the Russian bombs that split America and broke the back of its government like other places had. No, New York had been captured. Sadder still, it had been collared. If this could happen to New York, Sarah could only wonder with increasing dread what was going to happen to her and Margaret. To everyone. She leaned out the side window and looked for a glimpse of the camera bot. She thought she saw a small black dot in the sky above her, though it was also possible the dot was merely a trick of the eye. A tear warping her vision.

•

They followed Broadway until they came to a small park with a large porticoed building at the center. It had the unmistakable look of officialdom, a tall, sweeping set of stairs, and the dome of a rotunda topping the stately second story.

"End of the line," the kidnapper said.

"What is this place?" asked Sarah.

"It used to be City Hall. Now it's something else."

They left the car on the street and followed a wide stone path to the steps, the captor holding Margaret by the elbow, Sarah's bag slung over his shoulder. Margaret hadn't said a word since the roadblock in Pennsylvania. She gave the large man no resistance or even a glance as they walked.

"Raise your hands. Both of you," he said when they reached the top of the stairs and the metal-clad door. "Make sure they can see all your fingers." He pushed a dirty button on the wall near the big door. With a mechanical whirr a camera swiveled in their direction.

"Lonny!" the kidnapper said to the camera.

A moment later came the sounds of lock bolts turning and the big door slowly swung open. An incredibly dark Indian man stood in the large threshold, the white of his teeth in a Cheshire grin, a roll of duct tape in one hand.

"The prodigal son," said the Indian.

"I need the bomb team right now. My hand's got nothing left."

The Indian pulled a long strip of tape from the roll, bit the edge with his teeth, tore it free, and gave it to the kidnapper.

"To be honest, Kino, we never thought we'd see you again." The Indian man looked Sarah and Margaret over. "I'm happy not to have to hunt you down."

"Well, you know how much I care about your happiness," the kidnapper said, winding the tape around his thumb and the detonator.

When the tape was secure, he sighed with relief. "You have no fucking idea how much pain I'm in."

The Indian grinned wider. Two men with small machine guns walked up behind him. "This is her?" the Indian asked with a nod toward Sarah.

"Yeah."

"Okay," he said brightly. "She and her things come with me. You and the other one can go with the boys here to, um, unpack."

"Why can't we stay together?" asked Sarah.

"Such a happy family. You're separating because you need to stay alive, and Kino, who never fails to confirm my overestimation of his intelligence, has chosen to wrap the young lady in actual explosives. We'll do our best."

"I don't give a shit about him. She's my sister. I won't cooperate if anything happens to her."

The Indian pulled a gun from the waist at the back of his pants and prodded her toward the large foyer beneath the rotunda. "Young lady," he said as they walked, "a little advice. Your biggest worry now should be focused on what will happen to *you*."

They said nothing to each other the rest of the way through the quiet marbled building. The only sounds Sarah heard were the thumping of her heart and a metallic jingling that rang in time to the Indian's steps, like coins.

38

A collection of thirty-one people from throughout the ship's departments had squeezed themselves into the captain's private conference room adjacent to the CC. They were analysts, flight control managers, research scientists, people from across the spectrum of services and disciplines of the *Kalelah*. They were men, women, old, young, and somewhere in between. Together they represented seventeen different home worlds that stretched across the galaxy that spawned the mother world of Origen. Yet this diverse group had some important things in common. Language, of course, and religion. All peoples that could trace their identity to Origen shared those traits, which was all peoples of the universe, as far as Origen was concerned. The one notable exception being the people of Earth. This hand-picked assembly, however, shared one additional and distinctive characteristic. A special kind of relationship with the Code. This ad hoc group was known as The Divers. And this was their first meeting.

Trin had placed a small metal box, barely big enough to stand on, in a corner of the room. He stepped atop it once everyone he invited had arrived.

"My thanks to everyone for coming on short notice. Why we're packed into this box together, the one place on ship we can speak without cameras and mics, will make sense in a moment. Perhaps some of you have started to figure it out already. We all know who we are, what links us. I've reached out to you because I need your help in finding Sarah. So let me make sure you know who she is.

"Three years ago, I took Sarah from one world and dropped her into another without even the slightest shred of preparation. A world so foreign she didn't know up from down. She didn't understand us, and we sure as shit didn't understand her and the billions she represented. Until she got here, until we met her, until we heard her speak, we denied she was even human. We couldn't even use the word *people* for Sarah and her kind. The *population*. That was our word. To Laird, to most of us on ship, to the Plan, they were literally just a number, like a counting of species of trees. She knew some of this, some of what she'd be up against when I asked her to join us. Captain Argen had told her. She came anyway. She could have believed her own people when they told her Argen was lying. She could have believed her own people when they thought they could simply fight us and win. Sarah believed Argen instead. Even though we didn't believe in her, she believed in us.

"She put her life on the line to stop the Correction, more than once. Not only to save her own people, but to save us as well. To save us from where we are right now. When the pilot ripped the gloves from the ship, she fell with us, she was standing right outside these doors when we went down. Actually, she was already on the concourse floor, because Laird had beaten her half to death by then. While we didn't succeed in stopping the Correction before it started, we needed her help to save the lives we did. To save the billions we did.

"Now she's out there somewhere, off ship. I don't know where, but I know how we can begin to find out."

Trin paused and let what he'd said sink in. The looks he saw on several faces told him at least some in the crowd were tracking. A woman from Flight was the first to respond.

"May I ask, sir, if you've already tried what I think you're ordering us to do?"

"I'm not ordering, I'm asking. And yes, I've tried. The captain has tried too. We've found nothing."

"XO, you and the captain are the best Divers on ship," the woman followed up. "If you can't find anything, maybe there's nothing to find."

There were several nods of agreement to that.

"That's possible," Trin conceded. "But both the captain and I think the Code has information that will help us find Sarah. For whatever reason," he paused here to search for the right words, "she's not making it easily available."

A nervous buzz went through the crowd.

Fuck. Wrong words.

"Permission to speak freely!" a research scientist shouted.

"Please." Trin addressed the crowd. "We're talking among shipmates, that's it. For the purposes of this discussion, forget rank."

"Okay. Then I say the minute we start doubting the Code, thinking she's hiding something, is the minute we start doubting everything. In fact, having this conversation here in this room, the one room that won't record it, we're the ones hiding something."

Wildei pushed her way toward Trin's corner. "I get where that comment comes from, Doctor Tenit. The relationships we each have with the Code are incredibly useful and often quite meaningful. The XO isn't saying we shouldn't trust the Code. What we both want to say is that something is happening with her we don't yet understand. Over time we'll figure it out, or she'll tell us. We need the Code and she needs us. We're her purpose, and I don't believe she'd knowingly abandon that. In the meantime, though, we need to find Sarah."

"If we all went at this together, in a coordinated way, I think we could break through," said Trin.

Silence.

After a beat, a young analyst with a tired look on his face and a premature shock of gray going through his dark hair spoke. Although his words were simple and concise without flourish or hyperbole, like storm clouds swiftly gathering on a red horizon, they got everyone's attention. Trin knew he had no good response to the young man other than the truth.

"You want to stage an attack on the Code?" the analyst asked.

39

In her imagination, the man she expected to meet, the king who called himself Mayor, looked the part of the villain, scarred and menacing. The kind of man who would send another to beat a woman and tie her to a bomb in order to capture her sister would have to look that way. Repulsive and obvious. The mobsters and cruel men of history had been all those things. Their mug shots and news clipping photos always gave them away. Their strange hair, facial markings, and their dark-ringed eyes always proclaimed, *you've got the right guy*.

Instead, Tom Nader was a strikingly handsome man with a generous smile. *Beautiful*, she thought at first glance. He was fit and well dressed, standing in the center of the room. Sarah thought there might be something about his eyes that were off. But the room was large, and from where she stood, the first impression he gave was that of a prosperous CEO. Only the man next to her with a gun told the truth of the scene.

"Hello, Sarah," he said graciously. "I'm Tom Nader." He walked over to shake her hand, as if this were a regular business meeting. He was tall, so he bent a bit when he offered his hand, bringing his eyes more in line with hers. She was right, they were off. Camera one and camera two. Mismatched. Still, overall, the handsomeness was winning out over the villainy. He pointed to a seating area behind him—two sofas facing each other with two club chairs at the wings, and a large glass table in the middle.

"Please have a seat...anywhere you like."

Sarah took the center cushion of the sofa that faced the door to the room. She wanted to have a view of what else might come through it. The Indian set her bag on the carpets and looked ready to leave.

"Lonny," said Nader, "a word before you go." The two walked over to the bag on the floor and talked quietly.

Sarah looked around the room for the first time. It was like she imagined a mayor's office of a big city would look. The only glitch in the picture was the large red and black flag furled in the corner behind the desk. It put a shiver down her spine.

Nader came back, took a seat facing Sarah, and threw an arm over the back of the sofa. He sat there and looked at her for a long moment, silent. It was like a therapy session she'd seen in the movies. The shrink's stubborn silence versus the patient's anxious desire for permission to spill. Except she was a prisoner, not a patient. All she wanted to talk about was her sister. She debated which eye to focus on. Before all this, when she'd encountered someone with a lazy eye, she'd make an effort not to favor one over the other, but to focus on the bridge of the nose. She'd always thought that was the polite thing to do. Now she didn't care if her pick of the green eye—the one angled off to some space to her right—was the eye to aim for or not, or if her choice of it made him self-conscious in some way.

"I find it impossible not to think about your name," he said at last.

She wanted to scream, *where's my sister?* Except everything about the situation told her things, whatever they were, were not going to go according to her timeline. She glanced at the door, closed now, perhaps even locked.

"It's just a name," she said.

"No," he said evenly. "Jane is just a name. Sally is just a name. Sarah is something much more, isn't it? I've always thought her story, the story of Sarah, Abraham's wife, to be a cautionary tale." He paused to flash a smile like a preacher on TV. "Her destiny, which God relayed to Abraham who then relayed to her, was to be a mother of nations. Sarah didn't believe her future, and her lack of faith caused all kinds of problems."

"It wasn't only lack of faith. She thought she couldn't have children," Sarah said. "I know the story."

"Of course you do." The smile again. "Then you know that Sarah's real problem wasn't fertility at all. Her problem was that she only saw the world with her eyes. From that perspective, the world was a place where women gave birth in their teens, were old by their early thirties, and died before their mid-forties. Sarah, blinded by her own eyes, couldn't imagine living long enough to be *ninety*, let alone giving birth to her first child at that age. She was so convinced she'd never give Abraham a child, she gave him her maidservant, Hagar, to bear one for them. Think about everything that happened next."

"Do you have a point here?"

"A question, actually." Nader uncrossed his legs, leaned forward off the back of the sofa, and rested his elbows on his knees. "Are you ready to see with something beyond your eyes?"

"It's hard for me to see anything right now except for my sister's face. Which is swollen and frozen in a permanent state of terror. Why are we here? You have the guns. What more do you want?"

He smiled. Sarah stayed with the green eye, hoping it hurt him in some small but cutting way.

"You're right!" He banged upon the glass tabletop with the knuckles of his right hand. "I nearly forgot. Let's look at the guns." He walked to the bag and took it to his desk. "Join me."

Sarah got up from the sofa as he undid the bag. By the time she got to the desk he had the thing open.

"Impressive," he said, his smile now looking particularly real.

He took a duster from the bag and examined it as if it was a thing that had fallen from the sky. Which made sense.

"The cleanliness of line is remarkable. What's it called?"

"A duster."

"A duster. This is the weapon you used in the park?"

"Yes."

He gave a small nod of approval. "A good name."

He took the gun by the handle, pointed it out the window, and looked down the line that went from his arm to the ejector end of the gun. "Boom," he said. "Or is it *zap*?"

"It's neither."

He pivoted his arm until the duster was aimed at Sarah's head. "I've heard of you, you know. You were semi-famous for a few minutes. The geologist from a little town in Ohio who discovered the ship and then went to live on it. The news window didn't last long, only a day or two. The world has been too busy falling apart to care much about you since. But I was so intrigued. The things you must have seen...like meeting God himself. Now here you are. Well, there you were, in Lancaster to rescue your sister and take her back to the ship. So said your friend. The French woman."

"You didn't have to kill her."

"She betrayed you. What else should I have done with her, a person who can't be trusted?"

"She was harmless."

"Not to you. Apparently."

He kept himself behind the duster, looking down the length of it.

"What do you want?"

"Weapons."

"You have them."

"I want more. I want you to help me get them."

"What makes you think I can?"

"Yeah," he let the word draw out. "You're a mystery, but there's no mistaking the presence of you, Sarah. It's so obvious I saw it through a nervous video on an ancient iPhone."

"Maybe you're just seeing things. I can't help you. Besides, even if I could, I wouldn't."

"You haven't heard my pitch yet. You don't understand the power you have. When you do, I think you'll see things differently. You'll come to understand that it's the right thing to do. The only thing to do. I know this. I feel it at a cellular level. I'm never wrong about my feelings, Sarah. Never. I trust them completely. Which is why I trust you."

He lowered his arm, turned the gun around, and offered it to her handle first. "Show me how it works."

"What?"

"There's no trigger that I can see. So please, show me how it works. I insist."

She took the gun, not because she knew what she might do with it in that moment. She took it simply because he told her to. "You toggle this switch while gipping the handle." She flipped the switch, and the gun came to life in her hand. The casing pulsated with a soft iridescence and a nearly musical hum pushed forth from the machine.

"That's new," he said.

She thought about the door behind her, and the people behind it, and the guns they surely had. She tried to move the pieces of the chess board in her mind. A part of her knew the board was his and the squares weren't true. But she had the gun in her hand. She raised her arm and leveled the ejector at his face.

"I want my sister. Now."

Nader neither blinked nor moved. He somehow looked around the weapon to her. To inside her. "How many people are you willing to kill to get her?"

"I only need to kill one."

"Then it should be easy," he said, his green eye suddenly snapping straight. "Shoot."

She shot.

He was faster than she could think. The eye. *The fucking lazy eye*. It had distracted her. Not for long—only a fraction of a second. A fraction of a fraction. It was all he needed.

He swatted her gun hand with his left just as she managed to get off the shot and hit her hard in the face with his right. The punch felt like a cannon ball. The surprise of it hurt most of all. How could anyone be so fast? A second later she lay on the floor in front of his desk. She could see the cuffs of his carefully pressed trousers, and beneath them, his polished brown cap toe shoes. She watched them pivot as he turned to face the wall behind him.

"Now *this* is one damn fine gun," he said from a far, far distance as the light faded from her eyes and the room went dark.

40

Three years before, when the *Kalelah* had awoken from its extended Skip and finally rubbed the catastrophic sleep out of its eyes, getting a slot on the Omniscience Team had been among the most prized assignments possible. Its location within the CC was prime, right next to the bridge and Flight and it reported directly to the captain, no middle management department head bullshit. Argen, often with Trin in tow, would be poking his head in every hour, and getting to work with them both in that way, in those early hours of the crisis when nobody knew what was going on, had been a rare thrill for Lukas.

Omni's job was to achieve as quickly and completely what the field manuals called "Immersive Awareness," or as Trin would call it in those days, *what the fuck are we into?* At Lukas's disposal was an arsenal of intelligence gathering and interpretive probes to paint a picture at near granular detail of the world around the *Kalelah*.

The first investigation had been cautious, a single probe launched while the ship was still in its undersea hiding spot. The tiny silver ball, no bigger than a fist, had propelled to the surface water, extended an antenna, listened for twenty seconds, and then descended once again to its launch tube within the nanotecture of the *Kalelah's* skin.

It was in that quick look that the full horror of what had occurred was revealed. Captain Argen's worst-case scenario had been proven true. Against all laws, objectives, and odds, the population had not only managed to survive without Guidance for one hundred and twenty thousand years, it had acquired alarming levels of technology.

Mere hours after that discovery, Argen gave the order for full deployment. Every probe on the ship went out. Visual capture, audio capture, mapping, microwave and radio frequency interceptors, conductive wire spies and computing sniffers, water and air samplers, even the tasters. The Omni Team had swelled to more than one hundred analysts and Lukas was on the ride of his life.

The level of incoming was off the charts. No one on ship was prepared for what was pouring in. The ship should have awoken at Epoch Check 2. The population, had it survived in any numbers at all, should have been relatively small and nomadic, confined in territory to the original seeding continents, and in the early stages of tool use. Instead, the ship had awoken at E-37 and the population had exploded to more than seven-point-three billion and was generating data at the speed of a level-six civilization.

The Omni Team's Spectrum Wall, a long expanse of fiber generation web able to display images and sounds with far more fidelity than float projection, had literally gone down twice in those early hours from the surge of information it was asked to show and catalogue. The constant pulsing and strobing of colors and lights from the thousands of images displaying at once had caused headaches and fainting among the staff. Lukas himself suffered from bouts of dizziness during that time and often had to touch the edges of workstations as he walked to help keep his footing. Eventually medical and engineering staff simply moved in with Omni to keep everything and everyone up and running. Most of the team had stayed awake for days straight to handle that initial learning curve.

That seemed like eons ago now. Lukas, the most senior member of the radically downsized Omniscience Team, the only member, swiveled his chair away from his workstation to survey the rows and rows of abandoned workstations. He looked at the Spectrum Wall and sighed. Like the room itself, the giant wall was mostly empty, the images mostly static. Data generation had fallen to level two—an emerging data culture. He knew that classification was simply based on numbers. In reality, the world outside the *Kalelah* wasn't emerging at all. It was declining. Signals popped up from time to time, but few instances were anything more than fleeting. Theoretically, his job was still a crucial one. Few aspects of the civilization outside were more telling than its technological state. But on a shift-to-shift basis it had become soul crushingly dull.

It was time to do a manual check, to walk the Wall, so he hoisted himself from the chair. He started from the oldest detected signal, a terrestrial broadcast band that popped up three weeks ago in the southwestern sector of Continent three. It wasn't a particularly strong signal, but it had shown remarkable staying power and had so far set a record for the longest sustained broadcast since the Correction. It was a continuous loop of video content twenty-two minutes long. It featured a man and a large hoofed beast that looked uncannily similar to an animal on his homeworld, a *flantura*, and the two appeared able to converse with one another. Lukas wasn't cleared for language learning, no one was that he knew of, so the meaning of the content was a mystery to him. He found it amusing anyway. He especially liked the song that played at the start of each loop. Lukas lingered there for a moment, watching the flantura thing stomp its hooves and speak like an intelligent being.

Emlin walked up behind him, the scent of her hair arriving in advance and teasing his appetite. She slipped an arm around his chest and the other to the front of his pants. She had a thing about surprises, and he was always happy to indulge her things, whatever they were. Her job in Flight had become even more uneventful than his.

"Miss me?" she asked.

He turned within her embrace and put his arms around her. "Don't you have work to do?"

She kept her hand at the front of his pants. "I do. In fact, I'm incredibly busy."

This was her new thing, breaking shift early. It had started out as shaving the edges off the clock, a few minutes at first, nothing really to worry about. Over the weeks, though, she'd grown more brazen, cutting shift a solid hour early. They'd been lucky so far. But in the back of his mind, he wondered when their luck would run out and they'd get caught. It wouldn't be pleasant.

"You know I have to check the damn Wall."

"Yeah, and the Wall hasn't changed in two weeks."

"That doesn't matter."

"It's bullshit make-work, right? Like everything we do around here lately." She put her chin on his chest and looked up at him, the dark of her eyes and the roundness of her lower lip reflecting back the soft light of the overheads. "Take me to my pod and make me do bad things," she said in that voice she used when she wanted her way.

"What kind of bad things?"

"The good kind."

"I should stay."

"That's what you always say," she purred and pressed herself to him more completely. "But a part of you always disagrees. Whatever's on the Wall now will be here in the morning. And if it isn't, who cares?"

Who was he kidding? He could never say no to her. "Yeah, who cares?" he conceded.

"Then say goodbye, Wall."

They untangled and Emlin and Lukas left to begin their night together, leaving the Spectrum Wall unchecked. By a cursory look at things, that night's breach of protocol was no more irresponsible than the previous night's breach, or the one before that.

Because Lukas had already known the total number of signals up on the Wall. That total was the exact same total since his last walk of the Wall. Four hundred and thirty-seven. However, within the composition of that total there had been changes.

A small radio signal, less than fifty kilowatts, from the northeast sector of Continent one had stopped sending. No one would ever know exactly what happened. The equipment generating the signal could have been vandalized or fallen victim to fire. The antenna could have come down in a storm. A dozen other reasons could have explained its sudden absence. At some point a cross check would be made with other activity monitoring for insight into its disappearance, but lost signals never received the same urgent attention as new arrivals. What Lukas had missed by not walking the Wall was that among the four hundred and thirty-seven total signals, one had just arrived.

It was a grainy aerial image showing the roof of a large building set within a small park.

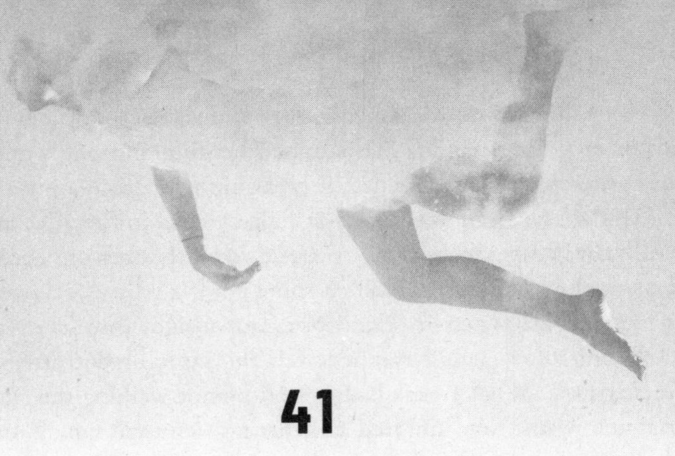

41

Sarah opened her eyes to the slightly fuzzy visage of a woman's light brown face framed by long, dark hair. Her expression was serious, her lips tight, her brows furrowed. Sarah grunted softly and the woman's face relaxed, her mouth turning to a small smile as the picture sharpened into focus.

"Hi, Sarah," the woman said warmly. "I'm so glad to see you awake."

The side of Sarah's head throbbed. "Shit." She reached up to touch her face.

"No, leave it be. I have some ice. Can you sit up to swallow an aspirin?"

"Where am I?"

"The residence."

"Who are you?"

"I'm Kelly. I work for the mayor. How do you feel?"

"Like I got hit by a train."

"It's not too far from the truth. Here, c'mon, sit up."

Sarah sat up slowly. Every bone in her body hurt. She was wearing a light cotton robe. Her clothes hung from the back of a chair next to a desk by a large window. "What's my face like?"

"He got you good."

"Fuck. Why does everyone hit me in the face?"

"So you can't pretend it didn't happen," the woman said. "It's lucky he hit you *there*. Don't you think? In the face, I mean."

The woman handed her some aspirin and a glass of water and got up for the ice pack on the dresser. She was Asian and very pretty, dressed in a tight skirt and high heels.

"How far along are you?" the woman asked.

Dammit.

"I don't know exactly," she said. "Nine weeks, ten, twelve. Somewhere in there." That was the truth, she didn't know. That only added to the feeling of chaos around her life, a feeling like falling that never stopped.

"See?" the woman said. "Lucky." She came back with the ice and sat down on the edge of the bed.

"What do you do for the mayor?" Sarah asked.

The woman waited a beat to answer, as if figuring it out herself. "I do whatever the mayor wants."

Sarah looked at the woman's manicured nails, her elegant clothes, her precisely painted mouth. "I see."

"No, not yet. But you will." She smiled and gently placed the ice against Sarah's face. "Hold that there for a few minutes and I'll get your shower ready." The woman got up off the bed again and walked to the en suite bath.

"Do you know where my sister is?"

"Your sister's safe," she called back.

"I want to see her."

"First shower, then dinner, then sleep."

"Why are we being held? At least tell me that."

The woman came out from the bathroom and offered Sarah help with getting up from the bed. "The mayor's a great man, Sarah. Everything he does he does for a reason. I think you'll find you and he have important goals in common." She brightened her smile and pointed to the small sofa at the foot of the bed. "I picked out some clothes for you."

"I'll stick to mine, thanks."

"Yours smell. The shower takes a minute to heat up but should be ready now. I'll be back to help you dress."

The woman stepped toward the door.

"The mayor doesn't know anything about me or my goals," Sarah said.

The woman paused at the threshold for a moment, but she left the room without another word.

•

By the time the woman returned Sarah had already gotten dressed in her own clothes.

"Kind of defeats the purpose of a shower," the woman said. "You know, most people would kill for a Michael Kors dress. That one hadn't even been worn."

"I don't have time to kill for a dress. Thanks for the clean underwear, though."

The woman led her through a long hall that took them to the rotunda. They were on the second story of the building and the space opened up dramatically, with the underlit Romanesque dome curving above them and a view below of the grand staircase and the main foyer. They kept straight and stopped at a set of large wooden double doors on their right. She put her hand on Sarah's arm.

"He's a powerful man, Sarah. Be careful."

"If I get a gun, I won't hesitate."

The woman offered a sad smile. "Listen," she said, "I know what it's like to—"

"No, you don't."

"Okay, Sarah." She licked a finger and smoothed a few of Sarah's hairs into place. "Maybe just think about making it through the night."

The woman pushed the big doors wide. Nader sat at the center of a long wooden table that could easily accommodate forty people. Two other place settings were waiting. One next to him, and one directly across. He stood and motioned to the single place at the opposite center of the table. She took the seat.

"How are you feeling?" he asked.

"I'm fine," she lied.

"Good to hear. Can I offer you a drink?" He pointed to a green bottle of something called Pastis. She had no idea what that was, but it looked boozy.

"I'm good with the water, thanks."

"Oh, right. My mistake."

Sarah cast a quick glance to the Kelly woman but if she understood its meaning, it didn't show. Nader poured some of the Pastis into glasses and followed it up with water. The Pastis transformed from a brownish transparent tea color to a milky yellow when the water hit. He gave a glass to the Kelly woman and raised his in toast.

He smiled. "To chemistry."

The table was elegant, the lighting soft and mellow, and whatever was going to be served smelled heavenly. Her stomach ached for a meal. It also sent a warning. There was a pattern with this guy. Hit you with the good silverware and candlelight, then hit you. Sarah wasn't sure if she'd make it to the main course. So she saw no reason to be polite.

"How much bullshit before the food comes?" she asked.

The Kelly woman had her glass to her lips but froze before taking a sip. "Sarah, please."

Nader seemed not at all put off. He smiled and knocked the table hard with the knuckles of his right hand. "Let's eat then. Robert!" he called, still looking at Sarah. "Bring it all. We've become very hungry."

A minute later the food came. Warm rolls, a red leaf salad, roast chicken, tenderloin medium rare, carrots and potatoes. She did her best to eat slowly. She failed.

"It's good, isn't it?" Nader asked.

Sarah nodded. "Yes."

"I want you to know we're not the only ones eating like this tonight. Thousands of people throughout the Kingdom eat just as well. Those who can't dine like this still have access to food. They may not eat richly, but they eat. Dozens of office buildings have been converted to hothouses and chicken houses. Nearly everything we consume is produced on the island, or on nearby farms we own and protect at great expense." He paused and took a drink. "Outside the Kingdom it's a different and dangerous story. Which, of course, you know."

"That's why you need the weapons, to protect yourself? Protect the...um, *Kingdom?*" She saw by the Kelly woman's face that throwing a little shade here was playing with fire, poking the bear. She didn't care. She wanted him to know she wasn't buying into his bullshit. Even if it meant another bruise on her face.

Nader let it go.

"The Kingdom can protect itself. For now. But the chaos around it is a waste of human potential, and a future danger if left to fester. There's a leadership vacuum that needs filling. That's what the weapons are for. Phase one. The real work is what comes after, Sarah. For that I need something more. A gift from the gods, if you will. A lightning bolt of progress."

"I've already told you," she said, "I can't help you."

There was no anger or frustration on his face. He took her refusal as if she'd thrown an idea out to the table that was something worth grappling. The Kelly woman pushed her eyes in his direction. Sarah was really starting to hate this woman. Nader took another bite of his food and chewed it slowly. When he'd finished with it, he took a sip from a glass of wine and finally spoke.

"Have you ever heard of the term *social resilience*?"

"No."

"Social resilience is a society's ability to cooperate and act collectively for common goals. Our world feels and acts collapsed because we've lost our ability to do things together. Every society in our human history that's suffered a collapse did so because it lost social resiliency. Now, you may think that your ship and the Russian bombs were the cause of this state of collapse, but they weren't."

Sarah arched an eyebrow but kept at her food.

"Don't get me wrong," he continued, "they were terrible shocks to the system. The loss of Asia and its supply chains in particular. They could have been survivable though. They *should* have been survivable. On their own, they didn't need to lead to the collapse. Except we were already working toward it long before those things happened. We were rushing toward the cliff all on our own. All part of the natural cycle. All we needed was a few good shoves to push us over."

"You're saying this would have happened anyway?"

"Maybe not three years ago. Perhaps ten years from now, or five. But we were on our way."

"I don't believe it."

"You should, because this is a pattern that has repeated itself all throughout history. We seem to be drawn to violate the limits of our natural cohesiveness. The clan was really as big a group of people we've been able to successfully hold together for any great lengths of time. It was homogeneous, united by shared genetics and family ties. It was simple. It was small. Yet the human spirit isn't easily contained or satisfied. The human spirit wants more. More land, more wealth, more diversity. It's who we are." He grabbed the Kelly woman's hand and kissed it. "So we build cities, we chart trade routes, and we create new, exciting genetic pools. To manage it all, to replace the binding agents of family, we add institutions, artificial forms of authority and chiefdom. Religion, government, militaries. We add *complexities*.

"For a while, they work. Our cities grow, our technology grows, our empires grow. Our civilizations become more powerful than their founders could have ever imagined. Still, in every case, even without alien ships and nuclear bombs, they all eventually break down and die. The Incan, the Aztec, the Roman, the Persian, the Mayan, the Greek, the Chacoan, pick any of them and the reason for their collapse is always the same. The cost of civilization—of the institutions, the complexities—simply becomes too great."

"You're saying this is all about money?"

"Everything in life is a cost-benefit analysis. At some point, every civilization so far, in the end, chose not to pay the freight of its own survival. It gives up on itself. Why? Because it had lost its social resiliency."

"Before the Correction, the world was richer than it had ever been."

"Not too rich to stop fighting over oil and cobalt and diamonds. Complexity, Sarah, is expensive. Consider Rome. The empire was able to grow rich by conquering its neighbors and forcing them to pay tribute. With that wealth, it built great cities and developed what were, for the times, incredible technologies.

"Yet the bigger the empire got, the bigger the army it needed to hold it together. Eventually, the cost of the army grew beyond the value of the tributes coming in. It had fallen victim to one of the most important laws of economics: the law of diminishing returns. People began to ask what was in it for them. Powerful people began to ask what was in it for them. It didn't take long after that before selfishness entered the system and became a kind of institution of its own. A counter complexity. Rome stopped investing in the things that had helped make the empire successful in the first place. Rome grew weak. It grew vulnerable to attack, from without and from within.

"Think about our own country before the bombs and the alien ship arrived. Did you think of it as a nation united in common cause? We'd been unable to pass a single large piece of public investment legislation for decades. We fought over how to pay for schools, how to pay for roads and bridges, broadband and healthcare. We argued over the legitimacy of our elections, and we did nothing about any of it. Our resiliency had run out. How much longer do you think we had?"

She took a drink of water to give herself a moment. She knew what was happening. Like a flatlining patient experiencing an out-of-body perspective, watching her own last, desperate moment from the operating room ceiling, she was able to see what he was doing to her. She was completely aware of the recruitment process underway.

Only she didn't know how to stop it. Should she get up from the table and risk a walk-away? Should she stab him in the neck with the silver-plated knife in her hand? His carotid artery was no more than thirty-six inches away. Could she be faster than him this time? She picked up the knife and gripped the handle tight. Margaret's tear-stained face flashed in her mind.

Sarah stayed in her seat and cut a bite of chicken.

"I didn't see it that way," she said, "like what you're talking about. Collapse."

He waited a moment before he continued. Maybe he saw the flush in her cheeks, or the way the color likely drained from her hand when she squeezed the knife. Who knew what a man like him could see?

"People are so afraid of danger," he finally said, "they do all they can not to see it even when it's right in front of their eyes. A man builds a house by a river. The insurance company refuses to issue a policy. The man looks at the river. It's so beautiful, so peaceful. He thinks, forget the insurance company. He furnishes his home and is very happy there for many years. Then one day a storm comes and the rains don't stop for a week. Until the moment his furniture floats out his front door, he disbelieves the danger. But, of course, it was obvious, and was there all along, right in front of his eyes."

Sarah pushed her plate away. "I'm done. Thank you."

The mayor dabbed a corner of his mouth with his napkin. When he finished the task, he smoothed the cloth flat on the table before returning it to his lap. "Not quite," he said, his face a portrait of seriousness, the politician smile nowhere to be seen. "I want you to think hard about this next question, Sarah. How many babies did you encounter on your travels?"

"What?"

"Babies, Sarah—newborns, infants, toddlers. How many did you see?"

"I don't know. I can't remember."

"Would you say they were a common sight?"

"I don't know. No, no I guess not."

"Did that seem odd to you?"

"I didn't think about it."

"Right. Why would you? You had other things on your mind. Yet babies, Sarah, are the canaries of civilization. Their presence, or not, is a measure of a society's belief in itself, belief in its own longevity. When a civilization begins to die, when it's under stress, it loses population on both ends of the spectrum. The very old and the sick die as they always do. In a crumbling civilization, however, those deaths aren't offset by births, and it's not just the young choosing to have fewer babies. Fertility actually drops. It's like a collective, psychosomatic reaction. When our minds can't imagine a future fit for children, our bodies go along. Soon, the population is unable to reproduce itself. Yet, there you are, Sarah. A push against the norm."

"You're connecting dots that don't exist."

"Whether you realize it or not, you see a future. I do too."

She hated the way he kept equating the two of them, joining them together. He didn't know her. He *couldn't* know her. "Enough! None of what you've been saying excuses what you did to my sister and to me. It doesn't excuse the armed men on the corners, the colors, the flags, the garbage trucks patrolling the streets like tanks. The killings at Ellis Island. I don't want what you want. All you want is control. And you'd do anything to get it."

There was a soft, barely audible groan from Kelly.

Nader, for his part, kept his seemingly unflappable composure. There was even a hint of a smile in his eyes, as if what she'd just thrown at him were compliments.

"Manhattan Kingdom is the safest place on Earth. If you want to call control the ability to sleep at night without the fear of marauding gangs, that's fine with me. As I said earlier, Sarah, control is just a means, a necessary one, but it's not the goal."

"Then what is the goal?"

"A new kind of civilization, one that can transcend the natural cycle of ascendance and decline."

"Oh, you want to start a new kind of civilization?"

He gave a small nod of understanding. "You think that's...what? Impossible? Crazy? Not mine to do?"

She thought there was almost real humility in his words. It both struck her and confused her. "Umm, yeah. Probably."

"What is it you want to do, Sarah?"

"For the ten thousandth time, this isn't about me."

"Are you sure? Only you among us all have lived among *them*. Only you among us all can build a bridge and walk across it."

Beneath the table, Sarah put her hand to her belly. She thought about the pilots in their planes who kept watch over the *Kalelah*. Carlos, Jürgen, Nigel, Elouise, Greta, and Luca. She recalled how she had pleaded and sobbed to them and anyone else who might have been listening through the float. She flashed through her arguments, her rationales, her descriptions of the daily miracles of the ship, the magic that could be transferred to restart and reinvent the world.

Why did the only person to hear her have to be this man?

"What I want," she said, her voice tired and soft, "is to get my sister, go home, and try to live my life."

He got up from his seat and walked the long journey around the big table and sat down in the chair next to hers. "Sarah, that alien ship can never be your home. At some point, it won't be a home for anyone, because that ship is no different than us. It's dying too."

"That's not true. You don't know the ship."

"I know it's surrounded by hostiles. I know it hasn't reached out with its weapons beyond the crash site since it fell. The ship is either too damaged to be of any real danger, or its people are. It either can't attack, or it won't attack. It doesn't matter which. The ship either needs peace with us or wants peace with us. On the other hand, do you really think the people of this planet will simply let it be? Do you think we'll ever not dream about peeling it open and taking what's inside? Even as we flail in our twilight, we won't let the ship rest. We'll keep banging on the door until we get through. Eventually there must be a reconciliation between our two worlds. If not, there will be a reckoning."

"The ship can do things you can't understand. It can survive on its own."

"Maybe under the sea, when no one knows it's there. But out in the open, knowing what it knows? Knowing what it was? Can it survive without purpose?"

"Survival's a purpose."

"No, it's not. Almost no living thing on this Earth exists merely to exist. Almost everything has a job to do. For humans, the job is to grow, to build, to create. Human nature abhors boundaries. Eventually the ship will grow too small, exactly like the close-knit clans of our ancestors did. Just as this island we're standing on now will. When it comes to people, these things follow predictable patterns. Most of history is simply variations on the same tragic theme. New and truly surprising things are rare. It's a lie what they say, that history has an arc. History is a circle. An ever-spinning loop of growth and decay, of golden eras and dark ages. Of peace and war. Either we will spin ourselves into the ground, dust to dust, as we're on the path of doing right now, or something will come along to stop the spinning and make something truly new."

"That's you?"

Tom Nader leaned back in his chair, changed the crossing of his legs and smiled in a way that was without lie or cynicism. It was the smile she imagined a proud father might offer, a smile of unconditional belief.

"No, Sarah, that's you."

42

By the time Lukas realized the Wall had changed, the new signal was no longer new. It was nine hours old. Ancient. And it was weak. Its field strength was in the microvolt range, almost too little for the relay probe three hundred miles away to even pick up. Yet despite the miniscule size of the signal, it was able to display a characteristic Lukas could not ignore. He shouldn't have left his post early. He should have stayed last night to walk the Wall.

Even if the curious nature of the transmission ultimately proved to be an artifact of a line-of-sight problem or some other kind of interference, there was no getting around it. He was going to have to escalate this up the chain. He kicked himself for letting Emlin do her usual on him. But it was nothing compared to the ass kicking he was about to get when he reported the signal. Nine hours old. *Nine hours old!* What was he thinking? He vowed he would never break shift early again. Never.

In the meantime, he was fucked.

The captain was in the CC confronted by a phalanx of early briefing floats. Not the best of moments but waiting longer would only make things worse. Besides, better her than the XO. His kick was considerably harder.

"Sir."

Not even a twitch from her in his direction. "What is it, Analyst?"

"There's a new signal on the Wall, sir."

"Can it wait until later?"

"Practically? Probably. Technically, no."

She sighed and pushed a float away to make room. "Bring it here then."

He pulled the float.

"What is it?" she said.

"I'm not entirely sure. A structure I think."

"Yes, okay, I see that now. From above. It's awfully grainy." She squinted at the float for a bit until one of the briefings still hovering lured her eyes back in its direction. "Bring it back when you've cleaned it up."

"It's a very small signal, sir. This is as good as it gets."

She looked at Lukas for the first time. It wasn't a happy look. "Lukas, darling, tell me why this mess is in front of my face and keeping me from my work."

"Because it's ours."

"Yes, so what? We have probes all over the planet sending us signals. Clearly this one needs repair or repositioning. You don't need my authorization for that. Get on it."

"Sir, it's not a probe."

"What do you mean?" She went back to the signal float. "Then what is it?"

"It's a bot."

"A bot?"

"Personal bot."

"Like a follower? A recorder?"

"In all likelihood. It's a very weak signal so—"

The captain was now leaning into the float, trying to decipher as many of its details as possible. "How long have you been tracking this?"

His throat went dry and he covered a small cough. "Nine hours."

"Nine hours?"

"Yes, about that, sir, I wanted to say—"

"Push the nearest probe closer to those coordinates and get me a better look at that area. Also, get the XO."

Lukas stood there.

"What are you waiting for, Analyst?"

Now that he'd said the worst part, the nine hours part, he felt he had to say the rest. "Sir, I left my post early last night. That's why this report is nine hours old."

A flash of concern on her face. "I see. Were you ill?"

"No sir."

The captain sighed and her concern turned to anger with more than a small hint of disappointment mixed in. Like he didn't feel bad enough already. "Then what could possibly inspire you to leave your post, Analyst?"

"My girlfriend, sir." *Shit*. "No, I mean...I wanted to be with my girlfriend."

The captain looked him in the eyes for an eternity. "Thank you for your honesty, Lukas. Do you love her?"

"Sir?"

"Do you love her?"

"Yes, sir. I think I do."

"Have you told her?"

"No."

"Then that's the third thing you'll do today, understood?"

"Yes, sir."

"Also, if you leave your post early again, I'll cut your balls off."

"Yes, sir."

"A lot of good love will do you then."

43

The Kelly woman stood at the limestone-capped railing of the balcony off the governor's suite. The mayor had gone to bed and left Sarah with Kelly and a few guards. It was cold and her breath clouded in soft puffs of white as she spoke.

"What I wanted to tell you earlier was that I used to think the mayor was crazy. Then I started to think that maybe all people who change the world, or want to change the world, are crazy. That maybe crazy is what it takes."

"The world can't stay like it is," Sarah said. "The mayor's right about that. Things will get worse if nothing happens. I just don't think it should change his way."

The woman turned toward the park. "Listen to the city for a minute and tell me what you hear."

Sarah looked out toward the lawns and the stone paths where the lampposts were lit. There were electric lights in several of the buildings she could see from the second story of the old city hall. She listened to the sounds that traveled on the breeze from the streets and sidewalks and open windows beyond her view. The motors of cars. Footsteps on the pavement. A barking dog. Nearby, a bicycle with a rattling fender and loose chain peddling down Broadway.

"It's quiet," she said.

"Yes, it's quiet. Before the mayor took over, you had to hold your ears. Not because it was loud, but because it was scary. There were gunshots every hour. The crash of doors being bashed off their hinges and windows breaking. Not anymore. People know what it means to step out of line."

"And what does it mean?"

"Your chicken becomes beans. Your clean, comfortable job gets mean and dirty. Or much worse. The mayor doesn't believe in incarceration."

"Does the mayor believe in justice?"

"The mayor believes in order. What justice is there in being too frightened to walk the streets?"

Sarah shoved her hands in her pockets.

"Don't judge him by the standards of the past," the woman said. "The past is gone, burned away and turned to dust. For all it matters now, it was a dream that never really happened at all. We have to let go of it now."

"People can't just forget."

"They already have. If there was an election, if that were possible, the mayor would win it. Do you know why? Because most of us would rather fear the costs of breaking the rules, than not know what the rules are at all."

Sarah thought about how much of her own future she couldn't yet predict. How hard the not knowing was. "Will I ever see my sister again?" she asked.

"It depends. The people on the ship...will they come for you?"

"I don't know."

"Let's hope they do. The mayor's counting on it."

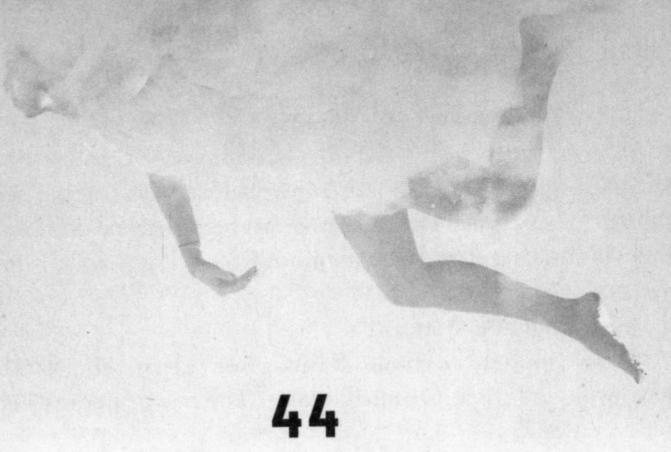

44

Wildei leaned into the cockpit while Trin buckled into *18*. "You are to avoid conflict. Period," she said, her face as serious as he'd seen it. "I don't like that location. You'll be boxed in, and up's the only way out. We are not soldiers. Fighting in close places is not what we do. So no fucking around."

"Wildei—"

"Promise me, Trin. I'm not losing anyone else, and I want these transports back safely. One more thing..."

"What?"

"Most of the Divers have come up for air."

"And?"

"Nothing."

He nodded acknowledgment and began toggling through his launch sequencing.

"Which means no diving for you. Not until you're back. Understood?"

Trin smiled. "I got it. I'm on my own."

She smiled back. "That's right, darling. Now go get our girl."

Four transports shot into the Russian night, *18, 12, 5*, and *1*. It was hardly a show of strength. But, really, what strength was there to show? Sending the entire fleet of transports wouldn't have made the team any more potent. Only *18* had a gun. Wildei was right—the other pilots were security guards who drove transports, not really pilots at all, and certainly not warriors. No one on the ship had any real combat training. Crowding a bunch of transports in that box would only increase the chance they'd crash into each other. In fact, Trin had argued that he go it alone. Wildei had almost agreed. In the end she'd hedged her bet. Four transports meant four sets of comms and four pilots meant four holstered dusters. Four was better than one, she'd said. And if everything went to shit, losing four was better than losing thirty.

They flew a route designed to steer wide of the launch coordinates of the missiles. The night was moonless and black as ink, and the demarcation between sky and land, easily seen during daylight flights, was nearly erased by the dark. There was almost no electrical power on the ground within this sector and apart from the occasional spot of fire, it was hard to tell up from down. The transports were all cloaking so none of his four view floats offered much of anything to actually see. They were just four black rectangles. He folded them away and sat for a bit. His Bridge Maker was tucked into its usual storage spot—a vertical chest pocket on his jump. He thought about plugging in to kill some time, but for once he took Wildei's warning seriously and kept the maker in the pocket. The transport was on auto. The floats were worthless. He did a quick comms check with the other transports and closed his eyes. It would be nearly night again by the time they got to Continent three. A little sleep would come in handy.

•

If he hadn't been buckled in, the blare from the transport's detection system might have tossed him from his seat. *Missile launch* it screamed.

A second later the *Kalelah* was on the comm.

"All transports, you have unknown incoming. Closure in twelve seconds."

"*Kalelah*, this is *18*, repeat closure."

"*It's right there*, 18, *and you're out of our strike range.*"

Trin brought his floats back. One, three, and four were dark still—nothing. Two showed a circle of light, growing fast.

"Where did this come from?" 5's pilot shouted.

Trin slowed his transport and quickly pushed the craft toward what he guessed might put him and his gun between the missile and the other ships. Before he'd made it halfway through the maneuver he knew it wouldn't matter. The coming danger had already arrived.

"*Oh God*," someone said.

12, Trin guessed as a metallic taste flooded his mouth, and everything went wrong.

The explosion was sharp, taut, and so concussively loud it knocked the wind out of him. For several seconds his vision was smeared, his stomach woozy. When the audio alarms managed to break through the ringing in his ears and the panicked chatter on the comm, Trin understood why. His transport was spiraling. He reached into his chest pocket for the maker, jammed it into the side of his head, felt the surge of fuse, and choked out the word, "Control."

He switched off the alarms and with their shrieks quieted, he could hear with sickening clarity the unmistakable sound of falling. The wind was forcing its way around the contours of the ship from all the wrong directions. As the Code tried to manipulate a hundred variables at once, the little vessel, battered by the turbulence of its own making, banged and shuddered like it was bouncing down a set of concrete stairs hung from the sky. He was sure the thing would tear apart at the welds.

There was nothing Trin could do but hold on and wait out the ride.

Another bang, this time much louder and more ominous, shook the cabin and then only the sounds of the comm.

He received the Code's analysis in his mind, "*Flight dynamics stabilized*." He sat still for a moment to catch his breath and let his heartrate settle down.

•

12 took the punch hardest. Her cabin caught fire and the pilot was burned beyond the capability of the transport's docbot to treat. A hole was shot into *1's* pulse generator causing a critical leak. All the ships lost their cloaks, millions of mirrors were burnt away, and thousands more were loosened from their network bindings and fluttered impotently in the transports' slipstreams.

It was decided that *12* and *1* would turn back around for the *Kalelah*. Without their cloaks, all the transports would now have to fly as low to the surface as possible to avoid hostile radar. Trin's *18* and transport *5* would soon enter the relative safety of a path over water. *12* and *1*'s path back to the *Kalelah* was over land, and with the sun due to rise soon, they'd be visible and vulnerable to a million potential dangers. The costs of looking for Sarah were escalating beyond what Trin had imagined. If he was right about the signal, that it was her asking for help, there was nothing he wouldn't give of himself to answer that call. He just hadn't planned on others paying his bill.

The two small ships continued west, leaving land for their route over sea. They communicated in sparse, technical language over the comm. Mostly they kept to themselves, choosing to lick their wounds in quiet.

Five hundred miles later, Trin gave the floats another try but the animator had developed a stutter so severe they were as good as dead, another aftershock from the explosion, no doubt. He folded them again, and with no pretense of stealth left, he opened the view through *18's* windscreen. They'd flown into daylight long ago, but the sun stayed low and never reached a mid-day height. He'd left night behind only to chase it going forward. Around him was water as far as the eye could see. Like the big star sitting close to the horizon, he, too, was flying low, nearly skimming the liquid surface, and from this perspective the strangeness of the alien planet vanished. The clouds of white, gray, and pinks rested on the break between ocean and sky in accordance with all his memories of home. The water, blue and green and gray, with small wind-blown caps of white, looked as familiar as anything he'd known. Nature, undisturbed by the ambitions and vanities and evil of humankind, seemed even here, on this place where so much had gone wrong, to go about its universal ways. For a long time, he was able to dream of walking under the warmth of a real sun.

When the buildings came into view, rising up from the water like a distant forest of gray and leafless trees, he shook away the mist of his dreaming and reconnected with the tasks of piloting. He looked over at *5* as it moved closer his way to tighten their approach. The little ship looked beat, blackened and pocked, with unadorned nanowool showing where its gleaming mirrors ought to be. He knew *18* looked much the same. They flew toward the Kingdom of Manhattan not at all like things born of miracles and mystery, things to frighten and awe. Instead, they were exposed and vulnerable. Already half beaten.

With the fight still to come.

45

Three years ago, after the bombs and the fires that erased Asia from the Earth, and the governments of America's East Coast had failed, the airports were among the first things to be picked clean for parts, food, and materials. Nader had gotten his share of the stuff that came easy. Two hangars crammed with four heavily vandalized Delta 737s—with almost enough parts between them for one potentially air-worthy plane—were his and still costing him a fortune to protect. But he hadn't yet gotten his hands on the real prize, a radar. The dishes and their component parts were seen as particularly valuable when the opportunists with guns and followers began sketching out their plans for a new feudal era. No one had even the smallest beginnings of what it would take to form an effective air force, but all had known the strategic importance of controlling the skies above their little worlds.

One of the Newark systems was supposedly up and running and in the possession of King George. It wouldn't be for long. Now that Nader had Sarah's guns, he'd soon have that radar, and more. In fact, if the only alien weapons he'd ever manage to get were the ones he already had, he could take down George and every other king up and down the coast and right up to the fuzzy edges of the hot zone.

Of course, Nader had no intention of stopping there. Or anywhere.

The only way to save what was left in the world and make something of it again was to take it all. And for that, he needed what he was sure the alien ship possessed. Magic. Or at least its equivalence, the quantum leap.

In the meantime, he relied upon the radar he did have, a network of men paid to watch the city and the skies above it linked together by Motorola radios. While it wasn't the swiftest or most impenetrable of systems, it managed to keep him informed. With that system he'd been able to deal with every significant breach of Kingdom airspace and shoreline since his own consolidation of power. Now his ragtag radar had come through again. Two strange-looking flying objects were spotted heading toward the Kingdom from the east. They were neither plane nor copter. They were coming low, made no noise, and moved like nothing his people on the ground had ever seen.

He had known where they were bound, or hoped he knew, and had given strict instructions to let the craft be. Watch them, he'd said, don't shoot them.

Not yet.

He had Kelly take Sarah to the old aldermanic rooms on the second story. Between them they offered the most windows on the park. If the objects were tracking Sarah somehow, the park around city hall was where they'd land. If landing was what they did. Who knew how the objects actually worked? He simply knew they'd come. He'd known it from the moment he'd seen the video of Sarah. Around the lawns of the park he had assembled a large array of guns. Not the dusters; he didn't want to disappear the ships. He wanted to capture them, at least one of them. It would make everything easier. It would make everything faster. And time was running out.

"Stingrays, they called them," Nader said when he entered the room.

"What?" Sarah said.

"Stingrays, like the fish, but in the air. Flying stingrays. There are two. They've entered the Kingdom. I think you're about to be rescued, Sarah."

He ushered the two women toward a large window.

"When the sun is just right and you know what you're looking for," he said, pointing to an elegant apartment building of reddish brick and limestone ornamentation across the park, "you can see the barrel of a MK19 grenade gun behind that window. Third floor, two in from the south corner. See it? It's quite the beast...can punch through armor up to two inches thick. But wait, there's more," he said with a showman's theatrics. "There are dozens of .50-caliber rifles pointed down at the lawns of this park from various heights. Some are as high as twelve stories above." He quieted for a moment to savor his preparations and think. "Will the stingrays land?" he asked.

"I don't know," she said warily.

He watched her face as she scanned the area, perhaps trying to find the other hidden guns.

"How many will there be? People, I mean."

"Not many."

"Ten, eight?"

"Less."

"The stingrays. How come I've never heard of these things before?"

"They have cloaks. Stealth tech. I don't how it works, but they're not supposed to be seen."

"So why, do you think, they want to be seen now?"

"You're asking me like I know the answers."

"Is it to frighten us?"

"I don't know," she shot back.

Sarah moved closer to the window and put her fingers on the glass, her gaze toward the skies. Nader thought she was nervous. The talk of guns had shaken her. He pressed on. "Are these stingrays heavily armed?"

"They're shuttles, transports," she said, her breath fogging the glass. "That's all I know, okay?"

"Okay, Sarah. I've got enough."

She turned to him, angry. Scared. Exactly how he wanted her. "What are you going to do?"

"I'm going to find out just how much you're worth."

46

Kino thought he might be on the verge of passing out. The bomb guys were taking their time disarming the vest he'd put around Margaret. Despite the initial relief the duct tape had given his hand, the pain had come back with a vengeance. He needed the fucking detonator out of his grip. He needed out of the stink hole he was in too. He and Margaret had been escorted at the ends of several guns to the basement of a low-slung building a block away from the old city hall. If by mistake or otherwise Margaret's vest were to explode, the mayor and his world would be untouched. The disarming was delicate work and the bomb guys didn't want him in the same room while they worked so they locked him in a dingy space that had once been a prep room for a restaurant on the first floor. It stunk like hell of onions and rat piss. Between the stench and the cramping in his hand, he was lightheaded and sick to his stomach.

The room was poorly lit and only barely furnished. A steel table and a heavy metal stool with an adjustable seat were its only occupants besides Kino. He got up from the stool to clear his head and walk off the urge to vomit. The room already smelled bad enough. After several laps around the table and stool he heard the tumbler of the lock on the door turn. Seconds later Lonny walked into the room, a jingle of coins in his steps.

"The vest is off," Lonny announced. "All clear."

"It's about fucking time." Kino began to pick at the tape around his hand.

As he worked, Lonny slowly pulled a Ruger Super Blackhawk .480 from the back of his pants. The giant gun hung down well below the man's knees, looking more like a small rifle than a pistol. Lonny producing a weapon wasn't particularly surprising. The mayor's forgiveness was never a guarantee. A Super Blackhawk though? That was unexpected. The .480 seemed like overkill, even for a killing. Kino wondered if Lonny possessed the strength to keep the Ruger's notorious kick in check.

When he'd gotten enough of the tape peeled away to move his thumb freely, he acknowledged the heavy, Old West styled revolver suspended at the man's side. "That's not your usual piece."

"No. But this is a special occasion. I thought, seeing as we are old friends, I would help you go out with a boom."

"Bang, Lonny. A person goes out with a *bang*."

Lonny shook his head and closed the door behind him. "Thank you for making this easy, Kino."

"I got the mayor what he wanted, Lonny. And then some." The rest of the tape was off, and he stretched the digits of his hand. "Don't tell me he's pissed about the car."

Lonny laughed, his white teeth gleaming against his skin in the dim yellow of the room. "No, he is not angry over the car."

"Then what?"

"The game, Kino."

"The game?"

"The one you and the mayor played. At the start of this adventure."

"What's the problem?"

"The problem is you won." Lonny raised the long barrel of the Ruger with his right hand and pointed it at Kino. "At least you are off The List, old friend."

"This is a mistake, Lonny."

"This is me following orders, Kino. And enjoying it, I might add."

"No, Lonny. The mistake is thinking you can shoot that bazooka straight with one hand."

47

The late daylight hit the roofs and glass of the buildings at a steep angle and sent shards of color and flash into the world. Trin marveled at the city's scale. While he'd seen dozens of images in the Omni data capture, it was another thing to see it with his own eyes. Its primitive nature was evident in digital and it was there in person, but the captured information compressed its enormity and dimmed the obvious genius of its architects. In facsimile the vibrance of their ambition and dreaming had been drained. Now, seeing what was made and what had been unjustly lost cast a shadow on him as long and dark as those the giants below him threw upon the ground.

The forward console showed the source of the signal as a red dot slowly pulsing and surrounded by data detailing its various geographical characteristics. When his coordinates and those of the signal finally matched, the dot turned green. He was much higher than the bot, his view more expansive. He recognized the footprint of the large building over which the little bot hovered so diligently. The place where Sarah was. He could also see the nature of the box he was in.

There was little movement on the ground. Other than some light traffic of vehicles along the broader streets, the park around the building looked empty and quiet.

He descended to a level closer to the bot, and when he reached the point where he no longer had line of sight to the streets, he halted. Transport *5* followed his lead. They waited there to see if their presence might alter the activity around the building in any way. The sun kept on its descent and soon the building was plunged into shadow.

"I'm going in for a closer look," he said.

"*Negative,*" from the comm. "*Captain asks for Worlding before any additional actions.*"

"*Correction,*" Wildei's voice now. "*This is* Kalelah *actual. And I insist.*"

Trin didn't reply except to turn the scanners on. A beat later he confirmed their operation. "Replication active."

He pictured the CC's great imaging column, the giant tube of holographic light ringed by a bank of workstations with Wildei at the center of it, nervously pacing around perfectly replicated versions in fractional scale of *18* and *5* and surrounded by exactly the environment he was. As long as *18* and *5* could scan in all directions, Wildei and the CC could share his world in three dimensions. It was the kind of babysitting that invited opinion, slowed things down, and drove him out of his mind. This time, though, he liked the call. After what had happened to *12* and *1*—the way that missile had come fast and by surprise—maybe a little company and some extra eyes couldn't hurt.

"It looked bad in the mapping, and I don't like it any better in the real," Wildei said.

It was what they'd all thought it would be, a tight box with tall sides, and he and *5* at the bottom of it. "There's always the chance it looks worse than it is," he said.

"How's our luck been lately?"

"I'm too close now to leave, Captain."

"I know, darling. But no feet on the ground. Keep an exit open. It'll be a while before we have a pop count and detailing."

"*5*, Captain's right. This box looks like shit. Go home. This is my hunt anyway."

"*Negative*, 18. *The whole point of four transports instead of one was redundancy. Now we're down to two. You need me. Besides, it's not just your hunt, sir. I fought with Sarah three years ago. It's my hunt too.*"

"All right, 5. Then let's say hello."

They guided their vessels in a descent toward the open space of the park just below the roofline of the large stone building, where they stayed to wait again. In that particular spot between the ground and the sky they were nearly even with a long row of tall windows. Although the rooms belonging to those windows were dark, there was the unmistakable presence of people. The unmistakable sense that he and 5 were being watched. The watchers were no more recognizable than figures of silhouette. Faceless, colorless, dark cutouts that rocked on their heels, put a hand to a featureless face, or turned to address one another. Only by their shapes and stature could he guess even their genders. He counted five men, two women. If they were friend or foe, Trin could not say. If one was Sarah or not, he could not say. He'd said hello. That was all he knew.

The transports held that same position without movement and the two parties continued to watch each other until the sun fell fully beyond the grasp of day and the night returned. Large lamps set at intervals along pathways in the park went white with electricity and punched holes of detail and color into the dark. Other than the still unrecognizable figures solemnly guarding the windows of the big building, Trin saw no one in any other window or on the ground. He calculated the actual distance between himself and the small group of watchers. It was mere meters. In that long moment of waiting, a moment of stubbornness or fear or contrivance, that distance seemed as far as he had traveled in all his life. Lightyears.

The comm broke in. *"Transports, we have an early pop count. You've got a big audience there."*

"How big?" asked Trin.

"One thousand and forty-two so far within the scan lines."

"Shit."

"Exactly. That's the thought on this end." Wildei's voice. *"Two transports hovering for hours and no one shows their face?"*

"I'm going to open the hatch," Trin said.

"Negative. It's been long enough, darling. It's time to come home."

"This is the right place. I know it."

"Then, tell me, where is she?"

"I don't know."

"Yes, you do. We both do. We talked about this scenario. The bot may have been hers, but it may not be anymore."

"Give her a little more time."

"Trin, if that's what's happened, then the box isn't a box anymore. It's a killing field."

He took the holster from its stowage and buckled it around his waist. He gestured the hatch and a thin shaft of white lamplight fell across his face.

48

Now that the moment had come, Sarah was more regretful than relieved. It was a mistake to have launched the bot. It brought help from the *Kalelah*, but with it had also come trouble.

How small the transports looked away from the reflected enormity of the *Kalelah*. There, lined up in numbers enough to be called a fleet, they looked like soldiers at the ready, united in form and cause. They were part of the sweeping magic of the place, enchanted and spellbinding. Here, they looked less like magic and more like magic tricks, like quaint deceptions for the purpose of entertainment. PR stunts. Minivans floating in the air, a promotional freezeframe from an action movie about soccer moms. Only their injuries gave them any dignity. Their beautifully mirrored skins that would reflect the dock lighting in such bewitching ways were broken, burnt, and torn. She had done this to them. She had done all of it.

She walked away from the windows and sat down against the wall with her arms around her knees. On her way she passed the Kelly woman, who had an anxious pall to her face and stood nearer to the back of the room than the windows. The others present were security details, large and silent men charged with keeping Sarah where the mayor wanted.

Nader sat facing the window in a club chair near the glass, his legs crossed, his suit freshly pressed, and his eyes never straying from the situation outside. Spread as they were, those mismatched eyes, taking the world in from divergent angles, Sarah imagined they enabled the mayor to hold two equally divergent opinions at once. A man who could comfortably be of two minds. He might be a person who could happily switch sides in any argument because he knew that either side was his side. If that were true, could anyone ever truly negotiate with such a man?

"So, what do we do now?" the Kelly woman asked.

"We wait," Nader stated.

"For how long?"

"Until they tire of waiting."

"What if they're thinking the same thing?"

The mayor sat for a minute before responding. "What's your opinion on the matter, Sarah? Are they patient? Or are they ready to rip the doors off this place?"

"They don't know anything about the situation; they're only responding to a signal."

The mayor turned in his chair to face Sarah, who remained against the back wall. "A signal you sent."

"That's right."

He smiled. "A signal you sent for us. To advance our cause."

"I don't have any cause with you," she said incredulously. "Now I'm sorry I did it at all."

"That's only what you tell yourself."

"You're out of your mind."

He smiled. "Why did you leave the ship, Sarah?"

"You know why. I left to get my sister."

He adjusted his place on the chair and faced her more fully. "That's your story. Though maybe not the honest one."

"I know what I did."

"Bear with me. Who leaves the relative comfort of a miracle from another world to slog her way through the wild wasteland that has become our little corner of the galaxy? A person with a sister in distress, you say. It might be so, but there are other possibilities that could describe that person. In fact, when I first saw that beautifully murderous video of you in Liberty Park, I went through a fascinating litany of exactly who the perpetrator of such elegant erasures might be. You were Sarah Long, of course. *The* Sarah Long. That much was obvious. But were you Sarah the escapee who broke from her alien captors? Were you Sarah the fugitive who ran from the claws of alien justice? Perhaps you were Sarah the spy sent to blend in where her alien patrons cannot? More than likely, I thought, you were one of those Sarahs. Then something about the French girl's story got me thinking. When it turned out to be true—there really was a sister in Lancaster, Ohio—well, my train of thought really picked up speed."

"You think too much," Sarah said.

He got up from his chair and found a bottle of wine on a polished high top, poured a glass, and drained it half away in one drink. With the hand that held the glass he pointed to the window. "The truth is right out that window. You could have retrieved your sister the easy way. You had things of magic all around you. Why didn't you borrow one of those stingrays out there and get her? If you couldn't borrow one, why didn't you simply ask for a ride? Clearly they would have given you one. They came all this way just because you sent a signal. You chose to do it the hard way, including a trip on my wretched boat. You know what that's called, Sarah?"

"No."

"The hero's journey. Sarah, you chose to suffer."

"I needed to go alone, that's all."

"No, Sarah, it isn't *all*." He put the wine down and grabbed the edges of the tall table as if it was a podium and he a minister of some deranged congregation.

She had that feeling she'd had before, that his eyes, those divergent eyes, saw the pieces of her and rearranged them as she was, and it frightened her like almost nothing else had ever frightened her.

"Do you know why you took the path you did?" he asked.

"Why don't you tell me? You're going to anyway."

"Because it was the only one that would lead you to me. Which is the only one that leads you to you."

"That's not true," Sarah said softly, the words ringing in her ears. "It can't be true."

As she stood to move away from him to end his crazed sermon, a loud gasp took the air out of the room and the Kelly woman ran to the glass from her spot near the back. "Oh my God," she said.

An opening began to cut its way through the skin of one of the transports. It traced a path to a perfect rectangle, and when it was finished the shape slowly pushed out and to the side of the ship.

Then it was Sarah who ran to the glass. She pounded at the window to get his attention. She screamed his name over and over. He didn't hear her.

The mayor walked to the glass and stood next to her. His eyes focused on the open hatch floating above the park, his face lit by a smile. "So this must be the proud father. Handsome fellow." He raised a radio to his mouth and into it spoke a single word. "Rifles."

49

The hatch door opened wide and cool air, moist and redolent, rushed into the cabin. Trin stepped closer to the sill of the opening and waited. He ignored Wildei's cautions that continued to sound from the comm. Something had to break the stalemate. Something had to give him an answer. He surveyed the darkened windows before him and one in particular caught his attention. The lights from the lamps below threw orbs of white upon the windows, and on one window the orb was bouncing just a little. Was that window vibrating? He stepped onto the sill itself to see if he could get a better look.

The punch hit before he heard the sound. It was hard and sharp, and it shoved him back into the cabin where he collided against the seat of his chair and fell to the nano floor of the transport.

"What the fuck?"

"Trin!" Wildei's voice. *"Close that damned door!"*

He pushed himself up and grabbed the seat back to take the weight off his leg, which burned like fire and was suddenly unwilling to take orders from his head. A noise filled the space, loud and percussive, disorienting, like hail made of titanium bearings. It echoed off the walls of the tight quarters, building on itself as if a storm of long-suppressed anger suddenly found the will to express itself.

He crawled his way back toward the hatch away from its opening and gestured the door closed. The storm outside continued to rage while he sat up against the wall next to the hatch and tried to get a grip on what was happening.

"What do you see?" he yelled above the din.

"*Projectile bursts, multiple origins,*" from the comm.

"How's 5?"

"Holding up. What's your status?"

"Checking."

It took him seconds to determine his status was shit. The right side of his jumpsuit was soaked red from the thigh down, a hole the size of a fist in the fabric.

As suddenly as the storm began, it stopped. In the quiet, the pain had him all to itself.

"Fuck me."

"What happened?" Wildei's voice. *"Are you hurt?"*

"Something tore a hole in my leg."

"That's it. 18, 5, *get the fuck out of there."*

"No. I saw something," Trin said.

"I don't care, Trin. We're done. Deploy the doc, stop the bleeding, get out."

"Captain, please—"

POOM!

A thunderous blast exploded outside the transport and pushed a sickening wave of shock through the little cabin.

"5 *report!*" the comm shouted.

POOM!

Another thunderclap. Trin was tossed to his side, his leg trailing, unable to help control his slide, and in such pitiful agony as to bring dancing specks of light before his eyes.

"I'm hit hard!" 5 screamed through the comm over the panic of sounding alarms.

"For God's sake, get out!" Wildei's voice pleaded.

POOM!

Deafness.

Darkness.

Feedback in both ears.

Flickers of light.

Crackles of static through the comm.

Nausea.

5's alarms through the comm: *"Critical system failure. Critical system—"*

"Fiiiiive!" Wildei shrieked.

The cabin lights dimming, brightening, dimming.

A crash.

Silence.

The sound of his heart.

His parents' house. Lamir nine years old, laughing in Trin's room so hard juice spurted from his nose. His schoolmaster at the float. His father before the launch. Argen waiting in the CC, the white light all around him, the worry in his eyes. Argen's head on the metal table, his blood in a pool, the tears in Ganet's eyes. The acrid smell of powder. The Keeper at the chains. The fire from the cannons.

Sarah.

Sarah.

Sarah.

"18, *report!*"

...

"18!"

"Reporting," Trin coughed.

"Thank God," said Wildei. *"Status!"*

"What hit 5?"

"Can you fly?"

"Yes. What hit him?"

"Three projectiles."

"Points of origins."

"One."

"Send me the coordinates."

"Trin, just get out."

"Send me the fucking coordinates."

He went for the floats again. The stutter was worse now. A red smear of a heat signature was all he could make out. Worthless. He pulled himself across the floor to the stanchion that anchored the seat to the ship and hefted himself onto the chair. He was dizzy and parched. He tried to punch in a translation order at the console, hoping the ship itself could lock in on what Wildei had sent, but he kept fumbling the sequence.

He took the Bridge Maker from his pocket and placed it in his ear. His spine tingled and she was there. The conversation took almost no time at all, covering all the ground he needed. *Find the target*, he told her, *and fire at will.*

The ship swung around and the rain of projectiles began its attack once more.

Why did you block what you knew about Sarah? He asked her. *Why did you block it from me most of all?* They talked about it at some length as the plasma fired from Yorn's handiwork and the entire park and all its surroundings burst bright with midday sun. The dust of the reddish brick building fell through the darkness and the rain of projectiles silenced for the last time.

Trin turned the ship back around to face the big building with the recorder bot hovering above. There was a balcony on the long side of it. A group of people had assembled on the short slice of railing that faced the ship.

Sarah was among them.

"Deploy the doc," he said aloud.

50

The mayor stood behind her, his left arm across her chest and his hand gripping her shoulder tight. Sarah felt the cold of the gun against her temple. On either side of her were the large men from the room where they all had watched the transports arrive. Their guns were leveled at *18.* Trin's ship. But there was much she couldn't see and didn't know. Everything beyond what was directly in front of her or in her peripheral vision, as far as the mayor would allow, was a mystery. She could hear Margaret's heavy breathing and sniffling from somewhere behind her. She didn't know who was with Margaret or where the Kelly woman was.

The rush to the balcony had been so well coordinated it almost seemed rehearsed. When Trin's ship took out the red apartment building Sarah was instantly swept up by the security detail and brought outside. The efficiency and swiftness of it took her by surprise and subdued her before she could even think of a counter response. There was no shouting of instructions, no panicked questions from the underlings to the mayor. It was as if a switch somewhere had been flipped. She was at the windows, then like a cut between scenes in a film, she was at the balcony. Everyone on their marks, every gun in position. Trin would be up against something he wouldn't understand.

The transport flew to a position that allowed its stairs to lower onto the balcony. She flashed to the last time she saw this moment, the hatch opening and Trin walking down to the deck of the *Lewis*. This was different. When he came to the stairs now it was all she could do not to scream from the sight him.

His duster was out of its holster and pointed at the crowd. The look on his face was pure anger. His jumpsuit was covered in blood. His hands were covered in blood, and the one that held onto the railing shook with fatigue. His steps were tentative, halting, one leg clearly unable to bear any weight at all. The mayor let him make it all the way down.

"Does he speak English?" the mayor asked her.

"Yes."

"Welcome. My name is Tom Nader."

Trin leveled the duster at the mayor's face. "Sarah, are you hurt?" he asked, his accent present and obvious in even four small words and it broke her heart.

"No."

"What is this?"

"This is a game," the mayor replied.

"What?"

"It's called, which one of us dies first."

"Is this a joke? You've seen what our weapons can do."

"Yes. Damn fine guns. I'm lucky to have acquired several of them."

A flash of puzzlement crossed Trin's face. Sarah heard the click of a radio button behind her and then the Kelly woman's voice: *"Now."*

A beat later a string of plasma shot from a window behind them to the other transport. Trin nearly stumbled from the light and surprise of it. He shouted a profanity in a language only he and Sarah could have understood and lurched closer to the mayor as if his leg was miraculously made whole again, his gun arm stretched straighter and longer, his eyes blazing and his face in aguish. The mayor's security men reacted in kind, moving quickly and shoving the nuzzles of their guns right up to Trin's head.

"There was an innocent man in that ship," Trin growled.

"There are no innocent men in this world, Trin," said the mayor. "Not anymore."

The group stayed locked in that dangerous huddle of guns. Trin was sweating and his chest was heaving. His breath clouded around him in bursts of white. The security men were doing no better. Sarah was tight up against the mayor's chest. His breathing was quiet and slow.

"Trin," she said, "you're hurt. He won't stop."

"Kelly, bring Sarah's sister here, please," the mayor said, as if to underscore the point.

Sarah watched Trin's eyes make sense of the moment.

The Kelly woman did as she was told and Margaret was suddenly in Sarah's view, her face a swollen mess and her eyes filled with fear.

"I want you to understand something." The mayor moved his polished revolver away from Sarah's head and leveled it at Margaret. "The greater good is everything to me. This," he cocked the gun, "is nothing."

"Wait!" Trin took a hobbled step back, lowered his weapon, and placed it on the balcony floor.

The mayor nodded in approval. "Good game."

Whatever the rules to the game were, whatever constituted a good and meritorious example of it, Sarah would only ever know that fair play had nothing to do with it. The silver gun went off like a bomb and her sister crumpled to the ground.

51

A table and chair had been brought out to the balcony and the mayor sat comfortably there drinking wine and examining the Bridge Maker taken from Trin's ear. Sarah was on the ground, her back against the railing next to Trin, imagining the many ways she'd like to see Tom Nader die.

"Now that the question of Margaret has been answered, I hope we can get down to business," the mayor said.

Sarah looked away from him and laughed. It came up and out of her without permission, tinged with tears and soaked in exasperation. "You're a monster," she finally managed.

The mayor set the maker carefully on the table and smashed it with the handle of his silver revolver. "Not true, Sarah. I'm a janitor, and if the clean-up on aisle four is unpleasant, if it makes us all hold our noses, the fault is in the nature of the mess. If you had finished what you'd started none of this would be necessary." He gestured with the gun in a way that said by *this* he meant the world around them. "You've left me no choice because you left us as you did. Half alive, mostly dead. Ants only partially crushed and spinning in circles trying to get their footings. That, that *negligence* was a crime crueler than the one that preceded it."

He swirled his glass in the light spilling from the open doors that led to the balcony.

"I'm going to give you the opportunity to make amends for that crime."

"Fuck you," said Trin.

"Still on the fence, I see. Okay. Then let me provide a few additional details. Be my ambassadors to the ship. Secure for me the weapons and technologies needed, and I will do your dirty work. I will straighten out the mess and take the garbage out. After that, well, we'll have generations of mistakes to guide us to a better place."

Sarah closed her eyes and fought back her tears. She'd come for Margaret and had lost her in the worst way possible. She'd been crazy to have taken this chance. The only question left in her mind was this: How many more will she let die?

"No," Sarah said. "The power you crave, the things you think should be yours, the weapons, the people, the dominion...we won't let you have it. None of it."

The mayor smiled and cocked an eyebrow. "I think you misunderstand the situation here. Most of all, Sarah, you misunderstand *me*. The things you think I must have, they're not the point at all. Possession is merely a road. Travel it with me, however, and you'll get to the real destination. Redemption. Isn't that what you want? What you and the people on your crippled ship need most of all? I'll provide it. I will redeem you. Do you understand? In the eyes of all the world, and in the eyes of God."

He pushed back in his seat as if he'd settled the thing, grabbed hold of the end of his tie, and with it began to polish the mirror finish of his gun. In the brief moment between words, a noise in the far distance, subtle and maybe not really there at all, crept into Sarah's awareness.

"I'd leave God out of this if I were you," Trin said.

"Who are we to leave God out of anything?" the mayor frowned. "Besides, it just so happens that I know Him well. Someday, in the fullness of time, or sooner, you will too. The question is how will God know you? As destroyers? As the breaker of things, the stealers of souls? Or as something holy and eternal, something, Sarah, to honor your name? That's the opportunity I offer you and everyone on that cursed ship, if you can see it. An opportunity to shape the contours of that meeting with your Maker."

He got up from the chair, walked over to the railing, and knelt down with the gun, holding it casually between his knees.

Sarah was sure now the noise was real. Still far, but there. Like thunder from an ocean storm too distant to see. In the mayor's face, a small tic of the green eye's brow made her think he'd heard it too. He pushed on with his point.

"You've set this decision in motion," he said. "Now you must make it. Will it be two bullets?" He gently touched the end of the gun's barrel to Sarah's forehead and then to Trin's. "Or will you help me?" He looked Sarah in the eyes, his own mismatched pair suddenly aligned in direction and piercing in their unnatural way. "Help me, Sarah. Live to see through the promise you already hold in your womb."

"Wait, what?" Trin said.

A cruel smile emerged on the mayor's face. "You haven't told him, have you?"

The noise now, she knew what it was. A plane. No, not just a plane. A jet. And coming their way.

Trin turned to her with a look that broke her heart. She couldn't believe this would be how he'd learn he was a father. Yet another thing she'd managed to ruin. She opened her mouth to speak, to tell him the truth, all of it. Except the noise had suddenly grown too loud for anyone to ignore. And before she could say the thing she wanted to say the most, "I'm sorry," before she could take his hand and press it to her belly, the hurricane scream of a jet airplane exploded from the night sky. The jet shot out between a gap in the surrounding buildings low and fast, a calamitous riot that shattered window glass, shook the ground, and pounded her like a wave. Too loud to talk or even yell over, it moved across the park from one end to the other, like a howling demon, pushing its way through the void left by the dusting of the red brick apartment house.

As it rocketed by Sarah saw a shape catch just enough light from the windows and moon to separate itself from the night. A triangle of gray. The delta wing of a fighter plane. A French fighter plane.

Elouise.

The plane used the streets as canals of travel through the thicket of buildings and arced itself upward and back toward the park. Just as the sound ebbed it grew terrifyingly loud again as the jet raced toward the old city hall building. Trin threw himself in front of her. A burst of light flashed from the plane and before she could connect the dots of what it meant, the rocket and its payload hit the rotunda, exploding the central core of the building outward and blasting dust and debris through the broken windows and doors of the balcony. Anyone who was standing was knocked off their feet.

Dust. That was all she could see, breathe, and taste when she came to. She had no idea how long she was out. A minute, an hour, a lifetime? She felt a pull at her arm. Trin. He was yelling at her. And maybe not for the first time since the rocket. "Are you hurt?" pushed its way through the dull ringing in her ears.

She shook her head.

"Get to the transport!"

"No, both of us!"

"Just go!"

She stood up slowly on shaky legs. The air was thick and painted white by drywall, brick, and the ancient hopes of a city turned to powder. She grabbed Trin under his arms and helped him off the ground. He screamed with pain when he put both feet down, but stayed upright, which was enough to get them both moving. The trick was picking a direction. She was disoriented by the blast and dust. Trin was in too much pain to navigate. She decided to wait before expending too much energy in the wrong direction. They stood there together, holding tight to each other. She looked up to find a break in the dust and a star in the sky, something to give her hope.

As if on cue, a gentle breeze began to blow, a wind so subtle it was barely there. Or maybe it wasn't there at all. Maybe it was just her longing playing tricks upon her perception, giving her what she wanted. Only when a patch of night began to push its way through the haze, did she trust herself. A moment later the ringing in her ears allowed the distant noise of a jet to make itself heard. Within the clearing of black above her, like a painting in a frame, Elouise passed between the moon and Earth and Sarah felt a shiver run through her.

How much did Elouise know when she'd first called out to Sarah? Tears spilled down her face and the journey she'd been on these past weeks flashed in fragments through her mind. Poor Dwayne and his mother and the Honda. The buck and the roadblock and Bobby lighting a cigarette the way she'd seen him do it a thousand times. Gabi and Solli. Her mind took her all the way back to the beginning, to the deck of the *Lewis*, when Trin, still shocked by Argen's death and improvising in the moment, picked her of all people to return with him to the *Kalelah*. Her of all people. *Then you'll find something else. Or something else will find you*. Heather's words.

Sometimes the killed have special jobs to do. She remembered that too. Heather did hers apparently. And Margaret, Sarah suddenly understood, had done hers as well. Without Margaret, there'd have been no journey at all. No way forward.

The air cleared enough to make out a path through the debris to the ship. She didn't dare look anywhere else. Until his voice turned her around.

"I can do this without you, Sarah," the mayor said, his words clear and strong, as if the rocket had never been fired. "I have enough weapons to take what I need."

He stood amidst the rubble between them, one side of his face and body lit by the muted glow from the park lamps below, the other side in shadow, except for the green eye. It shone like an emerald, illuminated from something within the man's soul, if indeed he had one. The silver gun was down by his side. Trin's duster was in the mayor's shooting hand now, the ejector blade leveled at her.

"But it will be better with you. More complete. More as it should be. Think of the greater good, Sarah. Because none of you are getting on that thing."

She shook when the weapon went off. The mayor's hand dropped first, then the mayor himself fell. Among the hundreds of impossibilities all around her it was the most incredible of them all. A moment later Kino stepped out of the shadow, a long-barreled Old West style gun in his hand. He bent and took the duster from the mayor, turned it off, and walked it over to Sarah. She took the gun and offered her kidnapper a nod she hoped would say everything that needed to be said. That whatever they both were before this moment no longer mattered. There was work to be done and she would need his help to do it. He nodded back and started toward the blown-out doors that led to what was left of the main part of the building.

Trin put a hand gently to her belly and she looked up into his eyes. They held each other in that embrace a few minutes longer as the world rearranged itself once again. She had only the vaguest sense of what would come next, but she knew they would greet it together. The three of them. This much was certain. This much was everything.

She walked to the mayor and knelt where he lay. His eyes were open but had resumed their divergent positions. His face, still handsome, was framed by a circle of black blood. She thought he could see her, that he knew it was her kneeling there. Before his eyes finally closed for good, he managed to push from his mouth four last words.

Years later she would think back on that moment and allow the possibility that she had heard it wrong. The man had not more than a whisper left in him. But at the time, with the dust falling and the hopes and fears of the city all around her, she was sure the words he spoke were, *"Sarah, mother of nations."*

THE END